NINTH DIVISION
GLOBAL INTELLIGENCE DIRECTORATE
WASHINGTON, DC
SPECIAL AGENT-IN-CHARGE, GREGORY MASON

ETHER

ISBN: 978-0-9833317-4-2

Cover illustration, book design
and layout by
Erik J. Kreffel.

ETHER

The Second JauntWorld Thriller

ERIK J. KREFFEL

Books by **ERIK J. KREFFEL**

JAUNT

ETHER

AGENT MAYA SEASON ONE
Graphic Novel

**AGENT MAYA
AND NEPTUNE'S DEADLIEST RING
AND THE MOONS OF ICE AND FIRE**

Edited by **ERIK J. KREFFEL**

OCCULT DETECTIVES, VOL. I
John Silence, Physician Extraordinary

OCCULT DETECTIVES, VOL. II
In A Glass Darkly

OCCULT DETECTIVES, VOL. III
**Carnacki, The Ghost Finder
& Other Ghost Stories**

For Dad

In the midst of the 22nd Century, humanity struggles to overcome 70 years of a dim age, where a series of global economic meltdowns have precipitated the collapse of the People's Republic of China, the Russian Federation, the Dominion of Canada and other BRIC states. Billions starve and die in environmental and political distress. Technological progress grinds to a halt. The dreams of prosperity languish in a near-medieval nightmare.

Nationalistic factions seize the spoils of formerly great powers and carve fiefdoms throughout the globe. Regional warfare convulses the bastions of freedom. By deliberate action, the last free powers lock down many conflicts, creating a second Cold War. Uneasy tensions build. The United States and Canada merge into a single entity—the United States of North America. Russian generals and oligarchs fuse a new Eastern European empire in the form of the Confederation of Independent States. China consolidates a wide western bulwark, a second Bamboo Curtain—the Central Asia Conglomerates.

A near century-long ban on nuclear weapons causes the few nationalistic powers, enflamed by megalomania and schemes of conquest, to experiment with far deadlier technologies in the years to come....

CHAPTER ONE

"Have you asked yourself why you do certain things?" he wondered aloud in imperfect English, heavily accented by his native Russian tongue. His lips curled into a smile as she unbuttoned his shirt. "I mean, who would think a beautiful European girl, in my hotel—"

She placed an index finger on his lips, her skin brushing against his day-old stubble, which didn't amount to much owing to his early twenties' age.

"Shh...let's not ruin this now, Andrei." A giggle escaped her mouth. "What's that word again...?"

"*Myod*," he said between kisses. "What you call 'honey.'"

Pushing him to the mattress, she put one hand above his head, holding it down with her right hand. She took the other and clasped them together. "Now, how much do you love sexy young Western girls?"

His eyes bulging, Andrei Ilichev growled playfully; astride him, the half-naked girl with the raven bob and heart-shaped face reached behind her back and put a small red capsule to her lips. *Crazy, absolutely crazy! Me, a simple physics research assistant!*

"What is that, *myod*?" he giggled, his doe eyes following her mouth down to his.

"A little kick I got in the clubs back home...makes things ten times better."

"Heh...you naughty *dyevooshka*." Andrei reached forward and kissed her, placing the capsule onto his tongue.

"That's right, good *maltsik*. I've got one for me, too...."

Swallowing the capsule, it metabolized within seconds of contact with his esophagus, tingling as it went down. Andrei's body grew warm and languid, quicker than any vodka he'd ever drunk before. "I...I'm sleepy, sexy *myod*...this is ten times better...?"

"Trust me...everything will be better."

Andrei went limp underneath her, his arms now dead weight in her hands. She rose off him and stood next to the bed. Laughing, her assumed central England accent slipped into a broad northern California one. "What an easy date."

She retrieved her shirt, trousers and pumps, donning all on in swift succession. Walking to the dining table, she unlocked the briefcase lying there and rifled through it, extracting a palm-sized cylinder which she then stowed within her purse. Exchanging his cylinder with an identical one, she placed the briefcase back to its original state.

She blew a kiss to the sleeping man and toggled a voxlink hidden in her purse. "Little lady to Stone man...my date's just been consummated."

"*Roger that*," the voice on the line answered. "*Let's go home.*"

Λ

"How was your date?" Special Agent Lisbeth Feltham asked the incoming junior agent, Natasha Kindred, at the hatch threshold, a smile creasing her face.

Kindred ducked under the starboard hatch of the manta-ray shaped, C-255 Grasshopper jumpjet *Green Scream* and took her seat inside the cockpit. Removing her wig and letting her short hair breathe again, she answered, "Best filet mignon I've had in years. Oh, a little going away present."

Unzipping her purse, she produced the cylinder and handed it to her boss, Special Agent Greg Mason, sitting next to his newly minted partner, Feltham.

"Just what you ordered, Stone man," Kindred said. "On time and under budget."

Mason held the encrypted data cylinder up to the cockpit's dorsal illumination. "Fantastic, Sha." Gesturing to the pilot and co-pilot ahead, Mason signalled the go-ahead for liftoff.

"Thank you, sir. Sorry I didn't bring back any pictures for the rest of the Company."

Mason let out a chuckle. "This'll do just nicely."

Λ

The chrome-framed glass and steel skyscraper basked in the sunshine of a late autumn Washington, DC, day, the latest in a renaissance of sparkling slivers to burst forth from the banks of the Potomac River's Federal Quarter, which housed all the United States of North America's civilian and bureaucratic denizens in their professional lives. Now, thousands of long-suffering Department of Justice agents, managers and staffers enjoyed the fruits of new digs; the stuffy and ancient basement quarters they had known for years was the rubble for this new tower, named eloquently enough for a man long forgotten, Charles Lee Memorial Building, or as its denizens dubbed it, the Glass Castle.

Emerging from the curving shadow of this new giant, the VTOL-capable *Green Scream* descended a hundred meters towards a crevice at the northern foot, where a hangar reserved for DoJ use lay. Gazing out the portside cockpit window, the trio of Intelligence and Investigative Agency agents watched the spectacular facet draw nearer, then envelope them.

They were home.

Λ

"Appears your double agent had a few secrets of his own."

Global Intelligence Directorate Section Manager "Chief" Grant Louris reclined at the sweeping, parenthetically shaped desk in his office. Gathering round him, the three squad members of his Ninth Division—9D—struck puzzling glances.

"Take a look at what Keegan and Moore found this morning after sifting through everything in that cylinder."

Tapping a button on his holographic computer interface, Louris brought up the assorted data files on the display hovering before the group. Nondescript quantum data strings scrolled past, until his avatar cursor paused over a square image, not more than a hundred by hundred pixels.

Mason's eyes narrowed to discern just what they were seeing. "Um, I'm not following."

"Neither was I, until they magnified it."

A reddish white blob lay within a black field, dominating their view. The image continued to magnify until only the blob appeared, its individual pixels soon betraying a spiraling matrix pattern over itself.

"Pixelated quantum encryption, huh?" Feltham said, her fingers brushing the holographic image. "Maybe some Mandelbrot thrown in for good measure, a steganographic fractal. Our guy sure was paranoid."

Mason's brow arched; having known her for the better part of three weeks, his partner's twin degrees in Quantum Cryptoanalysis and Behavioral Science had yet to be put through their paces. What better gift than to receive a case to potentially do both at the same time?

Louris reclined, his fingers combing his hair, silvery temples showing through the otherwise well-kept sandy brown waves. "Keegan and Moore can't be certain what the image actually is, but they've run the matrix through the code cracking QPUs...it's all in Russian, something about a '*Proyekt Efyr.*'"

"Project Ether," Mason said, roughly translating the words from Russian. Stroking a cheek in thought, the phrase tumbled in his mind. "This isn't just about neutronic transfer technology, is it?"

Louris shook his head. "Our friend Andrei had the goods from Yastanni's labs all right, but I think Yastanni himself may be dabbling in something entirely different."

"Think the Confederation has any clue?" Kindred asked.

"Hard to say," Mason answered. "One thing's for certain: we need to pay some people a visit."

"Oh?" Feltham said. "Who's first in your list of 'acquaintances?'"

Mason stared back at the blob for a few seconds before looking to his partner. "Yastanni himself, and a friend in Ottawa about this Project Ether."

Louris stood. "I'll make the travel clearances for Yastanni's lab. I also have an agent in mind for your slot, Greg. I'll see if he's available for operative status."

"Thanks."

"Ottawa?" Kindred asked, after Louris exited the office.

"The theoretical studies laboratory, an adjunct of the DoE. My old partner Gilmour and I contacted a Doctor de Lis some time ago. If anyone can tell us more about this Ether business, it's him."

"What kind of contact?" Feltham asked.

Her blue-grey eyes studied Mason's face, finding a hint of the ulterior recesses that he masked with a shit-eatin' grin on occasion; reading him was as easy as tea leaves some days, despite their new working relationship. Louris assigned her the hallowed mantle left behind by Gilmour; Lis Feltham aimed to secure a place in the annals of the Company in general and the Global Intelligence Directorate in particular and to prove at her age—practically Mason's little sister at 28—she had what it took.

Mason gave her his best grin. "The spooky kind."

CHAPTER TWO

"Still relegated to an underground bunker, Doctor?" Mason quipped, his arms folded. He watched the man in the tweed jacket ahead of them shuffling papers into a manila folder, so consumed by his task that even the puzzled looks and queries from the staff in the corridors failed to stir him.

Startled by the familiar voice, Doctor Richard de Lis stood dumbstruck in mid-turn, his eyes blinking involuntarily. Papers flew from his hands and landed to the tile floor.

"Don't be so happy to see me...."

"Agent Mason—I...I didn't expect you here again so soon." De Lis stuck his hand forward and shook Mason's. The agent, his sandy hair cropped short and dressed sharply in blue jacket and tie, hadn't changed since their last meeting nearly a year prior. De Lis waved towards his office. "Please, come in, all of you. Welcome back to the U Complex."

Feltham and Kindred followed de Lis and Mason inside U5-1, the hexagonal-shaped laboratory at the crux of the U Complex's fifth level, astonished by the melange of cheap, prefabricated walls and the ultramodern translucent fullerene glass delineating the individual offices therein. It was some Frankensteinian government operation, all right; Kindred half-expected a laser beam to bore a hole through the walls at any moment, followed by disheveled grad students in lab coats cleaning up after their latest awry experiment.

"These are the members of my 9D team, Doctor, Agents Lisbeth Feltham and Natasha Kindred," Mason said.

Feltham and Kindred, barely containing their mutual awe, distantly nodded towards the doctor before again devoting their gazes to the extraordinary structure they found themselves in.

De Lis nodded. "Pleased to make your acquaintance."

He steered the agents to the right to his own office, U5-3, one of six rooms within. A pass key in his hand admitted the group inside, whereupon their entrance a pleasant feminine voice intoned, "*Welcome back, Richard. How may I be of service to you and your guests? Perhaps some refreshments from the commissary?*"

"Thanks for asking, Salus," de Lis answered, "but we're good for now. Back to sleep."

"*Have a pleasant afternoon.*"

"Nice girlfriend," Mason said, his lip curling slightly.

"Yes, well," de Lis said sheepishly. Taking his seat, he proffered the three chairs at his desk to the agents. "What brings you to Ottawa, Agent Mason?"

Mason handed the cylinder to him. "This. Some interesting data on it we obtained in a recent op. Seems our crack analysts at the old IIA found more than we bargained for."

De Lis lowered his spectacles, scrutinizing it. "Let's take a look, shall we?"

Loading the cylinder bottom first into a receptacle on his desktop, de Lis tapped a button on a flat panel, causing a holographic display to blossom between the four in mid-air. Branches of data streams flew outwards from a central point, extending for several seconds until a tree stood fully formed, appended by miniscule text boxes.

"What we're interested in is located...here," Mason said, pointing his index finger to a particular branch, which rippled under his touch.

Zooming in at lightning speed, a thumbnail of the image in question eclipsed the data tree, revealing itself to de Lis at maximum size. The mysterious blob hovered above de Lis' desk ominously, its secret origin and purpose tantalizing all in the room.

"Interesting," de Lis said finally, stroking his chin. "I can discern a quantum encryption matrix starting here," he paused, pointing to the spirals Feltham saw in DC. "Someone's coded message dispersed within the image's picture elements."

"Which is odd, since pixels ceased to be a characteristic after the holographic imaging industry put physical monitors and displays out of business decades ago," Feltham explained. "Unless this is older than that...."

Mason scanned over the blob again. "You think Yastanni is dabbling in old research?"

"Old perhaps, Agent Mason," de Lis said, "but also forgotten by all but those who deal with extra-forces research, like the theoretical studies lab."

Mason nodded. "Than you know about Project Ether?"

"Not by name, no, but 'ether' is applied to a very specific theory in cosmology and astrophysics. It relates to dark energy."

"Dark energy...the stuff in galaxies and things that no one can see but seems to have super-gravity?" Kindred asked.

"Not quite." De Lis reclined and ran his hand through his thinning, silvery hair. "Dark matter's what you're referring to...I know, we in the scientific community have great nomenclature, right? Quintessence, Einstein's Cosmological Constant or Lambda, dark energy, all are variations on a theme attempting to explain why the universe appears to expand at an ever greater rate as it ages."

"Someone's joke," Mason said, chuckling after realizing the reference. "Outer space in the nineteenth century was thought to be filled with fluid, or æther."

"Correct." De Lis leaned forward again. "You mentioned Yastanni... Doctor Nouri Yastanni?"

"The same," Mason answered. "You've met him?"

"He was a research acquaintance, back about fifteen years ago at a conference in Bern. I peer-reviewed several of his papers in various science journals over the years. He's bright, has some interesting ideas...unfortunately, his Iranian nationalism seems to have gotten the better of him since then."

Mason added, "And given him a bad habit of dabbling in research that he shouldn't."

"Bitter, are we?" Feltham tweaked her partner.

Mason wrinkled his face. "Goddamn Confederation got him off in back-door dealings with the UN Secretary-General...." He held his thumb and index finger a centimeter apart. "We were this close to beheading that neutronic trafficking ring of his."

De Lis frowned. "Than it would appear he is on to something potentially more lucrative."

"Hold on," Kindred said, raising her hands. "Just what is this thing? What's the big deal on dark energy, or æther, or whatever you're calling it these days?"

"The big deal, Agent Kindred," de Lis began, "is that dark energy has hitherto been wholly inaccessible to humanity's devices, probably to the benefit of life on this planet."

De Lis rose, and circling round the holograph, looked out over the suite of offices ringing U5-1, his gaze piercing the fullerene glass.

"Ninety years ago, a French, Iranian and Russian consortium was contracted to build a covert research facility deep inside what was once North Korea, on invitation of the then-ruling Kim Dynasty. Nothing is positively known about the events that occurred there, but a devastating accident killed scores."

He turned back to the agents. "When I was an undergrad in Toronto, I heard rumors circulating amongst the students in the physics track about the North Korean incident. Well, you know as well as I that urban legends are part and parcel of these sorts of things, but something niggled me in the back of my mind. Being young and less...*methodical* about my prying, I asked around the faculty, and was met with skepticism, of course, but also quite a bit of selective ignorance. That should have given me pause, but I knew an incident that toppled a war-hardened, despotic regime nearly overnight must have had substance to it. It wasn't until only the last decade that colleagues I shall not name discussed with me the possibility of dark energy being the culprit."

"You afraid this Project Ether is your dark energy goose chase?" Feltham asked.

De Lis nodded. "Yastanni's interest in it can't be just circumstantial. And if he pieces together a methodology to manipulate dark energy...."

"You don't have to say it," Mason said. "I believe Yastanni has to be neutralized."

"I agree," de Lis said. "Agent Mason, I know this is IIA business, but do you mind if I provide some...assistance on this issue? At the scene?"

Mason smiled, finding de Lis' eagerness to provide all he could gratifying, in light of his occupation's toll on his time. The agent also wasn't about to deny the good doctor the opportunity to put the pieces of his career-long enigma in place if it went a long way towards solving their newfound case. "Your assistance is more than welcomed, Doctor, it's encouraged. That's why I dragged our sorry selves all the way up here."

De Lis steepled his fingers. "Thank you...I've been waiting a long time for this."

Λ

"Yastanni's last known operational facility was in the Zagros Mountains, on the Iranian side of the Iran-Shi'ia Republic of Iraq border," Mason said, his hands tracing an arc over the holographic cartograph occupying most of the airspace in the jumpjet's aft compartment. "His fanatical support for General Kermani ensured the state's purse strings were continually open for his research, and he has the digs to show for it."

Gathered around the pedestal which emanated the holograph, Mason, Feltham, Kindred and de Lis's faces glowed a bluish green. A magnified aerial point-of-view of the Zagros Mountains lay just below their abdomens, slowly flowing past them and disappearing off the squared edge of the holograph.

Tapping a seemingly bare patch of land at the foot of the Zagros, Mason zoomed in on a squat set of buildings built into the side of the mountain range, heavily reinforced with barriers and partially covered by earth.

"This compound has a deep subterranean structure, at least a hundred meters below ground, both outside and within the mountain chain," Mason said, his index finger highlighting the building's image. "Global Security Network satellites have penetrated the surrounding soil with radar and lidar scans, producing this real-time image."

With meters of crust peeling away like a layer cake, the compound's subterranean structure was revealed to the group, showing a rectangular cavern with numerous orbiting chambers connected by interweaved corridors. Two long corridors jutted away from the main complex and proceeded some dozens of kilometers northwest to a sister compound.

"UN inspectors found nothing worth noting in their decadal report in spring '41, but most people in the know will tell you it's a cat-and-mouse game with suspected perpetrators," de Lis explained. "Yastanni may not have had anything at these sites, but he has a competent network able to swiftly transport matériel from one to the next, always a step ahead."

Feltham looked to Mason. "What's the plan, boss?"

"Chief's cleared us to enter Kermani Iranian airspace through the Turkish and Kurdistani corridors. Since UN and IQEA inspectors have license to tour sites on a need-to-know basis, we'll be doing some disguised recon work. This is your area of specialty, Lis. Create some identities for us."

"Will do."

"Excellent!" Kindred smiled and rubbed her hands together, eager to stay out of the Glass Castle's overtly business-like atmosphere; the more she was in the field, the better. "I've got a whole new wardrobe for us to play dress-up in, Lis! And something I've been wanting to see you wear, Stone man...."

CHAPTER THREE

Weaving a jagged horizon against the late afternoon sun, the Zagros Mountains rose above the whitewashed UN cargo helicopters which descended into the southwestern Dasht-e-Kavir desert plain. Sandwiched inside a 750-square-kilometer, low-lying peninsula of earth—walled in on three sides like a mountain fortress of medieval times—a rectangular speck in the distance resolved itself into Yastanni's laboratory compound. Rimmed by perimeter razor fencing, the compound was a stubborn plot of civilization cordoned off from a desolate and deadly wilderness.

Riding inside the leading helicopter, the three agents gave last minute adjustments to their subtle cosmetic disguises. For his benefit, Mason received a radical facial makeover before leaving Ottawa; having accosted Yastanni himself in the not-so-distant past, the last thing they needed was recognition. Only de Lis remained unscathed, recognition being very much in his playbook.

Mason's nose caught the aroma of dry dirt tinged with pine, a dichotomous melange of scents he associated with the sense memory of his many training exercises in the harsh Mojave Desert as a rookie agent. Nothing could quite match the memory of a sudden skydive with a passel-load of fellow greenhorns dispatched to survive three weeks alone. Leaving his Hampton Roads, Virginia, home for the first time to a wholly opposing clime sent a ripple of dread and excitement throughout his system as a young man, to which Mason had been addicted to ever since. The fact that he'd met his first west coast girl after the fact was equally a matter of pride.

He fiddled with the soulpatch grafted under his lower lip. It'd been too long since his field work required a beautician, and the hair weave he sported and morning shave he'd forgone for his shaggy, bohemian and un-Federal-agent look started to rankle him; Kindred was going to pay....

Sidling beside the battered foothills, the crafts' rotor washes blew ochre dust into the compound's encampment, irritating the aging security vehicles nearby. Below them, visible through the starboard windows, a security detail leapt out of a banged-up jeep and jogged towards the fencing meters away, in obvious haste.

"That didn't take long," Mason said, tracking the jeep.

Unbuckling her seatbelt, Kindred chuckled. "Maybe they don't get visitors very often...they could be happy to have some company, Stone man."

"Should be lucky they didn't shoot us down," Feltham added, pointing out the anti-aircraft battery stationed a hundred meters to the south.

"Nah...Global Security Net'd fry its electronics before they'd let go of the trigger," Mason said.

Blissfully aloof of Feltham's observation and the others' small talk, de Lis headed towards the cockpit as the pilots set the helicopters down on the hardpan earth. "Follow my lead, agents," he said, turning to face them. "Remember, we're just one happy scientific community...."

The four gathered their officially stamped "UN" briefcases and disembarked their helicopter, ducking under the dying rotors. De Lis led the way to the security tower looming over the fence's entrance, bearing a smile as fake as any Mason had glimpsed on the man.

"No UN! No UN!" a plump guard in a ragged uniform shouted in broken English, sounding like he'd learned it from watching dubbed Mexican telenovelas. He waved his arms outwards, trying to ward them off.

De Lis continued his smile, nodding excitedly. "I am Doctor Richard de Lis, visiting from the Ottawa University Particle Physics Department! I heard my old friend Nouri Yastanni was in today!"

The guard wrinkled the fur growth that had hijacked his upper lip. "No UN visitors expected today...Doctor Nouri said so."

"Ah, so he is in! I'm looking forward to meeting with my old friend!"

Giving the four a skeptical glance, the guard toggled the voxlink earpiece he wore, then spoke in Farsi.

Mason raised an eyebrow, looking askance to de Lis; sneaking in would have been less painful than this. The doctor gave Mason a confident smile; surely Louris' UN contacts had reached Yastanni's cronies by now.

The guard finished the conversation, wearing a distasteful grimace. Gesturing to the tower above, he gave clearance to the facility's entrance. "Doctor Yastanni will meet you inside," he said to the group finally, his voice croaking its displeasure.

"You're a good man!" De Lis clapped him on the shoulder, handing him a few bills to "grease the skids" in proper rural Iranian fashion, hopefully making their visit a little less eventful.

Λ

Escorted inside by the portly guard, who the group learned answered to the name Shadmani, they entered a large motorpool housing more rusted equipment and non-essential detritus on steel tables than anything else. Shadmani grunted when queried about amenities; the legendary Persian-Iranian warmness towards guests obviously needn't apply to research facilities.

A uniformed figure caught Mason's eye before disappearing behind a wall some distance down a nearby corridor. Dressed in black, it could've been the Iranian secret police, *Savak*, or the more shifty FSB, although anyone fancying themselves with a paramilitary force or militia could rent mercenaries as toy soldiers. Yastanni didn't seem the type to play with fire, but whoever's bill he was on may have been keeping him on a short leash.

Shadmani took them to an office suite, more like a rundown roadside motel, than left them there, muttering something akin to "Wait here a moment," but with the sincerity of a laborer on strike. He leered at Feltham and Kindred, perhaps out of curiousity for their lack of hejab or headscarves rather than anything more consequential.

Feltham reciprocated the displeasure with a furrowed brow; she was less than impressed with their escort. She dared not voice anything, lest the suite walls have ears, but the other three caught her drift.

De Lis availed himself the opportunity to study the suite. Hundreds of scientific journals, their covers rolled under themselves, weighed down the shelf racks against the wall. Several framed plaques, degrees and mounted photographs occupied another wall. Kindred got a kick out of the ones showing Yastanni, in his finest—and apparently sole—beige suit posing with various heads of state from across the globe, particularly the CAC and South America. The doctor's gapped-tooth grin and hairy neck were enough to bring a smile to the junior agent's face.

"Venezuela, Uzbekistan, Pakistan...." de Lis ticked off. "Nouri's got quite the client list...."

"Then I'm certain he'll be eager to help us out. I could listen to him for hours," Mason said, eyeing the hundreds of holographic data cylinders lining the storage container adjacent to the QPU situated behind Yastanni's desk chair. "The stories I'm sure he'll tell...."

"Stories...ah, I have plenty," a baritone voice said, thick with his native Farsi tongue, but in well-spoken, European English enunciation; it preceded the appearance of a thin-framed, but full-bellied man dressed in the already spied beige suit. His salt-and-pepper sat on his high forehead, exposing his tanned skin. "Doctor de Lis, I take it?"

"Yes, Doctor Yastanni." De Lis took Yastanni's hand into his. "It's good to see you again."

"Ah, yes, the lecture at the LHC...all the ladies swooned over you in the hotel that night, I recall."

De Lis blushed, drawing stares from his companions, but swiftly regained control. "*That* was a long time ago." He gestured to the agents beside him. "Thanks for your accommodations, Doctor. I've been working in concert with the UN Council on Theoretical Physical Applications since last year, just to shake up my tired routine. These are three of my most promising *students*."

Mason bit his tongue to hide his annoyance; following de Lis' lead didn't mean giving him split-second carte blanche. "Bobby Stone," he introduced himself, loosening his inflections and body language.

"Renee Flores," Kindred said in turn, her south-of-the-border accent spot on. She had accentuated her Latina persona with mocha highlights in her leftsided, combed-over hairdo, keeping it short and slick. Deep rouge blush and lipstick completed her look; having been raised in California, it lent her credibility to disguise her decidedly English heritage.

"Jennifer Grant-Uhls, but everyone calls me Roxy," Feltham answered, reclaiming the Mid-Atlantic speech inflections she had dropped with Academy training. Perhaps the subtleties of the slight Maryland accent she grew up speaking contrasting with the standard, nondescript American English she spoke on duty were lost to the ears of Yastanni; it was good practice, though, since none of them wanted to broadcast stereotypically stiff G-man qualities.

"So," Yastanni began, circling round the group to take his seat. "Why come all the way to this old place? Surely the Japanese have much more impressive facilities than here," he said, employing false modesty.

De Lis smiled, resting his arm against the desk. "Yes, but I have an interest that goes way back...something not quite the norm."

Yastanni's brow rose. "Oh...I am eager to hear, dear Richard. Tell me, can I entertain you in the kitchen, okay? I know I am famished when I come here for my work season."

Nodding, de Lis played along. Yastanni stood and led the four out the office door and down the corridor, where Mason had spotted the figure moments ago. Yastanni may have slipped up when Mason and Gilmour snagged him last time, but the old doc seemed to have learned his lesson about subterfuge since then.

A grease trap greeted them, not at all the mess hall Mason expected. Unwashed trays towered over the nearby sink, surely the sign of a lack of a female presence. A few of Yastanni's security guards shoveled food down their throats and left hastily, perhaps ashamed to be seen by strangers in such a place; Mason couldn't understand what would possess them to be so modest, unless it was indeed the pair of females in Feltham and Kindred, their heads overtly unadorned with scarves.

De Lis was proffered a foldout chair by Yastanni at the dining table, then sat down. Mason's team did the same, careful to avoid stepping into the oil slicks permeating the cement floor.

"Amenities here are less than I'd prefer," Yastanni said, firing up the kettle on the stove, "but adequate for seasonal research in late fall." Picking up a tray with a large, flat bowl full of speckled red and yellow couscous, he walked over to the table and presented it to the guests, then took a seat himself.

All five reached into the communal plate and helped themselves to the lukewarm hand food, de Lis' team scarfing hungrily after the draining helicopter ride.

De Lis swallowed his bite and began, "Doctor, do you remember some talk about the Korean Feudal States...particularly Kanggye?"

Yastanni tried to stifle it, but a curve formed on his lips that de Lis perceived, almost as if by provocation. "So your interest is special enough to track me down, hmm, Richard? To be honest, I have a great deal at stake with my benefactors in the Confederation. I have been working on a series of formulae left by the Koreans after the incident, that if I can solve, will be the greatest source of renewable—no, free—energy the world has ever known."

"Dark energy," Mason said.

Yastanni nodded. "I abhor that phrase. I prefer Quintessence. The essence of the universe, that which binds space and time together, but also directs the evolution, the expansion of spacetime as well. It is true I have performed experiments—"

A cacophonous shriek from the kitchen drew Yastanni's attention away. Hurriedly rising, he leapt to the stove and shut off the gas to the kettle. Pouring hot water into another container, he created a steaming pot of tea, to which he parceled out to five glasses and brought over to the table on another tray.

"How successful have your experiments proven?" Feltham asked, her eyes twinkling as she took her tea from the tray.

Catching her gaze, he replied, "Enough to bring you all here."

That's just what Mason and de Lis wanted to hear.

Λ

"The Confederation has subsidized some of my research into Quintessence," Yastanni explained later, during a tour of the facility's cavernous underground. A cement corridor lined with electrical pipes and a safety railing led them for meters, until Yastanni paused beside a reinforced steel door, inscribed with a sign reading "HAZARD" in Arabic Farsi, Cyrillic and English.

"I was keen to get a piece of the action myself," de Lis said. "I thought this would be the perfect place to begin."

Yastanni produced a pass key from his pocket and slid it through the pad on the door lock. A green LED shone on the pad a second later. "Indeed, Richard. Than I have the perfect person for you to meet...."

Mason and de Lis exchanged looks as a rush of air from the swiveling steel door blasted past them. Yastanni walked through the threshold, inviting de Lis' team inside the vaulted room, a gigantic, spherical laboratory dominated by a metal cylinder ten meters tall. Surrounded by a single-story gantry, this cylinder was studded with viewing portholes that seemed to indicate a vast experimental device capable of extraordinary power; dozens of intricate electrical cords snaked up its exterior, a chokehold of mechanical vines that fed the resources of a dedicated nuclear reactor to it alone. Several lab workers hovered about the cylinder, checking and fine-tuning the variety of support structures strewn around the room.

Kneeling next to one section of the cylinder was an older gentleman tapping notes into a holobook, who stood and crossed over to the group at the sound of the their entry. His shock of receding white hair, bushy eyebrows and aged posture gave him the appearance of someone who belonged to a chess club better than this extra-forces laboratory.

"Richard de Lis," Yastanni said, gesturing to the man, "this is Doctor Vasya Zaryov, of the Cosmoscience Institute. He's wanted to meet you for some time."

Mason glanced at de Lis, just in time to see the blood drain out of his face.

CHAPTER FOUR

"Magnificent, is it not?" Doctor Vasya Zaryov beamed, a glint of pride in his old hazel eyes. "Many researchers dream decades for a facility. The secrets of universe are closer, dear de Lis, than before in history."

Still shocked by the dual surprises of Zaryov and the momentous cylinder, de Lis shook his head, failing to comprehend the doctor's thick Russian-tinged speak. A few seconds of cogitation re-engaged de Lis' mind. "Yes...yes, Doctor. I—I am impressed. No one at the UN talked much about your work here."

"My side project. Forgive me your ignorance."

Zaryov held out his hand, which de Lis took into his. Shaking firmly, the two old warhorses sized each other up.

"My team, Doctor," de Lis began. "Who knew we'd be in your inestimable company? Bobby Stone, Renee Flores and Jennifer Grant-Uhls. Post-doctorate students of mine at Ottawa. So, have you settled Park Yoon's problems of neutrino caging?"

Zaryov rubbed his chin. "We have stepped beyond boundaries Doctor Park couldn't in last century. Today, Nouri and I are perfecting Casimir entrapment."

"And has your technique reached 10^{-29} gram per cubic centimeter?"

"We soon will be, Richard," Yastanni said. "Your help would be invaluable. You have Casimir experience, correct?"

"Well, yes..." he stammered, "my facility employs the largest Casimir chamber in the Northern Hemisphere." He eyed the cylindrical behemoth before them, then smiled. "*Formerly.*"

"What kind of assistance can we lend you?" Mason—without

de Lis' consent—asked Yastanni, eager to learn all he could about their operation; right now, the fact he knew no more about neutrino capture than a second-year university student didn't faze him.

"Our Casimir has not been sufficiently tuned to reach our optimal target vacuum. Pooling our resources, we could perhaps achieve a breakthrough in a fraction of the time otherwise. What is your opinion, Richard?"

Sticking his hands in his trouser pockets, he rolled on the balls of his feet in thought. Mason's impromptu volunteering was the agent's detective instincts kicking in, but de Lis couldn't help but think it was a small dig for his earlier student comment to Yastanni.

"I'd like to see your Casimir in work first, perhaps analyze your post results, seeing where your faults lie," de Lis answered. "Is that possible?"

Yastanni smiled. "We will get started."

Λ

A cascade of a million billion neutrinos—spewing forth from the sun's raging surface towards the massive Casimir chamber in the incredulously short span of an atomic nucleus' spin—were a fleeting presence until Yastanni gestured to a lab worker, who activated the behemoth device. Blacking out the laboratory's overhead lighting, the chamber's portholes flashed a spectral kaleidoscope of magenta and umber hues across the assembled audience, awing all save the two who spearheaded the effort.

And despite this sight's familiarity, Yastanni felt a surge of excitement deeply within him....

Manning the holographic display controlling the floodgates of quanta, Zaryov tapped a sequence of buttons on the virtual keypad, beginning the Casimir vacuum sequence, a pair of nanoscopic metallic plates that, when triggered, are pushed together by the negative energy of spacetime itself. Bound nor attracted by nothing but spacetime's curvature, neutrinos ordinarily flowed unobstructed through matter; that was until this particular Casimir chamber was nearly perfected, enabling a handful of neutrinos to be temporarily "caged" inside the Casimir plates, eking out a miniscule measurement by Yastanni's QPU. Betrayed by the negative curvature of spacetime, the smaller but still enormous quantity of neutrinos could only wait until finding a fault inside the Casimir cage and fleeing once more.

Even in this universal, godlike blink of an eye, Yastanni had achieved a small victory...and de Lis, studying the plasma reaction powering the mighty energies inside, knew the game was afoot, but his opponent had written the rules, controlled the ball and was running away while he stood on the sidelines. Yastanni crept closer to harnessing the awesome power of dark energy and utilizing the power for himself and the Confederation on a whim; it was starting to look more and more like a viable blueprint for global domination.

Mason exchanged grimaces with de Lis. The agent itched to track the breadcrumbs to the origin of this mess, and that meant just one place...the Korean Feudal States, formerly known as North Korea.

Λ

"Neutrinos gain mass, and hence, repulsive properties, when driven apart, or better yet, isolated," de Lis explained *sotto voce* to his "students" a short time later, during a break in their reconnaissance when left to themselves.

"This Casimir of theirs nearly isolates neutrinos, then?" Kindred asked.

De Lis nodded. "Close, but still not there yet." He glanced to Mason, but looked askance to Yastanni and Zaryov a short distance away. "I need to find out what research they've done here. Your cover won't last much longer, I'm afraid."

Mason was a quick study, but not that quick for this heady subject. "You've got that right, Doc. My usefulness is limited here. However, I do know what we can do to help your cause."

The doctor raised a quizzical eyebrow.

"A little field work in the Feudal States...checking up on Park Woon's old stomping grounds. Or should I say, what stomped on him."

"I'll stay only as long as I need to. You know where to reach me."

Mason nodded. "Ditto. You'll be the first one I tattle to."

Gesturing to his 9D teammates, Mason excused them and exited the laboratory, escorted once again by the obliging Shadmani, who was perhaps more than eager to expunge the interlopers from his facility. Mason craned his head back and watched the receding facility behind them; leaving de Lis to explain their departure, he wondered just what the doctor could pry out of the two in cahoots physicists, and whether or not it'd give them enough of an advantage.

Just what this dark energy or Quintessence was capable of was another matter, he mulled over in the second UN helicopter ride back. A deep velvet sky painted the cabin in shadow, somehow mirroring his ignorance about precisely what the Confederation were planning. Perhaps Yastanni's experiments were all folly, a massive diversion of resources by the CIS to keep him busy within a gilded collar. Drawing a sizable paycheck from their coffers, Mason surmised, might keep Yastanni from aiding any other players in a potentially lucrative black market.

Or should he say, dark market?

Λ

"Zaryov? Vasya Zaryov was there?!" Louris said, rising from his office's desk chair. He scanned the visages of the newly arrived 9D, his own wearing disbelief and awe.

"Yastanni's built a massive Casimir laboratory," Mason answered, handing him a holobook. "It's all in my report."

Louris scrolled through the document for several seconds, then bunched his nose up. "De Lis stayed...? What does he hope to find?"

"If the Confederation can entrap neutrinos, they can possibly manipulate this Quintessence force," Mason explained. "Zaryov's providing technical support in the effort. That's quite a braintrust, from what I gather."

Louris walked out from behind his desk and paced before them. "Zaryov conceived, designed and built the Confederation's prototype *Strela* warhead...Yastanni is utilizing this Casimir to secure a stream of neutrinos as weaponizable particles. It doesn't stretch my imagination to know what they're up to."

"And what we're up against," Feltham added.

"Which is why we need to investigate the Feudal States, discover what exactly this Quintessence force is, and how powerful it can be," Mason said.

Louris paused. "I believe I've got someone who can help you in that effort."

Λ

"Special Agent Tommy Bell, sir. I'm pleased to be on the Ninth Division team." The young man, barely midway through his twenties, extended his right hand.

"I remember you, Agent," Mason said, shaking his hand. "Paris, last year. The Yastanni sting. I seem to recall you were wearing that same tie, though it appears you've loosened up a bit." He gave a disarming smile. "Am I right?"

"Ruh-right, Agent Mason," Bell stammered. *Was it really the same tie?* "Graduation gift from my grandmother, sir. Said I should look sharp at all times."

"Smart woman. C'mon, we've got work to do."

Mason led the team past the security checkpoint egress into the underground hangar bay, where the waiting *Green Scream* was in the process of preflight checkup by the flight crew. The hangar support personnel deposited the agents' collective luggage into a compartment at the rear of the craft and, seconds later, signalled to them that all was aboard.

Climbing up the hatch's lowered stepladder and finally entering the jumpjet, Mason took a seat looking forward on the cabin's starboard side, his discretionary spot as leader of 9D. Bell followed Mason closely, but drew stares from Feltham and Kindred when he sat himself directly opposite Mason, facing back at the senior agent. The two women shared a glance; poor kid was in for it now.

Mason cleared his throat and nodded to the seat to his left.

"Huh—oh...? Pardon," Bell uttered, rising and sitting in the appointed seat. A sheepish grimace covered his face.

"Feltham's got that one," Kindred explained, taking her seat opposite Bell. "You'll learn."

"We all do," Mason said, then dropped the minor indiscretion. "Biloxi field office, correct?"

"Yeh-yes, sir," Bell answered. "Originally from Atlanta."

A thin curve grew over his mouth. "Hope you packed your thermal pajamas...."

Blue skies and warm solar rays soon broke over the hull of *Green Scream* with the dilation of the hangar's ceiling iris above them, clearing a path for their departure. A sudden and tremendous blast of power shrieking from the twin VTOL ramjet engines lifted the craft, which bolted out of the hangar and traversed half of DC in less than ten seconds. Another ten minutes past their ascent, and 9D was eighty kilometers off the surface of the planet.

And with that, Mason reclined and took what he knew was going to be the best nap he'd get for quite some time.

CHAPTER FIVE

"Log entry, 1625 hours, EDT. We've plummeted five kilometers in just under three minutes, completing the descent parabola of our flea jump over the North Pacific to the Korean Feudal States. Chief has arranged, through his 'special' diplomatic channels at the State Department, an escort for us to the Chagang-Do Territory, ruled by the local warlord Daejang—General— Lee Gap-soon. Our first stop will be to the capital, Kanggye, for a hopefully brief situation update, which sounds suspiciously like a debriefing *to me, but if it greases the wheels...."*

Mason shutoff his data ledger and yawned. It'd been a long flight and the gut feeling that rumbled inside him reminded him the Koreans were most likely going to stonewall 9D's every move; it also was a not-so-polite cry for fuel. Rummaging inside his bomber jacket for a snack stick, he shredded the packaging and reveled in its granola goodness.

"So, what's General Lee's story?" Kindred asked, turning her attention away from the buffeting clouds just outside the cabin window.

"Fought a series of trench wars with other Korean field commanders after the demise of the previously 'democratically' elected leader," Feltham said. "Particularly adept at public executions to consolidate his power."

Bell rolled his eyes. "Great Terror, hmm?"

Mason nodded. "Same as for every other strongman in history. No reason to change that formula now."

"The question remains: can we do business with him?" Feltham said.

Mason leaned back and finished off his last morsel. "China's put some pressure on him, for whatever good that does us. More important, it's his backyard. He inherited the site when North Korea bought the farm. Plus Chief's given me some 'special' provisions to, how shall I put it, help our cause."

Kindred's chocolate eyes sparkled. "A little diplomacy in a bottle?"

"And then some. Seems the general, like all warlords, fancies delicacies that aren't so easy to come by in a cash-strapped state such as his."

Mason booted up his holobook, displaying a half-sized holograph of smuggled Caspian Sea caviar, which rotated before the quartet.

"Just have that stuff sitting at the office for times like this?" Feltham quipped.

"I couldn't scrounge up a bevy of young virgins on short notice."

Λ

A shell of a rural capital lay ahead of *Green Scream*'s cockpit, a carcass bereft of busy metropolitan arteries, reaching skyscrapers or a noisy populace. Row upon row of Soviet-era, concrete pillbox apartment rows and civil service structures were the signatures of Kanggye, hardly a jewel of post-dynastic Kim Korea. Forests dotted the periphery as far as the horizon, but no fauna could willingly call this dystopian graveyard home. Mud roads crisscrossed the brown fields under them, cut by deep ruts from the only reliable mode of independent ground transportation, heavy army lorries capable of breaking the semi-permafrost in the winter, and navigating the overflow from the distant Yalu River and its local tributary—the Changja—in summer.

"Charming," Kindred observed from her comfy seat. "Did somebody forget to tell Lee this is the twenty-second century?"

"The Feudal States are officially home to five of the top twenty armpits of the globe, Sha," Mason said, only half-joking. "Just be glad we're not going undercover on this one."

Gradually, the jumpjet circled round the municipal airport and set down on the single identifiably maintained tarmac. The pilots taxied the craft to the hangar, where a crisp, olive-drab-painted lorry emerged from the shade and parked in front of them.

Walking to the starboard hatch, the 9D team exited onto the airstrip and viewed their reception by a group of short—but not by North Korean standards—officials before retrieving their baggage from the aft storage area.

"Ah, here's our hosts now," Mason said, hoisting his baggage over his shoulder. Traversing the tarmac, he extended his hand to the head official, who looked vaguely authoritarian in his starched business suit and high-collar shirt. Then again, he thought, they all looked like some-body had pissed in their pool.

"Special Agent Mason...so good to meet you," the man greeted in stiff, heavily accented English, flashing a jaw full of yellow, decaying teeth. A sparkling Swiss timepiece on his wrist, coupled with his top-dol-lar suit, were completely incongruous with his hygiene. "My name is Im Hyong-jo, director of General Lee's diplomatic affairs."

Mason bowed, which was returned by Im. "Thank you for receiv-ing us so promptly, Director Im. This is my team."

Im bowed to the rest, then led the way to the lorry, which had additional seating behind the cab. "Please, follow me. Grand accommo-dations are appointed you in Koryo Hotel."

"Koryo? Isn't that in Pyongyang?" Mason asked.

"Ah," Im smiled, "ours is modeled on that magnificent gem. Please, all accommodations wait for you."

"Excellent." Mason started behind Im, looking over his shoulder to Feltham. "That was easier than expected," he whispered to her.

Feltham answered with an unimpressed grunt.

Λ

Journeying to the local Koryo Hotel amid the bombed-out roads in a lorry that had never known shock absorbers, the 9D team piled out of the vehicle with military precision after coming to a halt at the hotel's side street entrance. Once the luxuriously exotic pleasure quarters of the Chagang-Do Communist Party, this Koryo Hotel had fallen on rough times as of late, as evidenced by the shell holes, machine-gun ricochet blasts and grenade potholes peppering the property. At least the broken glass had been swept away before their arrival, Mason noted. Despite Im's exultation to the contrary, this Koryo was a pale imitation, barely reaching twenty stories and possessing no revolving rooftop restaurants like its famous namesake. But with the general in charge in these parts, he could name it whatever he pleased.

Im and his two colleagues—Hwang and Jeong—led 9D through the lobby and up to a tenth story ballroom-cum-lounge, where Hwang poured glasses of tea and presented small biscuits prepared in advance to the agents. Unloading their baggage on the floor in a heap, the agents then sat their aching rear ends on gilded, purple velvet-lined chairs arranged around one of several tables.

Im, in an awkward stance, observed his guests while appearing to be hiding a painfully gimpy leg, which didn't escape Mason's atten-tion; the agent judged the director to be in his fifties by countenance, but was most likely a good decade older, owing to the unusually youthful

Southeastern Asian constitution. An old war wound could have been the culprit, Mason figured; perhaps he had fought with General Lee, and when Im proved to be too lame, was provided with this cush appointment. His Company instincts kicking in, Mason contemplated how he could probe Im's psychology and worm his way to getting a bead—or better yet, an advantage—on Lee this way, if the pair's relationship did indeed stretch back many years.

"When do we meet with General Lee, Director Im?" Mason asked, sipping the tea, which seemed to consist of colored water disguising itself as oolong.

"The general greets you when we arrive tomorrow."

Mason nodded. "Ah, good. I have plenty of questions for him."

"Yes, the general has interest in the history of this incident. Frankly," Im shook his head sorrowfully, almost shamefully, "Our science community suffers great deal in the intervening years."

"I suppose it has....all the more reason for my team and I to get to the bottom of this mystery."

Im smiled. "Yes, of course." He pulled out a crumpled piece of paper and referred to it. "Unfortunately, the general determines certain areas off-limit, which we deem territorial security secrets. I hope not to offend you."

"We understand, Director," Mason said. "May I know which areas?"

Im gestured to Jeong, who handed Mason an emulsion photograph of the site, taken from orbital reconnaissance satellite. The large plot of land was squared-off and marked with red and black scrawls, looking as though Im had just declared parcels forbidden by throwing darts at the photograph. GPS coordinates were written on it as well, just to be safe.

"Now, we take our leave of you. Our hospitality is at your disposal, Agents. Whatever you require, please take advantage of us."

Mason and Feltham gave courteous smiles as the Koreans exited the room and closed the door behind them.

"Well," Mason said, reclining in his seat, "that wasn't as bad as I thought it'd—"

"I don't trust that coot as far as I can throw him," Kindred blurted.

Bell stroked his chin. "Maybe not, but we've got unfettered access to the unmarked incident site, right, Agent Mason?"

"For now," he answered. "Of course, that could change with Lee there. But that won't stop us from scanning for what we need...their experience with Americans may make them think we're suckers. That's where you come in, Bell. Go ahead and start setting up your equipment. Do a test run on this hotel and get some baseline readings. I want to be able to sort out the background radiation from the DU shells littering this joint from anything we might pickup tomorrow."

"All right."

"I'll start webdigging in the local nets," Feltham said. "See if I can bypass those firewalls preventing us from reconnoitering from HQ."

Mason nodded. "Good. See if you can also link to the Global Security Network and find out what exactly it is our intel says is off-limits. Meanwhile, Sha and I are gonna scrounge up some real food."

Λ

Bright dawn rays shone over their backs as the agents clambered into the lorry once more, a two-hour ride ahead of them to the outskirts of Chagang-Do, nearer to the Confederation border than was really comfortable. Despite the knowledge that five hundred meters of no man's land filled with sensing devices and landmines established during the Feudal Wars kept the peace between here and there, Mason's mind would be at battlestations the entirety of the investigation, especially since the Confederation's orbiting Geosync Array was in all likelihood monitoring their investigation.

Jostling in the rear cabin, 9D were left to review in their heads the discoveries they uncovered the previous night, if only to break the tedium presented by the ride through the unrelenting forests and despairing collapse of civilization here.

Feltham's foregoing of sleep to explore all known intel paid dividends, she had explained earlier, once Mason himself woke earlier that morning. For years before the incident, the Kim regime utilized the site as an underground biochem storage facility, until international sanctions forced the military to dispose of all accountable stockpiles of the weaponized agents. All areas designated off-limits by Im matched exact GPS coordinates as given in the UN Security Council brief from 2036. So, that possibly explained Lee's reluctance. But, another issue niggled at Mason, one he couldn't ascribe to the biochem hazard. De Lis said scores perished in the incident, but no one knew precisely how. Radiation exposure? Maybe. By now, that should have subsided. An explosion? Happens all the time, certainly in numbers de Lis described, but not generally worth ninety years' secrecy, even in a maximum security area known to the UN.

And this Project Ether business stood to be an entirely unknown quantity. De Lis and Yastanni explained it in vague terms, good enough for gee whiz contemplation, but in real life, what would happen? Mason's confidence in 9D's investigation and instruments was second to none, but could they even know the signs if they stumbled upon them? Louris felt Bell knowledgeable enough with the theories imparted by de Lis to lead the scientific survey, but Mason knew nothing short of the Ottawa theoretical physicist's presence could possibly do the investigation justice.

The one thing Mason knew wasn't in short supply was uncertainty; what they would find, and what they could possibly do about it.

CHAPTER SIX

"There was a facility here?"

Feltham stepped away from the lorry, her hand over her eyes to block the blinding sun. An empty green meadow, devoid of any structural remnants, spread out before her, broken up by a sprawling concrete sea until stopping at a treeline a hundred meters distant. Mason looked out over a series of bunkers to the right of the lorry, an area that fell within the off-limits zone.

Bell and Kindred however, departed to the south, left of the other agents and Im's contingent. A yawning crater, long since grown over with native shrubs, grasses and sickly trees, lay just meters away, like a long-lost mass grave or some uncovered Mayan cenote.

"Holy—Mason! Over here!" Kindred exclaimed.

Mason and Feltham walked around the obstructing lorry and over to Kindred's side. Less hastily, Im followed behind, pointing to the depression.

"Yes, main facility was located here," the director said. "Legends say it descends some ten stories into the ground."

Bell peered over the grassy edge. Kicking some loose gravel and grass clumps down the hole, he watched them fall until they were no longer lit by the sun. He let out a low whistle. "Yup."

The scrabbling of tires on gravel alerted the group to the arrival of another lorry, this one escorted by a battle-scarred but still service-able sedan, which seemed to run on ancient diesel fuel, judging by the noxious fumes. The sedan stopped with flourish, throwing up a cloud of dust; out of the left passenger door exited a surprisingly tall Korean man in army greens and military cap who wore shades and more brass medals and ribbons on his chest than anyone the agents had ever seen.

Im bolted towards the man, and bowing repeatedly and obsequiously, spoke excitedly in Korean.

General Lee Gap-soon strode gracefully past Im and shook hands with Mason, and without saying a word, nor removing his cap or shades, smiled widely and embraced the special agent. The general was well-tanned, his skin taut but with a frame built like an ox; little wonder Mason, thought, that Lee commanded with such a presence.

Mason uttered a meek "Hello" and clapped the general's upper arms, not fully comprehending or knowledgeable of traditional salutations in this land.

Lee spoke in Korean, to which Im immediately snapped to and stepped towards 9D.

"General Lee is quite happy to see you arrive safely," Im translated. "He wants to know if your stay is satisfactory."

"Yes, quite, thank you," Mason answered for the team. "I have some gifts for you, General Lee."

Mason walked to the lorry and returned with a briefcase, which he opened and presented to Lee. Reaching inside, the agent extracted the can of caviar and handed it to the general, who received it with a toothy grin. Another extraction produced a bottled liter of amber hard liquor. Upon this second offering, Lee doffed his sunglasses and inspected the bottle intently.

"A fine example of southern American hospitality," Mason extolled to Lee. "One of my favorites, bourbon."

Im translated for Lee, whose eyebrows jumped up in excitement. He held his hand out and exchanged a vigorous shake with Mason.

"Good going, boss," Feltham laughed. "I think you're his new best friend."

Λ

Mason repelled down the crater first, followed by Bell, then Feltham, all armed with hardhats, torches and equipment cases slung over their shoulders. Kindred stayed behind to man the wench rooted a meter from the edge, and also to keep a scrupulous eye on their hosts; an RT-01/9V nine millimeter semi-automatic pistol holstered inside her jacket kept her from feeling too insecure.

Once the trio were on solid ground, they swept the shaded area with torch illumination to provide a basic layout for them to proceed. Bell setup his instruments and took readings of the crater's dimensions: the agents were thirty-one meters below Kindred, and the crater itself loomed with a breadth and length of seventy-four and forty meters, respectively. The floor itself was the intervening nine levels and roof of the former structure, now pancaked into a jigsaw patchwork of shattered, overgrown concrete and periodic holes where the bare ground could be seen.

Mason inspected their descent wall; mosses and vines grew over and out of drainage pipes and skeletal support beams, but nature hadn't quite obliterated every scrap of the structure. Kicking up clods of earth and flora underfoot, he uncovered disintegrated plaster, decomposed conduit wiring, oxidized rebar steel scrap and shards of Plexiglas which crackled in such quantities that it couldn't have all originated from the crater floor. From the looks of it, whatever structure remained on the surface had at one point been bulldozed into the crater.

"Detecting a massively reinforced concrete substructure, pretty sophisticated for its time," Bell announced, surveying the area with his lidar cannon, which resembled a squat torch with a concave end. A rotating holographic schematic of the building shone on the holobook in his other hand. "I am going to hazard a guess and say this facility was built to withstand a nuclear detonation."

Mason glanced at Bell's holobook. "Well, we can tick that one off the checklist."

"A detonation from outside or above," Feltham said, "but from within? I don't think so."

"I didn't say that, Agent Feltham. Obviously something with awesome power gutted this place." Bell sighed. "No radiation...no chemical burns, or conventional blast residue, just the remnants of the materials. What did you say they researched here?"

"De Lis wasn't one hundred percent positive, but he had an inkling it was dark energy," Mason explained.

Bell's eyes bugged out. "Sweet Jesus, that Project Ether brief was no joke, was it?"

"If it was dark energy, as de Lis speculated, we need some damn good evidence to back it up," Mason said. "And proof positive that the Koreans didn't blow the place up later to cover their tracks."

Feltham clapped her hands. "All right, then, what are the telltale signs of an extremely exotic force of nature hitherto unknown in the entire history of mankind, and for all we know, invisible to our devices?"

A smile crossed Mason's face. "What we can't explain any other way, Lis."

Λ

"The soil under the foundation does seem to have been subjected to some extreme trauma," Bell said as he inspected a patch of bare ground on his haunches. Pocket knife in hand, he scraped through loose earth with the blade, exposing it to his lidar's concentrated laser scan.

"Really?" Mason knelt next to him, studying the results on Bell's holobook. "An impact?"

Bell shook his head. "Not any impact the reference library can discern. The atomic states of the constituent molecules have been scrambled—or, well, it's the best way I can describe this. Again, no neutron residue or radioactive isotopes are present here in vastly differing quantities than the background radiation I captured at the hotel. It's like a pressure wave acted on such a small scale that all matter here was traumatized."

Mason rose and booted up the holobook at his side. Toggling the holographic interface, he dialed de Lis' webaddress and waited for the doctor to answer.

Away from the two boys, Feltham inspected a corner of the crater where the landslide of debris from the surface collected into a pile, now under illumination by the midday sun. Wearing gloves and brandishing a collapsible shovel, she sifted and dug through the detritus, searching for possibly more of the papers and handwritten notes that were stashed inside several cabinets she discovered while reconnoitering the walled perimeter.

Clearing a sullied, twisted metal filing cabinet, she dislodged a corroded lock with her shovel, breaking open the door for the first time in nearly a century. Inside, a greater portion of written materials had decayed to a gritty slime, but moving towards the back of the cabinet, she revealed unscathed journals and binders.

She flipped through grimy printouts from ancient computers and handwritten pages, all in Korean—*hangul*—characters. Looking up to Kindred, she saw the agent standing sentinel over the area, without interference or prying eyes. Now was the time. Working fast, Feltham scanned the extant papers with her holobook, downloading all the text for later retrieval.

Finishing in haste, she ripped the pages apart and sprinkled them amongst the debris; just because the Company managed to get access, didn't mean the Confederation's own FSB couldn't as well. All the better to get as much of a leg up as possible.

Back in their section, Mason lifted a concrete slab from its mooring and pushed it to one side, allowing Bell to extract soil and other samples from deeper inside the crater, some ten meters from their previous sampling. Scrabbling within a pocket of rubble, the distinctive odor of rot pierced Bell's nostrils, forcing him onto his heels.

"Ahh—god...!"

Mason steadied the agent. "Wha—you all right?"

"Yeah...." Bell covered his mouth and nose. "Just...you'll smell it."

"I'm surprised after all this time...." Mason winced, putting his own hand over his face. "Well, might as well scan it, too."

Bell nodded, but not without displeasure. His holobook took in all the data from whatever's—or more precisely, whomever's body—had the misfortune of this horrendous death, crushed under all this mass, or perhaps, if they lucked out, during the incident.

A distinctive beep came from Mason's holobook. Tapping the interface, de Lis' head and shoulders materialized as a ten-centimeter-tall holograph, while Mason's own smaller avatar popped up right below. "Doctor, we're at the incident site. I need you to look these data over... and fast."

Data streams were sent up into the Global Security Network satellites, and redirected back to de Lis' location.

Scrolling through the uplinked data on his own holobook, the doctor replied, "Good work. I'm going to need some more time and a second opinion, but I think our supposition may be spot on. Does General Lee have any clue what you're on to?"

Mason craned his head back to the crater top. "If he does, he's been incredibly blasé. I helped our cause with a little 'diplomacy.'"

De Lis laughed.

"Doctor, this analysis is troubling," Mason said, his voice growing deeper and grave. "The more we scan, the more we're worried a weaponized version of this incident is the thrust of Project Ether. And the damnable thing is, it's almost impossible to discern any evidence that this was nothing more than a conventional or natural disaster."

"Evidence may just be stacking up, Agent Mason, but I won't elaborate. Get back safely when you wrap. De Lis out." The doctor's image shimmered, then faded.

Mason latched the holobook to his belt and returned his attention to Bell's investigation. Below the agents, after spending ninety years entombed in a concrete and steel deathtrap, were three remains, freshly exhumed. With skeletons shattered beyond traditional forensic reconstruction, the bodies cried out to tell their stories, after having been neglected by authorities for a century.

Kneeling down to caress a splintered femur in his gloved hands, Mason longed to have them give up their secrets about that fateful day, and warn the agent of what terrible experiments they had once unleashed. If he couldn't—or wouldn't—many millions more were sure to meet the same end.

Λ

Armed with terabytes of scanned data and materials samples, the trio of special agents clambered back to the top, in time to catch General Lee's soldiers prepping the lorries for the return journey to the Koryo Hotel before night fell and the assured onslaught of bandits, highwaymen and two-bit drug lords who prowled the outskirts fell upon the scene.

A fruitful investigation it had been, that much Mason could sleep on. In spite of that, the agent couldn't ease up until de Lis passed judgment on just what exactly the agents had discovered. A pre-dawn flight back to DC to get those answers ASAP was all that calmed his anxious mind; at least they didn't have to spend another night in this civilization vacuum. Im had been pleasant enough and accommodating per Louris's pre-arrangements, but the unsavouriness of General Lee's regime still left a bad taste, which he knew was the price of doing business in this corner of the world, particularly with their paramount concerns.

Sighing in relief as *Green Scream* ascended into the inky night, Mason decompressed in his cabin seat, accompanied by his 9D agents, all of whom relaxed as well when they saw the boss finally succumb to a nap. It was the barometer that all was well, for now.

CHAPTER SEVEN

"Yastanni and Zaryov are just weeks away from finishing this stage," de Lis pronounced, crossing his arms while standing in Louris' office. The sunlight streaming inside amplified his deep-set wrinkles and crow's feet, adding years to his visage and weight to his words.

Mason glanced at de Lis, than back to Louris. "What do you mean, stage?"

"You were on the right track, Greg," Louris said. "Weaponization can be the only answer. The State Department reviewed the consular logs of numerous diplomatic 'missions' in North American territories across the globe. They noticed an appreciative uptick in Confederation diplomats—FSB agents—accessing sensitive, but not high-level, data-bases on university theoretical physics projects relating to dark energy."

"Recruitment for out-of-country 'civilian sector' applications," de Lis explained. "Of course, this is a cover for the intelligence services."

Feltham nodded. "Nothing new there."

"Of course not. Doctor," Mason said, looking to de Lis, "if Yastanni is at Stage One, what's next?"

"I can't even begin to fathom. So, my next task is to replicate Yastanni's results, despite being months ahead of us."

"Do you have time for that?" Kindred asked. "His setup looked pretty damned intricate, let alone expensive."

De Lis smiled. "I've got a few friends in the community willing to part with a few days' worth of lab time, and equipment, to assist me."

"Good...sounds like we're going to need it." Louris rose from his seat. "What are your plans?"

The doctor toggled a button on Louris' desk interface, producing an eye-level holographic display. An image of the Chagang-Do crater hovered, then zoomed in to show a detailed schematic of the facility's structure as it most likely looked prior to the explosion. Situated inside the lowest sub-basement floor was a massive cylindrical mechanism, not too far removed, design-wise, from Yastanni's Casimir device.

"I contacted Doctor Valagua back at the theoretical studies lab and instructed him to recreate Park's facility from 9D's scans," de Lis said. "Now, based on the molecular damage the grounds experienced, we ran a few scenarios with conventional explosives attempting—the equivalent of several hundred megatonnes of TNT—to simulate the implosion."

Before them, a pressure wave detonated from within the cylinder, shooting an explosive column upwards into the above-ground levels, rapidly dissipating in the myriad corridors and punching a narrow hole into the facility's upper levels; the implosion was deadly, but nowhere near the calamity the agents saw firsthand.

Kindred's eyes were wide. "Wow...."

"Impressive, but not what did the deed," de Lis said. "My aim is to recreate this. Controlled, of course."

De Lis tapped a button, which reset the holographic structure. Now rolling forwards again, a second, far larger pressure wave erupted outwards, rippling through the facility not in an explosion as before, but in an expansive bulge of matter and space that stretched the structure outwards and then rebounded so violently the facility imploded within a half-second.

Unlike the conventional explosion, the entire facility, from top to bottom, sat in ruins, left to decay and become subject to the floral overgrowth, as experienced a day ago by Mason's team. The five agents gasped, leaving no doubt as to the perceived horror they had just witnessed, even in a simulated, holographic form.

"And that's an exaggeration...with your scans, Agents, it appears all the atoms within this structure, regardless of molecular composition, were merely 'nudged' out of place by less than an atomic nucleus' radius. You can see how much destruction an accident caused. In the olden days, we'd see this sort of destruction by a nuclear bunker buster. In modern armaments, this is equivalent to at least two neutronic devices."

Mason stroked his jaw. "Death by brush of a feather."

"Indeed. The only reason the destruction wasn't greater is because the miniscule tau-neutrinos responsible decayed in a split-second," de Lis explained. "But, therein may lie a chink in its effectiveness. Controlling these tau-neutrinos is quite difficult, nearly impossible until now. So, the potential for a 'dud,' if you will, is great, possibly as high as fifty percent. If anything, this is equivalent to the first atomic devices constructed by Los Alamos two centuries ago."

"Huh," Kindred blurted. "A roll of the dice."

De Lis nodded. "That's my mission, Agents. I don't envy yours."

"Just take care of your end of the bargain," Mason said, smiling. "Leave us the whys and wherefores."

Λ

With de Lis trotting back up to Ottawa under orders to report his progress at regular intervals, Mason and 9D set to work rifling through the State Department's reports and Company confirmations on the alleged FSB involvement in physicist pilfering. Expanding the investigation out to known diplomatic spies in the FSB and suspected civilian projects supervised by North American-recruited scientists, the agents drew up a list of activities across the globe that could involve either construction of or conversion into dual-use facilities for large scale testing of dark energy applications. Subterranean targets were given special attention, and the North American Geological Survey's scans of these areas were updated on a constant basis, whether for unnatural seismic activity, geological transformations or other unforeseen anomalous events.

Target tracking on this large of a scale resulted in nearly the entire Earth becoming subject to their investigation, but some could be blue-prize winners over others deemed lower priority. Occam's Razor assumed the Confederation would choose sites within their purview, for obvious reasons. For this purpose, Mason dug into known or suspected Confederation military maneuvers for the past year, with the intent of seeking any patterns indicative of major shifts in personnel, material or vehicles conducive to manning or constructing said facilities.

And with a week's worth of parsing, deconstructing and splicing together the innumerable reports, Mason formulated his candidates for immediate investigation.

Λ

"Our first assumptions were that the Confederation were doing this in-house, in Asia, preferably within its borders," Mason said, leaning forward as he sat at Louris' desk. "Plausible denial makes me suspect they'd go outside the country."

Louris scrolled through Mason's holobook. "The South African Republic and the Kuril Islands...the first seems less conspicuous, but the Kurils—"

"Hear me out, Chief. Japan's penchant for nuclear accidents isn't a dirty secret. Russian scientists can easily slip the necessary materials into the islands and perform experiments with reasonable assurances that whatever goes boom there is by result of the Japanese nuclear system, not anything the Confederation is doing. Hell, they've occupied the islands for two hundred years. I don't see it as a stretch."

"Agreed. This won't be a breeze, though." Louris scanned over the report once more, than caught Mason's gaze. "What's your plan?"

"I've outlined in the brief to split up 9D. Feltham and Bell will go to the Kurils, while Kindred and I go to South Africa."

Louris nodded. "All right...I'll get to work."

Λ

"With all respect, sir, may I request a change in your field assignments?"

Mason set his holobook onto his desk and looked to the rookie, Bell. The three teammates stood at their boss's side. "Is there a problem?"

"No problems, sir. It's just that I spent two years in Southern Africa on a genealogical expedition out of school...my contacts may get us through the door easier."

Mason put his fingers to his lips. "And just how long were you going to wait before giving me this vital information, Tommy?"

"I wasn't going to actually allow Agent Kindred to board that jumpjet, sir, whatever it took," Bell said in a dry monotone, then couldn't help but crack a smile.

Feltham glanced to Mason. "Your understudy learns fast."

"Indeed he does. Mind going on some deep recon instead, Lis?"

"I thrive on it."

"Excellent." Mason pumped his fist. "Well, ladies, I bid you adieu. On to the Kurils with you, then."

The two women departed from Mason's small office with nods. Mason rose from his seat and handed Bell his holobook, patting it against the agent's chest.

"Sir?"

"Plot our course. Make sure those contacts of yours get us some primo accommodations."

Bell took the holobook into his hand. "I'll do my best."

"You'll do better than that," Mason said, his turquoise pupils gleaming. "You're taking the lead on this one. Congratulations on winning me over, Agent Bell. Now make me proud."

CHAPTER EIGHT

Departing the passenger liner, the two men carried their modest luggage out of Johannesburg International Airport and, hailing a taxicab, made their way to the posh Palazzo Inter Continental Montecasino hotel. Dining on the fine steaks provided by the five-star restaurant on the third floor, the pair had their fill and soon headed into the evening chill, this time setting out in a rented stretch limousine to the Melrose Arch Hotel, previously scouted by intelligence agents secured throughout Jo'berg.

The scheduled appointment coincided precisely with the nightly retirement of three scientists assigned to TauTona Gold Mine, seventy-five kilometers outside Johannesburg. Exchanging glances, the pair exited the limo and swiftly crossed the twenty-meter distance to the hotel's entrance and over to the registry desk.

Dispatching any question about their business or identities with a quick show of badges and a handful of euro credits, the men tracked their quarry through the upper level of the lobby, trailing the unwitting prey across slick marble floors and wide, sweeping stairsteps, where the refracted chandelier light lent a fuzzy glow to the corridor.

Spying their trio of targeted rooms, the pair nonchalantly approached with naught an audible footfall. Leaving his partner to survey the corridor's only cross-section as a lookout, the other one produced a lockpicking passkey, which he employed on the door panel, accessing the room and shutting the door behind him.

Returning to the corridor, he repeated the procedure for the second room, and when that task was complete, he turned to the final room, this one closest to his partner. Closing the door silently, he skulked into a corner, listening to the putterings of a man in the bedroom who sang, rather badly, a Russian pop song from too many years past.

"Andrei Ilichev...."

Peering into the shadows, Andrei dropped the crumpled shirt from his hands, his eyes bulging in horror. "Who let you in?"

Walking forward, the tall man's buzzed, blond hair shone in the low light, blotting out his visage. He wore an immaculately clean and pressed undershirt like a noose around his neck, faint impressions of blue ink in his skin barely concealed by the collar. "I am called MOLOTOK. You have done a disservice to your colleagues, your field, and most despicably, your country."

"Don't you lecture me, you bastard! I have only done what my country has ever asked of me!"

Andrei threw a chair at the sinister figure and ran for the door, screaming. The intruder shrugged off the assault and with a single motion kicked Andrei in the kidneys, felling him. Reaching down, the intruder grabbed Andrei's hair and pulled him to his feet.

"No one can hear you," the tall man taunted. Sinews rippled and danced under his flesh as he now held the boy at arm's length in the air solely with his right arm; fingers squeezed an utterly vulnerable windpipe, an inhuman rasping springing from his forearm as muscles contracted.

Turning ashen faced, gurgles trickled from Andrei's lips. "Gggaaahhhh—gggkkkk...."

"Slime such as yourself are weak...did you really think a young girl would throw herself upon you, with your pockmarked face? Shit like you aren't fit to represent my country."

Producing a narrow ampule from his jacket, the intruder held it to the light before Andrei, studying it. "What secrets did she extract from you, slime? Was she a good lay? Or did you even get it up, hmm? TELL ME!"

"Nnngaahhh...."

"Ultimately," he said, his yellowed teeth glimmering inside a malignant smile, "it's not important. You're disposable...a drain on our resources. Your time has passed anyway."

"Gaahhh—"

The ampule entered Andrei's neck, its contents emptying via a nanoscopic hole tinier than a pore in the research assistant's neck, potently ending his resistance.

Releasing his grip, the tall man let the body collapse to the floor before him, a convulsing heap that no longer posed any obstacle to their operations. Lowering his arm, he winced at the continued firing of neural impulses into his muscles, only alleviated after a few seconds of applied pressure to his forearm, ceasing the relentless tension.

A moment later he walked down the corridor, where his partner stood in wait.

"It is done."

"Our contact will be very pleased."

Λ

Stepping off the tram car, Mason and Bell donned sunglasses and hoisted their equipment bags as they set foot on the gravel road leading to the office building a block away in Carletonville, a small town with the population of a city in near northwestern South Africa, home of the world's deepest diamond and gold mines.

Dozens of foreign workers from Lesotho, Mozambique and Zimbabwe shuffled past the duo, queueing up for the smaller trams to take them to the various mine shafts sprawled throughout the complex. If the arriving throng wasn't a commotion unto itself, then the mass exodus from the completed third shift put it over the edge. Hundreds of exhausted miners, hardhats and lunch pails in hand, commingled just a few meters away. It was a well-choreographed swarm to all but Mason and Bell, who could only look on, baffled by the complex simplicity.

Ahead of them, dust clouds from each passing vehicle billowed into the azure sky, the late-season drought rendering the landscape bone dry, only increasing the multitude of hazards associated with one of the most dangerous professions in history. If the heat of the sun didn't kill you, hell's depths would.

Unbuttoning the top two buttons of his cotton shirt, Mason let out a tired sigh.

"Don't go weak on me now, sir. Take a look at these guys," Bell said in admiration, "this is like the arctic compared to those mines."

Mason wiped his brow. "I knew it coming in, but you'd think I'd be used to this heat in DC. Guess I need to step out of the office once in a while."

"Not much longer now." Bell shielded his eyes with his hand, and sighting an ancient vending machine, pointed to it, to his mentor's relief. "Bet you we can cool off with some of that."

With refreshments guzzled noisily, the agents crossed over to the Western Deep Levels Mining Corp offices, a four-story, thoroughly modern glass and steel structure haphazardly constructed in the middle of an intersection of two gravel roads, seemingly plopped down from above by the whims of an architect who had never actually seen the plot of land.

The W.D.L.M. Corp owned and managed the Western Deep Levels mines, but contracted responsibility for the employment of miners out to various firms. It was a complicated and often sordid mess, stemming from the National Union of Mineworkers and the Department of Minerals and Energy competing over who wronged whom whenever an accident occurred, and the government in general having to answer to families when public outcries rose to deafening levels. Mason's research prepared him for the potentially "explosive" job ahead of them in piecing together TauTona's part in the Project Ether investigation, but until he and Bell actually got down there and dug around for real, he couldn't fully appreciate the politics quite yet. All that was certain was that Confederation activities here were just noticeable enough to warrant 9D's immediate investigation; whether Zaryov had a second Casimir lab under construction, masquerading as a section of TauTona, or some other, unfathomable operation was still up for speculation.

Opening the entry door, Mason and Bell were greeted by an invigorating wind gust, not only drying their perspiration but removing the buildup of dirt and irritants already finding their way into uncomfortable areas where the sun doesn't normally shine. A security guard at a check-in desk rose and welcomed them inside.

Putting his hands on the circular desk, Bell said, "We're here on appointment to meet Director Heydenrych for consultation."

"Ah, yes. Please sign." The young man, who wore a blue shirt two sizes too large and appeared to be barely out of school, handed Bell a digital ledger and stylus.

Bell and Mason signed their cover signatures as William Jackson and Bobby Stone, then waited at a nearby bench seat for Western Deep Mines' director of facilities, Errol Heydenrych. Mason knew little of the man, save for Bell's initial impression of him when webbing Heydenrych back in DC. Appealing to Western Deep Mines' bottom line, Bell presented the agents as potential suitors for investment in further deepening of TauTona, an ongoing project that had the nasty habit of eating revenue and killing miners at a prodigious rate. All the better to get hands on with whatever was lurking deep underground.

Of paramount importance was getting to know what activities the Confederation and other groups were or could possibly be participating in; if Zaryov was busy developing a weapons program out of Project Ether in TauTona, who else had a stake in this mine? The implosion of the Kim regime and subsequent exodus of matériel and knowledge after the Chagang-Do incident out of North Korea almost guaranteed hostile, international interest in such research. If 9D's luck meant they were a good decade behind less-than-savory regimes getting access to this dark energy weaponization, North America would have a serious crisis to confront, if not outright combat. Mason only hoped de Lis' pronouncement that Stage Two had yet to be activated was spot-on.

Past the check-in desk a set of doors opened, admitting a thin man with greying, short-cropped hair, his skin a permanent beet-red from the overbearing solar rays. Gliding over to the two agents, Errol Heydenrych tilted his head, greeting them with a lightly accented "Hello" that seemed to come out of some exotic European city that never existed.

"Good morning, Director," Mason said, standing. "Sorry, we're a bit early."

"No worries, gentlemen. Good to see you arrived, although I must apologize for the dreadful drought. Makes matters somewhat unpleasant." Heydenrych gestured to the doorway. "Please, let us go to my office upstairs. We can do business in the cooler air."

The agents followed Heydenrych up a set of stairs into a corridor lined with windows overlooking the TauTona site. A twenty-five-meter tall, squared-off structure—the winding tower, the entry into the mine itself and means of ore and spoils retrieval—dominated a skyline over which fairly low-key buildings and other administrative structures and facilities blanketed the area, broken up by pepper trees that suffered in the sweltering heat. In the distance, visible now thanks to their ascent, they viewed an ashen pyramid composed of mine spoils, rivaling any natural mountain around. It was a magnificent vista, alien yet beautiful in its utilitarian purposes and angled designs.

Heydenrych swept open the doors to his private office, where a desk and a handful of chairs laid in wait. Many photographs of the director with various heads of state and ordinary miners hung on the walls, orbiting a large satellite image of the Western Deep Levels mining sites directly opposite his desk. Citations and awards denoting his years of charitable services and humanitarian works lined a table next to the chairs, a welcome change from the unscrupulous Yastanni.

Mason and Bell sat opposite Heydenrych at his desk, finally comfortable after some time in the outside oven.

"We've been interested in a commercial partnership for some time," Mason said. "TauTona is the most promising candidate with your rather open relationships with international businesses."

Heydenrych stroked his chin. "Yours will be the first North American firm in almost fifty years, Mr Stone, to apply here. I have to caution you that several Confederation companies own a nearly ninety-eight percent advantage in international-designated gallery space.

There's no guarantee a free gallery will be available, or that the other companies won't buy up the open space to keep other internationals out, particularly since you do represent your country with your presence."

Mason waved his hand. "I realize there's nothing in your laws to stop that, but I would still care to see for myself. My firm does possess considerable assets, that, if it came to an auction, could sway the Department of Minerals and Energy to grant us a license, despite any opposition."

"Far be it from me," Heydenrych said, smiling, "to deny the opportunity for business here. I am certain my superiors would be open to new blood, so to speak."

Heydenrych stood and crossed over to the far wall and activated a holographic display. Tapping a series of buttons, the display brought up a lateral schematic of the mine, a complex of long shafts and wide galleries that looked more like an ant colony than anything constructed by humans. Red text boxes affixed next to the blue outlines of the numerous deep shafts dotted the holograph, smearing it with sensory overload that even Mason's practiced and studious mind had trouble following.

The director placed an index finger on a gallery, which blossomed larger, filling the display. "Gallery one-four-five-T has been little explored...it was excavated fifteen years ago during our last major sinking. Depth is forty-six hundred meters. Purchasing the license to excavate this gallery will come at a steep price, pardon the pun."

Mason looked to Bell, who nodded.

"That should do well," the junior agent said. "We're looking for someplace out of the way...our bosses back home will be more than pleased, Director."

"Oh good," Heydenrych said, clapping his palms. " Shall we go down, then?"

Mason rose from his seat. "Certainly...I want to see our new gold mine!"

Λ

"It is only a matter of time before American intelligence uncovers our efforts, due to the supreme indiscretion of Ilichev," the monotone, bass voice over the voxlink rumbled.

"Liquidating him and his associates was difficult enough as it was...we risk exposure if Americans are missing, especially here."

"Then you must dispose of any agents inconspicuously. Surely you can accomplish this, MOLOTOK? You have been handpicked by me for that very purpose. The time is still too premature, our efforts can be thwarted. As it is, we have every reason to suspect Yastanni's allegiance

may not be to the Confederation alone."

MOLOTOK laughed at that rather obvious truth. "Your *Savak* friends aren't too trustworthy, either."

"Leave them to me. I'll leave the Americans to you. And do not forget your place."

"Understood."

Toggling the voxlink off, his eyes met the reflection of his face in the restroom mirror. Tensed muscles spasmed in his neck, eager to crush the life from all whom stood in his way, perhaps even those who dared speak to him as a subordinate.... He composed himself, stepped out and crossed over to his partner in the Palazzo Inter Continental Montecasino's lobby.

"Our new orders?"

"Impossible...so we will follow them to the best of our abilities."

The pair walked among the bustling crowd.

"What good does that do if we alert every intel bureau of our presence?"

"Don't ask me questions I am not meant to answer, ZAMYESTITYEL. We must trust that our contact's plans are sound. Now," he said, pausing before the hotel's front entrance to don solar blockers, "reconnaissance and elimination are our orders. The Americans' best are surely to be here, if we give them credit thus far. We will deal with them as commanded."

"What do you have in mind?"

"Quite an unfortunate loss. Contact our civilian advisors here and tell them to...take a holiday."

Λ

Set off the breezy waves and northeastern coastline of the Sea of Azov, fifty kilometers southwest of Rostov-on-Don, lay a sprawling, three-floored *dacha*, one of only a handful scattered across ten square kilometers. Constructed in the era of the Soviet premiers and once housing a succession of Communist Party bosses, the country house now fully embraced the ideals and philosophies of an entirely different ruling elite, or more appropriately, broker.

The suited man smoothed his blue and charcoal pin-striped Italian suit jacket, concealing the voxlink around his wrist, which blipped offline. Stepping out from the portico, he placed his solar blockers over his eyes and walked to avoid the rampant juveniles roaring across the *dacha*'s green fields.

In the glints of the early afternoon sun, a retinue of distinguished guests lounged twenty meters distant, imbibing flutes of free-falling

California wine on a terrace overlooking a shallow, figure-8-shaped pool. Scantily adorned, pearlescent young women milled in the pool, concerning themselves with nonstop chatter, the adult equivalent of the giggles erupting from the children around the suited man.

His sharp threads and chiseled jawline elicited whispers and winks from the girls, which he ignored as he walked past—business took precedence this time around. Even in this heat, he preferred the armor a well-trimmed suit provided, his own expertise and qualifications subtly enhanced by the masculine and masterful image the suit projected, and vice-versa. The uniform of psyops, perception, a truth.

He moved towards the old man reclined in a deck chair centimeters from the pool, a wide-brimmed sun hat and beach clothes adorning his wizened yet wiry frame. An icy glare from the statuesque platinum blonde hovering about the old man sent waves of rage up the suited man's spine.

"Ah, Dymtra." Looking up, the old man called out the visitor's sobriquet. He folded the e-ink newspaper in his hands, waved off the blonde and wiggled his finger, beckoning, "Latest?"

Dymtrus Shvinskilli's slick and immaculate ebony hair reflected the sun as he stepped up the terrace, his attention decidedly not on the departing woman. He rubbed his palms together, drying the glints of perspiration from his pores. "MOLOTOK and ZAMYESTITYEL are in the pasture as we speak."

"Mm." The old man—Genndy Unat'kolarev—perused the flirtacious girls, his own advancing years and hairline not dissuading their attentions. "It has been a long road..." he continued to his major domo, "a shame that we shall have to leave this fertile field after so many years. I have grown...fond of the Azov, my friend, in our long exile. But we must not stray from victory. This is decadence, a pleasant diversion, admittedly."

"Yes, sir." His wrist voxlink chimed. Reaching down, he toggled it. "Yes?"

"Colonel General Mattarov is requesting entry."

"Good," Shvinskilli answered. "Send him to the terrace."

Unat'kolarev rose from his chair. Both men looked to the shaded portico, where a moment later, the flamboyantly decorated and attired form of Colonel General Viktor Mattarov—commanding officer of the Russian Confederated Ground Forces, North Caucasus Military District—exited and trekked to the terrace, a steel briefcase cemented in his right hand. His widely peaked cap silhouetted his sunken eyes and high cheek bones. The three gold-starred epaulet boards on his shoulders were like wings for the well-decorated army man.

Unat'kolarev planted osculations on the general's face. "Viktor, it is good to see you again. You brought us a gift?" he asked, more statement than query.

"Yes, sir. I present the command codes and encryption keys to all quantum systems of the North Caucasus Military District." Mattarov proffered the briefcase to the old man.

Unat'kolarev nodded, hiding his exulation save for the glimmer in his widened eyes; Shvinskilli noticed the old man possessed an energy not witnessed in years. Now he effectively held control of one-sixth of the Russian Ground Forces in his arthritic hands.

"Excellent, Viktor, excellent." Unat'kolarev clapped the general's arms and embraced him. He then rested his palms under Mattarov's cheeks. "I task you with the post of Chief Marshal of Ground Forces, my friend. Soon, sclerotic St. Petersburg will no longer be an obstacle to your supreme command."

"You are most generous, sir."

"Your loyalty over these years should not go unrewarded," he held an index finger in the air, gesturing to the Motherland beyond. "When the time arrives we will stand united, arrayed against our enemies. And you will be our vanguard."

Mattarov nodded with vigor.

"Nadya, my child," Unat'kolarev said a moment later, calling over the platinum blonde.

"Sir," she answered, pursing her thin, peach-hued lips. Her blue eyes betrayed no hint of affection for the man who claimed her as his daughter. The cold visage and short, right-side parted coif, however, left no doubt of her paternity.

"Please escort Marshal Mattarov to the room set aside for him on the second floor. He is to be shown the greatest hospitality for our feast this evening."

"Of course."

Nadya bowed minutely and obediantly. She turned on her heels without a second look to the men and led Mattarov to the *dacha* once more.

Unat'kolarev studied the unexpectedly thin equipment case, its reinforced carbon-carbon trim shining in the midday sunlight. A sophisticated T-ray beam identification lock, just on the exterior of the clamshell cover, would have to be modified for his exclusive use, but otherwise the object and its contents Unat'kolarev had coveted since the early days of countless struggles now lay in his grasp. Soon, the rest would follow.

The old man entrusted the case to Shvinskilli. "Secure it on the *Shinkansen*. Tomorrow will be quite a busy day."

Shvinskilli loosed a rare smile, which came easier in the company of the beauties at the pool. "Indeed, sir, indeed."

Λ

Rumbling over the gravel road in a rugged, jury-rigged golf cart, Heydenrych, his driver, Bheka, and Mason and Bell drove past the ore-sorting facilities to park beneath the pepper trees, just within walking distance of the winding tower. Swatting the biting flies from their faces, Heydenrych, Mason and Bell emerged from underneath the trees and into the baking sun; looking upwards, the trio were shaded by the silhouetted tower, providing some relief. Hardworking air conditioning units—audible from quite a distance—chugged away inside a nearby concrete bunker; Mason hoped the AC units cooled the mine as well as they made that cacophony.

A corrugated awning with locked double doors denoted the entrance, overseen by another young security guard fanning himself with a straw hat. Reaching for his set of pass keys chained to his belt, Heydenrych waved to the guard and then slipped the passkey through the lock pad.

Acrid, rusty air mixed with rock dust, diesel exhaust, grease and the stench of stale ionization from exposed electrical circuits smacked the noses of Mason and Bell upon entry of an anteroom more office than mine shaft. It was painted a dull orange, and adorned with safety signs and warning posters; one featured a (presumable) miner breaking some unspecified code, with the universal "no-no" symbol of red circle and slash superimposed over him. Scaffolding crisscrossed above their heads, while I-beams and bare grating clanked under their boots. It seemed to be under construction, but was most likely just function over any sort of form, with no reason to pretty it up for the nonexistent public consumption.

Heydenrych took the pair round a corner, where a smaller compartment of solid steel walls two-meters wide stood, bearing a single-paneled door with a keypad lock.

"We should be wearing these," Heydenrych said, pointing to a cabinet behind them where scuffed, torchlight-fitted hardhats, clear goggles and rows of reflective safety vests hung.

Passing the kit respectively to the agents, Heydenrych donned his, and after a quick lesson in proper adjustment and safety checks, he strode over to the compartment door.

Admitting them deeper entry into the sanctum, the director stepped down a set of wide metal stairs into an increasingly dim corridor, to a subfloor that was equivalent in size to the anteroom, most likely the shaft station. Tiny pinpricks of illumination against a velvet cavern were the only light sources until the trio adjusted to the abrupt change from day into night. Rubbing their eyes, the agents gathered their bearings before following Heydenrych deeper inside.

"Sorry for that," the director said, "visitors not acclimated always have a difficult first few minutes inside. Now the heat will be your next biggest worry."

Waiting ahead, a wide steel cage sat adjacent to a gigantic, dust- and grease-blanketed motor, the hoisting engine: a monster seemingly summoned from the bowels of some distant, industrial era. They set foot in the cage, less than eagerly in the cases of Mason and Bell, and proceeded downwards upon a simple press of a button by Heydenrych on a control pad.

Grinding against the support girders as if in complaint, the cage picked up speed after several slow-going moments, eventually settling into a groove Heydenrych said was twenty meters per second, and judging by the cool breeze upon them, Mason concurred. The breeze was a lifesaver, in fact; mine dust and the building heat began to work on the agents' bodies, wearing them down faster than a day spent in the blazing sun.

Strobing lamp upon lamp just centimeters beyond the cage blended in a nonstop blur, bathing the trio in pulsating sodium illumination for a poor man's dance club experience. Mason thought himself hallucinating, and began to wonder if they were anywhere near the end of the first shaft, for fear of vertigo overtaking him then and there.

"Four more minutes to the first gallery," Heydenrych announced, glancing at his wrist chrono. A wry smile crossed his lips. "The ride gets better only from here!"

"How much longer to our prospective gallery?" Bell asked.

"An additional fifty minutes to the rock. You didn't have any place to be, did you?" Heydenrych half-quipped.

Mason sighed and gripped the side of the cage. "No, of course not...."

Subjected to the infernal pit's not-quite-air conditioned tertiary shaft for the next hour, the trio finally finished the remaining leg of their descent after two subsequent cage changes, the perspiration beaded up under their hardhats and the cage's incessant vibration having turned their brains to mush along the way.

They stepped out of the cage and onto the 140 level, some four kilometers below the surface of the Earth. Mason and Bell's innards heaved under the hot, heavy air, like swimming in a deep ocean, where a breath was drawn with much labor; the very cavern they walked below seemed to be exerting a supernatural grip upon them, assisted by the eerie dark that was penetrated only by the sound of distant rumbling and the smattering of suspended orange illumination.

"We're here," Heydenrych announced, none the wiser to the palpable depths. "I'll go slow, but you both must keep a safe distance with me."

Mason nodded meekly, his throat unable to elicit an acknowledgment until his strength returned. The smells first detected above were magnified tenfold down here, robbing him temporarily of his other senses.

Heydenrych compelled them forward, giving the agents no choice but to acclimate. The trio walked down a four-meter-wide corridor hewn from the rock, a squared-off, organically crafted space for the smooth transport of mine cars and, to a lesser extent, human beings. Red and white reflective spray paint adorned the floors and walls in alternating blocks, reminding one to adhere to the corridor's path and not to crash into a stone wall ignorantly.

"Not much longer now," Heydenrych said, his lamplight swaying from side-to-side across the gallery's walls. His tightly focused lamplight's aperture shone on the succeeding demarcation signs, which started at one-four-five-G towards the provisional one-four-five-T.

Slightly narrower than the main gallery, these named adjuncts appeared to house equipment of some sort, but Mason couldn't discern what the Confederation had down here. Playing dumb, he took closer peeks as the trio walked past, seeing a vast array of equipment dispersed among two of the galleries; despite plastic blankets and a hanging plastic sheet to secure the area, Mason knew he was glimpsing a virtual double of Yastanni's neutronic caging set-up.

"What's the Russian contingent study in your mine, Director?" Mason asked, finally regaining the use of his speech and lung capacity, helped along by his insatiable curiosity as to just what else the Confederation could be doing to further Project Ether four klicks below the Earth's surface.

"Research relating to physics, I believe," he answered without pretense. "For a definitive answer, I'm afraid you must ask my technical expertise representative."

"Ah," Mason said, sauntering up to Heydenrych's side for the first time since setting foot on the lowest gallery. Something more pressing swiftly came to his mind. "I just noticed that no one appears to be working today."

"Hmm...." Heydenrych paused, and putting his hands to his hips, nodded. "Quite correct, Mr Stone. I thought traffic was less a chore than I remembered. Unoccupation for a certain length of time while under normal operations could be punishable by levying a fine. I will have to investigate further."

Bell turned to Mason, both of whom thought precisely the same thing: *Surely the Confederation hadn't wholly proceeded beyond Stage Two?* Yastanni himself was still a finite length of time from completing his research; abandoning this stage would be peculiarly premature, even for an accelerated, crash-course program.

A chilling possibility flashed in Mason's mind, but he hoped their investigation-cum-surveillance wouldn't swiftly morph into an altogether different operation, one leading them to watch their backs for a more prosaic reason.

CHAPTER NINE

"Something's damned odd," Mason intoned, shedding the safety kit outside the cage compartment. Hanging the items back inside the cabinet, he ran his fingers through his dishwater blonde hair, loosening the grit from his scalp.

Bell watched Heydenrych secure the cage behind them. "I've been waiting for you to say that ever since we left the gallery," he said, *sotto voce*. "Did someone get to these scientists before we could?"

Mason shook his head. "Whatever's gone down, there's no doubt they've been on the same track as Yastanni...all that equipment, even though it was covered in plastic, was essentially similar. De Lis'd have a cow if he saw it all."

"What's the plan, boss?"

"Get back to the hotel, web Chief about our findings, and then get ourselves back down there to scan everything for dark energy signatures. And if we can sneak a peek at the Confederation equipment, all the better."

Heydenrych locked the compartment door behind himself and paused next to the agents. "Thank you for your interest, gentlemen. I believe your bid will be seriously considered soon."

"Thanks," Mason replied. "One more thing...after I speak to my superiors, I would be grateful for a second tour of the same gallery. They're particularly exacting when dealing with new investments, and...."

"One tour per day, Mr Stone, is my employer's limit, but another can certainly be scheduled for tomorrow, the same time?"

Mason smiled. "We'll see you here."

The trio exited the winding tower, and after a short journey back to the offices via Heydenrych and Bheka, the agents departed for the considerably longer sojourn back to their Saxon Hotel suites for the briefing, and relief in the hotel's opulence.

Λ

"It's definitely Stage Two, Chief, but where they've gone is anybody's guess," Mason spoke over his holobook, Louris' image frowning before him. "So far we haven't encountered any resistance to the investigation, nor any signs the Confederation is aware of our presence."

"Smells funny...I don't like it," Louris said, his demeanor saying the news was next-to-worse case scenario. "Doctor de Lis is reporting some progress in his investigation, however. He should be making some headway in the next three days, if analyses of his duplication of Yastanni's experiments are accurate."

"Any news from Feltham?"

Louris glanced at his desk reports next to him. "Delta code of a successful insertion onto the grounds. I don't expect another communiqué for twelve hours."

"I can only hope the Confederation moved Stage Two there, or that TauTona is a redundancy," Mason said.

"There's still time to extract them," Louris offered.

"No, give them the investigation. If we can cut off as many avenues as possible to a dark energy weaponization program, we should do it."

Louris nodded. "Give me an update ASAP on your intel. Louris out."

Mason flicked off the device and set it on the night table next to him. The quietitude of the place disturbed him, if only because he had sent his partner and fellow agents into the hornet's nest that was the CIS, and here he was, waiting for some signs of life from the enemy away from their turf. If the Confederation was playing games, Mason didn't want his star players involved. Bell stood nearby, wiping the perspiration from his brow, his jacket hooked on his other hand over his shoulder.

"C'mon," Mason said, pointing a finger to the door and rising, "let's enjoy a four-star course on Uncle Sam's dime while we still have the time to ourselves."

Λ

The roaring tram rocked across the rails of the drought-stricken territory again, ferrying Mason, Bell and the next day's miners to Carletonville. Having wised up and donned straw hats along with sunscreen, the pair contemplated yesterday's conundrum while swatting at the thirsty horse flies in the late morning's ochre sun.

"I guess the odds of the Confederation outright cancelling the project are about nil, aren't they?" Bell mused openly, his eyes shifting over the passing mountains in the distance.

"That all depends on what they consider a priority," Mason said. "I doubt the time and expense they've put forth so far make it worth their while to. That old bureaucratic stone doesn't just stop rolling on a whim."

"Mmm. Buying all the resources, funding the research, hoarding all that data...killing it would be too good to be true. Plus," Bell smiled, "that'd make it too easy on us, and put us on the streets."

Mason laughed.

The tram stretched over a wide arc to the southeast, bringing them within sighting distance of TauTona's winding tower, which rose over the tree-lain horizon, a rectangular sentinel.

"Here we are now," Bell said, looking out the window.

Mason turned his head over his right shoulder, catching the sight in the corner of his eyes, now less than two kilometers away. Dust clouds lifted off the ground and blew over the tram, forcing the pair to fan the air with their straw hats.

"Hell of a wind today," Bell said, picking the sand from his lips.

"Yeah, just—"

Bell's eyes peered over his lowered sunglasses. "Huh.... Oh my...."

Craning his neck, Mason saw the treeline flutter in the dust cloud, obscuring the winding tower completely. Now a gale-force wind flew past them, rocking the tram, but seconds later—barely competing with the unexpectedly powerful quake that rattled through the earth—the tram leapt upwards and was tossed off the rails.

Landing on its portside, the tram skidded across the gravel-lined berm, its momentum sliding downgrade for a few meters before rolling over twice and slowing to a stop, cars haphazardly jack-knifed.

The horrendous din of grinding, snapping and collapsing tram cars was soon drowned out by a crescendo of rattling debris that grew to a thunderous roar. Over the scattered tram's remains, a cloud of earth, tree limbs and assorted metallic debris crashed to the surface, a pyroclastic flow of flotsam destructive not by its rather moderate temperature, but its seemingly random descent trajectory.

A glass pane from a car window tumbled end over end a few minutes later; a grubby, shaking set of fingers, then a hand, crawled out, grasped a bar and pulled itself up, revealing the visage of Mason, grey by dust and earth, red splotches lining his brow, cheeks and chin, his wounds caked in grit.

Tumbling onto the gravel below, he grimaced, cursed between clenched teeth, then reached inside the reeling tram to feel for the form of Bell, who was motionless and equally battered.

"Tom...Tommy, wake up...."

Cradling the younger agent in his arms, Mason rocked repeatedly, allowing gravity to give him a helping hand in retrieving Bell. Dropping into a stretch of scrub grass, they entered the company of the surviving miners, all with similar escape methods, their moans balancing out the creaks of the dying tram.

"Gregggg....what the—gahhh...."

"Don't move. Can you feel all your limbs? Is anything numb?" he demanded.

Bell paused, forcing his limbs to twitch in spite of the shock his body had just gone through. "Yeah...."

"Good."

"...But my leg's aching like crazy," he added.

"Damn. May be broken. Don't move." Mason looked at the general direction of TauTona. "Stay here and rest for a few minutes. I'm going to check out the mine...something's telling me this isn't right."

Coughing, Bell let out a weak "No shit" as he wiped his cheek with the back of his hand. Mason sprinted past the head of the tram, and was now lost in the underbrush beneath the pepper trees.

Protecting his head with his hands, while also squinting from the dust-laden blowback pelting the branches, the agent emerged from the treeline, bobbing and weaving to sight the damage to the Western Deep Levels Mining Corp offices, but unexpectedly finding nothing in the swirling waste. Scanning the sky, he thought he'd perhaps lost his direction, but the sun shone high in the north, just as it should be for the Southern Hemisphere; his senses had to be scrambled.

Another step forward and Mason found himself flat on his ass, having stumbled backwards as the land beneath him gave way, opening a half-meter-deep maw. Around him, the dust slowly filtered away, revealing nothing, save the catastrophic rubble just dozens of meters ahead: the former location of the TauTona Mine entrance, and most horrifying, the splintered winding tower, reduced to smoking debris.

Scrabbling out of the pit and racing ahead on all fours, Mason screamed his lungs out, a sudden jolt of adrenaline galvanizing him. The heat from a massive fire, most likely an internal explosion deep under the surface, held him back, but only just. Every fiber in his body compelled Mason to race ahead, duty still the first priority. TauTona died before him...there was nothing his devotion could do to stop it further.

My god, the miners, the thought hit him. Thousands of souls pulverized, four kilometers deep, as if the mouth of hell had swallowed the mine, the offices, the people in one volcanic action, the Earth taking back what humanity had been excavating for nigh two centuries.

Mason rose, feeling the trickling moisture running from his eyes, his simple, standing frame dwarfing the height of the field of destruction strewn about him. One phrase burned in his mind, causing his jaw to clench in anger.

Chagang-Do, 2145.

CHAPTER TEN

Clasping their RT-01/9V sidearms close to their chests, Feltham and Kindred—attired in "borrowed" Confederation army officer winter uniforms—staked out the security perimeter of the Makarov Base at the rim of the Tao-Rusyr caldera, Onekotan island. The dormant volcano Vulkan Krenitzyn, smack dab in the middle of Kal'tsevoe Lake, which filled the caldera, rose high into a cloud of fog, bathed in a silvery sheen by the setting sun.

Having slipped aboard a Confederation naval cruiser with false flag papers back in the Okhotsk Sea, the two agents then rode a large cutter through a narrow channel and up several locks for four hundred meters to Kal'tsevoe; this was courtesy of the Russian Engineering Corps, which had detonated tonnes of earth twenty years ago to build this snaking system, all for the express purpose of utilizing Vulkan Krenitzyn's four-kilometer-wide summit for the clandestine neutronic testbed site WT847, code-named ALEXEI by the USNA DoD.

After completing small-scale neutronic device test detonations over the last decade, the Russians converted the flattened summit into Makarov Base, and being the good Russians they were by retrofitting something old for new, easily switched gears from neutrons to dark energy, or so the Company seemed to believe. The only way to know for certain was to gain access to the grounds and sniff them with lidar.

Emerging from the dense fog that rolled down the volcano's slope, the pair scampered over a concrete causeway, bypassing the charred, ancient lava, which could still, remarkably, slice a thickly soled boot in half. Ahead, the causeway widened, forming a level that ringed the lower segment of the base like a concourse, itself poured over the remnants of the volcano's once-pristine bounty of tundra lichen and guano. A layer-cake of subsequent levels rose to Krenitzyn's summit above them, disappearing to become one with the everpresent clouds while deterring prying eyes from the coasts.

Feltham paused just outside the scanning region of an infrared sensor affixed to the base's metal wall. She produced an IFAR—Infrared Active Reflector—from inside her leather coat, and toggling a switch on the thin edge of the five-centimeter-diameter mechanism, flashed it at the sensor. Now having temporarily fooled the sensor's receptors with false, cooler infrared readings, the agents were cloaked long enough to bypass it and cross over to the side entrance, where a quick swipe of a lockpicking pass key gained them admittance.

They walked down a pre-memorized corridor, their uniforms and flesh reflecting the mustard sodium illumination, until coming to another doorway several meters beyond. Another quick lockpicking and the pair were inside the base's main vertical shaft. Pausing a moment to scan the immediate area for lifesigns with Kindred's holobook, they detected only a handful of stationary signals, all located well away from the main target: the suite of laboratories clustered inside the summit of Makarov Base, four levels above. According to the latest DoD intel at their disposal, Makarov Base was presumed to station a select few security forces and scientists only, due to the extreme remoteness of Onekotan, and what the Confederation presumably perceived to be the lack of interest by foreign powers here; Feltham was banking on Mason's Occam's Razor bet to pay off with an easy deep recon.

With Kindred gesturing the way to Feltham, the agents ascended the first flight of grated metal steps, beginning the trek above. Step-by-step the agent's footfalls reverberated against the solid concrete wall shaft, galvanizing them further to reach the target before discovery, even with the minimum Confederation security.

Sidearms drawn, the pair stepped onto the final level, surveying the cross-corridor thoroughly until deemed clear. Feltham eyed the suite of doors, six in all, half on the left and the others on the right. Each door was labeled in shorthand Russian signage; an obvious giveaway that contents were critical or classified in any situation was when nothing was labeled plainly.

Feltham swiped the pass key of the first door on the left, its door emblazoned "*Shikarnyy*" or translated roughly, "splendid." Shaking her head, Feltham hoped it was. Poking her torch past the threshold, the agent illuminated the small office suite, adorned with pinned recruitment posters on its walls and fading printouts that revealed nothing of interest.

Closing the door, she went to the second, *"Pristoynyy"*, "decent." Again, a suite that housed nothing of much import, and the niggling notion that perhaps all was not as it appeared, or more ominously, that the DoD intel was faulty.

"Not much of a laboratory," Feltham whispered to Kindred, who nodded.

Running her lidar cannon through this suite as she had the first, Kindred shook her head at the lack of inexplicable readings. "Nominal," she reported. "Maybe it's the wrong tree?"

Feltham bristled. "Open the others."

Kindred went across the corridor as ordered, scanning all in quick succession. Negative on all fronts, she shook her head again.

"Sonuvabitch," Feltham hissed, punching her palm in frustration. "Skim any printouts you can find," she commanded. "We need to know what *did* go on in this place."

Rifling through the assorted folders in a filing cabinet, Feltham's eyes darted over the various personnel and project files, all meticulously sorted by date, leading back to the late twenty-first century. She marveled at the clippings and photographs collected within, but had to remind herself of the unreliability of technology in the intervening years, due to the prolonged crashes affecting the world at the time. Storing data digitally was great when all was well, but access to it could be problematic when electricity was scarce, and holographic media needed competent analysts to read it, even in the best of times. Over the eons, the Egyptians still had the edge with paper. Feltham knew one thing: the Confederation was as concerned with a paper trail as Park Woon's scientists were back in Chagang-Do.

The next room over, Kindred hacked a data storage cylinder with her holobook, leeching the information directly into her possession, decrypting and translating it within seconds.

Finding and replacing the cylinders one by one, Kindred sifted through a stack of thumbnail images, all seemingly of various geographic locations across the planet. Many were of North America, and were either deep mines, or inexplicably, mountain chains; green isobar blobs superimposed over the landforms made no immediate sense to her, and the legend the isobars represented wasn't apparent to her, even in translation. *What the hell was all this about? Were these potential Stage Three locations, like de Lis explained?*

An insistent alarm from her holobook went off, focusing her attention on it. Toggling the holographic interface, her eyes widened at the proximity alert; they had company.

Exiting into the corridor, Kindred bumped into Feltham, the shadows concealing themselves from each other.

"Ahh—good, I hoped that was you!" Feltham exclaimed, having received her own alert. "Appears the boys found us."

"Too much to ask to...have a few more minutes," Kindred said between breaths as the pair reversed course and headed for the stair steps.

Rounding the landing for the next set down, the pair paused to listen, their ears picking up the faint footfalls of boots clapping on hard concrete and metal, and dangerously enough, just a few meters from the first flight.

Feltham gestured her right hand skyward. "Up!"

Scrabbling backwards, the two agents cleared the landing, avoiding the first volley of particle rounds, which ricocheted off the metal structure, spraying sparks into the half-light. Following just two flights behind, three Confederation soldiers brandished compact Kl-374w semi-automatic rifles on shoulder straps, aiming squarely for the shadowy interlopers above. A sergeant bringing up the rear of the squad grunted instructions, his left arm gesticulating wildly.

"*Locust*! This is Roxy!" Feltham yelled into her voxlink, broadcasting through her secure channel to the waiting jumpjet. "We need an immediate extraction! Repeat, *Locust*! This is Roxy! Extraction at ALEXEI!"

Pausing over the railing at the landing, Kindred let loose a barrage of gunfire from her sidearm, forcing the squad to cover, giving the agents time to spare. Three meters to her left, Feltham worked on the exit to the fourth level's exterior concourse, trying to open the way to *Locust*'s LZ.

"Do you have it?" Kindred asked Feltham, her sidearm and sight still trained on the soldiers below.

Feltham's arms pulled on the doors' stubborn handles. "Bitch is stuck! I'm gonna need your help!"

Kindred saw a glimmer of metal between stairsteps, and shot at it; a yelp from the area, and she knew the round had found its target. "I'm a little busy at the moment!"

"SHIT!" Pointing the barrel of her pistol at the door handle, Feltham fired several rounds until the corroded metal fragmented and subsequently unlocked. With an upraised boot sole, the agent kicked through the right door panel, unleashing a deafening reverberation throughout the narrow corridor.

Kindred winced at the din, but her eyes bulged at the ballsy attack by Feltham, the agent impressed by her superior's show of force. Abandoning her defense of the level in a heartbeat, Kindred flew out and onto the wide concourse.

There, Feltham stood adjacent to the blown door, waiting to ambush the squad. Hearing the approaching footfalls, Kindred reloaded her sidearm's magazine clip, then stood opposite Feltham on the other side.

A salvo of particle shots exploded upon the closed door and obliterated it, causing the agents to cover. Seconds later, the familiar tink of a cylinder rolling out of the corridor on cement was the only precursor to the discharge of charcoal smoke from a grenade, obscuring the soldiers' exit. Relying on sound alone, the two agents blitzed the evenly matched squad from behind, battling for their lives where shoot-to-kill was the law.

Kindred fired off several rounds towards what she thought was her opponent. A knee to her thigh sent waves of pain through her leg and pelvis, but she lowered her sidearm and fired again, thinking the torso had to be in there somewhere. The smell of iron and taste of salt rewarded Kindred's instincts, and she fanned her arms wide to help clear the air for *Locust* and Feltham.

Feltham's jaw flexed under the brunt of leather from a soldier's coat, a mistimed punch. She flipped the butt of her pistol upwards, cradling the barrel in her palm as she swung back, then felt and heard the vibration of metal on metal, two weapons meeting in the grey fog. Three rounds left the soldier's rifle, just to her right. Guesstimating the rifle's distance, Feltham reached out with her left hand and grappled the rifle's short barrel from underneath and pulled down hard, throwing the man off balance and closer to her.

A clearing in the smoke bomb presented the craggy face of the sergeant to Feltham, as well as the agent to his surprised visage. The two hesitated—sizing each other up—before each raised their weapons of choice, and Feltham squeezed the trigger—

And heard a series of gunshots from over her shoulder place three rounds right through the sergeant's heart, dropping him. Turning around, Feltham breathed heavily, and watched Kindred step into the clearing.

"Good shooting," Feltham said, a weary look in her eyes. "We need to get to cov—"

Gunshots from below sparked off the concourse floor, making them hustle closer to the wall.

Kindred picked up her man's dropped Kl-374w and held it near. "Where the hell is *Locust*?"

"Can't be more than a half-klick...."

The gunfire shifted from the concourse to another target, this time behind the base, where the two agents were blind. The deafening roar of two VTOL engines, coupled with the downward wash of searing air, passed high overhead and descended before them, answering the agents' pleas. *Locust*'s slate grey and metallic green exterior parted the gunfire from the pair, allowing them to clamber aboard the starboard hatch's outstretched stairsteps.

Three concourses down, a squad of five Confederation troops lined up with *Yastryeb* AV-8554d short-range chopper-killer rockets on their shoulders, all aiming at the jumpjet.

Bracing inside the cockpit, Feltham and Kindred watched the incandescent yellow exhaust trails of two *Yastryeb* rockets soar through the air. Bouncing off *Locust*'s fuselage—thanks to the thermal and magnetic countermeasures, which would prove to be fleeting once the squad figured out how to override them—the rockets exploded upon impact on the floor below. Pitching forward under the nearly full power of the VTOL engines, *Locust* cleared the concourse's edge as three more rockets glided past, and several more were readied.

Having enough of the game, the co-pilot assumed the instrument controls of the dorsal cannon, opening a single bay door ahead of the cockpit. Sloping down from its bow cradle, the meter-long coilgun fixed on the squad below and let loose with a flurry of tungsten-tipped osmium rods, disintegrating everything in its killbox, roughly ten square meters of concourse and all contained within.

Feltham grimaced at the carnage, but knew she'd wouldn't be joining them this day. "Good timing, boys," she praised, clapping each seat.

Joining Kindred back in the cabin, the agent strapped in while *Locust* blasted out of Onekotan airspace with abandon, ascending several hundred kilometers for the long fleajump across the Pacific homeward.

After finishing the intense navigation of the jumpjet to international waters moments later, the pilot was finally able to ease up and relay a message overhead. "Agent Feltham, we're receiving an Alpha query from Company HQ...signal code's identification is Chief Louris."

"Thanks, Captain, I'll take it over my voxlink." Toggling the device under her unbuttoned Confederation jacket, Feltham linked up through *Locust* back to DC.

"Lisbeth, Sha, ETA." Louris said curtly and without

acknowledgement; hell, he didn't even ask for a situation report.

Feltham was taken aback."Five hours. Sir, we've had a sit—"

"Your mission's just changed. From what the Global Security Network's reporting, and the NA Geological Survey, we may have reason to believe Mason and Bell are MIA, or worse...."

"Chief...?"

"TauTona," his voice trembled, almost breathlessly, " is gone."

CHAPTER ELEVEN

That can't be right. Mason and Bell wouldn't have fallen so easily, but....

Feltham's fingers rubbed circles into her temples. She and Kindred spoke nothing on the flight back to North American airspace, allowing the pair to mull over the numbing possibility that they were now the sole members of 9D, and had to pick up the flag for Mason and Bell. It was an unsettling prospect, one Feltham didn't need, let alone want. Shoot, she'd just begun to work with her new partner; she didn't really believe she could break in a new one.

Carry on they would, whatever had to be done. Louris was sure to be calling in as many favors as possible—friends and foes alike within the DoJ and DoD—to get the latest on TauTona's condition; his reputation at the agency as a velvet-gloved iron fist and an agent's agent would most certainly be felt again.

Locust veered towards the Glass Castle, bathed in the fading gold of a late sunset. Above the tower the first glimmers of stars in the velvet sky beckoned the agents' thoughts back to their comrades, wondering if Louris's communiqué was about to send them on a recovery mission.

Riding the elevator to the twentieth floor, both women, without words, took it as the longest trek yet throughout their headquarters. If it wasn't quite a house without a family anymore, it was the next best thing, or worst.

Louris paced in his office suite, one hand perched atop his frizzled head of hair, the other clutched around a worn holobook, locked in a fervent voxlink dialogue. His back turned to the holographic display mural across the widest wall, he lurked in the eye of the data hurricane, the axis of a less-than-healthy information overload that even his administrative assistant, Yoko Nishiyama, at Louris' side, looked overwhelmed and troubled.

Feltham and Kindred stepped by them and watched the web feeds on the display. Staring transfixed, their eyes jumped from one website's feeds to another's. Talking heads sat below images of grey smoke. South African men and women screamed, stood aghast, or just wept, while miners who hadn't reported to work milled outside. Emergency response vehicles blared traffic horns and glowed in red and blue illumination. Drone news craft circled round for better angles, their navigators, back in news offices, safe from harm, directing them from afar.

Superseding them all by far for sheer enormity was the Global Security Network's orbital footage, magnified thousands-fold: a decimated and cracked scar stood in place of TauTona and Carletonville. Pitch-black smoke belched forth from the new crater, exasperated by orange balls of flame. Yellow rings of fire pocked the region. If anything, or anyone, was within walking distance, they were dead, either by the explosion, the heat, the debris, or the sheer air pressure.

And yet, only one question was in Feltham's mind: *why?*

Not what, for that seemed premature. Motive. Was Mason on the path? Did he get too close? Or, she said finally, for the first time out loud, "Who found out?"

"Pardon?" Kindred asked, her mouth locked in a grimace.

"Did someone suspect we were in town? Breathing down their necks?"

Kindred placed her hands over her mouth and nose, in shock. "Did it get too hot?"

"Sha, I think we may have been duped."

Kindred looked askance at Feltham. "By whom?"

"The Confederation. ALEXEI...was it real?"

"Those rounds were real enough for me," Kindred said, her mouth letting out an exasperated gust of air.

"No...did the Confederation think we'd bite on one and not the other, or did what we find at ALEXEI mean to lead us off the trail?" Again, did Mason get on the path?

"Agents," Louris said, finishing his words over the line, "we need to talk."

Λ

"We haven't been able to trace or track Mason's or Bell's voxlink frequencies," Louris said, cupping his head in his hands. He leaned over his desk, the stack of holobook reports growing deeper by the moment. "I've got the NSA working overtime to triple-check every communiqué in and out of the African continent, but so far, zilch."

"What's the incident elapse time?" Feltham asked.

He glanced at the holobook in front of him. "Seven hours, forty-four minutes."

"Then they could be assisting in evacuations, or trying to get out—"

Louris interrupted Kindred with a curt, "Greg Mason has been a friend and colleague of mine for over a decade. If anybody's going to find a way out, it's him. We're not giving up, agents."

The pair nodded, half in confidence, and acceptance. The best they could do was trust Mason's abilities and Louris' trust in the mission.

"Now, I've weblinked Keegan and Moore your intel. We should be hearing back soon from them." Louris tapped a button on his desk interface, accessing a holographic display. "But this isn't the only pressing news. Just got this from de Lis before the world went to hell."

De Lis' holographic head materialized between the three, his visage hovering amid a backdrop of a control room in the Sudbury Laboratory. "Agent Louris, my first results from Sudbury are positive... we have a working neutrino cage. Now, please realize that this is rudimentary, but the process by which Yastanni and Zaryov has proceeded is viable. I suggest 9D work with all due diligence to pursue the shutdown of the Confederation dark energy operations at once...because I'm afraid this will only be the beginning."

The doctor stepped out of frame, and the holographic webcamera panned over to the neutrino capture cage, a spindly, two-meter-tall chimenea-shaped chamber centered in a stainless-steel clean room. Zooming in, the camera spied a metal test model inside the chamber's viewing port.

Audible through the recording, a low hum graduated to a piercing squeal, and after a scant five seconds, magenta fluorescence inside the chamber spotlighted the superstrong model's sudden and violent implosion from a rigid, hourglass structure into an inwardly shattering rubble pile.

De Lis was brought back into frame, his fingers unplugging his ears. "That was one thousand kilos of tempformed steel, easily able to withstand the crush depth of triple-hulled submarines to the bottom of the sea. With enough time, money and experimentation, we could equal what Yastanni has done."

Louris switched the hologram off, his eyes meeting the agents' shocked faces. "I believe Mason and Bell may have just found our Stage

Two, or what's left of it."

"Something still's bothering me, Chief," Feltham said, TauTona's smoking remains seared into her mind's eye. "Are we dealing with one set of foes, or two? I mean, why else would the Confederation destroy their own research in such a haphazard manner?"

Louris rubbed his jaw. "It's too early for speculation just yet. Investigating what the Confederation was doing in TauTona, and what they had accomplished, is the speed at which we should run."

Feltham nodded, but didn't wholeheartedly agree. Louris may have been the boss, but that didn't mean she was loath to peruse that line of investigation in the back of her mind, sans any word from Mason or Bell.

"Let's get started," Feltham said, rising from the desk.

Λ

"Get de Lis on weblink! Now, Yoko!" Louris commanded, suddenly rising from his seat. Gathering his numerous holobooks beside him, the 9D chief started sorting through the avalanche of data, cross-indexing half the world's mass in quantum bits in mere seconds.

Nishiyama's fingers swerved over various holo-buttons on her desk's interface, webbing the secure IIA link to the DoE in Canada, and patiently waiting for de Lis' response. Finally, the doctor's visage appeared before Louris in a coalescing column of light over his desk.

"De Lis, Louris here. Just received the intel debrief from my analysts...what do you make of this?" Louris tapped a single button, relaying the same schematic Kindred pulled from the data cylinders inside ALEXEI.

De Lis' eyes scanned the topographic material, reading the English-translated legend just below the cartographic relief. "Yucca Mountain, Agent Louris. I'm familiar with the site, but why would the Confederation be interested in this? If nothing else, it's simple intel leftover from the twentieth century."

"Yucca is more than just a relic from the nuclear waste storage days," Louris said, his tone barely concealing concern. "Thanks to this TauTona incident, I've got Solicitor General Rauchambau breathing down my hindquarters to solve this...but that also gives me quite a bit of leverage to crack open some long-lost, ancient history relating to Yucca and a certain Vincente Kweiksman."

A nerve twitched deep within de Lis, causing a reflexive snarl to form over his lips. "Kweiksman!" he spat, uttering the name of the notorious physicist caught selling secrets to the Russians some sixty years prior. "Kweiksman's been dead for decades...."

"He still seems to be giving the Confederation a helping hand, after all these years. These data came bearing Kweiksman's code-name, 'MYSHINYY.'"

"Yucca Mountain wasn't part of his prosecution, he just wasn't there," de Lis said, shaking his head. "I can't see how—"

Louris crossed his arms. "Who said he was ever there, Doctor? My digging indicates more were involved but didn't face public scrutiny because they aided federal prosecutors in exchange for immunity."

De Lis furrowed his brow. "Immunity for what...?"

"Continued pursuit at all costs of their initial research at Yucca Mountain: Little Neutral One."

"*Neutrino.*" The doctor's jaw lowered in shock, his brain racing ahead, already making connections where none were known. "My god, we had our own dark energy program, years after Chagang-Do...why? Why didn't they answer me?!"

"Doctor?"

De Lis punched a fist into his left palm; decades of frustration, questions and obfuscation reached a critical mass, allowing his ire to surface, a rare event indeed. "My mentors lied to me...ridiculed me. And look where we're headed! I could've prevented this catastrophe, Louris! Goddammit, goddamn them...what reason could they have had to lie to me?"

Louris didn't want to answer, didn't think it was worth answering, worth paining de Lis further. Perhaps fooling themselves into buying their own lies, de Lis' professors—mentors, for chrissakes, by his own admission—hoped to make their mistakes go away, willed away, becoming in essence a sin by feigned ignorance.

And along came this young acolyte many years after the fact, probing an issue about which he knew nothing of its history. Louris could only imagine the looks on those old fools' faces when *that* question was asked.

"Look, Doctor, all we know is that Yucca was the base for experimental research into dark energy. What I need to know is this: can the Confederation possibly have any use for these data now, after all this time?"

De Lis scrutinized the holograph before him, dozens of green isobars centered on southwest Nevada, the Yucca Mountain Repository being ground zero in the cartograph. "I just don't know. I found it highly doubtful as a site for Stage Three, let alone a current area of interest for them. Perhaps it suits as model topography for their own site."

Or a map to explain what went on down there, Louris figured, for Russian consumption. The schematic vexed the chief, its amorphous blobs burned into his retinas. Right now, Louris really wanted to chuck the whole thing into his computer's trash bin; it really was getting too late in the day.

"I'm sorry to upset you," Louris continued, eager to end the debate for now, "but I had to give you access to this. It's too important otherwise."

"I appreciate it. Please, don't hesitate in the future." De Lis turned to toggle off his end of the line, but he hesitated and looked back with weary eyes, adding, "Bring Mason back, one way or another."

Louris nodded, his resolve thoroughly transmitting over the web. "You have my word, Doctor."

Λ

"Brilliant! Nothing could have survived that! Nothing!" Grinning ear-to-ear, Shvinskilli's typically low voice raised in pitched excitement that victory's grace was soon to be upon them.

Unat'kolarev paced in the dank room. The stark necessity of meeting in an EM -hardened sub-basement lent it a claustrophobic air, but he believed it hardened the heart for the continual struggle. This *dacha* served its purpose on the outside for benevolent pretense, while the truer battle he waged belonged in the rat holes and dark spaces. After several decades, nothing could be left to chance; suspect everything, trust no mind not sullied by these trenches. Seated around him, his dozen advisors—borne of every stripe and rank through the strata of Confederation society, military, corporate, black market and political—looked on, engaged in such small ruminations he wondered if they staked anything other than sycophancy to the cause anymore.

"No, my friend," Unat'kolarev countered. "MOLOTOK's methods were crude...my explicit instructions were tossed away, like so much rubbish!"

Shvinskilli snickered all too easily; his recent fear of his superior now diminished into haughtiness.

"Your allegiance to this underground 'subterfuge' has grown tired," he railed. "The True Peoples desire action, sir. What better way to eliminate the Americans than the destruction of our own experiment? Sitting idly by while our patriotic deeds go anonymous is hardly the True People's way."

An arthritic index finger was flung his way. "Remember, I alone steered the True Peoples out of the wilderness, and having steadfastly gathered our strength in the blindspots of five Premiers is not insignificant. Your lecture is misplaced...what about *your* loyalty? Your affectations are not patriotic. Perhaps too long you have enjoyed the accompaniment of *devushkas* at the expense of your sense while here."

At that, the otherwise engaged audience went silent, experiencing for the first time in perhaps decades the open voicing of dissent; they had seen many briefings, and many differing opinions, but none so boldly proclaimed.

"My loyalty is to the True Peoples of Russia, sir," Shvinskilli said, his lively hands put to rest. "Please forgive me."

Unat'kolarev took his seat at the head of the circle of leather chairs. He let forth a great sigh, the weight of the years pressing down, a strange gravity on his frame. "What's done cannot be reclaimed. MOLOTOK's aim fell far long of my wishes, but he will not be punished. The webmedia are tripping over themselves to broadcast this tragedy. Have the arrangements been made to plant Vinogravich partisans among the recovered dead?"

Nadya's voice answered from the rear. "Yes, sir."

"Sir, if I may," Mattarov said from mid-circle, his epaulets shining in the dim light provided by an antique chandelier.

Unat'kolarev nodded his acquiescence.

"Stage Two's loss is not without merit...the timetable for Zaryov's Stage Three has been accelerated upon your approval. Yastanni's continued 'work' on Stage One still leaves much in our favor. Your strategy is a resounding success."

"Agreed," Shvinskilli said, publicly papering over their prior disagreement. "The Americans think Yastanni is our only hope with his application...it provides us plenty of opportunities to deceive."

Unat'kolarev trimmed the end of his cigar, then lit it, releasing a plume of smoke that only added to his dim surroundings. "But of course it has. And I have always had great ideas for dear Doctor Yastanni. His continued participation gives me great...pleasure."

CHAPTER TWELVE

"Over here! *Over here!*" Thrusting his arms towards the vents of smoke and flame rising from the shattered ground, Mason directed the aerial fire crews to apply their suppression foam in wide arcs over the smoldering crater, suffocating it in the tarry liquid. Dozens of plumes belched throughout the kilometer-wide sinkhole, as if plucked straight from the *Divine Comedy*.

Overhead, the media drones whizzed by annoyingly, interfering with the emergency rescue craft now making their way to the area. A few media lorries parked at the crater mouth, the reporters inside disembarking to grab the best scoop in person. Several trekked across ground zero with no regard of the dangerously unstable soil, at first looking as if they were here to assist, but Mason knew better; they were adorned in completely the wrong attire, merely readying to setup interviews and angling to get dramatic backdrops for their webeyes, the vultures circling for the feast in their multicolored webchannel logo jackets and hastily applied makeup.

Behind them, locals began filtering in, gasping at the rising smoke plumes, their exclamations drowned out by the din of collapsing debris and aerial craft. Some clung to the side of the crater pit, desperate to reach the men inside, but held in check by the newly arrived South African army and Carletonville constabulary.

"Hey! Hey, you! Are you one of the miners? You trying to help out your friends?" shouted a youthful reporter, stupidly oblivious to the carnage. A blue light on the side of his head was his webeye beaming the images to every corner of the planet, the ignoramus unaware of the extent, nor ethnicity of, the death below.

Mason, covered in grime, perspiration, dust, soot and his and Bell's own blood, turned towards the voice, narrowing his eyes. With the hot breeze blowing his matted hair against his scalp, the agent sneered, but quickly realized the opportunity that had just presented itself and allowed the lad to approach.

"You live?" Mason asked, meaning the webeye. "Come here."

Thinking he'd get the first on-site interview, the eager reporter crisscrossed the flattened corrugate siding under his boots and made his way to Mason. "How bad is it?" he blurted out excitedly.

"Thousands of miners are probably crushed under four kilos of rock," Mason said, with no trace of giddiness nor pandemonium in his voice. "Is that good enough for you?"

"Do you know—"

Ripping the webeye headset off the lad's brow in haste, Mason scrutinized the device's specs as the reporter soothed his skull from the agent's manhandling.

"Hey...! That hur—"

"Shut up!" Mason tore off the outer housing of the cheap, mass-market webeye and rooted inside the electronics, soon finding the device's transceiver. Performing some rudimentary jury-rigging, he directed the webeye to broadcast an alpha channel, coded communiqué back to Company HQ.

Holding the webeye at eye-level, Mason peered into its lens and said, "I'm alive...Jackson's got a fractured leg. Request assistance out of this fiasco ASAP. Stone out." With a single motion, Mason cracked the device in half, rendering it into junk, then handed the pieces back to the boy and began to walk towards the crater lip.

"What are you?!" the reporter protested, handling his dismantled webeye. "You can't just destroy Web447 News property! My bureau's litigation team is gonna hear about this!"

"They can suck it," he said without stopping. Right now, in Mason's mind, the greenhorn was lucky he wasn't spitting out his teeth. This new version of Chagang-Do curdled his guts, giving him no reason to treat the boy any better.

Striding through the newly arranged cordon placed around the crater by the constabulary and army, Mason fended off more media and civilian waves—his departure unnoticed thanks to the spectacle below—until reaching the tram line, where Bell sat propped against a fallen tree trunk, his leg halfway bandaged with his shredded shirt.

"We have to get to back to the hotel...I've got an Alpha out for extraction," Mason explained, pulling Bell up by his arm.

Bell grimaced as he put most of his weight against his good leg. "I saw some transports headed back that way...you sure they got it?"

"Don't worry," the senior agent answered, smirking. "I commandeered some equipment. I think I got my point across."

"Uhh, I hope so." Bell sighed. "I'm sick of this operation already."

Mason furrowed his brow; Louris said Bell was the man, the only agent for this op, and here he was, allowing a minor beating to defeat him in the midst of this catastrophe before the real hard work began. "You gonna pussy out on me *now!*"

Bell tried to defend himself, but mustered a meek grumble instead.

"That's what I thought," Mason, putting his best contempt on display. "Next time just stay back in the hotel, where—"

"Screw you! I'm the reason we made it this far, Mason!" Bell's face blushed, the blood in his veins pumping overtime. His embarrassment shaming him, he let his spine do the talking now, damning the torpedoes. "I may be the baby on this op, but I worked my Georgia ass off to get this high! So fuck off!"

A hoarse laugh bellowed from Mason, succeeded by a clap on Bell's shoulder. With the younger agent's bewilderment covering his face, Mason responded, "Not so soft after all. You'll do just fine...."

Λ

"You sons of bitches! I thought you'd both bit it!"

Escorting the crutch-ridden Bell through the Glass Castle's Global Directorate corridor, Mason could only smile morosely at Feltham's exclamation.

"Credit the trams for being five minutes late, or we would've."

Louris brought up the rear of the 9D greeting party, stepping around Kindred to shake the wayward agents' hands. He spied Bell's soft cast. "Welcome back. All in one piece, mostly?"

"Doc Miyuozaki says I'll need this through the night, at least until the fossa enzymes knit me back together," Bell said. Wrapped over his right knee and calf, the cast resembled a translucent pillow that held the limb straight as a pin.

"Any ideas 'bout what the hell's going on?" Louris asked, following Mason and Bell into Mason's office.

"My only theory is—" Mason paused to wheel his desk seat over to Bell, who sat down in it, "is that we got too close to Stage Two."

Kindred exchanged looks with Feltham, then looked to Mason. "So it's certain, then. TauTona was it."

"Oh, yeah. Scaled-up equipment like we saw at Yastanni's lab. No one was there, though, strangely enough."

Louris crossed his arms over his chest. "It was abandoned?"

"We hadn't gotten that far," Bell said. "Our next recon was to ascertain whether the Confederation was still using it, or what—well, you saw what happened next."

"They must have blown it remotely," Mason added. "Perhaps that was their intention all along."

Louris circled round the group, his mind digesting this new information. "You may have been on the right track, Lis."

Mason raised a curious eyebrow.

Λ

"Having a decoy site is almost too much for even me to believe," Mason said to Feltham a short time later, his hands clasped behind his head. "The resources required to dupe us are just too—"

"It's a former neutronic laboratory," Feltham replied. "Simple to refurbish, man with a small garrison, and bait with just the right clues to ferret out our interest."

Mason sighed. "I know what ALEXEI was...there has to be a good reason why we were led to believe it *was* Stage Two." He looked to Feltham. "Unless someone else wanted us to. Psyops...keeping us off our game by informing us they knew what our government did years ago, and capitalizing on it, principally by rubbing our noses in it."

"Look, I'm not ruling out a third party. But we have no substantial evidence of it," Louris said at last. "We can go on and on, theory versus theory for weeks, but we can't build a case on it. The point is, agents, we have data suggesting the Confederation is well aware of our own government's supposed clandestine dark energy research, and worse yet, is building their experiments on that knowledge. Yes, ALEXEI may well have been intended to catch us with our hands in the cookie jar. And, what was found there does corroborate the confidential court files relating to Kweiksman's activities. So, where do we go?"

Mason and Feltham looked into each other's eyes for several seconds, before Mason said, "We need some more answers from Yastanni."

"And how do you suppose we do that, stone man?" Kindred asked.

"I think it's time we lean on de Lis a bit more...and perhaps, just get Doctor Yastanni working for us."

Λ

"I'm not exactly in the most inviting mood, Agent Mason." De Lis shook his head, his eyes drifting down and his mind someplace else. "Beyond my lack of trust in Nouri, what Agent Louris informed me of earlier is giving me plenty of pause in furthering anything remotely approaching research with him, as well."

"I understand, Doctor," Mason said, looking at the remarkably good self-doubt in de Lis's holographic visage. "But I don't want you to build a weapon...I want you to perform intelligence for us. You've already done enough to be proclaimed an honorary Company agent."

"Well, I—" de Lis halted, a subtle smile crossing his face. "How thoughtful, Greg. Where's my badge? Don't I receive one?"

Mason snickered. "It's in the post. Promise."

"Sure. I'll lure him in for you. Won't guarantee everything you may want, but I'll see what I can wrangle."

"Excellent." Mason rubbed his hands together. "We'll be monitoring everything, Doctor. This is too important to leave well enough alone."

A grim countenance again fell over de Lis. "I know. Trust me, I know."

Λ

"And what benefit does my research receive, Richard? If I am not mistaken, I am at the very least three years, possibly more, ahead of Sudbury." Yastanni crossed his arms, his posture not long for patience standing in front of his office's holo-camera.

De Lis leaned close, employing the best showmanship he could muster. "The benefit of the most advanced researchers in the Western hemisphere. And," the doctor hesitated for effect," the possibility of sharing in capital earned by this venture. Joint venture, I must clarify."

Yastanni stepped back, his eyes widening at the prospect; his laboratory could go private, without the meddling of the Confederation, perhaps even surpassing the largesse of the Kermani regime. Throw in the chance to team with de Lis' considerable scientific might and the rehabilitated credibility it would lend him after the botched neutronic affair, he would have to be a fool to think otherwise.

But, his current employers would be none too pleased. Zaryov wasn't just the greatest physicist in all of Russia, he was a political officer, to boot (granted, that was all but impossible in the Confederation, but alas....) and the eyes and ears of whomever employed him to guide the dark energy project. Walking away wasn't just simply done; in all circles, he'd be a traitor, and his life potentially at risk.

Still, *inshallah*, the rewards would be great, indeed.

"You drive a difficult bargain," Yastanni said at last.

"Hard bargain, that is," de Lis corrected. "But open to you still. Why languish with your overlords when the sharing of our collective knowledge could lead—hell, will lead, to such greatness?" De Lis cringed inside upon hearing the words flow so effortlessly from his mouth.

"All right, okay...I need to get out. How do I do that?"

De Lis smiled. "Leave that to my acquaintances."

Λ

"You want *us* to spring Yastanni? He thinks we're your grad students!"

"Then there will be no suspicions, Agent Mason," de Lis answered, a little too self-satisfied for Mason's taste.

Mason muted the holo-camera's vox. Turning to Louris, he said, "Since when did he get your job?"

"Looks like he took your honorary badge to heart," Kindred quipped.

"Don't start...." Mason pursed his lips, then activated the volume again. "All right. Let's do this."

De Lis nodded. "I'll alert Yastanni that you'll be on your—"

"No alerts. We're doing this under the cover of night, and under the noses of the Confederation," Mason explained. "Smuggling him out is going to be hard enough without them knowing we're there. We'll contact you when—or if— we're successful."

"Good luck. De Lis out." The doctor's image shimmered into thin air, leaving a pulsing ring of illumination on Mason's desk, the holographic display powering down.

Mason swiveled in his seat, looking to Louris. "Get us a ride on a Dragonfly, Chief. I want this op completed ASAP."

"You've got it."

"The rest of you, study up on your Farsi, just in case," Mason ordered. "And work up a report on insertion strategies. I need to know every nook and cranny by rote once we land. Let's do it, people."

The agents of 9D rose from their seats—save for Bell, who was helped up by Mason—and sprang into action, exiting Mason's office with no time to spare. All knew deciphering the secrets of Project Ether and bringing an end to the Confederation's attempts to harness the technology rested on their shoulders, whether they failed or succeeded.

CHAPTER THIRTEEN

Dropping from the blanket of stars and out over the Strait of Hormuz, the USNA Dragonfly hoverjet *Green Lightning* rocketed across Qeshm Island, penetrating Kermani Iranian airspace at well past five hundred kilometers per hour. Bombarding the primitive sea, air and land defensive arrays with scrambling lidar reflections, the hoverjet—one leap in magnitude larger than a lithesome jumpjet—moved in undetected, heading over the southern coast and plains.

Utilizing a reverse parabola arc to the main land, *Green Lightning* crept nearer to the eastern-most edge of the Zagros Mountains, approaching Yastanni's compound from its seemingly inviolably protected southern flank, where the tall peaks scraped the sky, and no eyes on the ground could pass. But these were no ordinary trespassers....

Tightening the straps on the ebony flight gear they wore, the agents of 9D headed to the "bomb bay" at *Green Lightning*'s midsection, which bisected the two bow and two aft VTOL engine pods of the enormous, elongated figure-8-shaped vehicle. Once opened, the bomb bay doors would release a waiting descent rover, named the Prowler, Mark VI, with the agents dropped to the earth and their own devices; after that, *Green Lightning* would circle the Sea of Hormuz until ready to retrieve the Prowler at the rendezvous point. Now, 9D prepared to descend, abandoning the relative comfort a slow landing aboard the hoverjet could provide to one that was liable to be a little "bumpy" in the harsh terrain of the Zagros foothills and its inky recesses.

All four donned helmets with oxygen masks and advanced towards the tied-down Prowler, nigh two meters tall and three meters in length, its six exposed wheel wells displaying the dune-buggy-like mechanics of the bare bones vehicle, more roll cage than chassis. Massive shock absorber coils connected to the deeply treaded tires dominated the front end of the Prowler, cushioning it from a fall of over a kilometer in the sky and allowing it to immediately traverse ground considered otherwise impassable by lesser vehicles. Just above the Prowler's cabin sat the cumbersome, detachable descent rocket bus and drogue chute system, capable of delivering the Prowler with minimal involvement from the mother hoverjet.

With the LZ nearly at hand, the agents hastily clambered into the enclosed cabin, buckling the Y-belts across their torsos for the descent.

"Descent crew aboard!" Mason shouted through the voxlink to the *Green Lightning*'s cockpit. Toggling the instrument panel before him in the driver's seat, he accessed the Prowler's power systems, firing up the computer's descent sensors.

"Affirmative," the pilot said. "Beginning descent procedures. Good luck, guys... ready on my mark. Mark!"

A numerical countdown on the Prowler's instruments appeared, starting at ten seconds. Mason girded himself, his hands gripping the steering wheel, while next to and behind him, the trio clasped onto the Y-belts with leather gloves on their crossed forearms, readying for a drop none of them had ever taken, let alone practiced for in simulations.

Mason focused on the display, watching the countdown tick off: "6...5...4...3...2...1"

A blast roared beneath the Prowler and reverberated throughout the agents' bodies, a thunderous wave that rattled them to the core, then nothing, save for the sudden sensation of blood rushing to their skulls, ballooning in their heads. A peculiar feeling washed over them, as if all the worst earaches they had suffered as children happened at once, a tingling boring painful holes in their ears. *Green Lightning*'s shaded interior gave way next to them, replaced by the rapidly magnifying terrain a less than a kilometer below.

Sublimely balanced for just such drops—neither end pitching forwards nor backwards—the Prowler descended like the hunk of bolts, alloys and composites it was, gravity giving it no quarter. Ten seconds in, though, the descent sensors detected the optimal height, announcing the drogue chute's imminent release with a piercing alarm audible through all four agent's helmet speakers.

A trio of air canisters above the cabin jetted the three parachutes upwards, blossoming their reverse midnight-grey teardrops into the sky. The agents' tingling feet now traded places with their upper bodies as the Prowler caught an updraft and was pulled tens of meters back.

His instrument panel displaying the Prowler's journey over the Zagros increment by increment, Mason couldn't help but think the four were powerless to the whims of air currents and blind faith in the soon-to-be deployed rockets to hopefully whisk them over the peaks and onto steadier terrain.

Their descent was too startling and swift for Feltham, who rocked her helmeted head back and forth while muttering the Lord's Prayer as fast as possible, ignoring (or pretending to) the five-second beeps sounding from the descent computer that informed the crew was just that much closer to the surface—or oblivion.

Picking up velocity again as the drogue chutes lost their lift, the Prowler plummeted to under two hundred meters, giving the agents pause.

Any second now, Mason's new mantra was. *Any second now....*

One hundred fifty meters...one hundred twenty-five....

Mason's eyes darted from the terrain cartograph's horrifyingly huge image of the Earth less-than-a-minute beneath them, to the descent rockets' numerical countdown:
"3...2...1"

A cable snapped, setting free the drogue chutes. Four abrupt pops broke the rocket descent bus from the Prowler's cabin, allowing the bus to fall upwards along its own cable. Orange tongues of flame shot downwards among the Prowler, visible even through the tinted helmet faceplates, as if breaking through the atmosphere from orbit, and continued firing for fifteen seconds, just enough to slow the Prowler to a "soft" landing.

"Ooooohhh ssshhhiiiiitttt...herrre weeeee gooooooo!!!" Mason bellowed.

The second cable snapped, giving the last few drops of fuel left burning in the rockets to push the bus back, freeing the Prowler to its final, shortened leg. Eight meters to the Earth, the Prowler and crew free fell, buffeting to and fro, until reaching the Dasht-e-Kavir.

And with a hard thump, crash and blasting of rocks and soil, the Prowler made contact, rose into the air a few centimeters, then contacted again, the superbly engineered shock absorbers bearing the brunt of the six wheels. A few seconds later, the agents watched the flaming out rocket bus smash into the ground meters behind them, exploding debris across the desert, in all probability never to be recovered or seen again by human beings.

Taking stock of their situation with curt calls out and responses, the 9D team pinpointed their LZ coordinates and plotted out the corrections to the pre-planned insertion strategy.

They discarded their oxygen masks and breathed in the vented Iranian air, reacquainting themselves with the sensation of solid ground, which, truth be told, felt better every second. Now, after the worst roller coaster ride in their collective lives, the real work began.

Λ

Shooting through the jagged, angled foothills, the nearby mountaintops silhouetting the much more distant stars, Mason played out his teenage fantasy of rally racing, pushing the Prowler to design limits in an environment its designers had yet to enjoy. Clouds of dust and rocks chucked out from under the tires were reflected back to the agents on the infrared and lidar displays, giving them an even better understanding of their speed than the rather clinical speedometer before Mason.

Switchbacks and sharp rises and falls across the terrain tested Mason's skill and mettle, but he'd long ago come to grips with the dangers inherent in field work, instead giving his mind's worries over to the op itself. Having arrived bearing the standard sidearms, but also the more rarely employed M-119 Marine semi-automatic rifle, the agents worked to ensure they weren't outclassed like Feltham and Kindred had been at Onekotan island, in case de Lis' extended presence made Yastanni's handlers nervous about future visitors.

Feltham pulled up a Global Security Network cartograph of the foothills surrounding the compound, manipulating the holograph with her hands to bring their current position into sight. Magnifying the selected box, the agent tilted the image orthrographically, mirroring the view out the forward windscreen.

"All right, boss, we've got a long, straight ravine coming up soon," Feltham said. "Forty-six klicks beyond is our first security perimeter."

Mason nodded. "Okay...Tommy, you got the EM scrambler set yet?"

"Accessing satellite GPS logs now," Bell said, working a console behind Feltham's seat. His helmet glowing softly in the yellow and blue illumination, the agent targeted all known sensing devices in the area using Global Security Network scans. Dozens of green blips appeared in quick succession on the interface, text boxes identifying each one. "Got them."

"Take 'em out."

On Mason's command, Bell brought the Prowler's omnidirectional EM scrambler online, enabling it to feed false data to each successive sensor planted within and without the security perimeter.

Minutes later, the Prowler drove past the first wave of clandestine sensors, knocking them out of the security network and allowing the agents to slip in undetected, swiftly and easily defeating the Iranians' remote eyes, ears and mouths.

Relentlessly dry desert rolled beneath them, kilometer after kilometer, unshifting, unchanging, save for the mountaintops above. An hour in and the glints of a tall, chain-link fence row lined with razor wire appeared ahead.

"Here we are," Feltham said, cross-indexing with the cartograph.

Steering for the center of a fence segment, Mason throttled up, increasing the Prowler's speed on the approach to the outer perimeter.

"You've wanted to do this for a long time, haven't you?" Kindred asked, cocking her head for a better look.

"You bet." He wore an imperceptible smile in the darkness.

"Next time I get to, stone man," Kindred retorted.

Growling eagerly, the Prowler's engine revved as it met the fence and blew through it, leaving a wide hole with relish. Behind the speeding vehicle, fragments of twisted metal cascaded to the ground, proving utterly useless in deterring, let alone slowing, the Prowler, or 9D's resolve.

Λ

"Ah, our old friends." Feltham pointed to the windscreen, where the pair of anti-aircraft batteries 9D spied on their first trek here stood as silent sentinels.

The rectangular compound rose dead ahead on the horizon, spotlit by sodium lights, lending it the appearance of a prison more than a physics laboratory. A tower with an automated search lamp loomed unawares off to the right, its guards most likely napping or in a drunken stupor; after their encounter with the hapless guard Shadmani, the agent's level of concern for resistance was about nil.

Slowing to a crawl, Mason brought the Prowler near to the inner security fence. Bell hopped out and began work on the perimeter with a laser cutter. A moment later, he flashed an "okay" gesture with his left hand and then kicked through the fence, giving the others access inside the grounds.

"Hold the fort," Mason said to Kindred, grabbing Bell's and his M-119s.

Kindred exchanged her seat for Mason's, passing Feltham's rifle to the departing agent. As the secondary lead, Kindred remained behind to keep tabs on the trio, but would also drive the Prowler to the extraction point once the escape was underway. While the trio breached the opening, she accessed the Prowler's computer, which displayed constant biosignatures synced with their individual voxlinks, allowing her to monitor her colleagues' health and GPS coordinates.

Cloaking themselves in the shadows, the trio jogged fifty meters to an open shed where a locked jeep was parked; taking a brief respite to catch their breaths and analyze their positions, they raced off again for the compound, pausing outside the entrance.

Constructed of reinforced concrete walls and vertical steel beams, the structure appeared to be able to withstand a concerted conventional weapons strike, having been built sometime within the last fifty years by the latest Kermani strongman, The Extraordinary and Most Glorious Naseem Majeed Kermani, in one of his many nationwide construction sprees when flush with grey-market capital. Thanks to their previous visit to the laboratory—which Mason and Feltham had meticulously scrutinized while de Lis played to Yastanni—the agents easily broke into the front door's security system, a simple, off-the-shelf automated alarm connected to the antique glass entryway, Kermani's faith in his defenses obviously misplaced. Cracking open the right door panel, the agents strode inside, confident their hack had prevented the sensors from communicating to the security network and alerting the guards of their presence.

Walking swiftly, but not hastily, the agents kept the M-119s at the ready, their flight helmets providing intermediate sensor sweeps of the corridor and relaying the data in miniature HUDs; they also served a covert purpose, as a layer of cover for plausible denial.

The trio found the elevator leading to the lower levels of the compound after several moments, where the main lab and Yastanni's quarters were located. The lift basket wasn't much more sophisticated than TauTona's, Mason reckoned, being purely utilitarian; grimy, oily and noisy. A simple sodium light bulb flickered above, giving the agents a poorly lit view of the shaft on the way down. Next to Feltham, a rickety alphanumeric floor counter rotated, albeit so slowly it was one behind.

Mason punched a large red button on the lift basket's railing at the sixth floor, the last habitable above the maintenance level. The doors opened ahead and the trio exited, watching for guards, though again, security was arguably nonexistent.

Deep within the bunker stage of the complex, the ceilings were low and cylindrical, a whitewashed corrugate that could have been stolen from some Cold War-era bomb shelter. Four rooms completed the tiny level, with "YASTANNI" written in both English and Arabic upon the door, while "ZARYOV" was scrawled in Cyrillic two doors over. Mason approached Yastanni's door and slid a lock-picking passkey through the lock; the panel refused to open when he turned the handle, making him run into it with his momentum.

"Locked," he said, looking to Feltham.

She gestured with her hands in the air. "Well, you could knock...."

Mason rapped twice, trying not to wake anyone else who may have been in the other rooms, specifically Zaryov. Waiting a moment, Mason knocked once more; he waited again, and deciding to chance it by breaking it down, he raised his right leg, the sole of his boot perched—

The door creaked open, a single eye tracking the darkened strangers through the crack. "What the—"

"*Sobh bekher, agha-yeh Doktor* Yastanni," Mason greeted and lowered his boot. "Your ride is here."

Λ

Tapping her fingers on the Prowler's door frame, Kindred had no other distractions save for humming a pop song and reciting to herself the laundry list of books she needed to download when the op finished and they were safely back in DC. Checking her wrist chronometer as she switched to whistling, Kindred noted the elapsed time was nineteen minutes, still well within 9D's strategic planning.

Her mental radio play evolved into a full-blown drum solo on the steering wheel, until her ears perked up at the second a more distant thump sounded through the vehicle. Scrambling, she retrieved her holobook and scanned the distant echo, verifying its identity.

Triangulating the object's distance, and reading its velocity with lidar, the holobook displayed a red isobar against a green background. Tightening the lidar's waves, Kindred sharpened the contrast and compared it to the USNA military database: Mi-132, *Akilina*-class Confederation troop carrier, approaching the complex double-time. Not good.

She throttled the Prowler up and made a hard turn left, concealing it behind a ridge twenty meters southwest of the compound's southern wall, where shadow would hide it from eyes from above, but only for a short time. Any enterprising Confederation officer surveilling the area could discern the vehicle's presence and know something out of the ordinary was afoot.

Now blazing with landing lights that bathed the grounds in white, the *Akilina's* monstrous twin rotors whirred, the giant craft circling for a good clearing to land. The surveillance tower's guards must have finally woken up, as they flung the security spotlights onto the descending craft, illuminating the bird's hull markings; one stood out to Kindred through the magnification scope in her hand: a bear's head grasping a skull in its jaws: 56th Guards Independent Airborne Brigade.

Bullhorns from the tower bellowed Farsi across the grounds, then repeated in broken Russian, the two pronouncements bouncing from wall to ground and back again. Kindred couldn't quite understand what the shouts were, since the sound amplification was shoddy, but it seemed to imply less than welcome tidings. Fumbling with her voxlink, she toggled it and blurted, "Guys! We've got company! *Akilina* bird just touched down! Repeat! *Akilina* bird's on the ground!"

Λ

"You're from Richard de Lis' university?" Yastanni asked before glancing out into the corridor and closing the door behind the mysterious trio. His eyelids drooped, the look of a man deeper in his work than his own health. "His department must be richer than General Kermani's mother-in-law to have mercenaries sent out for me!"

Mason's concealed face allowed him great brevity, as he lacked the patience for explanations. "We're no mercenaries, Doctor. We're…an interested party."

Feltham said, "De Lis made no bones of the fact that you are extremely valuable to his continuing research. And your safe extraction from this facility must be undertaken now."

The doctor shuffled back to his reading table, wearing a stained white tanktop coupled with powder-blue pajama bottoms, not exactly travel-friendly apparel. "N-now? I thought I would have contact—"

"There is no time, Doctor," Bell warned, stepping close to Yastanni. One sure move and the agent would have him out the door.

"Against your will, or not," Mason said, drawing his sidearm provocatively, "you will be—"

"*Guys! We've got company!*" Kindred's voice crackled over the agent's voxlinks. Akilina *bird just touched down! Repeat!* Akilina *bird's on the ground!*"

Without a word or pause, the trio were galvanized. Mason flung the door wide and motioned Feltham and Bell forward. Bell grasped Yastanni by the arm and whisked him away, the agent bearing his M-119 conspicuously in his right hand. Mason spied a suitcase and small briefcase lodged next to the door, surmising Yastanni had packed his personal effects beforehand for a fast getaway. The agent snagged both and fled after Feltham and Bell, making sure he locked the door behind him.

"We're going to need you to take us off the beaten path," Feltham said to Yastanni, who trailed nearby.

"I don't underst—who, what—"

Feltham forcibly parted the level's door panels, allowing Bell to load Yastanni onto the lift.

"It's simple as this," Mason explained, "we're no match for fifty Confederation soldiers intent on storming your lab."

"But why," Yastanni stammered, clasping the lift basket. "Why are they here now?"

Mason punched the lift's control button, making the creaking machine ease them back up. "No idea. Right now, I don't have time for questions…we need to get outta here in one piece."

"And how do you expect to do it?" Yastanni asked scornfully, his mouth trembling. "I—we haven't any craft that could beat them."

His elbow bent, Mason rested his sidearm against his collarbone. "Leave that to us."

CHAPTER FOURTEEN

Soldier after soldier poured from the *Akilina*, all equipped with wrap-around night-vision eyegear and armed to the teeth with AKM-6A70 fully automatic infantry rifles, guaranteed to put targets down for good with extreme ease. A lieutenant wearing an officer's cap and consulting a Russian-made holobook stepped around the LZ, flagging the men towards the complex with his left hand.

Bringing up the rear of the 56th Guards, a monstrosity nigh two-and-a-half meters tall ambled forward, silhouetted in the search lights. The monstrosity soon galloped into full view, topped by two Confederation soldiers.

Sitting in rapt attention in the Prowler's driver's seat, Kindred slapped her helmet with her gloved hand, hardly believing her eyes. The monstrosity she witnessed was a vehicle she had only seen in schematics: a GAZ-57009 *Kazak* light infantry quadruped, known in NATO parlance as a Centaur, for good reason. The Centaur rode like a mechanical horse, capable of crossing terrain fit for a beast of burden. This thing could put a world of hurt on a person in a split-second, with a dedicated aft gunner blasting hot particles out of a harness-mounted 12.7mm DShKM-2109b heavy machine gun.

"This is bad...this is so bad...." She brought her voxlink close to her lips. "You've got to get out of there now, Stone man. They're here in force for something...looks like they're assaulting Normandy out here."

Pacing in the lift despite its crotchety, lurching behavior, Mason said, "I get the point, Sha. We're going to try the long way out, maybe one of the bunkered corridors—"

"We have no hidden corridors!" Yastanni blurted out.

"Can it!" Mason grabbed the doctor's tanktop. "The UN knows about them. No use denying it now when there's nothing left to hide."

Yastanni pulled away, his face wearing indignance.

Mason continued, "Keep a trace on our voxlink signals. Who knows where this will end up."

Screeching to a halt, the lift basket opened, admitting the four-some onto the Laboratory level, still some nine meters underground. Holding their rifles to their cheeks, Feltham and Bell led the way through the dimly lit corridor, Mason and Yastanni bringing up the rear.

"Where's the entrance to the closest hidden corridor?" Mason asked.

"Through the main laboratory...we use it to expedite deliveries."

Feltham craned her head back to the weary Yastanni, pursing her lips. "I bet you do."

Mason hid his displeasure with Feltham's comment, instead keeping an eye on the doctor. "Where are your security guards? Will they put up a fight or are they gonna let the Confederation walk right in?"

"Security? I have but one guard, and he takes nights off."

Guess that'd be Shadmani, Mason said to himself. Big surprise there. "Then who're the guards at the perimeter?"

"General Kermani's private forces," Yastanni answered, "mixed with several agents of the *Savak*. Very cruel and dangerous. They have no time for warm hearts."

So, my hunch was right; Yastanni's leash was shorter than I expected. Mason allowed himself a little measure of sympathy for the physicist-for-hire. "Have you left this place since you began your present research?"

"*Agha-yeh* General Kermani has forbade it," Yastanni said, the wistfulness in his voice quite evident. "Yes, this is my life's work, but I miss Shiraz in the winters and the Alborz for skiing in season. The *Savak*, they have no time for pleasures. How things must have been in the olden years, under the Ayatollahs."

Mason couldn't know that; the *Savak*, on the other hand, he was a bit more acquainted with. Outside of the FSB, the Bolivar Venezuelan Guards, and the Crescent Caliphate of Indonesia, the *Savak* wore their reputations as cunning and ferocious desert warriors proudly, hav-ing efficiently and ruthlessly eliminated hundreds, possibly thousands, of General Kermani's perceived and real enemies across the globe. It didn't take a leap of the imagination to know they wouldn't tolerate any Confederation attacks, whether it be on them or whom (or what) they were contracted to oversee.

Pausing at the same reinforced steel door that, unbeknowst to Yastanni, he had shown them on their first op several weeks ago, the doctor unlocked and swung open the thick door, again revealing the laboratory where all the troubles of dark energy had been brought to the modern day.

Even in darkness, the cylindrical neutrino capture cage awed the agents, its massive size not diminished one iota. Yastanni walked to it in reverence, still not fully aware that with the Confederation infantry on the premises, time was growing short for a long goodbye.

Feltham and Bell briefly lowered their rifles to take in the view, but Mason was more pragmatic. His interest lay not in the hardware, but in what Yastanni could recreate with de Lis *back home.*

Yastanni placed a hand on the cage, his voice switching to softly sweet Farsi. He seemed, to Mason, to be wishing it farewell, as if packing his child up to give away. While hard to comprehend for the non-scientist agent, the sentiment wasn't wholeheartedly dissimilar.

Now, though, wasn't a great time for it.

A harsh shout emanated from the ring level above the laboratory, followed by the clacks of the overhead lighting coming up. Shielding their eyes, the agents and Yastanni looked towards the voice.

"He doesn't look Russian," Bell said, checking out the swarthy man aiming a rifle at them.

The man shouted Farsi again, his hand gesturing at Yastanni. His weathered face and clean-cut appearance suggested he was not a Kermani private soldier, but *Savak*, and mighty angered. The doctor, for his part, responded less virulently, almost calmly, apologetically.

"Doctor," Mason said, picking out words in the *Savak* man's heavily regional Farsi dialect, "finish your defense later."

Some distance down the corridor, footfalls coupled with audible scuffs on the smooth cement floor served notice that Confederation soldiers drew near. Feltham and Bell looked back, their rifles raised again.

Mason reached out and pulled Yastanni's arm, but the *Savak* agent fired a warning shot, which ricocheted off the metal floor grates behind Mason.

"*Kir!*" Mason shouted in anger, his left hand pointing his pistol at the *Savak* goon. "Fantastic…." he muttered, then glanced at Feltham and Bell. "Start heading to the corridor."

"Boss—" Feltham began.

"Do it! I'll follow behind soon."

Nodding, Feltham surveyed the far entryway out of the lab, motioning Bell onwards. The pair eyed Mason and Yastanni once more, then disappeared beyond the exit.

Mason stared down the *Savak* agent, and speaking in rough Farsi, asked, "Why are you still here? There are fifty Confederation troops storming this complex. This isn't your fight."

"You will die before you make it out," the *Savak* agent said simply. "Our business is not your concern. Yastanni is not to venture beyond the perimeter."

"This is his decision," Mason answered. "His free will."

The *Savak* agent gritted his teeth. "Yankee dog...the Russian mongrels have already beaten you. Their physicist has ties to projects to which you cannot fathom."

"That may be the case, but I'm not here to question Zaryov."

Now just seconds from entering the laboratory, the Confederation troops' footfalls accelerated, the sounds of low voices giving way to excited commands, no doubt aided by the *Savak* agent's gunfire.

"Then die of your own free will!"

Mason took that and ran with it, towing Yastanni along. The squeaks of boots and din of weapons clanging together threatened to burst through the entrance, giving Mason no reason to hang around. Running to the opposite end of the circular laboratory, the two fled to the exit, seeing five soldiers in black garb bring AKM-6A70s to bear on them.

A series of gunshots from above the soldiers rained down, felling three of them. Mason caught sight of the *Savak* agent releasing a second barrage, before another wave of Confederation troops punched past and dispatched him with enough firepower to blow apart the railing around the ring level, leaving nothing save a red and pink mist.

"*GO!*" Mason exhorted Yastanni, sticking a forearm into the Iranian's spine.

Volleys of gunfire splintered the exit threshold and the corridor wall opposite the lab. Craning his neck over his shoulder, Mason watched the troops' shadows grow crisper and shrink, the men just steps away.

Flinging Yastanni forward, Mason swiveled around and let loose a barrage of particle rounds from his rifle, warding off the soldiers for a few seconds more. Taking off again, he caught up to the slower doctor and rounded a corner with him, descending a set of stairsteps past a small portal that took them several meters underground.

Narrowing to about a hundred and thirty centimeters in width, and dimming to just above the light of the grounds outside, the corridor took on the appearance of a drug runner's escape route under some foreign border town.

"A big concrete block is just up ahead," Yastanni said, his breathing labored. "We can push it into the path and seal it on the other side."

"Sounds good...."

Moments passed before Yastanni paused and doubled over, putting his hands to his knees.

"C'mon, egghead, help me with this," Mason said, walking over to the stone slab standing along the wall. An alcove lay just beyond, chiseled out of the concrete not too recently, that could easily accomodate the slab when set wide in the corridor.

Both men got on the far side of the slab and slid it out a few centimeters. Mason took a deep breath and gathered his strength, then pushed the slab to the left, walking it over while Yastanni kicked it with the toe of his slipper, which did nothing more than force dirt into the air.

"Right there," Yastanni directed, pointing his index finger to a slot in the alcove.

Mason did as commanded, sliding the edge of the slab perfectly into place. The narrow corridor was now a smidgeon more secure.

Clapping Yastanni on the shoulder, Mason said, "I'd ask if you've done this before, but I think I've got my answer."

Yastanni merely raised a bushy eyebrow.

"Sha," Mason said into his voxlink, "you have my signal?"

"*I'm tracking you now, Stone man.*"

"Find where this corridor ends and meet us there."

"*There's a cross corridor about a thousand meters in length that ascends to the surface,*" Kindred said. "*I can meet you at the entrance.*"

Yastanni gestured towards the other end of the dim tunnel. "Another two hundred meters."

"Keep sharp, Sha. We've got some angry Russkies on our tails."

Λ

Standing guard over a locked overhead door at the end of the underground corridor, Bell and Feltham shined their torches back down the tunnel, waiting in silence, listening, scanning for any movement indicative that Mason and Yastanni had outran the Confederation troops. Both kept their index fingers at the ready on their rifles, hoping the split team wasn't about to take on twenty-five-to-one numbers.

"*Lis, I'm two minutes from the entrance,*" Kindred said over the voxlink channel. "*Anything yet?*"

Feltham's torchlight circled inside the narrow corridor, trying to tease out a glimmer, any bounce of illumination of her partner. "Standby...."

"I'm on borrowed time, here...they've got drones buzzing all ar—"

Clacks of footfalls echoed in the agent's ears, tensing their muscles. Two pairs of frantic legs approached the end of the corridor, leading Feltham to bellow, "Who goes there?!"

"Mason...good to see friends again."

Hiding his eyes behind an outstretched palm, Yastanni did a double-take, finally adding up the actions of the trio with their leader's identity. "You? North American intelligence? The ones who put me on trial!"

Mason unbuttoned his chin strap and lifted the helmet up, revealing his eyes and brow. "And the ones who put their lives on the line to bring you to the West, Doctor...."

Yastanni cursed in Farsi, the venom in his voice overwhelming his passions. "Why should I trust you? Why should I trust Richard?"

"Because you have no other choice," Feltham said, her rifle barrel squared on Yastanni. "We're going to help you atone for your misdeeds."

A thunderous roar beyond the locked overhead door distracted them from Yastanni's diatribe. Crossing over to it, Mason rattled the door's handle, futilely pulling on it.

"Open it," the agent commanded, shooting his gaze back to Yastanni.

"Go to hell."

"The Confederation will be more than willing to oblige you, but I won't." In his left hand, Mason held his sidearm to Yastanni's forehead. "Do it."

"Uhh, guys, now's a good time—"

"Working on it!"

Convincing himself his chances under the North American yoke would be much more to his advantage than otherwise, Yastanni clutched his set of pass keys and selecting one, slid it through an adjacent lock on the wall. Clanking inside the overhead door, the long bolt retracted, releasing it. The doctor reached over and turned the handle then pulled straight up, opening the clandestine tunnel to the outside desert and the waiting Prowler's highbeam lamps.

Mason waved the three on, holding the door's bottom panel until they seated themselves within the Prowler. Looking back one last time, the agent let go, allowing the overhead to slam shut.

"I thought you might've decided to camp out," Kindred quipped a moment later. Gripping the steering wheel and turning it counterclockwise—rotating the Prowler's omnidirectional wheels one hundred degrees—she whipped the vehicle around and headed back up the incline roughly the same way she came in.

Bracing himself in the front passenger seat, Mason watched the secretive tunnel recede in the distance. "Amenities were a little lacking."

Stomping her foot on the throttle, Kindred powered the Prowler up to a hundred and sixty KPH, blowing dust and rocks over the vehicle. She switched off the front highbeam lamps with a single voice command, restoring image control to the holographic HUD. Instantly, the windscreen transformed into a bright landscape ahead of her's and Mason's eyes, untouched by the dark of night, giving them a complete visual of their intended escape route.

Tapping a button on his HUD interface, Mason started to open an encrypted voxlink channel to *Green Lightning*, but was alerted by a beeping red alarm on Kindred's display. With the alarm punched, a satellite view appeared of an object closing in on the Prowler from behind. Mason's index finger circled on the interface, toggling the image to the Prowler's rear holo-camera. A hovering military drone sharpened into focus, tailing the agents at a parallel velocity. Hacking into the drone's transponder, Mason brought up its model and specs: KD-10 *Lammergeier*, a forty-kilo vehicle killer, equipped with six electropulse missiles and twin fully automatic ion cannon, enough to shred in half an armored vehicle and the occupants inside.

"Drone found us," Kindred said. "That's the first of at least four I saw."

Mason sent out an emergency extraction call to *Green Lightning*, then input an ECM command into his interface. "Readying countermeasures."

A small round hatch popped open on the roof, out of which a miniature rocket shot up at the approaching drone, then flew straight at the intruder, flashing a brilliant countermeasure device that blinded it. Forced to recalibrate its onboard computer, the drone was effectively disabled long enough to lose lift and crash into the desert floor.

"Great shot," Feltham said, craning her head back around.

"Thanks, I—"

Three loud thumps overhead served notice the fight wasn't over.

Sounding throughout the cabin, a second alarm displayed another drone, a third alarm for a third drone, then a fourth alarm yet again.

"Shit!" Manipulating the interface, Mason setup for another countermeasure, but could only launch one at a time, proving once again that government engineers didn't consult field agents often.

Analyzing the drones' attack pattern, Feltham shouted, "Do some fancy driving, Sha! They're trying to outflank and pick us off with cross-fire."

Kindred steeled her hands on the wheel. "Speed, Stone man?"

Mason's eyes darted from one drone's lidar-calculated velocity to the others. "Estimated at seventy-seven knots."

"Good...you ready?"

"Online."

Kindred nodded. "Hang on back there!"

The Prowler spun hard right, carving a ten-meter-wide half-ellipse. In the night sky, the three drones fired a fusilade of missiles, wildly missing the target and instead harmlessly pushing up a cloud of earth. A countermeasure rocket blasted up over the Prowler, which reversed course and raced back to the complex.

"Got it!" Mason crowed, watching the virtual drone disappear.

The remaining drones arched symmetrical double fishhook trajectories, coming about to trail the Prowler once more. Barrel flashes shone in the sky, the KD-10s pelting the Prowler with more cannon fire, which bounced off its hardened skin.

A fifth alarm sounded at Mason's panel. "We've got an EMP missile alert."

"I think I can outrun it."

Kindred's right boot stomped the accelerator, pushing the vehicle back up to one-sixty KPH. Swerving several degrees left-to-right and back again to force the drones to continually re-adjust their positions, the Prowler gathered speed on the devices, pushing them to their upper velocity limits. Kindred lurched hard left, giving Mason a good view of the electropulse missile as it closed in on the Prowler's former position and plowed into the ground.

"We can't keep evading missiles until they run out," Feltham said. "We'll miss the rendezvous point."

Mason agreed, but didn't respond, instead watching for more missiles.

"There's...there's a big tunnel," Yastanni said, seated between Bell and Feltham. "If you can get us to it, it is suitable for vehicle this size. We should be safe for many kilometers."

"How far?" Kindred asked.

Yastanni looked from left to right in the cabin, glancing to Feltham. "Map. Do you have map access?"

Feltham activated her console and a blue rectangular hologram blossomed over the laps of Yastanni, Bell and her. Beginning with a Global Security Network view of the Asia continent, it zoomed tenfold, zeroing in on the Dasht-e-Kavir. The Prowler's current coordinates blinked in green, trekking across the desert.

Yastanni traced a finger across the cartograph, orienting himself. Searching his memory, he drew a line from the complex to an undistinguished blot of terrain not more than two klicks soutwest. "Here," he pronounced, tapping the spot.

Feltham circled the area with her index finger, bringing up a textbox of coordinates. "27.483 north by 55.014 east."

The crew leaned to the left as the Prowler careened right in a wide arc, barging back through the open desert, with two drones firing missiles in pursuit. Kindred's adroit driving foiled the assaults, but it was only a matter of one connecting to put the whole op in dire straits.

"This tunnel of yours better be impressive," Mason said, his eyes catching the glare of a missile strike go off target. "You send transports this way to evade the hot sun?" he asked facetiously, knowing full well the real answer.

Yastanni struggled to respond; instead he looked at the windscreen, pointing out a three-meter-wide divet in the sand. "There! Head down!"

A detonation behind the cabin shook the Prowler, but again the electropulses had yet to disable the vehicle. Several more thumps from cannon fire sparked across the rear windscreen, causing Yastanni to duck.

Kindred persisted in her weaving evasions, even as the distance closed to just ten meters. "Everyone brace! I don't think it's gonna be smooth...!"

Gripping the handles under his seat, Mason girded, his teeth gritted. A blur of rock, scrub and earth flew under the windscreen before him, and after, a looming maw, dark even under the blue-grey HUD.

The Prowler growled under Kindred's throttle. Pushing harder, she launched the vehicle towards the maw, the tires leaving the ground and bridging the distance in a cloud of sand.

A thunderous crash above their heads knocked the five about, then a squealing bang underneath sent them against their Y-belts. Sparks from the cabin roof's hard contact with the entrance cascaded down the windscreen, shining the crew in amber.

"We're in!" Kindred said, throttling down.

Rubbing his head, Bell quipped, "Just barely...."

The Prowler slid down the gravel-lined tunnel, slowing to negotiate the narrow way forward. Its engine revving down to a mild purr, the Prowler halted a good half-klick inside moments later.

Kindred nodded and shook her fist, expressing her inner teen-ager. "Tax money well spent. I've gotta get one of these!"

Two dying pings on Mason's interface attracted his attention. "We lost 'em."

Feltham and Bell turned around in time to see the debris at the entrance pelt the earth. Between them, Yastanni let out a prolonged sigh.

"Boss," Feltham said, resting her head back, "can we go home now?"

CHAPTER FIFTEEN

"We ran into some old friends, Chief," Mason said, rounding the circular table inside the interrogation room.

Home again at the Glass Castle, 9D had unloaded Yastanni to the custody of the Company's experts in psychological profiling and interrogation, Agents Roberta Shaw and Jacob Diamond of Division 12, who walked behind Louris and Mason carrying armfulls of file folders and holobooks.

Louris rubbed his brow in thought, content his squad's return was fruitful, if only by the skin of their teeth, but less so in the brewing international escalation. "General Kermani is, as expected, asking through his under-the-table diplomatic channels why a North American intelligence squad violated his sovereign soil...the Confederation's attack is facing less scrutiny."

"Scrutiny...." Mason said in contempt. "Kermani's only concern is that we didn't pay a toll to get in."

"That may be the case, but the President and Rauchambau are tightening the screws, Greg. The State Department is having face-saving meetings with Kermani's circle in just two days, and they are pressing the DoJ to reign in extracurricular activities...I don't need brass breathing down my neck any more than you need mine."

"And Vinogravich?"

Louris sighed. "The Premier's anxious to get his hands on the agents who infiltrated ALEXEI."

"That should go over well with his fickle constituency. Nothing beats single-digit poll ratings like a good old rattled saber."

"Yeah, well I am not about to have two of my best agents sidelined with desk duties," Louris warned. "We have to be smart…and choose our lines of investigation well."

While Mason watched Shaw and Diamond prep their equipment, another thought niggled at him, shelving his worries over his own government-created problems. "Seems like two hands may be at play…one performing the research, and the other destroying it once we're discovered. At this rate, no evidence of any further stages will be left."

"Don't be too grim," Louris said, clapping the agent's shoulder. "Sometimes the least significant or most inscrutable fact often escapes deliberate attempts at obfuscation. We'll get there, doing what we do best."

"Ready to start, Chief," Diamond said, his file folder and holobook sufficiently collated.

Louris nodded and led the way to an observation gallery just off to the side, where he and the rest of 9D would watch the proceedings with keen interest through a fullerene glass wall.

A pair of beefy security guards led Yastanni in, then departed. Shaw gestured to the doctor to a take a seat opposite them.

"I want to start by saying that we're glad you are in good health, Doctor Yastanni, and we're eager to work with you," Shaw said with a cordial smile.

Yastanni's greeting was subdued, his hands resting palm down on the table. Though he wore a weary face, Mason noted, there was a child-like innocence buried beneath, as though the doctor felt betrayed, or duped into providing his assistance. A twinge of guilt for the mild deception stung the agent, a far cry from how Mason felt when first corralling Yastanni.

"Now," Diamond began, accessing his holobook, "let's begin with your work with Doctor Vasya Zaryov. When did he contact you about Project Ether…."

Over the next few hours, Louris and 9D took notes on Yastanni's testimony, studying not only his answers, but body language, and his willingness to openly discuss several pointed issues relating to the USNA and North Korean dark energy experiments.

Yastanni didn't appear to intentionally evade or downplay his role in the experiments, forthrightly admitting his involvement with neutrino capture, even though Mason fully expected the doctor to stonewall or adopt a haughty defense. Time spent in 9D's company had perhaps made Yastanni honest, or allowed him to keep better secrets under wraps.

Mason paced, his mind replaying the events in TauTona, and the other half's op at ALEXEI. His supposition of two competing

Confederation interests didn't sit well in the pit of his stomach, causing him to believe more was at work than just a superweapon. But what else was there? The Confederation's attack on Yastanni's lab complex created nothing but more questions; avenues split everywhere down this investigative road.

"The second team worked independent of my staff," Yastanni said, piquing Mason's interest.

Walking over to the fullerene glass, he stared at Yastanni; if only his gaze could elicit an elaboration.

"How do you know this?" Shaw asked, typing notes on her holobook.

"Highly experimental work this dangerous should be redundant," Yastanni answered. "I apologize for knowing nothing more."

Diamond sat forward. "Were they in Iran, too?"

"No...I would have known. Somewhere more safe, underground complex more fortified than my own." Yastanni shook his head. "But I am separate from them."

TauTona, Mason knew.

"Are they still in operation?" Shaw asked.

"From the report I read when brought to America, it is sadly destroyed. Many losses in the destruction."

"Is there anyplace else?"

Yastanni paused, taking a deep breath. "Stage Three is planned, but I am not privy to progress. I was not to be informed until my laboratory was scheduled for relocation."

"Given your experience," Diamond said, "what location would you consider essential for Stage Three operations?"

"Somewhere inaccessible, away from vulnerable infrastructure. Cosmic neutrino capture is not easy. Deep underwater, perhaps, or even in polar regions. That is only supposition."

Mason looked away, his feet carrying him to Feltham. "Get de Lis. I want his opinion on this."

Λ

"I have my doubts about his physics-for-hire philosophy," de Lis' holographic image said later, "but I'm hundred percent sure he's honest."

Mason leaned forward in his desk chair, the floating visage of de Lis bathing the agent's office and 9D in azure ribbons. "I was hoping you'd say this was all a fairy tale, Doctor...."

De Lis wanted to smile, but his mood wasn't in it.

"What can you tell me about Yastanni's Stage Three ideas?" Mason asked.

"They're all adequate for neutrino study, as all have roots in pre-existing research over the years," the doctor explained. "I can't fathom the staggering amounts of cash necessary to construct facilities that remote."

"Hmm, if it's one thing I've learned in this business," Mason said, "it's to never underestimate the Confederation."

De Lis nodded. "I have some contacts in various industries, Agent Mason. Putting out feelers for information on refurbished neutrino laboratories in the last few years may yield more clues."

"What about dual-purpose facilities?"

"I'll get to work on that as well."

"Excellent. Get in touch when you have any scrap of info for us. Mason out."

Λ

"There can be no doubt...North American intelligence agents were responsible."

Shvinskilli watched the flickering image of MOLOTOK over his display, mild amusement crossing his face. "I would expect nothing less from the IIA. Twice now they have defeated our efforts to dissuade them otherwise. Can we be certain you eliminated them at TauTona?"

"It does appear that...we failed, sir," MOLOTOK said, his voice deflated.

"Yes. However, if these agents are one and the same, they seem to possess a single-minded persistence, an arguably admirable trait." Shvinskilli narrowed his eyes, sending a steely, non-verbal message to his own agent. "And what of the *Savak*?" he asked, moving the subject back to the post-op briefing.

Not dissuaded or shaken, MOLOTOK answered without pause, *"Three were reported eliminated by the lieutenant, sir. All other resistance was remanded to the Kermani authority."*

Clapping his hands together, Shvinskilli rose from his seat. "Good. We mustn't upset our new friends. Have you located Doctor Yastanni?"

"No. We are endeavouring to trace the IIA spies, but internal security is surprisingly strong."

"Don't expend too much effort, MOLOTOK," Shvinskilli said. "Our highest priority is counterintelligence. The time is growing near, but your team's success is vital to the project. Your new assignment is waiting aboard K-670. Instructions will be downloaded to your cochlear brane modules in due time."

"Understood."

The suited man reached over and flicked the transmitter off.

Standing in the doorway beyond was Unat'kolarev, the wheels of machination turning in his mind.

"A change in plans?" Shvinskilli asked.

Crossing over to his long-time colleague, Unat'kolarev demurred. "No change is necessary. Yastanni knows nothing, yet his imprisonment is to our advantage, I have realized."

"I don't understand."

"His highest-bidder double game is over, the Americans have seen to that with no effort on our part. The chances our ally General Kermani can surreptitiously exploit our Project Ether technology for himself by his continued 'hosting' of Yastanni are now moot. We, my old friend, still have the best hand to play. And Nouri is about to play his part in it."

Shvinskilli adjusted his necktie. "Of course."

"K-670 is maneuvering per schedule, correct?"

"So I have been informed by Captain Kalinin." He coughed slightly and cleared his throat. "Trusting our operations to the sphere outside of the Ground Forces is the biggest risk we have yet undertaken."

Unat'kolarev circled the desk in the office, reflecting upon the oil portraits hung on the walls of past Tsarist, Soviet and Confederation strongmen, imparting their confidence with cold and steely countenances; one day, soon, he would be among Peter, Joseph and Vladimir.

"This enterprise was not entered into lightly. We are now emboldened, you may recall," Unat'kolarev said, reminding his lieutenant of his earlier, out-of-turn outburst, "to seize this initiative. Our forces have never been so strong, nor bold. We have paid the best contractors for their expertise on Western strategy, tactics and training for our men. Building capital by lending our troops to fight other men's battles will pay off by favors returned. Plus, your handpicked agents will guarantee our rewards are trebled by the risks, don't you believe?" He was not questioning his belief, but expecting his major domo to know that he knew this operation rested on Shvinskilli's shoulders, not his.

"Yes...yes, I do. Your faith in my abilities is most heartening."

Unat'kolarev clapped his subordinate on the shoulder. "Come, then, we have further planning to do for our future success."

Λ

Ochre rays of the dawn sun burst over the backs of Special Agents Major Dima Tereshkov and Captain Eduard Zamatin of the FSB Counterintelligence Subcommittee as they surveyed the exterior of the laboratory complex hidden among the hinterlands of the Zagros Mountains. The final review of the now-barren complex was an afterthought; concern here had been directed elsewhere, with the audacious kidnapping of Nouri Yastanni by, from all accounts, the IIA.

What on first glance was believed to be fortuitous stumbling by the North American intelligence agents into Confederation operations proved to be more than just that after two, and now three, incidents; Major Tereshkov himself calculated it wise to not rule out their opposite numbers' efforts to foil his superiors' operations. They would strike again, that much he knew. What remained a mystery was precisely *how* they anticipated—no, checked—each stage. It would behoove Tereshkov and Zamatin to respect their enemies...and perhaps, listening to the even more mysterious man who was their contact, emulate the North Americans.

A piercing pain in Tereshkov's skull soon subsided into a dull ache. Closing his eyes, the major probed his thoughts, soon penetrating the fog of his mind's memories to extract the details of an implanted set of commands in his brain.

"ZAMYESTITYEL," the major said to his partner. "New orders."

Zamatin stepped over the long shadows across the desert floor, meeting up with his superior officer. "Another yanked chain already?"

Tereshkov merely grunted. "Our work here is complete. Submit the report. We will board the *Lyagooshka* soon afterwards for the Old President."

"Understood."

Cruising over the Caspian Sea some hours later in the Vu-1024 *Lyagooshka*—the Confederation's own jumpjet, known in Western intelligence circles as the "Toad"—the FSB agents prepared and recharged for their next course of action. Per commandments from their superiors, Tereshkov and Zamatin ingested the various nausea and deep-pressure medicaments in their kits, readying their bodies for the rigors yet to come. Their shrouded and ensconced superiors tested them well, pushing the battle-hardened officers into acts any lesser man would balk at. Years in the crucible of foreign wars, of grimy urban climes and shell-shocked rural villages, were the best instructors money couldn't buy.

Dispatched once more to coordinates centered in the western Black Sea, the agents would strike forth on an errand of unknown capacity and destination.

And, customarily, no questions were ever asked, no order ever denied. They inhabited a world where no quarter was given, nor expected. Ruthless, callous and hard-hearted, Tereshkov and Zamatin were the sharpest edges of the FSB's longest knives, a reputation they hoped to extend towards ridding the world of the influence, and provenance, of the North American spies of the IIA.

CHAPTER SIXTEEN

"Solicitor General Sebastian Rauchambau has scheduled a briefing with 9D," Louris announced, standing at the threshold to Mason's office. He eyed each of the four inside. "His personal assistant just webbed me a few minutes ago."

Wheeling around in his desk chair, Mason rose to his feet. "Rauchambau is coming here? Himself? Too big to leave to AD Bourgoin?"

"Wow, when he says it, he does it big," Kindred said out of the side of her mouth to Bell, who smirked.

"That's the privilege of the distinguished Ninth Division, agents. I suggest you clear your appointments for a few hours, starting at," Louris paused, checking his wrist chronometer, "oh nine-twenty."

"How about a heads up?" Feltham asked.

Louris stepped away and started down the corridor, with no hint of victory. "The wrap party for our Project Ether investigation."

Λ

Settling into the folding chairs arranged in a semi-circle inside the conference room of the twentieth floor, Mason, Feltham, Kindred and Bell whispered vociferously, the agents' eyes askance at the incoming DoJ delegation. In the two rows beyond sat analysts Keegan and Moore, along with Diamond and Shaw, all anticipating accolades for their small parts in the investigation.

"...What the hell's wrong with these goddamn bureaucrats?" Kindred said into the 9D huddle. "Do they expect—"

Mason stuck out his right hand, palm down, to calm the young agent. "He's the big boss. And what he says, goes. No question."

"Doesn't mean you have to like it," Feltham reminded her.

"This ain't right. It's way too premature to call this one closed," Bell said.

Striding into the conference room with his personal assistant, Simon Kilbey, the DoJ departmental staff, Company Director Ike Harrelman, Assistant Director Erin Bourgoin and Louris was Solicitor General Sebastian Rauchambau, who took a seat at a maple wood table next to his entourage. Known for his Creole-flavored speech, hometown charm and outside the Beltway mentality, the Solicitor General was distinct in the annals of DoJ bureaucrats; being an appointed Presidential cabinet member, however, he still faced the cold-water sentiment of many lower level operatives, biding their time until the next regime change came down the pike.

"Greetings, everybody," Rauchambau said, placing his interlocked his fingers down on the table. "Congratulations are in order to the Intelligence and Investigation Agency and its Global Intelligence Directorate, specifically Section Manager Grant Louris and his Ninth Division squad. Without their persistence, and the analysis of the caffeine-fueled techs here in the IIA, Doctor Yastanni would still be aiding and abetting our enemies overseas. And that's why I've gathered all you here.

"With the counsel of our United Nations ambassador," he continued, smiling in triumph along with Harrelman and Bourgoin, "and our solicitors in the International Court, we've reached an agreement to take a new case against Yastanni to The Hague."

Mason had to replay Rauchambau's words in his mind. Doing a double-take to Louris, and then staring at the Solicitor General in disbelief, Mason's mouth was agape. Raising his hand, he said, "Excuse me, sir, but under what pretenses have you to try Yastanni again? In our opinion, he's just a cog in our investigation—"

Rauchambau nodded, but interjected, "Ah, Agent Mason, your squad has led an excellent operation, and I commend you on it. Doctor Yastanni's crimes are far-reaching and still pose a grave threat to the security of the Western world. His continued dalliance with neutronic transfer technology confirms our suspicions that, uh, he's up to no good."

"Sir," Mason said curtly, rising to reiterate his position, "Yastanni's crimes are not in doubt by my squad. But the facts are he has moved on to a larger threat than neutronic trafficking. In fact, his arrival here is *with* his consent. He was offered a position with Doctor Richard de Lis." The agent straightened his tie. "Sir."

Harrelman, Bourgoin and Rauchambau exchanged puzzled looks. All three turned towards Louris, whose face was sour.

"Explain, Agent Mason," Harrelman said.

"Gladly, sir. Doctor Yastanni has agreed, in principle, to assist us in tracking the postulated existence of a Confederation experimental research facility rumored to involve the destroyed TauTona lab, that, thankfully, Agent Bell and I survived."

"Go on," Rauchambau said.

"Frankly, sir, your subjection of Yastanni to a trial in The Hague jeopardizes all we've worked on to bring him into our fold."

Giving a great sigh seemingly magnified into a heave by the stonework walls, the Solicitor General stood. "Let's adjourn for a ten-minute break."

Mason swallowed hard and glanced down to his team with raised eyebrows that said, "Here we go."

Rauchambau wiggled his finger towards Mason. "Agent Mason. A moment, please...."

The pair broke away from the chorus of murmurs and walked over to the far wall.

"What the goddamn hell is going on?" Rauchambau spat in a far cry from his personable public image.

"Respectfully, sir, our investigation's just begun. We don't need this BS wrap-up and photo op with balloons and handshakes."

Rauchambau shoved his hands into his trouser pockets, as if restraining himself would save them a very messy cleanup. "And this Administration doesn't need more gallivanting intel officers violating foreign soil in very public fashion. 9D has the dubious distinction of being on the shit list of a dozen hostile nations." In afterthought, he added, "And State. One too many words to Congress from them cuts your funding and your lifeline. I'm under an explicit directive from the President to finish this."

Rauchambau watched Mason chafe under his directive, before continuing, "The Project Ether investigation is complete, Yastanni has been brought to justice. And despite the setback TauTona was, this 'neutrino capture' technique in the report appears to be so volatile, practical employment could be impossible."

"So, just to be clear," Mason said, his contempt manifesting as a twitchy nose, "we're throwing Yastanni—and all he can help us with—to the mercy of the international body politick to give us good marks?"

"In short, yes. He's on his way now."

***

Λ

"Nothing! It was all for *fucking nothing!*"

Mason slammed his hand down, causing a stack of holobooks and various trinkets on his desk to jump. Composing himself a few seconds later, he cleared his throat and smoothed his shirt, then straightened his back.

Startled by her boss' rare outburst, Feltham inhaled deeply to calm her nerves. Looking to her fellow agents, she asked, "Options. What do we do?"

"I suggest we revel in our success," Bell said, sounding like an earnest greenhorn fresh from the Company Academy. "Broadcast it wide over the web networks. Show the Confederation our hand."

"Or make them think we have," Kindred said.

Bell nodded.

"It would definitely signal our belief that Yastanni's the one and only culprit," Feltham said. "Especially if we emphasize his laboratory. But that still leaves us with the ALEXEI issue...."

Mulling over his team's options, Mason was quiet, staring into the distance of the Washington vista beyond. An unseasonably warm autumn afternoon reflected back at him. Crossing his arms, he stepped to the window sill.

"Stone man?" Kindred uttered, trying to catch a glimpse of him.

"ALEXEI was a mistake." Mason swiveled around, his voice flat, as if practicing, or, better yet, reciting a script. His eyes peered at every agent's puzzled visage. "But it resulted in the discovery of a long-lost, damaging, secret."

Kindred nodded. "Kweiksman...yeah, we know. What's the damaging part?"

"That's for us to know," he paused, a tiny curl growing on his lips and a gleam in his blue eyes, "and the Confederation to find out."

Mason, with sudden animation that again surprised his team, headed for the corridor, leaving the trio in a confused fog. Bewildered, but curious, they followed him down the hallway, eager to see where the agent's legendary leaps of logic led.

They turned the corner to the conference room in time to hear Mason ask Rauchambau for a chance to address the webmedia.

"That was a remarkably short turnaround time, Agent," Rauchambau said. "I figured another arm twisting was in order."

"I'm full of ideas, sir."

Rauchambau was slow to answer, instead probing the agent's countenance. The Solicitor General knew Mason had a trick up his sleeve, but couldn't discern the particular one he had in mind. "Give me five minutes."

Feltham put her hand on Mason's arm, getting his attention. "Boss...?"

"It's time to swat the ball back into the Confederation's court," he answered, facing her. "In public. Their turn to deny Yastanni, or deny Kweiksman. They can't have both."

"Denying Yastanni would mean we'd no reason to investigate his lab," Feltham said, thinking aloud. "But denying Kweiksman's stolen research as the basis for Yastanni's experiments would mean the doctor couldn't have been doing what he *has* been doing."

"Or why Yastanni's laboratory setup was suspiciously similar to Kweiksman's leaked Yucca Mountain data," Mason explained. Glancing back to Rauchambau and his upper Company management entourage, he said to his team, "And I'm about ready to ask the Premier and the Confederation itself that very question."

CHAPTER SEVENTEEN

Threshing the four-kilometer deep ocean, the dark vessel proceeded quiescently, in near completion of its polar loop. Having slithered for two months between continental shelves and braved the vast trenches of the Drake Passage and the roaring easterlies of the Antarctic Circumpolar Current, it plowed forward now in open waters, treading closer to the seafloor than any vessel before it, risking collision upon the earthen barite towers that vented their scalding black smoke. A silver cylinder—held vertically by buoyant stabilizers—ascended from within one of the hull's twenty dorsal tubes and gently floated up into the dark currents, away from the watchful eyes above....

Situated within the nerve center of this massive vessel, a holographic mural schematic of the rising SLBM—submarine-launched ballistic missile—showed a blue cylindrical icon hovering over a green line denoting the submarine's past course.

"You came up to watch, I take it," Second Captain Yuri Anikiyev, first officer of K-670, RFS *Boris Yeltsin*, said to the two new guests, sporting a proud smile. He sat in the skipper's command seat, surrounded by a half-dozen of the boat's senior crewmen. "I don't blame you...it's an awe-inspiring sight, this deep."

Tereshkov laid a hand on a nearby railing, steadying himself from the after effects of a long flight and subsequent descent. Adjusting to the array of consoles, interfaces and dim overhead illumination that created a dull sheen on every surrounding hard surface was a chore. "Indeed. It strikes at the soul for a centered calm. After all, is that not why we are here?"

Anikiyev bobbed his head in agreement. Next to him, an

holographic display glistened in the low light of the bridge, his fingers tapping one button sequence after another.

"*Istrebitel* ten ascending at twelve knots, Captain," missile technician Warrant Officer Rodionev reported, toggling his hard interface. "All seems nominal."

"Good," Anikiyev said. "Readings from enemy sonic devices?"

A towheaded youth checked a scanner display at his post. "Stealth sonar reflection frequencies operative at ninety-four percent, Captain."

To foreign surveillance nations, in particular, the USNA, the sonar signature K-670 gave off resembled a pod of whales, albeit with triple metal hulls, a measure of loss unforgivable in times of declared war; but for this operation, invisibility was not paramount, just deflecting obvious detection.

Anikiyev sighed. "Not great, acceptable, though. I will have Ammosov look over the system when we reach Novolazarevskaya." He faced his guests again. "I have been commanded to turn over control of the *Istrebitel*s to you, Major, upon reaching the Prime Meridian. You may…sit in the big chair when we arrive."

Tereshkov read the XO's mannerisms, noting Anikiyev was quite uncomfortable with the two secret services agents, but like any good submariner, followed orders to the letter. "Thank you. Until then, I would be most honored as your guest at dinner."

"Of course."

Some hours later, Anikiyev, his commanding officer, First Captain Vitaly Kalinin, Tereshkov and Zamatin sat at the small table in the officer's mess hall, dining on Caspian caviar, foie gras, Kobe steaks and California wine, all from Kalinin's personal stash. Having undone the silver buttons on the military jackets the four wore from their respective services, the officers sat back, relaxing to the throbbing drone of the boat's engines.

"…If you are to spend time in our companies, it is good that you become one of us, Major, Captain," Kalinin said, polishing off a bite of steak from his fork. Gulping it down with a swig of wine, he gestured, saying, "Our benefactors wish us all to know each other once the fruits of our labor have fallen off the trees and bonked us on the head!"

The four men laughed heartily, after working through three bottles of wine to dull the boredom of the last few hours.

"Than my colleagues, you will have the pick of the seas to sail, women to romance, and liquor to drink," Tereshkov toasted, holding his glass up.

Imbibing more wine, the four loosened tongues and blood

vessels, their flushed cheeks now rivaling their rosy Russian countenances.

"Tell me, Captain," Anikiyev said to Zamatin, "do children these days still play with toys, or have you gone straight to the services out of the womb?" An obvious jab at Zamatin's youthful, round features.

Zamatin feigned a smile. "Some of us have to do the dirty work, while others dine well on the backs of the workers."

Waving his hands, Kalinin moderated the rising tensions. "We are all comrades, serving a higher purpose...now, let us go forward as colleagues. Major," he said, "all goes well back home, yes?"

"Snow still falls, vodka still flows," he answered. Lowering his voice now, he asked, "And our cargo. Will it perform?"

Kalinin exchanged a concerned glance with Anikiyev, then cracked a wide grin, dispelling his faux seriousness. "We will get your cargo on its way." He yawned, allowing his eyes to glaze over.

Anikiyev threw down his cloth napkin and belched. "Why all this 'sightseeing' for two months on end? Wouldn't it have been worth our time to mix it up with the Americans? Have some fun! Seeding the ocean without a minute's glimpse of the horizon...for what?"

Tereshkov ran his hands through his blond buzzcut, all the more to keep from showing this boar a really fun time in the CMO's sickbay. "There is a fundamental weakness in their constellation, friend, which we exploit—with your seeding—from the Southern Ocean. Regional hubs coordinate traffic between hundreds of nanosatellites. Destroy the hubs, shutdown the constellation. Simple."

"And as usual, when the secret services require real work, it must be done by the navy," Anikiyev added, provocatively. "Send in the boats, yes, Captain?!"

Tereshkov made sure to smirk, getting his message across to the dullard. "Just get your boat in the right place...we'll do the rest."

A sharp whistle sounded over the mess hall speakers. Kalinin set his glass down and stumbled over to a desk; steadying himself, he reached over and toggled a switch.

"Yes?" the captain managed, trying not to sound too tipsy.

"First Captain Kalinin, we are approaching east zero degrees, sir," Third Captain Igor Yulachenko, the Second Officer, said over the intercom.

"We will be up shortly. Kalinin out." Toggling the switch off, he composed himself. "Major, Captain...."

Λ

"Captain on the bridge!" Yulachenko announced, rising to his feet from the skipper's chair.

Kalinin, Anikiyev, Tereshkov and Zamatin clambered up the grated steps to the left of the bridge. At attention, the crew were relieved with a half-hearted wave of Kalinin's hand, his heavy legs walking him to his command post.

"Major Tereshkov...the seat is yours," Kalinin said, gesturing.

Tereshkov gave Kalinin a nod. Walking past the assembled crewmen, the officer sat down on the warm leather upholstry. "Crewman, access display."

"Aye, sir," Rodionev said, punching a button on his console.

Ahead of Tereshkov, the mural holograph floated in mid-air, a soft blue glistening on its periphery. With the Earth seen from below, centering on Antarctica, ten green dots ringed the continent; zero degrees north sat K-670, denoted by a yellow icon, straddling the Prime Meridian.

Tereshkov lifted his arm, sliding out a data cylinder he had secreted away, then plugged it into a slot on the adjacent hard interface. "Communications," Tereshkov said into the intercom, "signal Sevastopol. Relay this message: All candles are in the cake. Blow out."

"Aye, sir."

The holograph went to a split-screen, displaying the Arctic Circle, where another ten green dots ringed it, mirroring the planted *Istrebitel*s.

"Receiving message from Sevastopol, Major," the radioman said over the speakers. "We have commit."

Tereshkov toggled the intercom. "Understood."

Ten simultaneous text boxes popped up on the Artic split-screen, displaying coordinates and launch velocities. Red dashes traced the migrating dots from their moorings, gradually expanding outwards.

Tereshkov glanced over to Kalinin with confidence in his eyes. "Let the fun begin."

Λ

A kaleidoscopic aurora borealis draped over the snowcapped roof of the globe, a velvety curtain of emerald, sapphire and copper. Peeking through this spectral night sky were ten orange cinders rocketing upwards, penetrating the noctilucent clouds bathed by aurora light.

Departing multiple thousands of kilometers per hour, the ten cinders pierced the upper atmosphere, clearing all lower and medium orbiting satellites, bypassing the rabble and decaying debris, towards the circling devices so far removed from the surface that none shone at night, even when struck by direct sunlight.

Widening their swath to cover the entire northern hemisphere, the ten interlopers ascended, but gradually working southward to a belt of satellites no ordinary eyes were meant to see, nor foreign powers meant to visit: the Global Security Network.

Mounted on the approaching rockets, small conical warheads that robotically separated at the prerequisite altitude of forty thousand kilometers blasted towards the premier eyes and ears of the USNA. Shadowed behind the Earth's terminator, one of several warheads drew the combined attentions of several satellite hubs larger than terrestrial lorries, which slew active sensors at the barreling interloper, immediately scanning the warheads for armament, manufacturer, launch coordinates and national origin. Single-use projectiles half the mass of a hub satellite cascaded towards each approaching warhead, but all coming to naught—

As a silent explosion spread streamers of brilliant phosphorescent material outward, overtaking each hub in a shell that expanded for kilometers. Each streamer in turn burned brighter than the sun for seconds, overloading all the unshielded satellites with billions of lumens, effectively blinding the constellation from the second act to follow and the real show.

Λ

Moments earlier, Tereshkov watched the false *Istrebitels'* icons glide farther into space, counting down the seconds on the holograph's mission chronometer, until whirring to Rodionev on his right. "Missile control, launch!"

"Launch, aye, sir!"

Rodionev punched a button, and beside him, his fellow missile technician punched on his interface for launch.

Thousands of kilometers distant, under the cold depths of the Southern Ocean, ten equidistant *Istrebitels* burst forth, the first rocket stages streaking across the bright summer night sky. Matching the first launches from the north pole, the true *Istrebitels* ascended past orbital altitudes, striking out for the sensor-disabled Global Security Network's regional hubs. Second stage rockets boosted the *Istrebitel* warheads upwards, where they rounded the great belt of nanosatellites and drove straight for the helpless hubs, blinded and unable to defend against this second sortie no nation on Earth dared dream possible.

Second by second, Tereshkov and Zamatin followed the enveloping umbrella they unleashed, both transfixed by the most audacious and bold masterstroke ever undertaken against the Western powers.

Connecting with such force as to punch the hubs out of orbit, the warheads plowed through the Global Security Network's weakness, shattering the devices into hundreds, littering the upper exosphere with glowing embers that were snuffed cold in microseconds. Now, the thousand-fold constellation of nanosatellites circled the globe alone, with no anchor to join them nor brains to transmit the final fleeting moments of the constellation's existence.

Λ

"Target eliminated, sir," Rodionev confirmed, reading the telemetry beamed back upon impact.

"Excellent!" Kalinin clapped Zamatin's shoulder, then Tereshkov's. "This...this is a great day."

With a racing heart, Tereshkov committed to memory this feeling, this victory, that he, the lowly factory worker's son, had executed in the name of Russia. In the name of the True Peoples....

CHAPTER EIGHTEEN

"...And it is through our diligent investigation that we surmise Doctor Nouri Yastanni knowingly and without hesitation trafficked in covert USNA research, exploiting hazardous work done nearly a half century ago, and sold those secrets to the Confederation, basing his subsequent research and experimentation on this very same covert work."

Mason stood at the lectern in the public relations conference room, feeling the gaze of dozens of assembled reporters, their webeyes boring holes through him; his hastily arranged press conference carried live across the globe, billions watched in realtime as the agent damned the torpedoes, calling the Confederation's bluff before them all.

"We allege the Russian government," he continued, "under the guise of the Confederation of Independent States, financed experimentation on stolen national priority research. Therefore, we have no recourse but to ask the Russian government, 'Why?' And further, why a disgraced Iranian physicist should be performing risky experiments based on USNA research in the middle of the Iranian desert, and then, with our government authorized to detain him for questioning granted under our UN mandate, Russian forces attacked the laboratory complex? Again, I ask 'Why?'"

A chorus of murmurs grew in the media gallery, followed by sharp queries thrown at Mason, forcing him to cup his ears just to discern the nearest reporters.

Pointing to a older woman, he asked, "I'm sorry...could you repeat that?"

"Is Doctor Yastanni the same Yastanni you yourself arrested eighteen months ago, Mr Mason?" she asked, her webeye keenly recording

Mason's every word, facial tic and gesture, even down to the open capillaries in his flushed cheeks.

"Yes."

"Then why have you decided to charge him again?" she responded, drowning out her fellow media members, then shot out a shrill, "Surely you can't expect the International Tribunal to even want to try him again!"

"Our evidence is concrete," Mason said, somewhat exasperated already. "The choice rests with the Premier to answer our questions when we attend Yastanni's day in court."

"And why should the Confederation believe our government's contention that this scientist is performing these..." another reporter said, pausing, "illegal experiments?"

"Because I know the Russian scientist who helped him," a voice very familiar to Mason said, preceding the man entering the conference room.

The agent craned his neck, almost disbelieving the sight of Richard de Lis mere centimeters behind him, joining Mason at his side. More fevered murmurs erupted from the gallery, sending several questions the doctor's way.

"I can also vouch for Yastanni's experiments, as I saw them myself," de Lis said, elaborating. "And have studied under the researchers who originated the government's projects."

"Who are you?" a third reporter shouted, rising to his feet. "How do you know about Yastanni?"

"Doctor Richard de Lis, adjunct to the Department of Energy. I have a vested interest in seeing this research brought to an end."

The reporters jostled to get within prime earshot of the doctor. "Why?" many asked together.

"Because...war as it is now will be akin to a child in a sandbox with the weapon the Confederation is building."

Λ

Calling for a brief pause, Mason, de Lis, Rauchambau, Louris, Harrelman and Bourgoin huddled far from the agitated media gallery, making the reporters stew over the seriousness of Mason and de Lis' assertions, all six privately mulling what the Confederation's response would be, and in what forum.

"Nice entrance. You never fail to save my ass," Mason quipped to de Lis. "I wasn't sure they were listening to me."

De Lis smiled sheepishly. "You just need the voice of authority more often."

"Than I'm glad you played hooky to jet down here so fast."

"Hooky—!" de Lis said, with feigned indignance.

Rauchambau clapped de Lis' shoulder, then shook his hand. "Good to see you again. What news do you have?"

Surprise flashed over Mason's face; had the two planned this little reunion?

"Well, sir," de Lis said, "after my last web with Agent Mason about dual-use laboratories, the best I can offer from my sources are the ANTARES Mediterranean Array and Antarctica."

"Yastanni's thoughts exactly," Mason said, turning to Rauchambau. "Seems he decided to play ball like I'd hoped. I agreed to a very public trial, sir, but it's risky. I hope you're in it for the long haul like...."

The six were diverted by a brief brownout of the conference room's lighting. Off in the gallery, several webeyes died, severing web connections with their media parents, rousing muttering and awkward stares at not only the equipment, but the supposedly sophisticated—and brand new, to boot—energy logistics system in the Glass Castle.

"Odd," Harrelman said. "Power's independent of ground-based blackouts with the orbital microwave generators."

De Lis looked out over the puzzled media. "Must be a solar disturbance."

"Crackers slice into the web?" Louris wondered aloud.

Mason toggled his voxlink, but the tiny device failed to respond. "Offline...." Furrowing his brow, he leapt from the front of the room to the lower gallery. "Who's got power? Anybody having trouble with communications?"

"Communications?! I got shit all nothing!" a wag shot back.

Another reporter double-checked his computer equipment. "Same here...you got dampers gone haywire?"

Mason pursed his lips. Motioning to Louris, the agent ran out into the corridor. The pair flew down the hall, skipping the lift and making for the internal stairwell shaft.

"What're you thinking?" Louris asked. His shoes clacked against the steel steps, echoing throughout the wide chamber.

Mason stormed out of view past the next lower level. "That we just got our answer, Chief. Time to reopen our investigation, wouldn't you say?"

A moment later, the two agents had gathered Feltham, Kindred, Bell and de Lis into Louris' office, each member of 9D promptly booting up holobooks on quantum battery powerpacks, attempting to slice into the civilian Weblinked Satellite Grid—despite its currently spotty performance with the media—to help ascertain why even simple communications through government-issue voxlinks would fail in a fail-safe system.

"Lidar uplink is having some trouble, Stone man," Kindred said, scratching her head. Her holobook displayed a flashing blue cone reaching towards the Grid icons, but stalling out before contact. "Nothing's making any sense."

Mason looked over her shoulder. "It's like the satellites have been nudged slightly out of sync...how the hell's that possible?"

"Transponders are still functioning," Louris said, pointing at a text box floating above the image. "Get a fix on its position, then try the GSN."

Bell tapped a series of commands on his holobook, then read the returning data from the Grid. "They're off kilter by a few tenths of a degree relative to where scheduled. Gyroscopes should have stabilized any atmospheric drag, though."

"Not receiving transponder signal from the GSN," Kindred responded, furrowing her brow. She ran her index finger over the holograph, directing the search to other satellites in the military-administrative constellation. "No signal at all."

"The possibility remains, however unlikely," de Lis said after a moment of mental calculation, "that something, or someone, has intentionally pushed, or—perish the thought—destroyed crucial hubs. A ripple effect, say a debris field, could knock the Grid out of commission, too."

"An act of war," Feltham said. "No nation's ever been so bold in peacetime."

Mason arched a suspicious eyebrow. "Who says we're at peace? Doctor, we could use your expertise in the halls of government on this one."

"Hold on," Louris said, walking out from his desk and over to Mason. "What are you doing?"

"How many 'incidents' before we take decisive action, Chief?" Mason threw up his hands. "Yastanni's been lost to open scrutiny by international tribunal. TauTona's been blown to Hell, literally. I've put myself on the line by publicly calling out the Premier. Now our best weapon against the Confederation has gone 'mysteriously' belly up. Our Project Ether investigation is nothing without it. If we're subject to bloody blitz attacks comparable to TauTona or Chagang-Do, and now the GSN, what next?"

"This isn't our mandate, Agent. DIA'll have agents crawling all over—"

"Rauchambau can get the NSC to hand us over investigative powers," he countered.

Louris shook his head, worn down by Mason's persistance. Acquiescing, he put his hands to his hips. "Okay...who's got STRATCOM's address? Cause it looks like we'll have to do this the old fashioned way."

"I have your man," de Lis announced. "An old acquaintance."

Λ

"STRATCOM? Wrong boys, Doctor," Army Lieutenant Colonel Benjamin Dark Horse said, standing at the threshold of his Pentagon office, distraction in his eyes. Wearing a black t-shirt and trouser fatigues, his salt-and-pepper buzzcut was decidedly biased to the salty side after thirty years in Army Intelligence and covert ops. Behind him, a holograph alternated between periodic static and an Armed Forces communications webchannel, attempting to reach every extended arm. "You're going to need the 460th Space Wing out of Buckley Air Force Base."

Taken aback, de Lis absentmindedly touched his forehead.

"STRATCOM just disseminates the data to the rest of the government, a glorified press corp. With this emergency," he added, an ear to his holograph, "the Mission Control Station is your best bet to figure out just what the hell's the sitrep."

Mason peered inside. "What level we at now?"

"DEFCON 3," the lieutenant colonel answered. "Last news I received was the Secretary had been briefed by General Khalfallah of the Army Space Command on the losses. Oh, please come in. I'm afraid I can't offer much right now...interoffice services have been halted. Trying to spread the word has practically forced us to revert to using pencils and any scrap paper at hand."

Mason nodded. "Not exactly a ringing endorsement for technology."

The visitors walked inside and drank in the colonel's decorated chamber, filled with citations, hanging portraits of past military commanders and his framed commision. An oak desk neatly tucked into a corner rounded out the room.

"Fortunately," Dark Horse added, "Pentagon power is independent of the outside. We just can't talk between levels with voxlinks." The holograph near the desk blasted out a burst of static. "Or keep a webchannel clear."

"The rest of the world's in the same predicament, we believe," Louris said, clasping his hands behind his back. "Funny how a constellation forty thousand klicks up can be knocked out without a trace."

Dark Horse swiveled sharply towards Louris, slightly irritable. "There's always a trace. It takes time to find it, though."

"We need to figure out if the 460th has any clue what mechanism is behind this, Colonel," Mason insisted. "An investigation into suspected Confederation espionage is at a critical stage."

Dark Horse harrumphed. "Join the club. A good friend of mine, a commander in Naval Intelligence, pinged a strange anomaly off the Indian Ocean about six weeks ago."

"What does the DoE liasion have to contribute to that investigation?" Bell asked.

"Plenty of friends involved in whacked-out experiments, Agent," Dark Horse said. He elbowed de Lis. "Including this guy. Normally, the service would just toss out the same old suspects, but I have the ears of a handful of men and women who know just enough to make the unbelievable sound plausible."

"And do you have a suspect?" Feltham asked.

"Something big, something deep, and something methodical. Didn't appear to be in a hurry, according to sensor equipment."

Mason rubbed his jaw. "A sub?"

"Not a boat this guy's ever seen, or found out about," Dark Horse said. "And definitely not ours. Couldn't get a bead on any of the typical Confederation codes or frequencies. A lot of subatomic particle interference, not out of the ordinary, but odd enough to take note of."

"Shakedown cruise?" Louris offered.

"Your guess is as good as mine. Now, back to your problem. What can *you* contribute to the 460th, to make a twist on your question," Dark Horse said to Bell.

"A little know-how," Mason said, "and possibly a motive."

"Motive?"

Mason drew nearer to the colonel. "For the willful destruction of the Global Security Network."

Λ

"Getting to Colorado won't be easy under duress," Dark Horse warned, donning his jacket and slapping his black beret on. Walking briskly, he led the group and an Army MP escort from his office to the Pentagon's subway system tunnel, three levels down. "They won't be in the mood to lead a tour, especially for civilian intelligence officials."

"This is business, Colonel," Mason said, pausing ahead of a checkpoint. "I'm expecting—asking—for your assistance."

"All right. I do have some sway with the 460th," he said, finessing his charcoal mustache. "We sign off on some of their bills out there."

"Well, that'll at least get us through the accounting department's door," Kindred quipped.

After full body scans for the six at the checkpoint, Dark Horse signed off on the short trek to Langley aboard the secured subway, away from public view and any questions the lingering media, who had massed in the Pentagon's press room after the GSN rumors came out, could have summoned for the group.

Less than an hour later aboard the Air Force-grade jumpjet *Blue Belle*, 9D, de Lis and Dark Horse had bolted out of Virginia in a fleajump several thousand kilometers high that lasted for a hundred minutes, allowing the Earth to rotate underneath them, then descended just east of a snowcapped Denver landscape.

Skipping past the peaks of the Rockies, a wide, rural expanse populated by blocks of residences and straight suburban roads stretched ahead of them, punctuated by several concave hangar bays sprinkled over a dozen acres. Glinting in the blazing late afternoon sun were eight geodesic domes—radomes, radar antennae capped by weather-resistant shielding—bloated golfball minarets that added unique character to this otherwise sleepy pocket of the west.

They swung south, curving back northeast to approach a three-and-a-half-kilometer-long landing strip belonging to Buckley AFB. Bypassing squads of grounds crew securing transient aircraft for the night, the jumpjet paused and deployed its vertical engine pods, setting thirty meters straight down adjacent to Hangar Four.

The group departed with efficient haste—owing to their lack of carry-on briefcases and equipment—flinging off their restraints and scurrying down the hatch. Touching down on black ice, the group noticed the weather was a far cry from balmy DC, doubly so since the only extra layers they had were grey Air Force flight jackets, which, to no one's surprise, Dark Horse shunned.

Greeting them was a single female airman in a parka, who ushered the visitors into the hangar office at the westside of the tarmac. She slammed and locked the steel door behind them, sealing them inside a garage.

"Welcome to Buckley, Colonel," she said, extending her hand. "I'm Airman Stansfield, pleased to make your acquaintance."

"Colonel Dark Horse." Gesturing to each in succession, he said, "Doctor de Lis, Agents Louris, Mason, Kindred, Bell and Feltham."

Stansfield doffed her parka and took the visitors inside to the heated offices. "Today's been rather exciting, sir," she said, looking over her shoulder. "Get ready for some activity."

"That's what we thrive on, Airman," Mason said, checking out the numerous closed door offices. Evidently, everyone was elsewhere, doubtless working on an investigation themselves.

Meters ahead, the cacaphony of utensils, dishes and scooting seats on tile floor sounded throughout the hallway, reminding Feltham and Bell that it'd been hours since breakfast.

"Ohhh," Bell cooed. "Bacon."

De Lis waved them onward from behind. "C'mon, you're holding up the rear."

Coming up on a stairwell, Stansfield stepped down the flight and brought them to a long, three-meter wide steel corridor, the walls caged in copper mesh, creating an EM-deflecting Faraday cage; broken light from the overhead illumination cast amorphous shadows on the floor.

"This underground corridor was constructed nearly a century ago," she explained, stopping at a reinforced door at the head of the corridor. "After the Global Depression worried the government that our space 'assets' were in danger of falling into the wrong hands, a dedicated, sealable command center for geosynchronous satellites was constructed."

Mason locked eyes with Stansfield. "The wrong hands may have found a way round that."

Stansfield raised an eyebrow. "Are you the ones to find 'em?"

"God I hope so."

CHAPTER NINETEEN

Vast expanses of stars drifted across a black velvet sky, their distant beacons guiding the meter-long craft up into the cold clutches of space. Scouring the ancient fields of man-made, sparkling detritus, tumbling end over end, the craft rocketed above and beyond, hardened ablative shielding deflecting the thirty-thousand kilometer per hour micro-bullets.

Deep within the craft's hull, silkworm-grown neural synaptics contained inside a centimeter-diameter sphere analyzed hundreds of petabytes of raw data each microsecond, plotting the stars against a comprehensive photographic database and every wandering object to a pre-planned rendezvous. Sifting through the evolving data sets, the craft honed in on a particular target, only to find...sheer darkness.

Λ

"Absolutely nothing, sir. It appears the hubs have been blown straight out of their orbits."

Colonel Maja Ainsworth stepped over to the Army specialist observer, who stood on a clear segment of flooring, below which glowed a grid of mini pyramids, enveloping his body within a holograph of black space. Stars winked over the curves of his figure, illuminating him in ochre, gold and blue.

"Nothing? Did you compensate for atmospheric turbulence?" she asked, putting her hands to her hips. Flanking him, the colonel's tan uniform had taken on a blue hue.

"Yes, sir. Hawks're reporting negative. Spectrographic data on orbital debris match positive for the hubs."

"Damn." *Screwed again and not even an invitational E-warfare kiss by these guys.* Modus operandi by most lowlife slicer scum who took potshots at the military was crude virtual vandalism or the ever-popular denial of service to the hubs for kicks. These people had another agenda this time and playing with qubits was the least of their weapons.

Furrowing her brow, Ainsworth walked a semicircle round the bunker-like chamber, crossing back to the visitors who witnessed the inner workings of this deceptively calm sanctum. A handful of other specialists were immersed in holographs as well, monitoring the cadre of Army XX-99 Space Hawk drones circling the planet.

"Space Hawks haven't failed a targeted survey yet, sir," Dark Horse noted, to Ainsworth's growing, but gnawing, concern.

The 460th's commander gave him a wary nod. "That's what I'm afraid of. Ben," she said, lowering her voice, "what the hell's going on? I've prepped for this scenario hundreds of times, and yet wargames don't ever answer the question of why."

"And that's the worst part," Mason said, just out of view by the colonel. He sidled over to the pair. "The Confederation's playing for keeps this time. I guess the real question should be, was this the objective, or is it just the first volley, maybe a sucker punch to our eyes and ears?"

"DIA intel still hasn't uncovered evidence for Confederation mobilization anywhere out of the ordinary," she said. "Even with the GSN hubs out of commission, our forces could still launch a coordinated counterattack if necessary."

Dark Horse growled a deep sigh. "Seemingly foolish of them."

"Unless that's what they want us to believe," de Lis chimed in, joining the conversation. "I vote for a distraction ploy."

Mason watched the holographs around them, catching tiny specks of floating debris over the faces of the specialists, all that was likely remaining of the destroyed hubs. "That's an expensive distraction, Doctor."

"Regardless, gentlemen, we have a remaining mission," Ainsworth said, ending speculation for the time being. "Our next task is track where these suspected ballistic missiles originated, and their make."

"And how is that done?" Mason asked.

Ainsworth walked them to a station, activating a holographic display which blossomed at eye level. Another specialist manned it, manipulating the branching menu with his index finger.

"Specialist Gelder here is tapping into an auxiliary line to the nanosatellites that are the backbone of the GSN," she explained. "While not a perfect solution, since they don't have buffers for memory storage, the nanosatellites should give us enough data for the last milliseconds to whittle it down to several candidates."

Gelder's fingers glided over the holograph, accessing the down-links of the nanosatellites. A watermelon-size blue globe floated before him, girdled on the equator by a vaporous belt of particles, each a representative of the GSN. With swift violence, ten spherical explosions tore through the belt, leaving gaping holes that slowly rotated around the globe.

"Pause," the specialist commanded, freezing the destruction. Placing his pinched thumb and index finger at a point of impact, he separated the fingers, magnifying a small window.

The magnified explosion displayed hundreds of particulates blasting out of the hub satellite. Run in slow motion, the hub disintegrated under the brunt of a kinetic ballistic missile until the image stalled upon reaching its memory limit.

"There!" Ainsworth said, tapping the kill weapon's image. "Simulate reverse trajectory."

A green line swooped backwards towards the globe, swinging south in a wide parabola. The two colonels, Mason and de Lis stood in rapt attention; each second brought the weapon closer to the surface, the quantum computer calculating the probable launch vector. Five seconds of anxiety culminated in the ten green parabolas converging in a ring around the Southern Ocean, all individual plots on the outskirts of the seventh continent, Antarctica.

"Son of a bitch," grumbled Dark Horse. His eyes narrowing, the colonel shook his head, a red dot just south of the Indian Ocean receiving all his attention.

"I think your friend's mystery is a lot less mysterious," Mason said, his gaze locked on the ten red blips.

"The question still stands," Ainsworth said. "Who launched these? What platform?"

Mason stepped away, looking back to his 9D team. Sifting his hair in his hands, he scrolled through a mental checklist. What had Yastanni said during the interrogation? The poles...the South Pole? And de Lis' dual-use laboratories....

"No sub our Navy operates," Dark Horse noted. "He didn't have any clue what flag it flew under. Confederation didn't—"

"Doctor," Mason blurted out, swiveling to de Lis, "what about your research on the Antarctica dual-purpose facilities. How many and what kind are there?"

"Numerous, in fact." De Lis crossed over to a nearby terminal.

"May I?" he asked Ainsworth.

The colonel gave an obliging nod, going so far as to key in her security clearance. De Lis produced a data cylinder and placed it into the terminal's hardware panel, a square alcove on the wall.

Forming like fog in mid-air, a cartograph coalesced at eye level, showing the southern hemisphere from orbit. Manipulating the holograph with his fingers, de Lis swung the hemisphere towards the group, centering Antarctica. Multitudes of text boxes blinked into view, denoting several islands and geographic features hosting international research stations, most dating back two centuries. Dozens were clustered along the Antarctic Peninsula, a comma-shaped archipelago of mountains and glaciers that reached towards South America from the western edge of the continent. Deeper into the interior, situated amongst the domes that are the continent's highest points, were another smattering of stations, all spokes on a wheel centering on Amundson-Scott Station, or simply the Pole; a long-term North American scientific outpost that stood sentinel on Antarctica, it was the focus—or target, some military experts would say—of the prime Confederation outpost, Vostok Station, 1,800 kilometers east, which lay over the largest submerged Antarctic lake of the same name.

"All contact, officially, between our stations and Confederation stations ceased decades ago," de Lis explained. Magnifying Vostok Station, a spider-like structure resting over the ice sheet, the doctor's index finger tapped the buried lake. "No one in the Antarctic science programs nor the civilian or military administrations knows exactly what the Russians have been up to all these years."

Ainsworth shook her head. "Literally anyone, anything, could be down there. On any given day, our birds would be swooping overhead once a launch had taken place. But now...."

"Chances are, we would be in the dark regardless," Dark Horse said. "Your birds can only detect what we program them to. If the Confederation's utilizing new hardware, novel systems we haven't even fathomed yet, the best we could do was figure out what the hell's going down way after the fact."

Mason's chin got the brunt of nervous fingers; de Lis might be right about a distraction ploy, but his investigator's sixth sense made him pause and take stock of another side. Shooting down the Global Security Network in itself was outrageous, certainly above and beyond any unilateral act his nation had ever committed against the Confederation. But, what if they were hiding something bigger than a dual-purpose facility? Blinding North America from an act, perhaps, not just a laboratory. Could it be that TauTona was the beginning? Obliterating evidence on that scale seemed beyond belief, but not for these people, Mason knew. Again, to the agent, it appeared two hands were at play, but in what capacity continued to elude, if not frustrate him. If one scientist in cahoots with the Confederation, even by singular association with another scientist, could shed light on what 9D could expect with this dark energy experimentation and its practical application, then they had to run with it.

"I think Yastanni's still the ticket," Mason said. "Even though he professes to know nothing past his involvement with Stage One, any applications of Project Ether would be worth noting. Doctor, would you mind following up on this?"

"Certainly...he trusts me as a colleague, and I have no misgivings with assisting in his defense, if it gives us a better chance to shut this 'project' down for good."

"Do it."

"De Lis and I'll catch the next flight to The Hague," Louris said, tapping himself for the assignment. He looked to Mason as he and de Lis headed for the corridor. "Get 9D on the trail of that anomaly Dark Horse talked about. If it has any connection to these launches, you know where to go."

"Already on it."

Λ

"Here, here, and here." Dark Horse's index finger circled a trio of blips on a cartograph of the Indian Ocean, south of the 90th parallel. "A thousand klicks off the Shackleton Ice Shelf, near Mirnyy Observatory." The colonel crossed his arms over his chest. "Three pings, three consecutive days. After that, silence."

Gelder synchronized Dark Horse's three blips and their dates with the simulated launch trajectories, overlaying both onto the plot of ocean. A roughly five-square kilometer diameter of uncertainty lay near the anomalous blips, well within error. Gelder connected the ten simulated launch plots, forming a fuzzy circular zone around the continent, creating a suspected course for an unknown, unmarked craft to follow. Much was left to speculate, but the picture was becoming clearer: something, somewhere, had deliberately and covertly carried out this attack, and knew full well how to evade the USNA enough to accomplish it.

Which led Mason to ponder perhaps the next most difficult question: How do they find it, and stop further attacks?

"Offshore launch sites bodes well for a submarine origin," Ainsworth supposed, noting the cartograph's plethora of data points.

"Prior to destruction, no abnormal or anomalous materials were detected."

"Mm-hmm," Mason intoned. "So, odds for or against ten synchronized submarines doing this, or a timed launch with these suspected SLBMs lying in wait in the ocean?"

Ainsworth tsked, "Both seem equally absurd. Had to happen in some way or shape."

"Bottom dollar the Navy is sweeping south at this moment, regardless," Feltham said. "I suggest we hitch along."

Mason inhaled deeply. "Agreed...but I think our investigation might be better served if we split again. Care to flip for shipboard duty or freeze-dried wasteland?"

Bell searched inside his jacket pockets, producing a coin between his fingers. Handing it to Mason, he replied, "I'll take that bet. Heads for Antarctica."

Mason flipped the coin in the air and slapped it on his outstretched forearm. Lifting his palm, he revealed the coin's reverse, or tail, side to the agent. "Pack your swimming trunks," he chuckled. "Sha, you're with me. Lis, I'm going to entrust your and Bell's accomodations to Colonel Dark Horse...see what you can do to make sense of those pings."

"Got it. Your contact in Naval Intelligence will be crucial in getting us a good ride," Feltham said to Dark Horse, buttoning her jacket up. "Preferably something cozy, with four-star cuisine."

Dark Horse allowed himself a thin smile, but ever the career military man, he quickly got down to brass tacks. "He'll get you two on a ship, no doubt about it. Accommodations, on the other hand, well, let's just say you do your jobs, they'll take care of you."

Feltham shook his hand with a gleam in her eyes. "Deal."

Leading his team out of the Missile Control System bunker, Mason paused to acknowledge Ainsworth. "Thank you for your team's work. It was a pleasure."

With a simple wave and a dip of her head, Ainsworth said, "Good luck. And get those bastards for us."

CHAPTER TWENTY

Solar rays shone through the glacier, blanketing K-670 in scintillating azure ripples. Berthed in secured mooring a kilometer off the Atlantic coast of the Antarctic Colonial Frontier, K-670 restocked supplies and exchanged waste materials from the Confederation outpost Novolazarevskaya Military Science Station. Venting fresh air for the first time in two months, the officer corps and crewmen were allowed to stretch their legs and breathe freely, and perhaps even enjoy themselves for a few hours.

Some duties did not permit such easy pursuits.

Stroking his newly shaven cheek behind the fullerene glass observation window, Tereshkov witnessed another, more covert transport arrive from the station in the form of a robotic submersible, docking inside K-670's wasp waist aft of the sail in Compartment V. Literally a structure resembling its nomenclature, the wasp waist was a narrow, inner chamber that displaced seawater from inside K-670, enabling the loading of cargo too large or delicate for standard entry hatches; even more important, it could stow cargo for long voyages away from the crew and K-670's intricate machinery and twin reactor cores.

Tereshkov felt the rumble of metal upon metal contact, the submersible's umbilical hatch mating with K-670, just mere meters away. Several smaller rumbles followed as the drone's gears offloaded the delicate device it harbored in a mechanized parastalsis. Relieved that his contacts' precious equipment was secured in its robotic cradle, the major walked back to the quarters he shared with Zamatin, where amusement from the foreign reports the pair received about their previous operation kept them focused on their next objective.

Kalinin cast the boat off less than an hour later, keeping pace with the lean schedule begun with the destruction of the Global Security Network and the ensuing efforts by threat forces to discover just who or what had smote it. Racing to American—but not K-670—crush depth, *Boris Yeltsin* fled northeast, availing for themselves the Antarctic Convergence, cruising for what would amount to a two-week trek to Îlots des Apôtres, nineteen bird- and rat-infested, ship-rendering islands and rocks inhospitable to humans or animals that couldn't scrape together a meal.

Unlike the leisurely circuit K-670 performed round Antarctica, this leg would be traversed with extreme precaution and all eyes open, with the constant companion of foreign intervention in the back of their collective minds. Fraught with uncharted rocks and shoals, the Îlots des Apôtres, along with its larger neighbors that composed the chain of Crozet Islands, were subject to foul fogs, hard rains and searing winds, creating a virtual naval gauntlet, arguably a greater danger than any other.

Zamatin downed another round of nausea tablets, easing the toll the Convergence's waters were taking on his inner ear. Being a lifelong landlubber, the captain's duty to take to the sea was difficult, but he did as ordered, if only to prove to Tereshkov that the major's choice to partner with the young man was not wrong.

Both FSB officers waited with impatience in the ensuing days, confining themselves to their narrow quarters, checking and double-checking each man's holobooks, reading news from home, briefs from St Petersburg and running diagnostics on the faraway device they brought with them.

Îlots des Apôtres weighed heavily on them. If this pile of useless, gale-blown volcanic rock formerly under the thumbs of the backstabbing French didn't live up to expectations, if all the works of the various scientists and the ministrations of the FSB didn't pan out, then Hell itself wouldn't be large enough to contain the souls the True Peoples would surely send there. A revolution demanded the utmost from its participants: life; theirs and those of family included.

Constructed in far away labs separately and anonymously, the device, after much blood—most spilled by Tereshkov and Zamatin themselves to keep its secrets unknown—and toil, lay dormant, ready for the fateful command. The two officers were entrusted with this duty, since no other Confederation branch possessed the will, drive, nor devotion to the True Peoples than they.

Tereshkov and Zamatin committed to this deal knowing that

there could be no road back, no doubts left in their minds. The time of equivocation was long past. If the future was to be one of a True Russia, then the decline of the West would be brought to its fruition on those tiny islands; an irony that the Îlots des Apôtres were so far from the USNA, yet the opening front in this long-anticipated war.

Λ

With a final shout out of thanks to Dark Horse, who stayed behind, Feltham and Bell departed *Blue Belle*, the jumpjet having deposited the pair onto the dorsal Special Operations entry hatch of SSN-1974, USS *Triton*, fast-attack submarine, which surfaced briefly to receive the pair. Diving back down to cruise depth after the agents were secured, *Triton* ramped up to its maximum speed of fifty knots, threshing the relatively warmer waters of the South Atlantic.

Triton was a well-known and somewhat celebrated boat among the silent service; it received its name and crest—two atoms for twin reactors, falcons for reconnaissance, and a hand rising out of the sea with trident—from a prestigious line of submarines dating two hundred years back, each distinguished in its firsts. This particular incarnation, being the fifth, successfully stalked and killed a supposedly undetectable Confederation drone sub—KX-94, *Oogor*—angering the lameduck Premier Vinogravich to no end, forcing him to down a healthy helping of crow; in the interests of aiding international relations with the Russians by allowing them to save face, the Navy refused to inform the North American public of the martial victory. And while not a member of the flamboyant, show-of-force warship catamaran fraternity the Navy paraded through the ports and river deltas of the world, nor the megapowerful, ballistic submarine "boomers" that were its actual iron fists of destruction, SSN-1974 happily sliced through the blue waters, a deadly assassin the Navy didn't want to hear, worry or know about: a hunter-killer.

A sensory wave overtook Feltham and Bell, filling them with the plastic and titanium odors of this sophisticated boat and her machinery and electronics. Ozone crept in their nostrils, too, as well as the taste of stale and salty air tingling in their throats. This "black pipe" was a melange of sounds bouncing off the cramped quarters and bulkheads, where constant reminders of the dangers of operating sensitive equipment and computers were on every vertical surface, pasted proudly for all to see.

Led into the small control center by Chief of the Boat Alex Tucker, the two agents were greeted heartily by the boat's skipper, Commander Freddie Mitchum, newly arrived from a subdued Line-

Crossing Ceremony—the old equatorial-crossing rite of the sea—held in the crew's mess; both agents were pleased to be excluded from the festivities. Having initiated several new sailors, or "pollywogs" as they were called quite vociferously throughout the corridors, Tucker wiped the remnants of shaving cream and motor oil he had applied to several sailors in his role as "King Neptune" of the "shellbacks," which he relished completely.

"Welcome aboard," Mitchum said, rising to his feet. "A little boisterous here, hope you don't mind." His bearded face flecked with red and grey bristles, the aged skipper looked quite at home, perhaps having spent his entire adult existence aboard one boat after another. Exchanging handshakes with the agents, he gestured to the control center. "I hear you've been working this angle for quite some time."

"Several weeks...everywhere from the Kurils to Kermani Iran," Feltham said, the exhaustion inherent in the long overflights emanating itself when she dropped her small pack to the deck floor.

Mitchum's face lit up in amusement. "Damn, Chief, these two have seen more vacation spots than our wives."

Tucker snickered. "C'mon. We set aside a meal for you."

"Oh, agents, my staff meeting is at..." Mitchum glanced at the bridge's station chronometer, "seventeen hundred. Chief here will escort you to the wardroom, where we'll brief on the sitrep."

Bell and Feltham tipped their heads and departed, following Tucker below deck.

Λ

"...Point of origin is unknown. Nationality is unknown. True intent is also unknown, but we've seen what they are capable of committing," Feltham spelled out, resting her knuckles on the wardroom table. Standing before Mitchum and his senior staff, the agent's eyes were red and drained, a dead giveaway from too much time spent staring at her holobook.

Hovering above the table's central recess was a smaller scale holograph of the Global Security Network, before and after the attack.

Seated next to Mitchum, XO Lieutenant Commander Danielle Song eyed the simulated attack. "An attack like this could be undertaken by any nationality with maritime forces, but with this degree of sophistication, only NATO forces, the CAC or CIS. I don't believe any other forces would bother."

"There are plenty of others who'd certainly want a go at it," Second Officer and Chief Engineer Lieutenant Commander Ken Longman said. "But you're right, Commander. No declaration has yet been received, though, correct?"

Bell shook his head. "No ideological or political statement has hit the Web."

"And STRATCOM has yet to report mobilization by any foreign threat forces, either," Mitchum added. "So, let's presume our anonymous threat is not quite ready for act two."

"Agreed," Feltham said.

"Priority A is finding them. Fortunately for us, and not so much for our foes," Mitchum began, steepling his fingers, "ship-to-ship network communications aren't deterred by the GSN's misfortune."

Song continued from Mitchum, switching the holograph to a wide aerial view of the Atlantic, where a flotilla of blue dots, each trailing a dashed line, appeared. "The Fourth Fleet's been dispatched south from CONUS, double-time, to track this mystery boat or boats. Here we are," she pointed an index finger to a pulsating dot, a text box with SSN-1974's coordinates and pertinent data suddenly popping up, "and here are our sister boats, *Proteus* and *Neptune*, sailing adjacent to us half-a-day's sail away. Each of us are actively combing blue waters, triangulating as we go."

"Recon drones, too?" Bell inquired.

"Sea and air," Longman said. "Stealth blue-water catamarans from Strike Force Zeta are launch points for them. Zeta's these ships...right here." The commander's fingers waved over seven dots on the periphery of the flotilla, some one hundred kilometers from the Brazilian coastline. "Our *Petrel* air drones drop subdrones like torpedoes," his right hand falling away from his outstretched left hand, "that can patrol the ocean waters for days at a time, up to several hundred meters deep."

"If nothing else, we should sniff them out," Feltham said, impressed. "I hope it's not too little, too late."

Mitchum grinned confidently, the edges of his eyes crinkling into crow's feet. "We're gonna make 'em think twice before doing that again."

There may not be much reason to do so, Feltham thought bleakly, but concealed her fears behind her steely demeanor. She and Bell were in, literally and figuratively, uncharted waters aboard *Triton*, and the last thing either needed was the perception that this was a fruitless exercise. Pinpointing this anomalous threat was the Navy's bread and butter, but uncovering and deciding just what the threat was capable of doing after the fact was the agents' domain, and more was riding on these two being on the ball than Mason's trust in them.

That was yet to come, though. For the time being, Feltham required shuteye, and a dose of anti-nausea meds to keep her wits about her as the *Triton* plunged ever nearer to the world's most hazardous sea currents.

Λ

Creaks and groans shuddered throughout the boat's inner recesses, driving home the point that they were entering a whole new world with its own rules and dangers.

"Why am I getting the sense we're under some giant's heel?"

Bell laughed. Putting his holobook on his lap, he craned his neck back to see Feltham grasping the wall of their bunk with both hands, very much resembling a homesick puppy in some cage.

"I mean, I know what my brain is telling me, but...."

"Are you sure you don't have anxieties about confined quarters?"

"Quarters?" she scoffed, pulling a fallen lock of strawberry blonde hair from her brow. "Just deep cold water. That's normal, isn't it?"

"We're not going for a dive, Lis. It's cosy and comfy."

"Still...." she whispered, scanning the concavities for the trickling seawater bound to be pouring in at any second.

Bell shook his head in amused exasperation. Dining on the last few morsels of a chicken salad sandwich proffered by the galley, he finished the preliminary Company report on the Global Security Network attack, then laid his head back on the pillow of the bunkbed the crew gave up to the agent.

"Are you sleeping...?" Feltham's incredulous eyes peered around his pillow.

"Trying...."

"Well, don't let me stop you."

"Thanks. I won't."

"It's just that I don't, well...can't sleep sometimes without music. You know how that goes."

"Actually, I don't."

"So are you one of those men that fall asleep anywhere?"

Bell flopped his forearm over his eyes. "Yep."

"How do you do that?"

"By not answering silly questions."

Taking the hint, Feltham popped her prescribed meds, shut her mouth and booted up her holobook. A pulsating green icon hovered above a dimmed desktop, catching her eye. Smiling, she tapped it and the icon blossomed into a viewer showing a recorded holograph of a man—her fiancé, Bryan—back at home in Maryland.

A shock of ginger hair adorning his puffy face, as he rather obviously recorded the message early in the morning, Feltham's body quaked with muted laughter at the sight.

"*Hi, Lizzy, sorry I can't say this in person...I know you're off saving the world like you always do. You'll probably get this at some odd time, but it's just six weeks from today for your big day, and I'm counting down the time till then. Please take care of yourself...I love you.*"

Feltham sighed and fingered the small carat ruby chained around her neck. He was a strong man to give her the space needed to perform her job, but the distances involved certainly put the strain on Bryan to maintain the homefront. A few more years of her stellar rise and the section chief slot would open up, Feltham knew, as all the voices in the Glass Castle murmured. And the webbed messages from afar would be days long past.

Personal matters had to wait, however. A second icon demanded her attention, a follow up on Doctor de Lis' brief report on his progress with Yastanni's case. Submitted to the Company by Chief Louris via auxiliary satellite link from The Hague's ICC pre-trial hearing in Alexanderkazerne, de Lis' speculation about the Confederation's intent darkened. Playing the appended hearing the doctor himself attended before webeye imagers, Feltham watched and listened to Yastanni's sworn testimony upon his initial arraignment in the Special Sciences Hearing Court, a forum adjourned to specifically investigate crimes involving state-sponsored techno-biochem-terrorism before the ICC.

A wide-angle holographic scene now ran on her holobook, displaying a formal courtroom and a panel of seated male and female officials, some prosecutors, others fact-finding associates of The Hague. Yastanni sat before them, coupled with de Lis, Louris and, on Feltham's first impression, Research Director and right hand Stacia Waters.

"...The Confederation, in the person of a Doctor Vasya Zaryov, of the Cosmoscience Institute in St. Petersburg," a sciences prosecutor named Josteen Geertman began, "came forward to you in Iran, appealing your help in this dangerous scheme."

"Correct," Yastanni said, dipping his head. "I have known Zaryov for decade."

Another prosecutor stated bluntly, "Just what did Zaryov, and generally, the CIS, expect you to deliver? A superweapon?"

"It is my opinion," Yastanni said, visibly chafing under their combined glare, "the Confederation believed I could."

"This is the second time you have been before us, Doctor," Geertman said. "I find your guilt, to put it mildly, beyond a doubt."

"Sirs and madams," de Lis interjected, "this isn't a trial, not yet. This is a preliminary hearing—"

The Special Sciences Hearing Court's magistrate nodded, raising his hand to quiet the panel. "Agreed, Doctor de Lis. Refrain from accusations, Mr Geertman."

Geertman acquiesced. "Project Ether, as described by Doctor de Lis' and your preliminary reports, is a resurrected twenty-first-century research project. Just what do you think the CIS' superweapon could deliver that warranted this, uh, extreme behavior?"

"Weaponization beyond current mass destruction programs, sir," Yastanni explained. "Since abolition of nuclear programs by all nations in Nuclear Ban Treaty of 2053, many nations strive to construct other programs—"

"Such as your neutronic research," Geertman noted for the webeye.

Yastanni's eyes drooped. "Research now I regret to this day. Project Ether manipulates dark energy, sir. Consequently, whole sections of earth could be obliterated with no trace."

"No one can do that," the other prosecutor cried.

"Not yet," de Lis warned. "But soon. Very soon. And with Yastanni's most assured assistance, I have vowed to stop it dead. Or we all *will* be. Boundaries don't matter. If we have no defense—by creating a strong offense—then it won't matter. Because the Confederation will obliterate everything we hold dear. And what we debate here about Yastanni, rightly or wrongly, won't be worth a damn."

CHAPTER TWENTY-ONE

"There they are!"

Sha Kindred leapt from her leather jumpjet seat and stepped over to the circular starboard window. Balancing precariously on her boot toes, her hands lodged into the tilted ceiling, she wore a wide smile of wonder, the bright, ultraviolet-rich sunlight bathing her brown eyes.

Mason crowded Kindred in the narrow space, butting under her outstretched left arm.

"How in the...it's like a dream," she marveled.

Three hours out of New Zealand across the easternmost Southern Ocean to the iceberg-choked Ross Sea of the USNA Antarctic Colonial Frontier, or USNA ACF, the Navy jumpjet *Captain Frostbite* pierced the swirling late austral spring clouds, banking to starboard to reveal dagger-sharp, glinting silver stilettoes and an emerald dome constructed off the coast, an incongruity of eyecatching hue dropped in a palette of browns and greys.

Three, four, eight, a dozen...in swift succession, Mason and Kindred witnessed the magnificent decadence of McMurdo City's skyscrapers exposed from ten kilometers' distance; it was a vista seemingly plucked off the face of the moon in this dry-air mirage. Each tower anchored in the dry slopes and coastlines straddling Mounts Coleman and Barnes, the City was the brainchild of several American and Kiwi moguls nearly a generation ago to develop the slowly warming Ross Sea and Island basin. Now devoid of most indigenous life due to the global climate shift, humans settled here in vaster numbers, helping to offset the South American cities growing on the Antarctic Peninsula, half-a-continent away; the English-speaking contingent was not about to be outdone by a consortium of upstart Latin nations across the Drake Passage.

"Or a nightmare," Mason retorted, a reminder of how far Ultima Thule had fallen in two centuries. Carved into wedges of mostly waste-land after the twenty-first century collapse of the Antarctic Treaty, the ACF was a modern-day Manifest Destiny. The USNA and Confederation, whose respective territories ranged tens of thousands of square kilome-ters, dominated the continental halves between themselves, leaving the rest of the world to divvy up the scraps.

"Welcome to the McMurdo Dry Valleys on the Ice," *Captain Frostbite's* pilot said over the cabin speakers. "Others call it Taylor Valley, but they like to call it MacTown. Things are done a little bit different down there on the ass-end of the world."

How right he was, Mason thought.

Captain Frostbite streaked through the pillars of fullerene glass and tempformed steel structures, which were cushioned to soften the wind's blow and collect the sun's rays for natural warmth. Despite Mason's misgivings—a psychological throwback even the normally pro-gressive agent had admitted to colleagues was strange—he admired the moguls' techniques. Each tower was self-sufficient, producing, recycling and repairing each construct from materials and resources at hand, a true, self-dependent and inter-reliable "planned metropolis" on the USNA ACF.

Like oceanfront property in Miami or Hong Kong, the City's spires curved across the sturdiest bedrock of Victoria Land, a crescent of towers overlooking McMurdo Sound, just a scant two klicks from the icy waters. Blocks of semi-developed terrain were underfoot, lined by paved roads leading into the continent, a strange dichotomy of develop-ment and savage wilderness, a true harkening back to the days of colonial America. Near the horizon, a magnificent backdrop of frosted moun-tains sat at the periphery of the City, origin points of the slowly carved brown "tongues" of silt and rock that are the Dry Valley's natural state.

Extending its reach above all the other towers was the seventy-story Prime Antarctica Complex, the center of all USNA government authority and trade on the continent. Crowned by two rows of four mini-spires, each atop its final tapering levels, it gleamed proudly in the clear air, a thousand mirrors reflecting the UV rays and jagged peaks out to all denizens and beholders, the masterpiece of architecture denot-ing—some would say flaunting—its civic, strategic and artistic merits to the rest of the USNA ACF neighbor colonies. All eyes from within observed the continent, a spider poised at the center of a great web, each leg monitoring a separate strand.

The Prime Antarctica Complex was flanked on its southwest and northeast by giant soaring wings of spires, a great bird descending into the Valleys, designed specifically to catch the roaming eyes of all passersby. Some resembled a New York City of the bygone days, with romantic art deco geometries and feminine curves, while others nicked Middle Eastern and Indonesian mosque architecture, multifaceted, precise exteriors mimicking floral ornamental fashions that lacked nothing for the eye to latch onto.

Opposite this grand tower was the emerald dome spotted earlier, a vast reservoir of biomass known as Broccoli City, with an ample amount of tongue in cheek; Kindred's research identified it as an extravagant showcase of modern biotechnological prowess, the zenith of USNA ACF's colonial ambitions. Containing the overwhelming majority of the continent's agriculture, this was a closed-loop system dreamt of just a few short decades ago by the same American and Kiwi moguls. Spaghetti strings of elevated trams within and without the dome's decks ferried personnel and civilians throughout the planned city's narrow lanes.

Kindred's nose pressed against the window, where twin moisture circles formed. "That is awesome!"

With bemused affection, Mason gently elbowed the younger agent.

Swooping past the towers of this waterfront downtown, *Captain Frostbite* flew over the sound and out towards Ross Island, where McMurdo Station, the Town itself, lay nearly five kilometers distant, its ancient foundations and contemporary scientific facilities beckoning.

If the City was the spit-polished, pretty face and civic heart of USNA ACF, then McMurdo Station was the utilitarian old grunt who lived and worked in the garage and only saw the sun once in a great while. Locked by most of the year in an ice sheet, McMurdo was tenuously connected to the mainland all but three months of the year, forcing aircraft to provide supplies on ice runways. Fortunately, austral summer was upon them, and *Captain Frostbite* had no such problems, allowing 9D to approach the nearby Williams Airstrip.

McMurdo wore the scars of a fifteen-decade occupation rather poorly. Several bunkhouses were rebuilt, leaving holes from previous buildings, while various maintenance hubs were expanded outwards from their original floorplans, lending a hodgepodge veneer to the island. Further back, blocking the low sun with its flat roof was the FNG Laboratory, a larger extension of the already substantial Crary Lab building. Handfuls of space observation domes dotted the lower plains, overlooked by Observation Hill, where, as they flew over, distant figures in parkas could be seen hiking the frosty trail to the summit. Low-flying, aggressive seagull-like birds Mason recognized as skuas swamped the back alleys, scavenging the trash barrels left out in the cold.

In contrast to the neatly cut roads in the City, the tracks from continual usage of heavy diesel lorries—Deltas—and construction vehicles gouged ugly trenches in wide swaths around the station, as if a hundred years' worth of dragging huge boulders against the semi-frozen earth had defaced the island. Biodiesel exhaust wafted inside *Captain Frostbite*'s cabin, despite the several hundred meter drop to the ground, greeting the agents better than any verbal introduction could.

With *Captain Frostbite* setting down with a soft thump, Mason and Kindred threw off their restraints, and before they could stand, noticed from the port window the arrival of a red lorry onto the tarmac.

"Now that's service," Mason quipped.

Walking towards the cockpit, he and Kindred sealed their parkas and donned fur-lined caps. The co-pilot kneeled down before the hatch and began to crank it open, but struggled with the obstinate door.

"I don't think it likes the cold air," he said.

Mason reached down, lending his strength, and together they pushed the hatch door outward, dropping the air temperature in no time; exhaled breaths misted in the cabin, while the inside windows frosted.

"Ready?" Mason asked Kindred, his hands on the hatch railing, a set of steps waiting below.

Kindred cocked her head. *Ready as ever.*

Two men strode over to the exiting agents, their dirty magenta parkas and stained tan overall leggings clashing with Mason's and Kindred's freshly pressed Navy blue lined trousers and iridescent IR-desensitized parkas.

"Welcome to McMurdo," the man bearing a patch labeled "TOWNSEND" shouted over the dull roar of the jumpjet engines. "C'mon inside." A grey baseball cap, embroidered with a National Science Foundation logo and battered by heavy use, concealed his scalp from the blustery day.

The agents trailed the pair up pitched wooden stairsteps and onto a ramshackle hut that looked to have been dropped next to the tarmac by chopper. Arriving at a paint-flecked door that betrayed scars from numerous kicks, the man jangled a ring of old-fashioned keys into the deadbolt, admitting the weary visitors inside.

"Woo! Winds're a bitch." He hurriedly closed the door, then removed his gloves and shook hands with Mason. "I'm Chuck Townsend, McMurdo Station Director. Make yourselves at home."

"Matt Moulton, Science Labs chief," the other man said, waving.

"Agent Greg Mason, IIA."

Kindred slid her cap back a few centimeters, her eyes scoping out the austere workshop. "Natasha Kindred. Quaint shack."

"Thanks," Townsend said, without a hint of brevity. "Moulton and I are the only winterovers to take care of the place until the summer beekers flock back."

Kindred raised an eyebrow. "'Beekers?'"

"Researchers...scientists," Townsend said with a smile. "Us!"

"How many winterovers right now?" Mason asked.

"'Bout two-fifty." Townsend circled round the two and headed for a boxy cooktop stove situated on a table near a sink. "Care for some coffee? Tea?"

"Yes!" Mason and Kindred chimed at once.

After a moment of splitting open several silver packages of dry mixes, Townsend said, "When Governor Remarque informed us we'd be receiving some highfalutin guests, I have to admit I wasn't thinking intelligence folks. Was worried I'd have to chaperone DVs who thought it'd be a month of midnight sun right now. But, it seems you need some assistance in the affairs of the ACF?"

"You could say that." Mason planted himself into a chair. "An advisor of mine said this would be our best bet in following up on a lead."

"Oh?" Moulton raised an eyebrow.

"Doctor Richard de Lis."

Moulton and Townsend exchanged glances.

"De Lis? Dickie Dee-light?!" Townsend snickered, barely containing his glee. "He sent you here? Wish he'd flown down, too. Think I owe him some money."

Now the two agents shot each other bemused looks.

"We did grad school together at York...damn, I haven't seen him in, well, a decade," Townsend explained. "Still got a way with the ladies I presume."

"We wouldn't know," Kindred blurted, jumping to end *that* conversation.

"Anyway," Mason continued, "we need your expertise in neutrino research."

Moulton gestured with his gloved hands to the tiny, frosted window at the near wall. "You've got the right place. We have five auxiliary high-speed cosmic ray detectors, plus IceCube at the Pole is still the best around."

Mason sat forward. "Good, because what we're looking for is a little out of the ordinary."

Λ

"A neutrino weapon? You've got to be kidding me."

Mason shook his head. Taking a sip of his steaming coffee, the agent looked Townsend straight in the eyes. "You're a specialist with these particles, you know what dark energy is capable of. And you know the Confederation's mined the ACF...now you tell me, what do you think they're doing over there?"

Moulton raised an eyebrow and threw his hands up. "For chrissakes, we didn't enlist in the NCF to fight a war, Agent Mason. The ability to do something and doing something are two different things."

"That's not what I'm asking. What I'm asking is if your teams have detected any unusual particle emissions or other weird goings-on over in the CIS ACF?"

Townsend rubbed his eyes and said, "A decade ago, IceCube observed a cascade of decay particles—tau-neutrinos, to be exact—through the atmosphere that coincided with a known neutrino event, a solar flare. A small reflective amount was detected—backscattering off the snowpack. The flare however produced less solar-type electron-neutrinos than subsequent decay analysis had reported, or so we thought, so we just chalked it up to randomness."

"None of us fathomed dark energy producing the excess..." Moulton let out a low sigh, "and no one here would even suspect, let alone admit, a connection with Kweiksman and that accident in Korea."

Mason's empty coffee cup plunked down on a tray. "We've seen enough to convince us that that's exactly what's happened. In fact, I almost died because of it."

Townsend and Moulton looked each other over, waiting for the twitches or ticks in the other's face that said Mason had won them to his argument. The pair treasured their neutrality in affairs of state, choosing to excel in the sciences for knowledge, not political advancement. And now both researchers were fully cognizant that sometimes, despite principles and ideals, failing to act was worse than choosing sides.

"I guarantee you, this won't be the end of it," Mason added, mounting the pressure.

"Allow me to get Governor Remarque's permission...he should be able to arrange accommodations for you," Townsend finally said, breaking his reservation.

Mason stood and clapped Townsend's arm. "Now, how close can he get us to no-man's-land?"

Λ

The penultimate level on Prime Antarctica Complex, Governor Remarque's stately office suite and penthouse lay directly beneath the eight observation spires, allowing the waxing austral dawn to filter into the hanging convex glass skylights and four mural windows, casting golden illumination over all in the twenty-meter-diameter office.

Led into the glowing stateroom by Remarque's secretary, Mason and Kindred felt rather underdressed, judging by the portraits, busts and assorted governmental knickknacks the office was adorned with.

Gathered round Remarque at his oak desk, several suited staffers eyed the visitors with vague curiosity, striking Mason that the regular joes down in MacTown didn't exactly call on the governor with regularity.

"Ah, yes, the IIA agents," Governor Jean-Michel Remarque greeted, rising to his feet. Two nods from his slickly coiffed head dismissed his staffers. "Please, come in."

Filing past, the staffers scrutinized the agents before the office's automated doors closed behind them. Kindred left a lingering stare back as she followed Mason to Remarque's desk.

Remarque rubbed his hands together, a sizable diamond-set ring on his pinkie finger catching the light. "I have been informed by Mr Townsend of your request, and I am sorry to say we cannot sanction an official visit to the DMZ."

"And do you have an 'official' reason why not?" Mason said, the scorn in his tone obvious.

"We must not antagonize our neighbors," Remarque said, circling out from his desk, "Agent...."

"Mason."

Remarque snapped his fingers. "Ah."

Behind him, a cartograph shimmered into view, displaying the confines of McMurdo City, which zoomed out to a multi-kilometer view of the Dry Valleys beyond. The tongue of Taylor Glacier between Mounts Coleman and Barnes crept northeastward for several moments, until reaching a red line denoting the edge of USNA ACF hundreds of kilometers away, butting up against the no-man's-land they shared with the CIS ACF. A blue line threaded through the cartograph, winding from the City all the way to the DMZ, several points in-between denoting campsites and fueling depots with text boxes.

"I cannot promise any USNA patrols beyond Taylor Valley's

easternmost mouth. So, if you were to be so foolish as to attempt this trek in clear violation of our good-neighbor pact, I would advise you to seek your own means of safety and travel," the governor explained, his language contradicting the exact instructions his cartograph told them to take. "Because the USNA ACF will not come to your aid."

"Very well, sir," Mason acknowledged, maintaining the hard edge in his voice. "Your refusal to assist in this investigation has severely hampered us, and I'm afraid any leads will now be lost."

"A pity. Please, thank Mr Townsend on your way out. Good day."

A curt nod by Remarque dismissed the two agents, who fled the office with zeal, practically leaving Remarque's staffers in a cloud of dust.

"Did you record that, I hope?" Mason asked Kindred when they were alone in the lift.

Kindred tapped her holobook's casing. "Don't you know it." She stroked the nape of her neck, soothing her strained muscles. "He seemed sure to have a mole in there."

Mason let out a laugh. "It's always good policy to doubt all your hangers-on, wouldn't you say?"

Λ

After stowing the required arctic gear in *Captain Frostbite*'s aft equipment compartment, Mason and Kindred locked down their twin IR-desensitized, camouflaged grey-on-white ATVs, performing the last pre-flight safety checks before settling themselves into the cabin. Having long since downed the altitude and medications they would need—a 3,500-meter high plateau awaited them—before arriving, the pair had readied their bodies as much as possible, and now all that was left was to get underway.

With verbal farewells from Townsend and Moulton at the starboard hatch, the two agents departed Williams Airstrip, *Captain Frostbite* taking them deep into the continent the long way round, via a wide encirclement of the City north of the Ross Sea, just for the sakes of any unfriendly onlookers. Past the Asgard Mountains, *Captain Frostbite* swung back south to Taylor Glacier, gradually merging with the travel plan Kindred received from Remarque, several tens of klicks down the line.

Above the multitudinous and jagged peaks, the sun was crisp, bathing the cabin windows and its two passengers, who took the last few hours of opportunity to clean their sidearms, refuel their bodies and memorize the lay of the land.

No-man's-land, or the Demilitarized Zone, as it was officially dubbed, stretched for a hundred kilometers ahead of them, past the outskirts of claimed USNA ACF territory. Smack in the middle of the continent, it was subject to the harshest extremes possible on the planet, equaled only in its warmest austral summer days by the worst recorded in the steppe lands of Siberia, a foreboding sign, as the CIS ACF controlled the vast majority of the lands beyond that.

Surreptitiously mined by the Russian Confederated Army on its CIS-bordered side, no-man's-land posed the most difficult leg of their Ether investigation, the geography notwithstanding. Automated micro-vibration sensors, magnitudes more sophisticated than those they encountered outside Yastanni's compound, stood sentinel throughout the DMZ as well, ready to report any activity since the cessation of a short series of skirmishes nineteen years earlier. Probing deep within the lands with modified snowmobiles, the pair would be easy targets if they didn't follow the most rigid of planning, lowering their profile as they made their to within investigative distance of Vostok Station, the old Soviet-to-Russian research outpost, rumored—and suspected by not only de Lis but Townsend—of being the Stage Three of Project Ether.

Lake Vostok, buried deep with the ices of the vast East Antarctic landmass, hosted a neutrino telescope of the Confederation's own, comparable to the IceCube telescope at the Pole. A massive volume of prehistoric water kept liquid by the weird pressure physics above, the 5,400-cubic-kilometer lake formed a natural filter for cosmic and solar neutrinos, allowing scientists to sift through the bevy of the nigh-mass-less particles bombarding every square centimeter of the Earth. Due to not only its remoteness but its inherent properties, Lake Vostok made the most perfect site for neutrino-cage development; the more neutrinos were segregated from the outset, the more powerful an Ether detonation could be produced. All the agents were left to do was scan the region for the suspected tau-neutrino decay particles a dark energy reaction would create, an exact replica of what Townsend and Moulton described from ten years ago.

Disengaging off the swung-down aft compartment hatch of *Captain Frostbite*, the two snowmobiles rumbled into the dry, snow-packed Arena Valley, their hydrogen engines choking out steaming water exhaust, which crackled into ice mid-air. Dressed to the nines in heated salopettes and socks powered by their bodies' electrical impulses, parkas, boots, arctic camouflage helmets and finally oxygen tanks, Mason and Kindred set out on the multi-day journey, the benefit of USNA ACF covert stashes checked by the lack of orbital support from the MIA Global Security Network, which the two agents would miss in the days ahead. They had no choice but to make the best of the worst case scenario; in their hands lay the only mobile force capable of staking at Vostok unseen.

CHAPTER TWENTY-TWO

TING....TING....

"Why, hello there...." Sensor Petty Officer Pryor placed his fingers on his SID—standard information display—bracketing a miniscule yellow amoeba-like pattern amongst a violet background field. "Chief, I've got a blip in section one-nine, bearing one-four-two, range six-two-zero meters off starboard of drone Zeta-five."

Chief Petty Officer Dawes, running the radio shack department ahead of the control center, looked over Pryor's shoulder. Noting Pryor's SID, and the trio of other SIDs in the radio shack, he toggled his voxlink. "Control, radio shack. We have a target, bearing one-four-two, range six-two-zero meters off starboard of drone Zeta-five."

Officer of the deck—OOD—Commander Longman's voice crackled over the shack's speaker. "Radio shack, control. Patch it the conn display."

"Patching to the conn display, aye, sir." Pryor double-tapped the bracketed section.

Coating the nightwatch control center's bulkheads and panels in a coruscating violet, the yellow blip moved ever so perceptibly forwards. With Pryor rotating his fingers on his interface, the object followed suit on the conn display, showing a three-dimensional orthographic image some days' journey distant. Cross-indexed against an object drone Zeta-eight discovered two days earlier, the blip came alive before the crewmen and officers.

"Well, looks like we have a winner," Longman said. Turning his head to his voxlink, he duly informed the captain of their findings.

***

Λ

Within the hour, Commander Mitchum's appraisal of the findings had *Triton* speeding full ahead at just shy of fifty knots. Watching the orthographic long view of the boat tracking the extremely far off target, Feltham and Bell gripped the semi-circular railing ringing Mitchum's seat. Bathed in the cartograph's pastel illumination, the captain and crew traveled as silent witnesses to the continuing passage of the blip through the distant Antarctic Convergence. Forging a red trail towards a speck of far southern Atlantic islands, the blip didn't hesitate in its single-minded determination southeast.

Blinking in thought, Bell glanced at Mitchum. "Captain, do you have a projected course?"

Mitchum wriggled his finger at chief of the watch Jee, who answered, "Well, current course seems to indicate an uncertainty cone containing the Prince Edward Islands, the Îles Crozet, the Îles Kerguelen, Île Amsterdam, Île St. Paul, all the way to the eastern coast of Australia."

"There's nothing beyond that for quite some ways, is there?" Bell added.

"Not unless our blip's circumnavigating the globe."

Feltham stroked her scalp. "I think I'm starting to see what you mean. Captain, that thing's averaging a speed of about twenty-five knots, pretty steady."

"Mm-hmm." Mitchum's lips had a slight up curve.

Bell tapped the Prince Edward Islands of Marion Island and Prince Edward Island on the cartograph, well within the cone of uncertainty. "Can we encircle Marion Island here, ensnaring them?"

"We're too far away to intercept at that point," Jee said. He swiveled in his seat, and reaching between Augustine and Whitman sitting at the planesmen wheels, highlighted the images of Îlots des Apotres and Île aux Cochons within the Îles Crozet, a group of three major islands and handfuls of insignificant, but steep, rocks.

Feltham's eyes followed the cartograph's magnification; the red trail stopped and became a series of red dashes within the uncertainty cone. Behind it, a blue series of dashes rounded the Île aux Cochons from the southwest and encountered the red blip before it could enter the open waters of the southern Indian Ocean and evade probable capture.

Jee continued, "At full, we can attempt a better intercept inside the Îles Crozet...at that point, our speed will long overtake their head start."

Standing at Mitchum's side, Longman crossed his arms, gesturing the cap on his head towards the image. "We can run at maximum until we reach five-one meters depth...slowing this boat down to keep from running into uncharted seamounts and other rocks is going to be tricky. It'll be harder to catch them."

"We'll leave it to you, sir, but the sooner we can rein these guys in...."

Feltham didn't have to finish; Mitchum raised his hand. "Mr Longman, set a course for the Îles Crozet, best possible speed."

"Best possible speed, aye-aye, sir," Longman acknowledged, turning to Jee. "Chief, best possible speed."

Λ

Cruising through the deep blue, USS *Triton* slipped past the flotilla, Mitchum relaying his intentions to their sister boats. The rest closed in behind, becoming a dragnet in the event any "friends" appeared on the scene to assist the anomalous blip, which had, in the course of the day become their "rabbit" to their "wolf."

Meanwhile, Pryor partnered with Chief Petty Officer and engineer Rubin in further analysis of the mystery blip at the cluttered consoles and shelves of the computer room under the control center. Sifting the hundreds of minutes of scans the drones received, they synched the captured images to library images of known foreign boats.

Pryor rested his elbows forward onto his station panel, steepling his hands over his chin. Flickering from text box to text box, his pupils were in rapt dilation.

"I don't have any ideas," Rubin said, shaking his head. "Length is huge...over a hundred and eighty meters. Whoever it is, they know how to build 'em big."

"Chinese...Confederation...Indian...." Pryor muttered, his mind rifling through each nation's roster of known vessels. "And I want to know is how anyone could build this without the spooks knowing."

At that, Feltham ears perked up; the agent had been filling out a metal chair at the rear of the room, ready for any expertise she could lend them, but mostly killing time. Crossing over to the pair, she now stood behind them. "How's it going?" Her voice was flat, her true concern being their diligence.

"No luck, Agent," Pryor replied. "Database for all known boats is drawing a blank...drones lost contact, but I don't think we've been evaded."

"Good, make sure that doesn't happen," she cautioned.

"Yes, ma'am."

Feltham nodded towards the schematic. "What else do we know about this mystery boat?"

Pryor called up a set of sensor logs. Several lines of text and numeric blocks scrolled down the holograph, and the petty officer highlighted several with the touch of his index finger. "Apparently, this boat displaces over thirty-thousand tonnes underwater."

"That's big?" Feltham asked, her brow furrowed.

"Very." Rubin punched a button, bringing up dozens of submarine images from the past. "Since the heyday of submarine designs dating back to the Cold War of the twentieth century, these being the second- and third-gen builds," he explained, pointing to images of Typhoon and Los Angeles class boats, "boats've been built progressively smaller, mostly due to advancements in materials and computer technologies. Take the *Triton*, for instance. Computerization has overtaken the need for nearly a third of the crew a fast-attack used to employ. This gal, whatever flag she sails under, is a different breed."

Pryor rotated the three-dimensional image between his fingertips. "And chances are good she packs a helluva punch."

Feltham twirled a lock of hair, her gaze disappearing into the object's yellowish-red surface gradient. "What's this blue indentation at the nose?" She tapped the image twice.

"We're hazarding a guess and assuming it's a navigational supercavitating mechanism," Rubin said. "If it's true, that's the first time I've ever seen one applied to a manned submarine craft."

"Does that increase speed?"

"You bet." Rubin held his right hand out like a sub, then curved his left hand before it. "Think of it as a bubble of air ahead of the boat, which drastically reduces the fluid drag."

Feltham shook her head. "Damn. Somebody knew what they were doing. Think we can still catch them?"

"With that much mass," Rubin answered, "it doesn't hold a candle to our engines, even with their state-of-the-art supercavitation. It's just simply too weighty. On the flipside, though, I wouldn't underestimate them."

Feltham craned her head back to the control center-interface SID; the rabbit proceeded along its single-minded course, while *Triton* pursued, several days to a week behind, but closing. The agent couldn't help but hope it would be sooner than later.

Λ

"There it is, ma'am," chief of the watch Jee announced three days later, his voxlink chiming with the voices of the reporting radiomen. His index finger was planted squarely on the image of Île aux Cochons at the planesmen SID. "Sighted by navigational sensors."

"Put it on display," OOD Song commanded. Sitting forward on the captain's seat, she put two fingers to her lower lip in thought. "A mass of rocks isn't too far from the truth."

Île aux Cochons was a rather large plot of land, capped by the cloud-covered Mount Richard Foy, perfect for the opportunity to surprise their quarry. The rabbit's sonar scrutiny would be rendered impotent, thanks to the island, and satellite reconnaissance ineffective against the fast-attack *Triton*.

Song checked the OOD's SID to her left, studying the ocean channels on the Navy cartograph. The rabbit was entering the Îles Crozet nearly due east, just north of the 46th parallel, and set to enter the ten-kilometer-wide North Channel separating the southern Île aux Cochons from the northeastern Îlots des Apotres. *Triton* had begun to veer south, parting from the chase course they had been following four days prior, ready to round the southernmost tip, the Pointe de la Houle.

It was a complicated maneuver, Song knew; countless explorers from the great age of Antarctic discovery had run aground in misty shoals. *Triton* stood in greater circumstances, despite the blinded GSN. In all honesty, the XO spoiled for some action, even if it was another prolonged rabbit chase; the experience gained by the crew and officers in the operation could only make them better in future engagements.

"All right, Chief, this is where our fun starts," she said, rising to her feet. "Speed one-five knots. Right rudder one-five-zero degrees."

Jee nodded and looked to his planesmen. "Speed one-five knots, aye, ma'am. Right rudder one-five-zero degrees."

As her planesmen acknowledged their chief's orders, she toggled her voxlink, raising Mitchum, who monitored the course change in his wardroom. "Permission to change course, Captain?" she asked.

"Course change affirmed, Commander," Mitchum said into her ear. "Steady as she goes."

"Aye, Captain."

The control center's main holographic display showcased the shift, a camera pan due southeast slowly curving to port, all made possible by multifunctional passive sensors on the mast, which constructed a virtual optical view for the benefit of the commanders. It was a decent replacement for the old-style periscopes, saving the problem of having to ascend to periscope depth and breaking the surface. All in all, a tactical benefit balanced by the unnatural spectra of color applied to the reconstructed image that the human eye could never see.

Aft and above Song, the cartograph team worked feverishly charting their new course on the plotting tables, all the while checking off the suspected location of the rabbit with details provided by the radio shack on the table-length holographic and redundant real paper charts.

The *Triton* would round the Pointe de la Houle for the rest of the day, creeping along so that, even though they knew nobody with current technology could detect them, it was better to cruise at a snail's pace the final few kilometers than be spotted by some freak displacement turbulence from their baffles, or worse yet, be intercepted by some damned Confederation *Oogor*. Only when the radio shack confirmed that the rabbit was within their grasp, and Mitchum felt comfortable doing so, would *Triton* streak out of the blue like a bat out of hell and incapacitate the sonuvabitch, or if necessary, sink it to the bottom of the ocean. Figuring out the rest would be the Navy's salvage division's problem.

Λ

Bell and Feltham tired of the endless drills Mitchum and Chief of Boat Tucker were placing on the crew. A nice stroll to the bunks for the pair transformed into a Chinese fire drill, completely upheaving any semblance of normalcy the agents could have expected. Hours after that, another drill had every buzzer, alarm and bell wired aboard the *Triton* sounding off, making the short time the agents had to themselves unbearable. When this drill was called off, Feltham and Bell were dragged back to the control center by Mitchum just moments later.

Entering the control center from a deck below, the agents crept around Mitchum and OOD Song at the plotting tables, where the senior and petty officers conferred under a rotating cartograph. A green Île aux Cochons rose above a blue sea, and circling by the island was a miniature blue submarine—the *Triton*—heading north-northwest, its exact coordinates kept purposely secret, even from the agents. Several kilometers away, even tinier blue dots representing the drone *Petrels* orbited the Île aux Cochons. A red blip, once shooting straight for the open ocean, had inexplicably veered sharply to port, unbeknownst to the *Triton* crew, while rounding the island.

His none-too-pleased face illuminated in blue-green, Mitchum crossed his arms. "We seem to have a problem, agents. Our enemy's decided to take a side trip."

"Where are they heading?" Feltham asked, furrowing her brow.

"The Îlots des Apotres," Jee said, tapping a button on the cartograph table, which highlighted the titular series of islands and rocks. "They're taking a big risk...the depth is less than a hundred meters. Battle space could be like shooting fish in a barrel."

"Not much diving, huh?" Bell said.

Mitchum nodded. "We're awaiting STRATCOM authorization to commit. *Petrel*s haven't detected any structures on the islands, so it's an open question what they're up to."

"Commander Song, a sensor waveform has been detected from the rabbit," radio shack chief Dawes reported over the XO's voxlink.

"Patch it to the conn display, Mr Dawes."

"Patching to the conn display, aye, ma'am."

Song and the others faced the holographic display a few meters ahead, where a green field of uninterrupted, low-level environmental static was periodically swamped by spikes.

"Your men have any ideas, Chief?" Song asked, the waveforms not recognizable to her from the various USN charts and graphs she'd memorized over the years.

"Pryor and Cohen think it's nothing but baffle interference from their supercavitation system, but Robison insists he's seen that waveform before aboard the *Dakota*," Dawes said over the voxlink. "Something along the lines of calibration maneuvers."

"Can you be more specific?"

"Any number of systems, ma'am. He believes the likeliest would be torpedo tubes."

Mitchum and Song exchanged distressed looks. Leaping from the navigation platform, the skipper bounded to his post's SID, switching to the boat's central library menu. Shaking his head, he scanned several lines of text before punching his voxlink. "Dawes, get me straight to STRATCOM! Song, set Opsec, condition Alpha."

"All hands, Opsec Alpha," Song said, her fingers toggling her voxlink, which patched through to a mike that broadcasted her voice. "Repeat, Opsec Alpha."

Throughout the narrow corridors and tight quarters of the *Triton*, the few officers, department chiefs and sailors aboard were roused to action over the next twenty minutes, silencing all equipment and powering down any non-essential systems to comply with Operational Security Alpha, the highest state of watch the boat runs under in times of engagement. Any sound capable of revealing the sub to the enemy boat was either silenced or lowered, no exceptions.

"Captain, I have STRATCOM ready for your communiqué," Dawes said.

Mitchum walked out of the control center, departing for the officer's wardroom in the forward bow, where he would communicate with his superiors discreetly and securely.

Feltham and Bell turned back to the cartograph, their eyes tracking the two objects performing the delicate dance in the North Channel. The rabbit advanced unabated, either unawares or unconcerned with the *Triton*; Feltham certainly hoped it was the former. Closing the distance gap made evasive actions less and less likely. If this throwback to an era of bigger and bolder submarines held true, Feltham didn't want to be around when it unleashed the brunt of its offensive weaponry.

Palpable tension amongst the control center during Mitchum's absence heightened with each minute, raising a sense of foreboding in Feltham; she and Bell were relegated to pacing behind the industrious crew, hands in pockets, still very much aware of their outsider status. If STRATCOM authorized the *Triton* to act, she hoped they'd hurry it up.

Λ

"ZAMYESTITYEL, shall we give them the show they have been waiting for?"

Zamatin's pride rose with the clap on the shoulder he received from Tereshkov. Both officers climbed the steps to K-670's control center, where Kalinin and his chief engineer, Second Captain Sergei Sapov, torpedo officer, Senior Lieutenant Konstantin Byorkin, and the junior weapons officers conferred in the CONN's aft compartment, a bank of stations and holographic displays, all probing the topographic complexities of the Îlots des Apotres, which drew nearer into view.

Tereshkov's calm gaze belied the blood pumping in his system. So close were they now, the taste of what was to come almost overpowered his disciplined mind. Byorkin's calculations were nearly complete, he could see. Selecting the proper coordinates for maximum yield and efficacy took time, the major acknowledged; this was the prelude to greater things, and tuning it precisely was of utmost importance.

The days racing to the Îlots des Apotres were busily spent by Sapov's crew prepping their clandestine device for the next phase of the operation. Years, if not decades, were coming to a head here, at these tiny dots of rocks; not just the two FSB officers but the officers of the *Boris Yeltsin* seized upon this auspicious time and relished it, knowing they would be ushering a new era, one they would rightfully claim as theirs. The glory of the Confederation Navy, spearheaded by this magnificent weapon, was to be restored to its rightful role as the world's greatest ever seen. And to have the honor of delivering the most awesome energies man had yet harvested swelled in their breasts. Heady times to be a submariner under this ensign.

"Captain, we have confirmation on targeting coordinates," Byorkin said, raising his head from his display. An holographic yellow grid crisscrossed his face and those of his torpedo team, casting their flesh in ochre.

Kalinin nodded. Turning to his XO, Anikiyev, he gave the command to proceed as directed. In turn, Anikiyev set K-670's navigators on course to the final destination. The Îlots des Apotres beckoned to them just three kilometers away, and they were not to be denied, even as a miniscule waveform shift, almost imperceptible to all but the most skilled sailor, crept silently aftward....

CHAPTER TWENTY-THREE

Staggering from the covert USNA ACF shelter on their fifth day crossing the vast expanse of snow dunes, Mason prodded his oxygen tank, positioning it correctly between his shoulder blades. Continuously wearing it as they ascended the plateau bruised his flesh, killing any incentive for continuing their operation, but the agent wouldn't entertain the thought. Halfway to Vostok, both he and Kindred were too deep to abort anyway; nothing less than the fulfillment of the mission would be acceptable to either agent.

"...Uh...I'd love...ah...bowl of...soup now," Kindred eked out over their comm system, an improvised two-way link jury-rigged due to the lack of voxlinks. The pair had consumed nothing more than anti-nausea meds and military-grade slurry rations manufactured to provide adequate nutrients and liquids, ostensibly feeding themselves, but lacking any gastronomical delights. In fact, downing the rations through slits in their oxygen masks with non-freezable straws was the exact opposite of dining. Unfortunately as well, what happened on the other end of matters was just as unpalatable.

Mason turned his entire torso around, more out of his body becoming one with his salopette than ease of movement, and proffered a hand to the supine Kindred. Taking it, she rose to her feet in the shelter's narrow doorway, her helmet reflecting the buttery sunlight.

"Or...a night's sleep...in this damn...thing...." she continued with labored breaths.

Mason goaded her. "C'mon...we can...sleep while riding...." Thanks to the snowmobiles' advanced geomagnetic modules and lidar cannon, they needn't be actively navigating or driving; this allowed them short bursts of shuteye, essential for maintaining cognitive functions.

Replicating the grand Trans-Antarctic Traverses of the twentieth century, which had been accomplished by giant tractor trailers and lorries, the agents were slicing days off their predecessors' times by utilizing the superbly agile and lighter snowmobiles, easily crossing dunes, drifts and partial fissures where larger vehicles had once been stranded. It wasn't effortless, comfortable nor ideal, but their more agile snowmobiles certainly kept the Confederation's sensors from detecting them; the last thing needed was to set off remote eyes by rumbling over the hardpacked ice and snow. Their lidar cannon performed double duty searching for planted mines as well, assuring the weapons were given a wide berth as they ventured forth.

Setting off once again, they drove over the nigh-infinite white blindness, their helmet's HUDs delineating the horizon where human eyesight would long ago have failed. The sun's glare refracting into their faces was a constant nuisance, offset only by the shaded faceplates. Removing a helmet for more than a minute in the high plateau of Dome B was an instant death sentence; aside from the pressurized oxygen they breathed, the cold stood at a hellish -85 degrees Celsius on the day, giving even the hardiest human pause.

A day out in the Antarctic wilderness stretched to a few, exacerbated by the growing sunlight, since the agents' bodies were heavily Northern-Hemisphere locked, training in boreal Canada and Alaska couldn't compare. Hours hunched on an snowmobile seat numbed the body, the sole arbiter of time being the HUD computer warning one in no uncertain terms with piercing alarms that it was break or shelter time.

And when the coordinates and schedule informed the agents their quarry was a mere two kilometers distant after crossing into the CIS ACF without so much as a shrug of the shoulders eight days in, the propensity to just keep on going another 1,800 klicks to the coast was a little inviting.

Mason's single-minded doggedness wasn't about to agree.

Stopping the snowmobiles on a snowbank, they approached a snow ridge and hunkered down, tuning their HUDs' binoculars to the coordinates. With normal vision, the horizon was limitless, and one was unable to perceive depth or distance, especially in the Antarctic. Shadows and forms blend into one, rendering eyesight less than useless. Zooming in on the target with lenses of a precision instrument revealed a far different story....

A depression hidden from the eyes of human beings stretched

from north to south across the horizon, at first glance a normal plateau no different from anything in the American Southwest, except for the glaciated snow blanket four thousand meters thick. Peeling layers of sedimentary ice apart, though, their HUDs' sensors adroitly unveiled the depression's true visage, being that of a frozen body of water the size of Lake Ontario amongst the landscape of the highest, driest and coldest desert on Earth: Vostok, the first and grandest of its kind.

Perched upon the lake at its very southern edge, Vostok Station was a frozen phoenix rising from icy ashes. Destroyed by fire a century previous, shaking off a formerly friendly American research camp once located there, the original incarnation lay under meters of snowdrifts, its current form straddling the icecap with a tall trio of implanted and spindly legs, a single cable radiating in from each leg to a central hub. Emanating downwards from the nine-meter-wide hub was a cylindrical penetrator that was lodged thousands of meters deep inside the icecap and threaded, essentially creating a giant bolt. Judging by its architecture, Mason surmised the penetrator could be extended on top and the legs ratcheted up to supplement the station during the inevitable ice buriel. A kilometer east sat two domed structures, likely camps constructed for the researchers during the peak summer months of habitation; currently, they looked unoccupied, save for the handful of rusty lorries parked off the ice some hundreds of meters beyond.

Kindred turned to Mason on her right, her labored breathing apparent in voice. "Wha...what the hell?"

"Gimme a minute." Mason adjusted his HUD, switching to another filter. Slicing through the penetrator's metal skin, his HUD made out a five-meter-wide inner shaft, with machinery constituting a lift platform. *TauTona all over again.*

"Ah...got it, Sha...our entrance."

Kindred did a double-take. "We're...going in...there? You know... where it goes?"

"Straight down."

Λ

Ditching the snowmobiles, the two agents trekked into the bowl of Vostok, walking across the glacial crust to the cylinder. They traversed the growing snowdrift at its foot and began climbing the series of vertical handrails towards a closed door panel on the hub twenty meters up. Breathing heavily, and suspended with all four limbs on four different handrails, Mason strained to manipulate the balky holobook clipped on his waistbelt in the meantime.

Underneath him, Kindred pulled herself up, the bitter wind

beating against her, working to rip her away. Clenching her teeth, she recalled every drop of reserve in her and held on, now just a step below Mason's own foundering form.

Pounding the holobook's interface with his ham-handed glove, Mason looked for weaknesses to crack in the door's locking mechanism. His holobook's spintronics picked the lock and a second later, Mason was in with a hard kick. A stiff breeze whistled out of the pressurized interior, swiveling the door away on its left hinge. Mason reached down, heaved Kindred up into the darkened hatchway and followed her in.

Switching on their helmet lamps, the agents illuminated the tin can's interior. The pair—ghostly forms in lumpy snow gear against the dark wall—were standing on a grated metal lip surrounding a lift that was ready for the next descent. Smaller auxiliary and maintenance lifts—like complementary U-shaped cutout puzzle pieces—were adjacent and the hoisting engine stood silently, attached to the interior wall. Peering through the lip's grating, a long shaft below them blew more pressurized air up, unsteadying them.

Mason turned to Kindred and tapped his helmet, saying, "Take off your oxygen mask."

Scrabbling with the latches at their jaws, the agents ripped the masks off and rubbed their raw skin, not having felt moving air since the shelter many hours earlier. Both gasped at the temporary ecstacy.

Raising her shaded faceplate, Kindred filled her lungs and glanced down the shaft. "All right, Stone man...you want to lead us down?"

Half-nodding, Mason opened the liftgate and stepped onto the lift, putting his gloved hands on the controls. Kindred closed the gate behind her and braced herself. Mason gripped the lever and pulled it down, engaging the lift with a jump. The hoisting engine roared to life, paradoxically without complaint despite the deathly cold temperatures.

With wind blasting against their faces, the agents' eyes were fixed on the broken illumination shining through the lift floor's grating, brightening tiny squares of the interior walls. Their ears, though, rang from the crushing din of compressed air.

"How far down?" Kindred asked, blocking the gale with her gloves.

Mason gave her a sheepish grin. "Thirty-four hundred meters."

"Ahh...shit."

"At least it's air-conditioned," he said, reminded of the terrible heat of TauTona.

"Wake me when we reach the bottom." Slumping on the lift floor, she rested her head in her hands.

Nearing the elapsing of an hour, the lift ground to a halt, lowering to a tempsteel-lined level. Inset floodlights in long skeletal girders and crossbeams burst to life as the lift softly connected with a wide beam, rousing Kindred.

Rising to her feet, Kindred followed Mason, who opened the lift gate and stepped out onto the wide beam, then down several centimeters to a narrow secondary crossbeam, interwoven with other girders. The two advanced a series of steps, blocking the illumination with their hands, studying the layout of the floor.

Mason put his hands to his hips. "Not much going on here."

"Wait, there's a ladder over there," Kindred said, gesturing to curved metal handles silhouetted at the edge of the crossbeams.

"Let's see where the rabbit hole leads."

Mason descended the rungs, careful to avoid wedging himself in the tight cutout. Pausing at the next level, the agent turned his torso, taking in a wide view.

Putting her hands on the railing, Kindred peeked downwards. "Whaddya say?"

Mason was silent for a second before answering, "We may just have our case."

Λ

Gun-metal grey decking rattled underfoot, broken up by two rows of meter-tall metal cylinders gleaming in the filtered light. The seventeen vertical cylinders, connected via thick cables to the crossbeams above, were plugged into the deckfloor at short intervals. Indecipherable piping and a bevy of bolts covered the cylinders' exteriors, but no printing or other markings could be identified. Three more unused cables hung from the ceiling, presumably missing their respective cylinders. A gentle hum permeated the chamber, evoking a living, breathing being.

Kindred ran her fingers over her holobook, actively scanning the first cylinder. An exploded view of the cylinder hovered above the device, slicing the individual components apart and reading the compounds and molecules within.

"Each cylinder has isotopic readings from differing regions of the world, even though they seem to be identical parts in the other cylinders," Kindred said, comparing the sets of chromatograph waveforms against one another.

Mason stole a look, studying the peaks and troughs. "Were they made in separate countries?"

Kindred brought up another file, synching it with the present isotopes. "These match your and Bell's TauTona scans, but these," she tapped a second waveform, "are matching metallicities from Eastern Europe, Central America, Western China, Canada...my God, these just keep going."

Mason furrowed his brow. "Minute radioactive counts are all over the casings. Looks as though these have been assembled from all over, too, and brought here."

"But what are they doing?"

Mason booted up his holobook and scanned the vicinity. "Lake Vostok is just centimeters below us, protected by this pressurized cap. The tips of these cylinders are locked into the water."

On his holobook, the domes were submerged some fifty centimeters into super-chilled and highly pressurized lake water that if released, would spew water capable of fatally injuring them.

"Damn this is odd...." Mason circled his torso around, casting more lamplight into the shaded corners.

"What's that?" Kindred asked, pointing towards a podium-type construct which had a trio of levers set parallel to the floor.

He followed her arm, illuminating the waist-high object. "Controls to something."

Mason walked over to it and placed his hands on the first lever, gingerly flexing his gloved fingers, almost as if debating himself.

"Let's hope this doesn't kill us."

He pushed the lever up, which groaned akin to a stubborn gear shift. The columns shuddered, then vibrated to a quickening pace from above. Pistons sounded around them, inching the cylinders from the plugs, separating from silicone prophylactic seals restraining the lake water within.

Pushing the middle lever forwards next, Mason began to extract the cylinders—ten on the left side, seven on the right—lifting them up. Climbing centimeter by centimeter, the metal canisters exposed their domes to the awed agents for the first time.

Mason stepped towards a nearby cylinder. "What the hell...."

"Oh, my," Kindred whispered, her holobook targeting a dome. "They're hollow inside, except for some really tiny metal plates."

"Plates?" Mason placed a gloved hand on the dome. "Plates... plates!" He grasped Kindred's collar. "Casimir plates! Neutrino-capture cages!"

CHAPTER TWENTY-FOUR

"Sonuvabitch!"

Kindred paced between the cylinders of the left row. "Each of these are a neutrino cage? Are they...warheads?"

Mason lowered his hands from his aghast face. "Nothing else fits. A handful could devastate whole continents. Sha, we have to destroy them. Now. Having them in the lake water, that's the purest form of neutrino separation possible."

"Like Yastanni was trying to do...purifying the quality of neutrinos, the less particles, the more powerful the yield."

"Yeah."

Kindred did a double-take, looking at the other row, counting the cylinders. "Oh, I'm not liking this, Stone man. There's housings for three more over there, but they're empty. Did the Confederation arm them already?"

Mason slapped his forehead. "Stupid...of course. Why didn't I see this? Yastanni was a fallback, a cover even. They did a good job keeping us occupied, that's for certain. We're chasing bogeyman in Iran and Africa and they've got perfectly serviceable warheads down here. That does it. We have to disrupt their operation somehow, make sure those three warheads are never used."

Kindred crossed back to him. "I've got an idea. Maybe—maybe we should smuggle one out. De Lis insisted on banning the technology, but if we have a working, weaponized warhead, we would be able to know how much knowledge the Confederation has, how to defeat them if it comes to a confrontation over them. Or better yet, evidence."

Mason gave it a quick thought and nodded. "All right, help me with th—"

A familiar alarm sounded on Kindred's holobook: the proximity alert.

Both agents swiveled towards the stepladder cutout meters away.

"EM counts are way up," she said, her eyes on the device.

"Drones!"

Mason clambered up the steps, just enough to spy the lift. Raising his E4.10c "Bull" sidearm to eye level, he popped his head up further, scouting for any telltale signs of the killing machines; the agent had no doubts the Confederation employed nothing but the best for their most secretive research laboratory.

He needn't wait too long, as a sequence of searchlights and blinking diodes emerged from the auxiliary shaft. Mason took one look and knew what they were in for—a KD-7 *Hornet* hunter/killer drone. At ten kilos, it was a personnel killer, the smaller cousin to the *Lammergeiers* that the Confederation had sicced on them in Iran. Developed for surgical effectiveness, the KD-7s wouldn't attack like the suicide-bombing *Tamils* employed in Indonesia; these drones had synthetic neural synapses engineered for tactical awareness, easily killing a target from twenty meters out to just a few centimeters.

The bulbous KD-7 wheeled its central gun barrel around, its constellation of compound lenses—like insects' eyes—scouring the field of view. Its searchlights swept the chamber and locked onto the ladder, illuminating Mason's pistol. He fired a volley of particle rounds, nicking the *Hornet*, but not deterring it. Rushing at him with the piercing buzz of side-mounted engines, two more followed behind the first, unloading their own particle rounds.

Fleeing into the cutout under a shower of sparks, Mason dropped to his feet and held his pistol at arm's length. "If you want that damn thing you'd better hurry!"

Her eyes widened, and body galvanized, Kindred redoubled her work. Releasing two latch rings at the top of the cylinder, she then ratcheted the cable downwards, slackening it so that the dome now rested over its plug.

Several meters away, Mason lay on his back firing round after round into the cutout, the silver flashes refracting throughout the chamber. The lead drone hovered nearby, popping scintillating ions at Mason.

"Almost there," Kindred said, unfastening the tethering system with difficulty due to the heavy gloves she still wore.

Mason let out a cry, but continued to fire, his rounds at last disabling the drone so that it fell out of the air, against the cutout's edge and into Mason's lap. Grasping the seared and smoking remains, the agent dropped his E4.10c onto his chest and flung the dead drone at the second buzzing killing machine, knocking them both backwards.

A final attack fell upon him from the third drone, again with more intense particle rounds. Mason was able to put the metal grating between himself and the drone, but not for much longer; descending quickly, the drone's engines whined irritatingly in his ears just centimeters away, desperate to burst through the cutout and finish off the agent, who was saved solely by his return fire.

The drone weaved in and out of the cutout, formulating a strategy to wear out the besieged agent with a combination of fire, then cover.

Mason held his ground, but the continual rolling out of the line of fire fatigued him; one slip-up snowballed into many more. The drone took advantage and slipped into the cutout, its barrel discharging, but held in check by Mason's left hand, which forced the drone upwards.

Buzzing furiously, the drone quaked, attempting to free itself. Mason set his pistol barrel against the device's skin and pounded two-centimeter-diameter holes into it. Mason shot off the left engine nacelle, making it lose lift, yet the particles still poured forward, intent on the kill. Floor shrapnel blew across Mason's gritted face, his eyes locked on the struggle, adrenaline sapping his strength.

Swiveling millimeters every few seconds, the drone's barrel worked its way towards Mason, the rounds zipping closer and closer, the ionized air warming around him. A particle flash tore through his parka half-a-head-turn away; just seconds more and the last thing he'd feel was—

An explosion blasted the drone apart above Mason's torso, scattering its debris over him. Shaking his head in amazement, the agent looked to Kindred, his breath pushing out of his nostrils and mouth.

Lowering her RT-01/9V sidearm, Kindred stepped over and kicked the metallic carcass off Mason, then proffered her hand to him. "Sorry I took so long."

"No problems...." Huffing, he took her hand into his and stood up. He gave one last look to the smoking debris and asked, "You done?"

"Yep."

"Good. We need to destroy the rest of these."

The pair turned to the remaining cylinders, all humming in the chamber. Mason paused to crack his neck after the tense firefight, then wasted no time in crossing back to the control podium. He put his hands on the second lever and pulled it down, which after a moment's waiting, lowered the cylinders into the plugs once more.

"Let's see what this one does," he said, reaching for the third lever.

Kindred held her oxygen mask over her face. "I'm putting my oxygen back on."

"You don't trust me?"

"I don't trust *them*," her voice echoed behind the mask.

Mason steadied himself over the podium, and after a deep breath, pushed the third lever upwards. Barely a moment followed before the deck shuddered, the plugs themselves vibrating violently around the enveloped cylinder domes, which seemed to come alive with groans and creaks that filled the chamber. Quaking, shrieking metal upon metal clattered inside the cylinders; great cracks jolted the skins, beginning from the plugs and rising higher. The prophylactic seals were repealed, the lake water given free reign to rush into the naked neutrino-capture cages.

Kindred faced Mason, her body language increasingly animated.

Mason felt the immediate sting of cold upon his flesh. His exhalations steamed in the air, tiny ice crystals glistened on his stubble. "The lake! Water's getting into the cylinders!"

Shrapnel launched into the air, blowing apart the decking and leaving craters under the cylinders. The agents ducked under the onslaught, blocking the flying debris with their hands. Geysers of pressurized water sprang up, coating the walls and floor in ice.

Kindred laid a gloved hand on Mason's back and yelled, "Let's get the hell outta here!"

Λ

Struggling onto the lift with the ice-encrusted cylinder, the two agents stabilized it by resting it on its top, allowing the dome to stand heads up. Kindred broke off the ice on her boots while Mason gripped the lift's lever and raised it, beginning the long ascent. Roaring to a start, the lift accelerated, jerking them downwards.

Glancing past Mason, Kindred did a double-take, her tired eyes suddenly fixed on something beyond the lift.

"W-what?"

"The cable's moving…the auxiliary lift."

"Shi—" Mason scrambled to locate his holobook, which had shifted on his belt during the scuffle. He booted up the device and scanned the vicinity. A flashing red blip descended towards the green icon on the interface, the distance closing minute by minute.

He looked up, his visage glowing. "Our 'friends' have found us."

"I imagine they'll want their toy back."

Mason patted his parka's left breast, layers above his shoulder holster. "Let's make sure they don't."

Underneath their feet, the lift swayed, its own cable beginning to fall victim to the attackers many meters above; tiny meteor-like embers rained on the two agents, residue from fired particle rounds.

Their lift soon to be put out of commission by the attackers, Mason decided to cast a tactical die and hasten its demise. Warning Kindred—who locked the cylinder close to her body—he braked the lift, bringing it to a screeching pause.

Now, Mason returned the favor, opening fire on the auxiliary lift's cable. He didn't want to destroy it; the lift was all too instrumental to his plans. Putting the fear of crashing feet-first into the disintegrating lower deck was more his style. Being this far down, and certainly aware of the cataclysm the agents had just created, the Confederation troops were more likely to head their way than back up. And Mason was counting on that very fact....

"Get down!"

Mason threw his weight onto Kindred and the cylinder, pushing her to the opposite side of the lift. A hail of particle rounds shot up the lift floor where Kindred had stood, raising Mason's ire.

"I'm good...." Kindred squeaked and removed Mason's arm from her shoulder.

Mason thrust himself back into view of the auxiliary lift and fired off a volley of rounds, holding the rapidly descending troops back. Their return fire from Kl-374w semi-automatic rifles did not target the agent, but the lift cable again, forcing him to get aggressive in defense. Sighting the squad with his sidearm's blue laser light, he took aim at the men just meters above, incapacitating one, but the others took cover.

A loud pop coupled with a stomach-churning tremble rippled throughout the lift, widening Mason's eyes. Flinging himself a meter-and-a-half at the auxiliary lift as it bypassed their larger lift seconds later, Mason landed on top of the squad, brandishing his elbows and ramming his helmet into the surprised troops.

Kindred slid on the lift floor away from the cable, its uneven level pitching her towards the controls. Behind her, the cylinder fell onto its side and rolled to a stop against a leg of the railing, clattering loudly. Ignoring Mason's actions, she charged herself with the duty of protecting and reclaiming the cylinder for their mission; she'd start with bringing this lift back under control. She grasped the first lever in her left hand,

and wrapping the crook of her right elbow over the railing, pulled up on the controls with all her remaining might. A horrendous squealing from the cable's mechanisms roared through the uprising air, threatening to snap the cable under the strain. After what seemed to be an eternity, the lift paused and hung in the air with uncertainty, leaving her to wait for Mason.

Landing a punch with the hard butt of his sidearm to the first Confederate trooper's jaw, Mason took him down by surprise, the sound of cracking bone and torn cartilage echoing in his ears even with the bellowing lift car. Whipping his left elbow upwards, he knocked over the second trooper, causing him to lose his Kl-374w, which clattered to the other end of the lift. A third trooper launched himself at the agent, grasping Mason's torso in a vigorous bear hug and throwing him two paces towards the railing.

Mason again felt the blitz of the third trooper, who clutched him and started to lift once more. Reaching his right and left hands round the Confederate's torso, Mason clasped the trooper's parka hard, and whirling around with all the strength in his back and legs, circled to his left and pinned the trooper's back against the railing. Palming the man's face, Mason inched him towards the interior of the rapidly descending interior shaft wall, nearer and nearer to certain agony.

Now, the second trooper had shaken off Mason's attack and poised his Kl-374w at the agent. Just beyond the third trooper's jawline, Mason spotted the other trooper and with a quick right boot, kicked the rifle away. A red cloud exploded from the third trooper's leg, eliciting a howl as he dropped to the lift floor. Mason sprang forward and fired a single round into the second trooper, who collapsed onto the railing, but still clung on, slowly sliding. Helped along by the fists of Mason, who pushed him towards the liftgate, the agent kicked him in the chest with a grunt, forcing the man's doubled-over form to slump backwards through the gate.

He looked over the edge to see the trooper tumble into the darkened abyss, acutely aware that the lift was rapidly approaching the disintegrating chamber below. Looking up to the increasing distance from the auxiliary lift and Kindred, beads of perspiration stung his eyes despite the chilled air blowing inside the shaft; he had to get this ride stopped ASAP. Stumbling past the outstretched legs of the incapacitated first trooper, Mason's hands flew at the levers, pulling on them with haste to ease his descent.

Dozens of meters up, Kindred glanced over her shoulder, eyeing the swaying cables and smoldering lift mechanisms which appeared ready to collapse from the ungodly strain the agents had tasked it with. Wild temperature swings—chilled dormancy and superheated descent and ascent—didn't help her cause any, either. She crouched down to secure the cylinder, eagerly scanning the pitch-black maw for signs of Mason's return.

Rumbling to life, the auxiliary lift crawled upwards, none too soon for Mason, as the pressure from Lake Vostok finally took the vestiges of the lower level to its doom. A powerful updraft brought debris and small shards towards the lift's bottom, clanging loudly beneath his feet. He rode the lift at full power (for it) ticking down the minutes and seconds until Kindred's hunched and shadowed figure was lit in the half-light.

Relaxing the lever, Mason slowed his ascent and joined up with the main lift, which, owing to its cockeyed pitch, sparked when the two met, creating a mild shudder.

Kindred stood uneasily, one hand on the railing and one on the now upright cylinder. "You're a little too heroic for your own good, Stone man," she scolded. "I'm not going to witness you for an honor bonus."

Straddling both lifts, Mason helped walk the cylinder over with his hands on its dome. "I don't need a bonus, Sha...just getting outta here in one piece is good enough for me."

"Amen to that."

"Let's blow this joint." Proffering his hand, he clutched her arm and pulled her onboard. Maneuvering the control levers again, Mason sent them both into the upper reaches of the shaft, one step closer to leaving the forsaken continent.

CHAPTER TWENTY-FIVE

"Control center, wardroom, we have commit to engage," Mitchum transmitted over Song's voxlink. *"Repeat, we have commit to engage."*

"Wardroom, control center, commit to engage, aye," Song confirmed aloud. "Mr Cox, ready tube two."

"Ready tube two, aye, ma'am." At the forward weapons control panel, Torpedo Officer Lieutenant Cox punched in the sequence to launch, first opening the shutter door for tube two and next sending instructions to the torpedo room.

This was really it, Bell thought, completely unaware of his fingers swiftly curling around a railing just under his waist. *Was it to be war? Or just another skirmish swept under the carpet of global politics?* He never imagined his first true assignment would devolve into outright warfare.

The calm maneuvering by the *Triton* command crew unnerved Feltham more than a frenzied mess of alarms, shouting and activity. Perhaps it was the idea that the crew and officers had drilled this so many times repeatedly and now performed the real thing almost by rote, as if planning the obliteration of a fellow sub, caused her concern. Even in her line of work, with years of dedication and discipline, the expectation of mass casualties sent her into a mild panic. Mitchum's steady handling of the situation, and his command staff, by proxy, did alleviate some of her stress; this was not a trigger-happy crowd by any means.

"Station the fire control tracking party," Mitchum's voice sounded over the sub's intercom, scrambling the best of *Triton's* best to their various posts, ready for battlestations.

Mitchum soon flew out of the wardroom and into the control center, where he moved past Song at the OOD chair and back to the plotting tables, overseeing the "playing field."

On commands from the CO, OOD Song instructed the planesmen to circle slightly to starboard, giving the imminent torpedo strike an out-of-the-blue surprise, keeping *Triton* invisible for as long as possible, until any of the rabbit's other "eyes"— *Oogor*, satellite or onboard sub sensors—discovered them. At that point, Mitchum would sink the boat in an emergency "angles and dangles" maneuver to escape retaliatory torpedoes, hoping the North Channel's shallow waters would hamper the rabbit in its strike.

A level below, the torpedo room's chief and petty officers shouted instructions to each other, manning the SIPs and coordinating the messages from Cox essential to arm and fire the torpedo at their rabbit.

"Target confirmed, Captain," Cox reported, looking over his right shoulder. A green reticule flashed over the rabbit's sensor image.

Mitchum straightened his back. Double-checking his navigators' cartographic plots, and seeing the *Triton* was in optimal firing position, he delivered his decision with an efficient lack of hesitation. "Launch number two torpedo, Mr Cox."

Λ

"Countermeasures! Two-zero degrees left rudder."

Vroot! Vroot!

Kalinin raced to his chair, his senior officers following to their respective posts. Dozens of holographic displays switched to incoming alerts, illuminating the bulkheads in a multitude of hues. Alert sirens wailed their irksome alarms, echoing in the captain's ears as he tapped his peripheral console to track the incoming torpedo.

Bracing themselves for the abrupt turn to port, the crew and officers shuddered as the *Boris Yeltsin* complied and groaned under the strain. Displays fluttered and returned to full order, still broadcasting the tick of an approaching threat.

"Sonar, control! Threat identified as mark fourteen torpedo from North American fast-attack submarine, Neptune-class!" sonar officer Captain-Lieutenant Chuchikov announced over the control center's speakers. "Passive sonar indicates the sub was in our wake."

Anikiyev looked to Kalinin with steel in his eyes, an anger tinged with determination. "Dammit...!" The XO fingered his voxlink. "Control, sonar. Where are those countermeasures?"

"Glitch in the computer, sir!" Chuchikov answered, his eyes fixed on the displays before his radiomen. A nod from one of the seamen brought relief to his face. "Quantum flux countermeasure system active, sir. Sending countermeasure signal...now."

Lowered into the shallow bluewater, the quantum flux counter-measure system undermast was composed of micrometer-sized piezo-electric tuners that pulsed spintronic signals capable of overwhelming and confusing threat weapons with superfluous data, essentially flooding and frying them.

Pulling within meters, the torpedo plunged through the bluewater, skimming just centimeters above the sediment-laden ocean floor to the hard-cranking K-670. Homed-in on its supercavitation propulsion, the torpedo's processors received a quick burst of data chatter which wormed into its guidance algorithms and forced it to change course. Seconds later, the warhead rammed into the seafloor, burying into several meters of sediment and exploding harmlessly.

"It's too late for them," Kalinin said, more to reassure himself than anything else. He pulled Tereshkov, who had been steadying himself on a nearby console, closer to him. "Your device is loaded...I suggest you commence the launch sequence."

Tereshkov nodded. Clapping Zamatin's shoulder, the two officers, being the only men on board with the secure launch codes, began the descent to the lower levels of Compartment Three.

Sailors squeezed through the tight corridors, pushing against the two officers, a mighty river of humanity, forward movement slowed to a fraction of realtime. Gripping vertical handlebars set along the bulkheads, Tereshkov and Zamatin fought their way to the lone stepladder, each step down seemingly an eternity.

Bearing the passkeys on chains around their respective necks, the two men's boots clanked on the lower deck, the launch bay aft of them filling with youthful sailors amid barking junior officers. Askance looks from the terrified newbies reminded Zamatin of his first time on duty, only less than a decade ago.

"Captain Tereshkov, I have received orders from Captain Kalinin and Lieutenant Byorkin to admit access to the launch station," Ensign Olgashvilli said, waving to the junior FSB officer. Olgashvilli loomed over an instrument panel, a sailor sitting below him.

Tereshkov swept Olgashvilli aside, and producing his passkey, slid it inside the instrument panel's slot and retrieved it in one motion. A verbal command from the terminal instructed the captain to verify his identity with a proteome scan, conducted by Tereshkov placing his hand under a T-ray beam, made all the more difficult by the bucking K-670. With that complete, Zamatin repeated the process, authenticating the pair to put their device to its fullest employment.

Updating Kalinin by voxlink, Olgashvilli set the armament of the prospective torpedo into play.

"Ensign Olgashvilli, torpedo five loaded into tube two," a torpedo chief announced.

"Proceed firing sequence."

"Control center to torpedo room, you have optimal distance to launch," Byorkin announced.

Just the words Tereshkov had waited long months to hear. His eyes found the sensor display relaying the images of the rocky cliffs of the Îlots des Apotres hardly an hour's cruise from here.

"Launch torpedo five!" Olgashvilli ordered, cradling his arms against his duty jacket.

Tereshkov felt the peculiar; a bead of perspiration above his brow, the very last sensation he'd thought he'd feel. Years of steely practice to drum out the anxiety seemed to desert him now....

Λ

A scream of unparalleled intensity cascaded in the deep blue, an unease borne by the dense metallic cylinder that seared the water behind. Rocks and shoals recoiled beneath the building pressure wave, the prelude to horrors yet unknown to the fauna of the Îlots des Apotres....

Λ

"Control center, sensor room! Rabbit torpedo away!" Dawes reported over his voxlink to Mitchum. "Target fix is three klicks away from the rabbit...." the chief paused, tracking the red line on his SID. "The islands, Captain. Îlots des Apotres."

Mitchum swiveled his head to Song; both officers had a deepening pit forming in their stomachs.

"What in the hell...." Song balanced herself in the OOD seat, the boat's angles and dangles forcing the control center to pitch forward. "Planesmen!" the word spat from her mouth, the tactician in her abruptly shifting tack, "Eight-zero meters!"

Confirming her command as echoed by Chief Tucker, Augustine and Whitman broke *Triton* out of the maneuver as swiftly as the boat would allow, the combined strength of both sailors pulling on their respective wheels to force them upwards again in a great U-shaped parabola, closer to the surface in a helluva lot more of a hurry than either cared for.

Creaks and moans trembled throughout the hull, as the complaints of the *Triton* were made apparent for all to hear and feel. Risky, dangerous and barely approved by the very engineers who ran the boat, the reversal gave much reason to cling to the sturdiest rail for fear of life and limb.

"They're targeting the islands but not us?" Mitchum pondered aloud. "Agent Feltham, any insights?"

"Not one, Captain." Welded to a station by her arms, she watched the virtual torpedo trace a red streak on the holographic display.

"Control, sensor room. Captain, sensors detect an unusual output signal from the torpedo," Dawes' voice said over voxlink.

"Sensor room, control. Can you elaborate?"

Dawes, hunched over Pryor and his SID, encircled with his index finger a radiating wave emanating from the launched torpedo. "Wavelength structure matches the frequencies emitted by high-energy neutrinos."

Mitchum furrowed his eyebrow, unaware of the two agents who exchanged horrified looks.

"Get this boat away from here! *Now!*" Feltham shouted, leaping to the captain's side.

Λ

Banking hard to port, *Boris Yeltsin*'s triple hulls bellowed under the immense strain Captain Kalinin had placed her under after their torpedo's launch. Officers and crew held fast, both body and mind assaulted by the acrobatics performed by the boat, her engines outpouring megajoules of power just to circle away from the target in the requisite few seconds.

Kalinin's dire hope was to be the champion in this test of wills, proving not only his loyalty, but his prowess in defeating the Yankee boat, which was unaware of K-670's true mission. And when the score was settled, he longed to be the first Confederation commander to haul back the gutted wreck of a North American fast-attack submarine to St. Petersburg, to the acclaim of millions.

"*One-zero meters....*" Tereshkov heard in his ears, a deck below. "*Nine meters...eight meters....*"

Magnified at full on the sensor display, the green circle flashed, inexorably drawing towards the hapless Grande Île of the Îlots des Apotres, that nondescript slab of rock seemingly raised from the sea-floor. With the span of measured time and distance slowing to a crawl in his mind, the flashing ceased, and Tereshkov soon quaked before power and destruction never felt nor experienced in the whole of human history.

CHAPTER TWENTY-SIX

A miniature sun erupted under the deep blue, vaporizing all matter within a two kilometer radius. The great rock that had just been the Grande Île shuddered and—in a reaction otherwise naturally impossible—disintegrated from the bottom to the three-hundred-meter-tall peak of Mont Pierre, atomizing in such succession and friction that individual particles burst apart in a flash of plasma, an explosive cloud briefly hotter than the sun's corona. Magma burst forth from a newly formed, three-kilometer-wide crater on the bedrock, vaporizing what little air was sucked into this cauldron of quanta.

Fervently replacing this sudden vacuum in a nanosecond came a seething rush of ocean, creating a column and rising mushroom cloud of boiling water several hundreds of meters tall—pressed inwards by the returning mass of waves—that soon settled into crashing whitecaps.

Beyond ground zero, temblors cascaded in concentric rings, uprooting seafloor, dislodging the minor rocks of the Îlots des Apotres, bolting them upwards as natural torpedoes in the now-hazardous ocean.

Pelted by these rocky mines and wrenched hard to port was the *Triton*, its screws spinning and fins maneuvering to extract the fast-attack sub out of the dangerous reverse undertow, saved from humanity's first wielding of the destructive power of dark energy solely by Feltham's plea, which turned the boat back from the cusp of instant death.

The ocean found new seams in the sub's hull, spraying the battered control center with brackish, steaming water, which burned the *Triton*'s crewmembers, all of whom stumbled in the dark, foundering chamber. Flooding the room to knee height, the seawater soaked into the delicate electronics and quantum computers, shorting out the power systems.

Mitchum fell on his left flank, clawing into the security railing with his hands. "Seal those hatches!"

"*Control center, Engineering! Pressure dropping below—*"

"All hazard teams to the pumps!" Song yelled, her voice carrying over her voxlink. "Clear the decks! Get this water out of here!"

Bell dove out of the water—having collapsed in the barrage—and traipsed up to the navigation table, where a waiting Feltham took him by the arms and sat him in a seat.

"I—I'm starting to think I'm jinxed," he uttered, his voice hoarse from the seawater he had inadvertently swallowed.

Feltham dabbed his face dry with a handkerchief, despite her own tousled and soaked hair. "Hardly...you're a good luck charm," she said. "You've twice taken their best shot."

Bell sighed, although the sound of his very breath was lost to the cacophony enveloping them. The two agents were the definition of fifth wheels, neither qualified nor knowledgeable of the boat's mechanisms to lend a helping hand, no matter how either were eager. They could only bear witness to the scurrying crew who flung themselves at the tasks necessary to bottle *Triton* up again.

The two agents' lungs took deep inhalations of the smoke-tinged air, which stank of burnt plastic and scorched metal, leaving an acrid taste on their tongues. Their ears perceived Mitchum's plaintive commands, his voice just denting the echoes of rumbling bulkheads, rushing water and clanging alarms, directing the planesmen to get this boat into deeper waters where the turbulence would be less and the margin for error a helluva lot more forgiving.

Feltham set the handkerchief down, and espying an accessed navigational SID, magnified the display image, a holographic reconstruction of what was formerly the Grande Île gleaned from the *Triton*'s mast sensors. Gasping, her outstretched hand found Bell's, and the senior-most agent died a little inside.

"No...it's, it's worse than I thought possible," Feltham muttered. "The whole island...it's been wiped clean."

Bell cleared his throat, his eyes flitting right-to-left on the image. "An Ether device. The yield, it must have been enormous, bigger than even Doctor de Lis had formulated."

"I—I have to reach him," Feltham said, her eyes narrowing. She stood halfway up past the table. "Get word out to the Company about this, Greg's gotta know, too."

Bell looked up at her. "Fighting our way back to the bunks won't be easy. Relaying it on this overworked grid will be next to impossible."

"That's why you'll be with me to help. You're handy with technology, right?"

"Hardware...and even I can't work miracles if the grid's gone to pot."

Having made up her mind, Feltham grasped Bell by his wrists and pulled him up. "C'mon. Time's already lost."

Fording the waters, both agents hobbled to the stairwell, where gushing seawater foamed as it splashed onto the lower decks. Their arms interlocked, the pair trod gingerly step by painstaking step, aware that any false footing would put them in a world of hurt at the bottom.

Settling down on their bunks, the agents wiped off the beads of perspiration and seawater that had collected over them. Loosening her blouse collar, Feltham gave her neck some air in the increasingly stifling atmosphere. Tapping her holobook once, it recognized her thumbprint and blossomed an interface menu.

"Web de Lis," she commanded.

A tumbling hourglass displayed before her as the device reached over the compromised web, the interminable seconds passing like minutes. Finally, a sketchy image of the doctor's face slipped into view.

"Agent Feltham...I'm just barely reading you—"

"I know. Listen, we've got a situation here. Get word to Chief, Rauchambeau, hell the Prez if you can. An Ether detonation's blown an island to bits...you read me?"

De Lis' garbled visage expressed incredulity. "Ether detonation? That can't be right—"

Feltham pulled the holobook closer, practically touching noses with the hologram. "Time's up! We're lost, dammit! Get every goddamn bomber to take out this—"

"—What'd you say?" De Lis craned his neck, almost out of view, distracted by a smattering of noise behind him. "No...NO! Agent, I— something's gone down...."

"Doctor? Doctor!" Feltham fingers tried to stabilize her connection, but the interruption was on de Lis' end, severing the line in a blast of static.

Bell glanced at the idle holobook, then up at Feltham, his weary eyes swinging from concern to downright fear. *What could've caused de Lis to sever the weblink? And after what Feltham had just said...?*

"It's all gone to hell."

***

Λ

"That's the...last time...you...choose to have—your side adventure...!"

Mason swiveled to look back at Kindred who, her chide notwithstanding, carried her half of the neutrino-capture cage cylinder.

"And another...thing...you and your...souvenirs...."

Regaining their stance on the ice sheet above Lake Vostok once again, Mason and Kindred lurched over the landscape, the senior agent bound for the pair of lorries they spotted earlier. Forging a trail out of the bowl, both labored under the mass of helmets, oxygen tanks and the cylinder on an inclined, frozen terrain, their quarry now lost to the near endless wall; Mason's only assurance was his chirping holobook providing the correct path up.

Mason reached the crater lip first, hunkering down in the hardpack snow, his left hand extended in front of him to assist Kindred, his right hand bearing the brunt of the cylinder. A grunt escaped his mouth and twinge in his lower spine served to remind him that no human was meant to cope with these conditions, giving his critical brain reason to go easy on his body.

They tossed the cylinder to the ground, relieving themselves of their burden for a few scant seconds. Hunched over, the pair panted before righting themselves and plowing ahead to the nearest lorry, a tantalizing hundred meters distant. It was an almost outrageous sight, a dichotomy of color dropped amidst a vast drabness perhaps only a painter could appreciate; a cabin ensconced in a dark, UV-protected windscreen, sitting spryly on a brilliant orange, cubical chassis with tall tires bordering on the obscene. MacTown inhabitants referred to the American versions as "Deltas" and these weren't too far from that lineage.

Reaching the Confederation lorry, which Mason henceforth named "*Deltsky*" in his head, they stowed the cylinder inside the *Deltsky*'s unlocked trailer, which accommodated it easily. The pair walked to the driver's side door, where Kindred placed her hands on the handle.

"Just how do you expect to get in this thing and drive?" she asked, her words flowing easier now that they had paused.

A jangly set of metal keys—a rare and unusual sight in these days of quantum encryption and pass key cards—were produced from one of Mason's parka pockets. "A little going away gift from our friends back there...grabbed 'em up before we stepped off."

"Fantastic. I've changed my mind about you."

His thickly gloved fingers fumbling the keys, Mason managed to manipulate the metal pieces in the cold lock, opening the cab door.

Kindred climbed up two grated steps and received a boost on the small of her back by Mason, who followed her inside. Scooting over for him, her legs hung over the edge of the flat seat like a toddler in a high chair, her frame quite a bit smaller than the usual occupant.

Mason found the starter keyhole on the rather narrow steering column and turned the key, praying the *Deltsky* had some life left in it, let alone diesel to get them where they needed to be: Mirnyy, for a date with the local Confederates. And he wasn't in the mood to take no for an answer from them.

"Hope you're ready for a road trip," he asked.

"Put the pedal to the metal!"

Coal-black diesel exhaust choked out of the vertical pipes behind the cabin, the engine rumbling the *Deltsky* awake. Gripping the vehicle's stick shift and stomping on the clutch, Mason put them into motion. A loud crunch could be heard as the *Deltsky* set out on the Antarctic ice-cap, flattening crystals underneath the huge, threaded tires.

Λ

"No! *Nouri!*"

De Lis hit the carpeted floor, dodging the chaotic tangle of limbs around him. A piercing chorus of shrieks and screams were in his ears, forcing his hands to cup the sides of his head. The doctor rose up and forded the river of flesh separating him from the fallen Yastanni, now blanketed by a horde of UN security guards.

Playing through the din in his mind, all he could remember was the mechanical whirring that emanated from the hearing room's upper gallery, and then several rounds of particles that streaked silver flashes towards the hapless man. A drone—yes, that was it—a hunter/killer that somehow had evaded the stifling security inside the ICC's main court-house in Alexanderkazerne to strike and silence Yastanni. The unthinkable galvanized him; even with Feltham's warning about the Ether explosion, Yastanni was de Lis' only concern at the moment. The physicist was as big a target as ever, and now de Lis' worries seemed destined to come true. The Confederation no longer appeared to have boundaries, and gunning a man down in the world's legal capitol was fair game.

Another wave of gunfire from the balcony came not from the drone, but from the Dutch gendarmes with semi-automatic rifles blasting the hovering device from two sides. Out of commission, the small drone lay in ruins on the balcony floor, disabled at last.

De Lis made it to the security detachment just as they cleared a path for medical personnel to carry Yastanni out on a stretcher. Low, rattling moans were buried under the crowd's commotion, but de Lis had spent enough time with Yastanni to recognize them as his. He couldn't see Yastanni directly, didn't know his condition, but couldn't stop from injecting himself into Yastanni's care.

"I need to go with him," de Lis yelled to a medic in his best, but provincially Canadian, French. He produced his USNA security badge and flashed the VIP ID on his neck lanyard.

The medic looked at him quizzically, then waved him forward, more to get him out of his hair than anything else.

Jogging behind the medics who parted the stunned and frightened audience, de Lis filed past the security detachment at the building's exit doors, racing to catch up to the fleeing team. Rounding a corner on the rain-slicked boulevard, the doctor paused with considerable edginess; his charge and sometime nemesis now slotted into a waiting medevac VTOL craft, it was difficult not to see it as Yastanni's fleeting, final moments. Much as de Lis tried to fight it, a sense of guilt began to creep into him, responsibility for putting Yastanni in the light of day, even anger for not having better protection. He'd never felt more vulnerable, but beating himself up wasn't going to help Yastanni right now. Getting Louris on the case—with all his available manpower—was the priority now.

De Lis pulled himself inside the craft, its dayglo orange strobe lights pulsing across every surface in a seizure-inducing frenzy. Strapping himself into a cramped cabin seat, not at all like the more comfortable jumpjets, his muscles tensed for the short flight to Alexanderkazerne's hospital complex, a few blocks distant. Producing his holobook from his jacket, he webbed Louris to greet him with the awful news.

Λ

Boris Yeltsin once again resounded with the cheers of a dozen crewmen and officers in the command center. Replaying the disintegration of the Grande Île in a holographic loop, the men privy to watch the explosion celebrated with song and smiles, all too eager to throw off the yoke of imperialist North America and enjoy the spectacle, a treat none of the younger men—most in their twenties—had experienced in this world of economic and political turbulence. Battered and deflated by the continual fatigue of a generation-long depression in their native Russia, the boys yelped with pride and accomplishment.

Surveying the celebration from a darkened corridor aft of the command center, Dima Tereshkov could hardly blame them. And waiver from this euphoria he would not.

Kalinin rose from his command seat and turned to see the major and Zamatin peering at the men, his own satisfaction muted by professional decorum. Crossing to the pair, he couldn't help but clap them both on the shoulder.

"Tonight we will toast this great victory, my friends," the captain announced. "Our benefactors will be pleased, no?"

"Yes," the major said, his chiseled face managing a soft smile. His eyes scanned the crew some meters away. "They performed admirably, even more so in extricating us from the detonation site in time."

"Have you any news of the enemy boat?" Zamatin asked, out of turn, but not provoking a rebuke from the quiet Tereshkov.

"Most likely crushed, but given time, and all things being equal, we'll find them as the radiation is filtered from our sensors."

Tereshkov nodded, his concern for the pursuit of the North American boat distracted by the replay. Focusing, he said, "I have instructions to proceed to Mirnyy at once."

"Mirnyy's a long departure, and not the amenities these men were promised."

Tereshkov grew to his full height, now a good three centimeters above the not-insignificant Kalinin. "Long dead are the days of gunning and running, dear captain," he bellowed, attracting the skewed glances of the crew, their cheers now muted. "Putting into Novolazarevskaya after showing up the enemy—as if that were a victory in itself—will not be this operation's crowning achievement. We are at war! These Yankees have destroyed the fabric of our culture! You would all do well to think upon what we have accomplished, and what we have yet to do. Now, Captain," his azure eyes were narrowed like fine blades, "set sail for Mirnyy. The next act of our operation is ready…in less than forty-eight hours, the world is ours."

CHAPTER TWENTY-SEVEN

Twilight hues lowered towards the horizon, the sun's austral spring rays hovering over the wide curvature. A glance up through the *Deltsky*'s windscreen by Kindred revealed a smattering of stars in the zenith, their crystalline light unwavering beacons through the driest atmosphere on Earth. Flecks of orange, red and violet flashed upwards into the sky from the distant north, as if stroked by a great watercolor brush.

"Would you look at that!" Kindred gasped, her oxygen mask limp by her right cheek.

Mason leaned over the large diameter of the steering wheel. "Aurora, huh? Funny we didn't see anything that brilliant on our first traverse."

Kindred fished around in her parka and produced a holobook. Aiming it at the aurora, she clicked several lidar photo-holographs, which she then fed to the device's projector. Creating a handheld holograph, Kindred studied the sparkling aurora in the comfort of the *Deltsky*'s cabin.

"Huh, particle flux is strange...."

Mason glanced at the floating holograph. "How so?"

Kindred rubbed her eyes, nearly disbelieving the data her holobook displayed. "It matches what Townsend gave us. Tau-neutron decay particles."

Mason's neck craned up at the windscreen again, this time in haste. "It's gone...."

"One of the four warheads...."

Kindred turned to see Mason floor the gas pedal, his right hand manhandling the gearshift, then felt a shudder. The diesel engine

rumbled beneath them, propelling the agents at a rip-roaring sixty kilometers per hour; good enough for one day's drive straight through fourteen hundred klicks. Mirnyy still lay nearly half a continent away, but she
knew the *Deltsky* was going to get there a bit sooner now. A brief pause
along the way would be called for when Kindred relieved Mason for a
quick snack break and nap, then a determined push to the coast of Cape
Davis and the Pravda Shore.

En route, Kindred memorized the layout of the Mirnyy
Observatory grounds, consulting her holobook's detailed schematics
acquired over years of reconnaissance from submarines and the USNA
ACF. A sprawling complex set against four ice-locked islands—not
unlike McMurdo in many ways, actually—meant the grounds were quite
formidable, perhaps even ridiculously difficult to breach. Devising an
insertion point would try both agents' skills and creativity; she could
count on the Confederation garrisoning Mirnyy's grounds with a comparable number of troops as ALEXEI, perhaps even more so. There would
be no jumpjet waiting in the wings to extract them should the agents
encounter resistance.

Plowing twin *Deltsky* tracks over the wasteland of Ridge B, Mason
and Kindred were truly alone, physically, if not spiritually.

Λ

"Agent Feltham," Chief of the Boat Tucker said, raising his voice over the
din of the control center, "Brantley has received an Alpha communiqué
from CONUS encoded to you."

Feltham stepped down from the navigation level and crossed over
to the radio shack forward of the planesmen. Careful to keep herself
balanced in the tilting cabin, she stepped gingerly through the standing
water. Feltham knocked on the door and was met by Chief Dawes, who
admitted her. Making space for the agent at his post, Brantley stood from
his seat and handed her a set of cordless headphones for confidential-
ity.

Nodding to the man, she placed the phones over her ears and
tapped a button on Brantley's SID. Squawks of interference—no doubt
a consequence of the many channels through which the Alpha were
relayed—sounded before the distinctive timbre of Chief Louris came
on.

*"Feltham, Chief here. Your message was successfully relayed. We
have scrambled a jumpjet from Strike Force Zeta to extract you. ETA is
thirty-six minutes."*

Feltham toggled the SID's voxlink. "Feltham, Chief. Roger that.
Sir, I'm sure you're aware of *Triton*'s situation, so I'll make this brief:

we're taking on water like a sieve. Bell and I are going to have to disembark. We'll be hot, Chief...there's still a wolf out here who may have our number."

"*Understood, Agent. We've got PACCOM's best eyes on that Grasshopper to spot you. Chief out.*"

"Feltham out." She closed the voxlink and disconnected the channel. Doffing the headphones, she thanked the boys and shut the radio shack's door behind her.

"Agent Feltham," Mitchum said, his hands akimbo as he stood over the planesmen, "I have the sneaking suspicion your time with us is short."

She smiled and waded across the deck floor to him. "Requesting permission to disembark, Captain."

"I'm not sure I can authorize that," he said, his eyes askance to Tucker. "Chief?"

"Captain."

"You have your chiefs ready for the agents' departures?"

"Aye, aye, Captain."

Mitchum nodded. "See them out."

"Fare thee well, sailor," Feltham said to Mitchum, stepping away.

"By the way, Agent, thanks for that tip. And keeping us alive."

The skipper tipped his cap to her, receiving a smile in return.

Moments later, Tucker led Feltham and Bell through the bowels of *Triton*, facing a veritable gauntlet of applause and whoops from an assemblage of petty officers and chiefs. Inside the "black pipe" the hoopla was deafening but the two agents reluctantly soaked in the gratitude; the sailors had saved their lives as much as the agents had theirs.

Fed continual applause, the trio reached the Spec Ops hatch—where the two Company agents had started this voyage—and stopped at a two-meter-tall ladder bolted to the bulkhead. Nowhere to go but up now.

"Control center, Tucker," the chief spoke into his voxlink, "are we cleared for opening the hatch?"

"*Chief, control center. You are cleared to open the hatch. Grasshopper* Jiminy Cricket *is awaiting our guests. Control center out.*"

"There's one final parting gift we haven't quite given you yet," Tucker said, the compartment now eerily quiet. "As our guests, we're obliged to give you an official send off...."

On cue, the contingent of sailors all revealed canisters of shaving cream from behind their backs and launched a sustained fusillade at the helpless agents. Spattered with foam, Feltham and Bell yelped but acquiesced to the sailors' exuberance.

Tucker wore a great grin as he clapped the foamy shoulders of the agents. "Now you're both extended family. Take care out there on the big, bad surface world."

Λ

After a quick cleansing, the two agents watched and listened in *Jiminy Cricket's* passenger cabin as Louris reported the update from the Glass Castle.

"...Suffice to say POTUS is not happy with the developments in The Hague, nor the sudden Ether detonation you two experienced," Louris said. Two bloodshot eyes blinked repeatedly, hint enough that Louris was due for a holographic communiqué breather. Particularly from the staff of the leader of the free world.

Feltham pursed her lips. "Tell us something we don't know."

"What's the latest from de Lis?" Bell asked, getting to the heart of the matter.

"Yastanni is critical. If he makes it through the next twenty-four hours it'll be a miracle. De Lis suspects Confederation proxies smuggled in a pre-fab personnel drone, probably one of those Venezuelan knock-offs. Cheap, but it evaded the checkpoints."

"I suppose it's too late to lodge a protest with the Dutch authorities," Feltham said with snark. "Perhaps we can upload a security manual to them for next time."

"That's for Harrelman to lose sleep over. Our job is to track down where that Confederation sub sped away to, and whether they have more of those goddamn devices aboard." Louris sighed, his normally unflappable and parted coiffure showing signs of ruffles. "On a personal note, the brass won't be so kindhearted in their public sentiments, but I at least am glad you're not swimming with the fishes, so that counts for something."

Feltham twirled her hair, the irony of her identical involuntary reaction lost on her. "Thank you, Chief. Finishing off the Confederation will be easier with an Alpha from Mason, though."

Louris shook his head. "He's too far from our auxiliary satellite link-ups, so you're to consider him neutralized until further notice. But if I know Mason, he's well on his way to getting to the bottom of it."

Λ

"I wish I knew where the hell I was going," Mason said, cranking the steering wheel hard left, pulling the *Deltsky* off a beaten traverse course and onto rougher, virgin terrain. A monolithic slab hundreds of meters wide loomed ahead, blocking the Davis Sea and the horizon beyond.

Leaning over the wheel, Mason strained to locate Mirnyy Observatory's grounds, seeing nothing but encrusted pack ice and scattered stratospheric UV. The *Deltsky*'s panoramic view was of an alabaster desert pockmarked by stony outcroppings and ice dunes, a field whose distances could not be measured by human eyes.

Kindred held up her everpresent holobook. Before the pair, two separate cubic constructs glowing in yellow were embedded in a blue mass. "It's hard to see the observatory grounds behind the ice buildup, but spectroscopic and thermal lidar cut right through most of it." An index finger tapped the lowest levels of the northernmost building. "Scans are inconclusive here, however. Thermal hits—most likely people—keep phasing out after a certain depth."

"My bet is they've shielded the area," Mason added.

"Perhaps. Then we know they've got something here worth protecting."

She switched the thermal image to a satellite-based view, clearly revealing the two-hundred-year-old facility, scattered over sprawling grounds. Zooming in, smaller trailers orbited the far-larger buildings, showcasing the helter-skelter construction method over the course of decades. An iceroad bisected the buildings, leading up a steep cut in the mountainface from a dock on the Pravda Shore and rounding to a route just behind their current position; where Cape Davis was once a monolithic, sheer cliff, the Confederation had blasted away millions of tonnes of rock to facilitate this improved seaside port. No longer a secret well-hidden from Western eyes, Mirnyy was now the forward operating base in the Confederation's opening front to a war.

"The best approach seems to be from this route, southeast here," Kindred said, pointing at the holograph. Right angles intersected off the buildings' many exterior walls, creating a mosaic of green and red triangles over the field. "These sensor shadows give us blindspots to creep up to. Park us just far enough that the perimeter micro-vibration sensors won't pick up the vehicle...and I'll do the rest with IFAR."

"It'd be easier if we could just tunnel in," Mason said, manhandling the gearshift. He turned the wheel again, pulling the *Deltsky* onto a narrow incline, the ridge dead ahead.

Billowing diesel exhaust into the frigid air, the *Deltsky* struggled upwards, its over thirty-hour, continuous trek wearing down the engine. Designed for the harsh Antarctic climate, the vehicle's advanced age regardless began to work against the agents, becoming more a liability than an asset.

Mason eyed the dashboard's engine display, a faltering yellow icon. "Something's telling me we won't be in any danger of getting too close...this thing isn't going to make it to the perimeter."

Kindred's shoulders slumped. "Hoofing it again...?"

"It'll be the least of our problems."

Mason finally killed the *Deltsky*'s engine at the ten-degree incline point, its hulking frame giving a great sigh in relief. Ice crystals formed thick concretions on the chassis that engine warmth had previously melted; soon it would be a mammoth waiting to be dug up from a snowy grave.

Wrestling his helmet over his balaclava, Mason followed it up with the oxygen mask over his stubbly cheeks. The aches of weary bones complained enough to make him forget that even his follicles were bitching about the abuse. He then grabbed a small tool pouch on the cab floor and buckled it next to his holobook on his waist belt. Meanwhile, Kindred secured her salopette and parka, and gave a thumbs up to Mason.

Completing the final equipment checks on each other, principally their oxygen tanks, the pair proceeded onto the pack ice again. The terrain sent cold waves of pain through to their feet as ice crunching commenced their latest travail; how anyone could voluntarily venture to this continent was beyond Mason.

Kindred clutched her holobook in both hands and pointed it at the peak, where the north building lay. To their naked eyes, the facility seemed to be no farther than two hundred meters, but lidar told a different tale; a fluctuating numerical readout on the interface flashed point-seven-three-four kilometers. *On a clear day one could see forever....*

Hunkered down, Mason and Kindred trotted across the distance, their forms soon mere specks from the vantage of the *Deltsky*. Following Kindred's prescribed approach, she led them to a bare outcropping halfway up the incline where they took a breather, then shifted to a lateral ascent due north. A direct route straight up the hill was no-go land, one of the red triangles open to easy Confederation detection. Moving laterally, the duo hid inside a blindspot created by a larger, foundation outcropping at the peak; it didn't take them too far north, just a few meters, enough to remain in the blindspot before they charged east up the incline again, the green triangle narrowing towards a point on the northwest foundation wall.

Racing—as much as they could in the bulky snow gear—up the remaining few hundred meters, the agents soon hugged the exterior wall of the north building and its utilitarian, function-with-no-form architecture. A dilapidated structure that once rose over the pack ice, but, like all other buildings in Antarctica, succumbing to a slow ice burial, the facility's flat-metal roof now towered a mere two meters.

Well aware of the dozen meters of pure ice below their boots, Mason and Kindred trod over the precarious terrain, gloves in constant contact with the cinder-block walls. Reminded of the Nor'easters he and his upstate New York grandparents periodically endured in his youth, Mason set one steadfast foot in front of the other, his arms out at ninety-degrees. Kindred marginally had it better, her lower height affording her greater stability, but with her California background, she knew she was most definitely not in her comfort zone.

Thirty minutes of numbing snow drifts later, the agents encountered the far wall, and the expanse beyond: the frozen, coastal cliff of Cape Davis. Glinting off the far waters and floating ice lozenges, the late morning sun ensconced the agents in ribbons of light before escaping behind clouds of haze. Kindred gestured towards the edge of the cliff, a hundred meters hence.

Evading the no-go zone, Mason and Kindred crossed the distance and paused at land's end, a steep and icy Dover, where only snow drifts and broken shelf ice could go. Fifty meters under their boots lay the frozen sea.

A roar erupted far below, loud enough to be heard in their helmets. Kindred yelped and turned her head sharply; from her vantage she witnessed a dark mass surfacing through an ice floe on the Davis Sea. The object floated towards the cape dock, where a narrow delta of jagged, black rock mingled with azure ocean water. Above the rocks, snow-covered gangplanks fingered outwards from layered platforms to meet the object. Seated at the dock end of the iceroad was a whitewashed Vu-1024 *Lyagooshka* "Toad," whereas further back, a trio of incoming *Deltskys* traversed the frozen avenue.

Mason tapped Kindred's left shoulder. "That can't be good...."

She unclipped her holobook and scanned the vicinity. Successive layers of matter peeled away as the lidar beam skimmed the dark mass. "*Kursk* class submarine. You suppose that's our mysterious launch platform?"

A chuckle left his lips. "I wish our luck was this good in Vegas. I'm also betting Feltham and Bell have made contact with it as well."

"Quantum analysis does indicate substructural trauma, just like Chagang-Do."

Neither of them had to say it; whatever tau-neutrino decay particles they detected on the traverse to Mirnyy, this Confederation *Kursk* class boat had been involved. And the presence of that Toad betrayed high-level Confederation interest twice over. Mason's instincts were resolutely focused on a singular task:

"We've gotta get down there."

Kindred craned her head around, noting the plethora of nonexistent trails around the cliff to the Pravda Shore, nearly half-a-klick distant. "I'll give you a week's pay if you explain to me how we do that without flying."

"I'll get back to you on that."

The two turned away from the cliff and started towards the northern building, certain that the Confederation's machinations on the coast were ominously connected to the activities the agents had disrupted deep inside Vostok. Mason just hoped their arrival wasn't too late; the world didn't need a repeat of TauTona.

CHAPTER TWENTY-EIGHT

"Everything we need to know is going to be down there," Mason said, huffing out breath that fogged his helmet. "And I think it all starts through here."

He and Kindred jogged the final few steps to the opposite side of the building and stopped, both reaching for their knees in exhaustion. Gathering his strength, Mason rose up and produced a collapsible shovel from the tool pouch.

"Where exactly is that old observatory entryway?" he asked over his voxlink, his HUD offline after several days of low juice in the power cells.

Kindred scanned the wall with her holobook. She waved her left hand several times to direct him. "You're going to dig with that thing? You might be there a while...it's a meter under this ice crust."

"Ah, you're not getting off too easy. You're gonna help me by marking a hole." Mason's hand dove back into the pouch and retrieved a photon saw, a ten-centimeter-long chrome pistol grip with a narrow handguard and short barrel. He turned and handed the tool to her. "Now don't bash it up, you'll need it to cut through the door when I'm done."

"Aye aye."

Mason trusting in her surgical skills perhaps a bit too much, Kindred thought, she nonetheless obeyed the command. Pulling the finger trigger she let the pack ice have the full brunt of the photon saw. Ice chips flew upwards from the nigh-invisible nanoscale beam of gamma-ray photons, each centimeter of her hands' movements slicing into the decades' old accumulation with ease.

Mason joined her in chipping away at the ice when Kindred was about halfway through her semi-circle. The pair broke a hole roughly fifty centimeters in diameter, uncovering more of the rusty corrugated wall first laid down centuries ago. Hacking for another twenty minutes, Mason scooped out enough pack ice to contact the top of the door frame. A bit more digging and he would have a space large enough to slide through.

After some help from the saw, of course.

Mason motioned Kindred over and pointed to the few exposed centimeters of the door panel. "Make us a new door, Sha."

She plopped her small frame inside the new hole and fired up the saw, placing its business end against the door. Iridescent sparks of freshly sliced metal bounced off her parka and onto the ice, sizzling and smoking until cooling into ground pepper-like droppings. Her arms and torso reverberating as a veteran steelworker would on any colossal construction, Kindred severed the panel from its frame without mercy. Perhaps owing to the extreme cold and therefore its inherent brittleness, the portioned metal slab conceded defeat and was no match for a final assault by the combined boots of Mason and Kindred.

In identical fashion as Vostok, the pressurized maw created by the agents blew out a great rush of air, flinging ice chips and metal filings back at the pair. Mason crouched into the hole past Kindred and went in feet first, his left hand grasping the intact door frame, the right his E4.10c "Bull" sidearm.

With Mason dropping into the dark abyss, Kindred proceeded as well, eager to leave behind the howling winds and disorienting Antarctic wilderness.

Two sets of boot thumps echoed throughout the room, a good two meters below where they entered. Outflowing air buffeted them, a squealing banshee that subsided once Mason and Kindred moved away from the wall. They drained the last few decent amps of power from their helmet lamps, bringing spotty illumination again to a space long since abandoned, if the flying dust motes and the rust stains on the ceiling were any indications.

Their flickering lamplights unveiled more prefab corrugate-style interior decoration, which the two were by now accustomed to. A group of office desks, filled with stacks of ancient printer paper and books, blocked the one entry door. No cubicle seemed untouched, let alone intact. Nothing short of a panicked riot to Mason.

"Looks like they didn't want anybody to work weekends," Kindred quipped.

Mason laid his hands on the desk closest to the door and pushed it several centimeters, creating enough space to squeeze through. Just that minor disturbance released a storm of dust which was quickly sucked out by their impromptu entryway. Clean tomes featuring a plethora of astronomical photographs now looked him in the eyes, reminding Mason that this was at once a true observatory, now perverted to Project Ether madness.

Lamp light in the corridor beyond soon yielded to near darkness, leaving the agents with one less sensory input.

"Damn, power's dead," he groaned. "Governor Remarque's equipment wasn't rated for an extended trek in the wild, I guess."

"We can make do."

Mason laid a hand on Kindred's shoulder. "Hold up—let's lighten our load and get these tanks of our backs. This atmosphere is pressurized and we're not halfway to space anymore."

Both agents undid the straps to their tanks and assisted the other in discarding the heft they'd been dragging around. Oxygen masks were detached as well and thrown to the floor. Mason lifted his helmet off and massaged his neck, cracking several vertebrae. He slid his balaclava up over his chin, then tugged it back in one swift pull.

Kindred eyed his matted hair, noting the upright spikes in the residual light. "Never thought I'd say this but you look better with the helmet on."

"Remind me of that next time you wear your bob again."

She shook her head and removed her own balaclava, content to join the frizzy party.

Stumbling in the narrow hallway while waiting for their eyesight to adjust, they walked a few meters, passing wall-mounted charts, discarded and smashed computers on the floor and spaghetti strings of cords and cables littering the corridor, some simply hanging from above.

Kindred's gloved hand brushed a long strand of suspended cables away. "Did they trash their stuff on purpose?"

"I've seen worse in dorms."

"Good point. Huh, Inauguration Day at the White House is just as fun."

Mason pointed to a door on the right a few steps away. Bolted to it was a sign printed in large red Cyrillic script. "Aha. Stairwell."

He wrapped his hands around the door's release bar and pushed it down. Jolting free with the ease of a decrepit tomb lock, the door hesitated before Mason's strength overcame the creeping corrosion and swung it towards them.

Kindred slid in after Mason, the two pausing to gather their bearings. No longer fearing a surprise resident, she booted up her holobook and scanned the descending stairwell. A virtual flyby of the stairwell zoomed past on the holobook's imager, giving the agents a bird's eye view as the scan descended flight after flight until reaching the bottom some tens of meters below.

"If nothing else it gets us in the right neighborhood," he said, the holograph's spectral glow reflecting in his face. "You ready?"

Her left hand unbuttoned her waist holster and produced her RT-01/9V pistol in a split-second.

"That's why I handpicked you."

The agents proceeded down the stairwell methodically; deliberate steps from each boot were positioned just right on the metal grating to reduce the footfalls in the exquisite echo chamber. Fifteen minutes' worth of steady, spiralling progress led them to the last flight, sealed behind another closed door.

"Large dock, an underground motor pool," Kindred said, her eyes watching the evolving holograph in her hand. Probing beyond the door, her holobook constructed a miniature schematic as if Kindred drove through the space herself.

Mason noted the display image, memorizing it for their next course of action. "Must have been built recently...I don't remember this dock appearing on the last intel reports."

"Surprise, surprise. They hid it from the Global Security Net. Our *Kursk* is just out the back door here."

"Let's not keep our hosts waiting any longer."

Mason manhandled the door release, pushing the door open softly, thanks to the newer, rust-free metal surfaces. Peering into the narrow crack, his eyes swept the loading bay up and down, left to right, examining the spacious real estate; it looked to have been blasted out of the very foundation of the observatory's grounds. The bay's roof towered nearly fifteen meters above and the walls spanned the same wide. Twelve loading drones—state-of-the-art automated cranes with arms suspended from low, half-level trusswork that dominated the right side of the bay, creating a small motor pool—were housed inside, ready to receive and process hulking hardware for industrial construction in the temperate zone. The left side remained fully open to the actual ceiling, allowing larger vehicles, terrestrial or aerial, to reside.

Beyond that, the forward doors were up, exposing it to the Pravda Shore. No vehicles—aerial or terrestrial—rested yet inside the ample parking lanes, giving him cause to think it was in the midst of a large operation, lending more credence to the appearance of that *Kursk* and Toad.

"All right, we can—"

Kindred halted Mason this time, her gloved hand pulling him back. "Stone man," she whispered, "I'm reading three more neutrino capture cages out there on the dock. Three of the four missing from Vostok."

His countenance hardened. A flat, determined sneer appeared on Mason for the first time in a while, Kindred recalled.

"Whatever they plan on doing, we're the first best chance to put an end to it. There have to be detonators or some sort of similar mechanism around here."

Kindred furrowed her brow. "What's the plan?"

He turned his head back to the bay again, bringing his E4.10c "Bull" up close to his temple. "We're gonna take it down. Nobody's ever getting their hands on this research again...!"

Λ

"*...You're to consider him neutralized....*" The phrase mingled with the half-a-million other musings and concerns in Feltham's brain. Twice in this investigation Mason, barely a month into their partnership, had been or was to be among the "missing," Company speak for KIA, he and Kindred two future stars on the Memorial Wall in the Glass Castle. It was a prospect Feltham could not accept and would not until she could go no further in proving Louris wrong.

And she was not about to allow the Confederation to stop her.

She simmered with righteous rage, the passenger cabin inside *Jiminy Cricket*, even in the crisp coolness of high-altitude flight, not dampening Feltham's edge. Hours into the parabolic jaunt to the ACF, she and Bell compared notes on their course of action and debated Mason's intentions and capabilities. Vostok Station had been his original goal, and if at all possible, the enigma of Mirnyy Observatory would be investigated as well, the two sites entwined in some perverse Chinese finger trap. Step into one, and the other inexorably pulled you in, too.

Mirnyy, by geography being the nearest target for *Jiminy Cricket*, lay less than twenty minutes away, making it Feltham's first priority. All logic pointed to Mirnyy as the closest refreshment and refurbishment point for the Confederation boat that had nearly sunk *Triton*, if such a maneuver were necessary. It went unsaid between the two agents, but Feltham believed payback was in store for the Confederation's provocative and outright senseless destruction of Îlots des Apotres.

Finding Mason and that damned thing consumed her.

Feltham took a chance on betting that the wolf sailed back to Antarctica, instead of pursuing the *Triton*. Even the half-mad Confederate sailors had to know that an USNAN flotilla escort was out there, ready to pounce should they decide to approach the South Atlantic. The only course *was* Mirnyy, not Novolazarevskaya.

Rising from her seat at the head of the passenger cabin, Feltham disregarded safety protocols and crossed the two meters to the cockpit, sounding the cockpit's approach chime. Steadying herself, she stood behind the seats of pilot Captain Thubron and co-pilot Lieutenant Cohen, neither of whom betrayed their surprise.

"Captain, we might be flying into an angry swarm of Confederates," she warned over her helmet vox. "I've got good reason to believe the sub that blew up the Apostle Isle is anchored there."

"Funny about that, Agent Feltham," Cohen said, flipping a button on his interface. "I'm tracking a wave disturbance here off Cape Davis. Been there for the better part of an hour now."

A small spike, nearly a gentle plateau in a waveform so similar to what Feltham saw in the radio room of *Triton*, rolled over a flatline on Cohen's holographic instrument panel.

That's it...I was right. "Great. Captain, I need to know your armaments. How long can we hold off a concentrated infantry defense?"

"We have the standard anti-personnel cannon, the type I'm sure you've seen in action on your extracurricular activities," he answered. "And we sure fly higher."

Feltham tried to smile, but a lame smirk grew on her face instead. "If worse comes to worse, I'll need your fancy flying to get us close. I'm betting my boss is somewhere near the observatory grounds. And you can be sure that damn wave is defended by troops eager to bring this bird down once we're spotted."

"We'll make sure we don't."

Feltham stepped back, bracing her left arm against the upper bulkhead separating the cockpit from the cabin. Toggling her voxlink, she raised Bell. "Tommy, break out your binocs and keep me apprised on the ground situation."

Back in his seat, Bell ripped open his equipment case and pulled out all-weather binoculars, small enough to fit inside his enclosed hand. Pushing his helmet's faceplate back, he looked through the binocs and scoped out Cape Davis, several dozen klicks distant.

"I'm squaring up the landmass now," Bell said, following five seconds of silence. "Looks like any other super-secret outpost we're not supposed to be aware of."

"What?"

Bell rephrased his answer. "I can't see shit-all."

"Then don't keep quiet once you can," Feltham said between gritted teeth. Slapping the voxlink, she severed the channel and sighed, making sure no one heard her discomfort. The last thing Feltham needed was for anyone to get any ideas about her doubting the prosecution of this op. If she had to suffer pangs of indecision—even in the throes of rage—she'd do so in silence, just as she'd done all her years.

Λ

Mason's back hugged the wall nearest their entry point, his feet walking onto the half-meter-wide catwalk, just ahead of him a short set of grated steps leading below. Kindred followed to his left, her eyes panning the expanse all the while. She had replaced her holobook onto her waist belt and now clutched her sidearm in both hands, her stance bent at the knees. Ready to sprint if necessary, the two agents slunk in the shadows of the bay, listening for the voices of troopers in-between the involuntary whirring and clicking of the various mechanical and electrical equipment.

Slung up like inverted sewing machine needles—albeit on a two-meter-sized scale—the double rows of loading drones gave decent head-to-torso cover to the clandestine pair, allowing them some maneuvering room as they stepped onto the half-level. The business end of the drones were electromagnetic claws, quite literally supersized needlenose pliers, perched on the ends of folded, extendable arms that dropped through rectangular holes in the half-level's flooring to any waiting vehicles.

Creeping between the double rows' narrow gap, Kindred fell behind Mason until her holobook chirped. Flipping the device up from her waistbelt, she grimaced.

"Our friends are back!"

Mason swiveled around. "Wha—!"

"Drones!"

Particle blasts ricocheted off the loading drone armatures, leading Mason and Kindred to jump off the edge of the half-level to the floor below. Ducking below the idle loading drones, the pair crouched under the rectangular holes, half-a-meter above. The loading drone's flying kin of six KD-7s descended via an open portal at the roof's apex, a nest of mechanical hornets with uncanny proficiency to seek out carbon dioxide exhalations. Hovering a slight meter above the half-level, but still out of sight, the KD-7s methodically circled the loading drones, probing and developing angles for attack.

With anxious breath, Mason squatted on one hand and knee,

tracing the rampant buzzing from ear to ear with his E4.10c. Meanwhile, at the next loading drone over, Kindred cycled through a series of holobook hacks, her fingers scrolling over icons in silent stealth mode. Her eyes darted up to the claw's stamped manufacturing data, clearly reading the Cyrillic script "translation" coupled with rows of Mandarin Chinese characters.

Perfect.

Discovering the exact model of loading drone with the IIA's and DIA's respective databases inside her holobook's quantum drive, Kindred accessed a zombie hack. Thumbing the impromptu arrow command key controls, she turned the loading drone directly above her into her proxy, bringing it to life.

Mason, startled by the claw near him rumbling into activity, saw the KD-7s' search lights slew over to the loading drone. Wasting no time, he aimed through a grate slit and squeezed a round into the only visible drone, blowing a hole into its main body, which crashed in a cloud of shrapnel. Another drone to his right dropped down in front of his E4.10c's barrel. Fixing his gaze on it, Mason shot it out of the air within a half-second before it could focus on him.

Still bathed in the spotlights of the KD-7s, Kindred's zombie drone rotated on its armature "elbow," its claws opened like a maw. The distinctive hum of an activated electromagnet brought a brief smile to Kindred. Thumbing the control keys again, she lunged the claw upward, bringing the powerful EM waves irresistibly closer to the KD-7s.

A screech and clunk signalled her first success. Mason peeked for his own confirmation, giving Kindred a thumbs up when the ensnared KD-7 was stuck face-first into the claw. She maneuvered the claw again, wheeling it from left to right, plucking a second drone from the air, and a third.

Mason peered around the armature above him, catching sight of one more KD-7 that apparently learned from the misfortunes of its brethren. Hovering two-and-a-half meters away, the drone probed the electromagnetic threat to its survival, bobbing and weaving about the EM field. Sizing up the claw, the KD-7 sighted its particle cannon and fired on it, doing nothing but bouncing particles off its metal skin. Strangely computing the claw as a bigger threat than the agents, the KD-7 didn't see Mason leap outwards and put two rounds through its fuselage.

Kindred ended the misery of her captured drones, instructing the zombie loading drone to close its claws, snapping and exploding the three KD-7s with vigor. She clipped her holobook to her waistbelt again and walked out next to Mason. Wiping her brow despite the subzero temperatures, she grinned. "That was fun."

Mason dusted off his parka. "Now let's go get—"

A barrage of shouts in Russian beat against their ears, but the two soldiers riding a charging GAZ-57009 Centaur, its biomechanical hooves clanging over the hard floor from the open bay entrance, hooked them. Mason and Kindred scattered as gunfire from its DShKM-2109b heavy machine gun erupted, pounding craters into the walls and floor. Chunks of charred metal and concrete created a whirlwind of shrapnel.

Mason clambered up the stairsteps, ascending to the half-level with his hands shielding his eyes. Kindred tucked her sidearm into her parka and leapt up. Grabbing hold of the rectangular hole above her, she pulled herself up and crouched amongst the loading drone armatures, drawing her RT-01/9V. Covered behind the mechanical forest, Kindred unloaded her sidearm at the Centaur, picking the driver off first with a hail of particle bursts.

Below them, the driver-less Centaur compensated for the fallen soldier by reapportioning its stance, its biomimical quantum brain taking control. The gunner slung the DShKM-2109b at the loading drones, smashing the machines apart with abandon and doing his damnedest to flush Kindred out.

Now Mason took the bow off the gift he'd just been handed. Lying flat on his back he aimed his E4.10c and squeezed several rounds, more than enough to put the gunner out of commission. The Centaur galloped riderless in the bay, circling several times in a bizarre sight guaranteed to give the agents the creeps.

Mason disregarded the display and spied another pair of soldiers meters out, drawing close, AKM-6A70s at the ready. With cover fire from his partner keeping the agents at bay, the third soldier reigned the Centaur in and climbed aboard, signalling with his free hand. The fourth soldier, carrying an equipment case, ran out some five meters onto the pack ice.

What's his story? Fearing these guys were sending the heavy artillery, Mason gambled and launched to the floor. Vulnerable to the quick-witted soldier who might just gallop up and put a round in his head, Mason rolled under the half-level where the Centaur would have more difficulty reaching him. His blue laser sight targeting for him, Mason struck the third soldier in the shoulder, who sounded out in pain. The agent rested on his right arm long enough to sight the Centaur's massive legs and put several rounds in them, severing the synthetic muscles inside. The Centaur crumpled under its collapsed mass not even a second later, burying the hapless soldier.

"Sha! SHA!" Mason shouted, looking up to her through the grating. "Get the one outside! Outside!"

Kindred skimmed her eyes along her zombie drone's outstretched maw to glimpse the fourth soldier twenty meters away on the pack ice. Going on instinct, she lined up the fleeing soldier in her RT-01/9V's sight, her height giving her a better shot than Mason. The motion blur of his off-white and grey camouflage and its blending into the environment notwithstanding, she pinpointed his legs and fired twice, hitting both in a flash. A puff of snow and ice rose from the ground where he crashed, an equipment case sliding out from his right hand.

One last shot from Kindred brought Mason back to his feet. Kindred flung herself over the half-level and landed, then swooped past Mason, sprinting onto the ice. Mason crossed over to the third soldier, who writhed on the floor, and pilfered his AKM-6A70; no sense letting the guy shoot him in the back.

On the ice, Kindred trotted towards the fallen soldier, his cries growing louder as she approached. Bearing down, and forgetting her own aching muscles, she closed the gap and halted a few seconds later. Mindful of any concealed weapons he may possess, she held her RT-01/9V at arm's length, targeting his head and upper body. Kindred walked over to the dropped case and picked it up, never taking an eye off him.

She studied the locks by the case's handle and knew the perfect tool for the job. Reaching inside her parka, Kindred withdrew a set of lockpicks and attacked the lock, making quick work. She set the case down and opened it, revealing a double-decker shelf nestled with three chrome-clad plungers, with room for twenty total, all in foam emplacements. The trio of plungers, each ten centimeters long, were topped by triangular molded metal and designed to be punched by hand into the nosecone of a warhead. Further digging produced a matching set of cylindrical timers on the bottom shelf.

"Mason, this is it," she yelled back at him, her superior inspecting his newly acquired weapon a few meters back.

He eyed the downed soldier with suspicion before walking over to Kindred. He'd fallen just a mere dozen paces from scaffolding that led to a precarious series of grated stairsteps, twisting and winding thirty meters towards the Pravda Shore below. Drab granite rocks from the removal blast formed a rough-hewn wall just to the left, to which the scaffolding had been bolted some time recently. The agents were literally standing on the precipice.

"Detonators and timers?" he asked.

"Yep. Course of action, *mon capitan*?"

Mason knelt down by Kindred and inspected the booty. Satisfied, he closed the case and allowed Kindred to take possession of it.

He jutted his thumb to the shore. "Blow this place to Kingdom Come."

Rising to their feet, the pair began to turn toward the loading bay until a low growl and heavy boot falls grabbed their attention. Ascending the stairsteps the fallen trooper attempted to take, a tall, hulking figure, his buzzcut hair glistening in the hazy sunlight, walked forward.

Pausing at the pack ice, the huge man clapped his bear hands. Chiseled eyes in a rockface visage glared across the short distance to the agents, his icy stare putting Antarctica's catabatic winds to shame.

Mason caught his breath, his boots squeaking beneath him, the footwear almost imploring him to retreat. He reached into his pocket and tossed a set of keys over his shoulder to Kindred. "Get to the *Deltsky*," he said, not looking back to her.

Kindred covered the case behind her back, keeping it out of sight. Her RT-01/9V trained on the looming Confederate, she stepped backwards, keeping an eye on Mason all the while. He didn't have to instruct her on what to do; the plan was set.

The two circled each other, sizing up their respective opponents. Mason fingered the AKM-6A70. The Confederate's neck muscles tensed, an odd pulse flexing in his flesh. A split-second later Mason's right arm raised the AKM-6A70 to fire, but the figure's left arm covered a meter at the same time, grasped the barrel and wrenched it away. Gripped in his hands, the AKM-6A70 shattered like glass and fell to the ground in pieces.

CHAPTER TWENTY-NINE

"I am called MOLOTOK—'hammer' in your barbarian tongue," Major Dima Tereshkov stated, his English chopped into practiced tones. "And I intend for you to find out why."

Mason stood a good fifteen centimeters shorter than the built Russian, even in the hardy Arctic boots Remarque provided him. This MOLOTOK needed nary the warmth of a parka; his muscle mass was quite evident through the ink-hued FSB overcoat draped on his frame. And how in the hell he shattered that AKM-6A70 like matchsticks god only knew, the agent wondered.

Additionally, Tereshkov's quickness took Mason aback. Determined not to fall victim to the huge Russian's arms, Mason put two steps between himself and his opponent. MOLOTOK didn't seem to brandish a weapon; his intimidation and mass were deadly enough.

"Coward," MOLOTOK said in Russian, his contempt quite apparent. "As an imperialist Yankee your dishonesty measures up well. I will crush you and your pretty friend next. Did your government believe you could stop us? We have already won."

"So much for a handshake." Mason's nostrils flared. "Now if you'll excuse me, we have a mission underway."

Mason in no way intended to allow MOLOTOK to pursue Kindred, hoping through his obstruction that he'd buy her time, and perhaps even suss out more intel from this monstrosity all the while. Any other Confederate may have been easy pickings for the agent, his training and intelligence quickly overpowering the typical operative.

Except Tereshkov proved himself unlike any other typical Russian.

Leaping forward an easy two meters, the major's outstretched arms, tree trunks in size, wrapped around Mason's head. Tumbling onto the ice, their mass flung chips into the air. Two predators now broke the brink to a furious engagement.

Suffocating, drowning, collapsing, Mason's mind shut off, his reflexes and training taking command. Drawing his E4.10c from his waist holster would take more energy than he could afford; MOLOTOK's hands choked the life out of him second by second. His left hand slipped his four-centimeter-bladed survival knife from an external pocket and plunged it into whatever soft flesh he could find.

A howl filled Mason's ears once enough blood flowed again within his skull to hear. Rolling over his left shoulder, he fled Tereshkov's grasp, chiding himself for his carelessness. Breath filled his lungs but there was no time to draw deeply.

Steam rose from the crimson pool on the ice. Tereshkov sat on his haunches, his hand enveloping the knife hilt embedded in his clavicle. Bellowing, he pulled the blade out and dropped it in his freshly spilled blood.

"Give it up," Mason's voice sounded behind Tereshkov. The obvious click of the agent cocking his E4.10c followed up his ultimatum.

"Intimidation is a concept you will soon learn does not frighten me," Tereshkov replied, rising back to his feet. He turned and faced Mason, the wound failing to crack his stony visage. "I have...eliminated opponents more worthy of my energy."

A deafening scream burst into the clear air—Mason recognized it as a *Yastryeb* AV-8554d rocket—and echoed over the artificial valley, causing him to flinch. Squatting to evade any flying debris, Mason's jaw and cheekbone couldn't dodge the solid treads of Tereshkov's boot. Landing on his outstretched arm, his E4.10c flung away from him, Mason lay sprawled out, his vital points vulnerable. Another boot connected with his ribcage, sending waves of pain into his abdomen.

Gathering his willpower, Mason started to roll onto his back to defend himself. A cramp grew in his gut when he doubled over to stand; an unexpected thrust into the air knocked the wind from his lungs. Suspended a meter off the ground by the hands of Tereshkov, the Russian's glinting cobalt eyes were Mason's last sight before being thrown.

The agent collided with the granite wall, his exposed flesh bloodied and bruised by the rough-hewn rockface. He tumbled amid the loose stones until his bones found the ground, ending in a thud. Shaking his head, Mason's senses were scrambled, his eyesight and hearing vibrating, the pack ice quaking under him.

Mason was propelled upwards a second time, the sharp rocks shredding his parka and slicing his scalp as his head flopped back. Head, neck and shoulders now flared with pain as his body contacted the wall once more, held to by MOLOTOK.

Tereshkov's right arm reared back and unleashed a backhanded punch, his knuckles flattening the bridge of Mason's nose. Directly drawing Mason's blood for the first time, the major's demeanor digressed from cold business to heated fervor.

Battering Mason under repeated punches gave him *enjoyment*; yet he hadn't even begun to mete out a punishment worthy of the MOLOTOK moniker.

A hand the size of a bear paw cupped Mason's face and slammed the left side of it against the granite, loosening the pebbles underneath. Mason felt cartilage and bone crunch before the stinging in his left eardrum ceased and all the world went silent in that canal.

"I have to admit, Yankee, your will is strong...others of your imperialist ilk have sung like nightingales with lesser punishment." MOLOTOK's cracked lips perched closer to Mason's one good ear. "I would love to hear your wail!"

Tereshkov grasped the agent's parka collar and dragged him to the edge of the stairsteps. Mason flailed his arms, trying to connect with Tereshkov, every finger crooked in desperation. His mouth gasping for air as his nasal cavities were starved, Mason's body spasmed. His will, however, still would not break—he'd be damned if he cried out for this mother's enjoyment.

One shove sent Mason below, a rag doll to the mercy of the cold planks. Blinding pain coursed through his limbs. Bones popped and cracked while his extremities splintered, the parka providing less of a cushion than perhaps hoped. His tumbling ended at the first landing, his bloodied face hovering over the next set of steps down. Blood-tinged drops stinging his eyes, he nevertheless scoured the environment below for his next move. With his peripheral vision, he followed MOLOTOK, girding for the next attack, but the powerful Confederate paused at the head of the steps.

Voxlink? Mason couldn't hear or understand it.

MOLOTOK's fingers toggled the voxlink attached to his jacket after just ten seconds. As his heavy boots had thundered on their ascent, Tereshkov's footfalls did the same towards the fallen agent again. The major loomed over Mason, his large shadow cloaking his prey. Any second now his agile arms could reach over and finish the job.

"A final question, *doorak*, before I end your suffering. Where is the case?"

Every wave of grinding pain made Mason's body beg for mercy. It would be easy to give in; hell, he was on his stomach like a baby. He couldn't possibly offer any threat....

"Heh. Heh-heh...."

"THE CASE! Where did she go?!" Tereshkov ground his teeth together.

"Ffff...uck...you!"

Mason powered his right leg, firmly kicking Tereshkov's crotch with the back of his boot.

For once MOLOTOK stumbled, reaching out to the railing to catch himself. Given wriggle room to escape, Mason propelled himself down the next stairsteps, face first, choking up saliva and blood. Tereshkov cursed and flung himself at Mason, narrowly catching Mason's left boot. The agent wrapped his arms around a step and pulled hard, making himself as much of a pain in the ass to MOLOTOK as possible.

Λ

"Come on you SOB..." Kindred stomped the accelerator, hopping in the *Deltsky*'s driver's seat, "Get up the damn drive!"

Heaving in fits and starts, the *Deltsky* struggled to cross the pack ice where Kindred and Mason had abandoned it several hours ago. The cabin vibrated as the massive diesel engine just ahead of her fired off-kilter; Kindred had less difficulty with plunging and arming the detonator into their pilfered Ether warhead than this vehicle had with its design purpose.

With the *Deltsky*'s engine finally heating up, an excited Kindred slapped the steering wheel as she cranked the vehicle round the ice road's wide bend and up the ridge. Her eyes looked askance to the old-style, dialed speedometer: fifteen kph, eighteen, twenty-five....

Brown exhaust rose over the ridge. From far below the opposite end of the ice road, the *Deltsky*'s engine grill and headlamps broke the horizon, before the entire vehicle summited and descended at a greater speed.

The lay of the land spread out in front of Kindred; the dock populated with the assorted snowmobiles but a smattering of soldiers brandished their AKM-6A70s and *Yastryeb*s towards the sky—not a great sign.

What're they shooting at—? Kindred crouched in her seat, craning her neck towards the blinding UV sky. The first *Yastryeb* minutes ago streaked up but hadn't hit anything from what she could hear. Nothing she could do about that. She returned to her objective, glancing at her chronometer...under five minutes. She turned her head, looking out the driver's side window, the terrain below slipping by, the ice a blur of grey and rainbow streaks. It'd be hard, probably bonecrushing, but Kindred put that out of her head.

Pravda Shore neared, now just about half-a-klick distant. Mason was out of view, and honestly, she couldn't focus on anything anyway, or even see that submarine now. Kindred hoped to hell Mason'd had the sense to stop his stalling tactic with that Russian giant and high-tailed it. At least she knew Stone Man wouldn't hold his death against her....

Λ

Tereshkov growled, pebbles and bits of ice flinging up into his nostrils and eyes. He wrestled with the insolent IIA spy until his acute ears heard the rumbling of a diesel lorry across the ice road. His synapses put two and two together...instinctively he scrambled to his feet. Sprinting over the supine Mason, Tereshkov bolted down the remaining flight of stairsteps and hoofed his way to a trio of idling snowmobiles, kept warm in the harsh climate. Mounting the nearest vehicle, he revved up its handle throttle and spun around to face the ice road's ascent, throwing a torus of ice shards and exhaust fumes about him.

Tereshkov roared up the ice road, his heart racing, imploring the snowmobile faster and faster. The snowmobile was no match for the lorry, but it didn't need to be; lidar-tagging it for a *Yastryeb* strike from the Pravda Shore would do quite well. Toggling the controls for the lidar cannon on the snowmobile, he marked the lorry's cabin, and now awaited the sensor's signal to his men on the shore to abide it.

Λ

The two vehicles closed the distance, neither giving way.

Kindred couldn't believe the other driver was insane enough to plow her head-on. A tiny snowmobile couldn't stop her now. Gritting her teeth, duty took over and in one move she opened her door and looked down.

Λ

Swiveling as one on the Pravda Shore, the Confederation squad looked down from the sky and repositioned the *Yastryeb* launcher on the shoulder of the launch specialist. Another soldier loaded a rocket into the launcher and clapped the specialist's helmet. Acquiring the lidar signal, he tapped the *Yastryeb*'s fire-and-forget display, soon feeling the heat and force of its sudden launch. A tongue of flame and white exhaust pierced the cold air and arced up in a parabola.

Hardy congratulations and another round of claps on his helmet were the last actions any of the troopers committed before a unholy screech cracked the air around them. Within seconds the smoke cleared to reveal a three-meter-diameter crater, chunks of which rained down tens of meters away.

Descending low over the devastation and wheeling around, *Jiminy Cricket* surveyed the damage their coilgun's osmium rods wrought.

"Killbox checked," Lieutenant Cohen reported, the square shifting from flashing red to quiescent green. He then magnified the trajectory of the *Yastryeb* rocket on his display and followed its arc, hoping it wasn't headed back to *Jiminy Cricket*.

Feltham stood over his shoulder, reading the holographic interface. "That lorry...."

Λ

"Oh shit!"

Kindred cranked the steering wheel hard left, giving the *Deltsky* enough space to try to clear the *Yastryeb* rocket. The continual catabatic wind gusts overrode the rocket's lidar targeting, sending the rocket to the roof of the cargo trailer. Exploding in kaleidoscopic balls of flame, the roof ripped away, exposing the neutrino capture cylinder to the bitter Antarctic once again.

Her sharp turn brought the *Deltsky*'s front left wheel in contact with the suicidal snowmobile. The subsequent impact launched the cabin upwards and back down again in a terrible clamor. With time nearly up, Kindred put all her mass against the door and kicked herself free.

Kindred tumbled for meters, ice chips and pebbles following in a vortex that continued on after her body lay flat. A tremendous cacophony—a million ocean waves or a swarm of grumbling engines—pounded in her head, drilling through her mind. She contorted in a grimace, the sharp pain graduating to the feeling of hot blood leaking under her salopette.

The *Deltsky* continued to trundle down the ice road, its blazing trailer billowing a smoke cloud all the way to the Pravda Shore. Rattling side to side in the vehicle's rear, the neutrino capture cage ticked off its final seconds, the detonator core prompting the end sequence of its reprogramming. Delicate mechanical chambers expunged the remaining molecules of atmosphere to form a vacuum, siphoning a select few tau-neutrinos from the solar wind and dutifully sequestering them. A process humanity foolishly and gravely experimented with now bore the fruits of a century's labor.

Λ

Kindred was mercifully semi-unconscious for the roar that blasted forth from the Pravda Shore, immolating the seashore and the dock works below. Expanding in a luminescent shell that reached a diameter of a hundred meters, the material of the former Pravda Shore boiled in a multi-attosecond concoction of quanta until nature slammed the vacuum shut.

A swirling tube of molten matter erupted towards the sky, inhaling its surroundings, pulling rock, pylons and other detritus into its funneled maw. Winds rivaling the tremendous Antarctic catabatic shoved their way towards the engorged detonation funnel, encircling the monster in a furious, secondary accretion funnel.

Darkness cloaked the shoreline, a mushroom thunderhead eclipsing the feeble sunlight. Arcs of violet electricity leapt from the smoldering crater into the rotating cloud. Liquefied rock erupted in the crater's bowl, the angry syrup of ultrahot matter illuminating the underside of the expanding cloud. Steam vents formed in the various lava pools, blasting the formerly frozen water into a lethal, pressurized sauna. Even this steam couldn't extinguish the flames licking the crater's sides and the lip, nor the fires flashing forth over the dock and up the ice road's incline.

Cannonballs of flaming rock catapulted onto the surrounding hills, spreading the havoc to the environs. Where the fires couldn't reach and what the detonation could not destroy the reverberating seismicity buffeted; overlooking the crater, Mirnyy Observatory teetered on a treacherous house of cards. Boulders broke away and slid down the mountainface, allowing rocks to roll onto the ice road, slugging it with a dark avalanche.

Vibrating pebbles danced across the snowy plain, pelting the downed Kindred, while airborne particles blanketed the ice road, portending disaster. A stone chunk found the agent and collided with her right flank, stirring her. She pushed up on her shoulders and arms, allowing her to see the imminent rockslide between curtains of blood-caked hair.

A dark shape poked through the wall of dust and plowed into Kindred, throwing her into the air. Knocked to the ground again, her vision blurred and began to fade. The grip of a colossus on the back of her scalp jarred her.

"Small girl...."

Kindred now looked straight into the eyes of the giant Confederate who Mason had quarreled with. His square face bore streaks of dirty crimson, the whites of his eyes as bright as headlamps. Despite missing strips of flesh from his neck and jaw, he maintained steadfast control over himself and Kindred, her limp form cowering before him.

"I am called MOLOTOK. And now you will know the meaning of PAIN!"

Tereshkov hoisted Kindred off the ground. He sank the fingers of his left hand into the nape of her neck, its smaller diameter yielding easier to him than Mason's. The right hand soon joined the left, slowly clenching her vertebrae and ringing her neck. Crooked yellowed teeth cut his face in two as he felt the impulses of her struggle.

Kindred gagged and gasped, her body spasming and legs kicking in mid-air. Each breath was successively smaller than the last. In desperation she wrapped her hands over his outstretched arms, trying to support her mass. *Goddammit I'm not checking out like this! Greg I—*

She brooked the crushing torment, reverting to instinct and the only way out; a wayward hand scrambled inside her torn-open parka. Shoving her left hand upwards a beam of gamma-ray photons sawed through the forearms holding her aloft. Pieces of sundered, burnt flesh and bone flew out before Kindred's eyes. Hot fluids splattered her skin and parka, steaming immediately upon contact.

Tereshkov staggered away in an apoplectic rage, holding his thrashing, sundered arms outwards. Bundles of silver fibers erupted from his hand-less wrists, the rapid uncoiling withering his once-brawny arms, an ebony fluid pouring forth and splashing below. He doubled over, seized by a terrible twitching that locked his upper body in a torturous rigor.

Kindred collapsed in a heap on the ice road, coughing herself hoarse. Her senses dulled, she didn't register the paroxysm just three meters away until her hand reflexively jerked, the photon saw it held still lit and humming peacefully. She wiped the salty and oily, bitter fluids off her mouth and nostrils with the back of her hand. Resting on all fours and breathing shallow gulps of air, Kindred tried to re-oxygenate her lungs, every breath stinging. The new, pounding migraine drilling a hole in her brain was soon dwarfed by the din of rotors in the howling air above.

Λ

Boiling rock flowed closer, releasing noxious gases that burned lungs from a distance. Molten metal rained upon the smoldering crater wall, pelting the blackened earth, cracking and sloughing off the glassy crust. Shards of silicates cracked under the trembling figure who clung to the wall, barely holding any leverage. Broken bones and blistered skin sent waves of agony to his brain, and every clenched centimeter of muscle cried for release.

From the air he was a nondescript speck of grey, twisted and ragged, a crushed seabird at the precipice of the crater. Obscured by vats of rising steam, even the crimson stains on his parka and the pinkish burns over half his face could not betray him, leaving him to the mercy of whomever had survived this catastrophe....

A penumbra blossomed through the steam curtain, then grew into a hole, through which another form lowered under a familiar clamor. Agent Greg Mason's watering eye narrowed, his vision denied by a gathering shadow. Metal clinked repeatedly, dropping lower until his body felt the buffeting of strong winds, cooling his seared flesh.

"I've almost got him," Bell shouted, his voxlink flooded by *Jiminy Cricket*'s VTOL engines. "More, just a bit more."

Bell, strapped into a harness at the end of a zip line, stretched his right arm out, his gloved fingertips clawing at Mason's shredded parka. Balling his hand into a fist, he grasped fabric and pulled himself over to the fallen figure.

"More! I need more!"

Bell's body descended again, his boots contacting the precarious wall and straddling the quarter-turned agent. Now angled a few degrees towards Mason, he wrapped his arms over him, grunting to lift the eighty kilos of dead weight. Hooking additional straps about Mason's torso and groin, he secured the clasps, essentially belting the fallen agent to him. Bell removed the mobile oxygen mask and canister he wore over his mouth and nose and placed them onto the fallen agent, giving Mason lifesaving air and a chance to survive the copious fumes. Satisfied with his labors, Bell gave the flight crew the okay to lift them both.

Meter upon meter of zip line cycled back to the hovering *Jiminy Cricket*, sending the two men past bubbling magma and the everpresent steam that showed no signs of abating. Rising further above the dissipating thunderhead, the pair were pulled towards the ventral hatch of *Jiminy Cricket*, where Feltham—strapped to the cabin wall—operated the winch that descended from the roof.

Strong updrafts blew against her flight suit, threatening to send her down the narrow corridor, but the agent held tight to the U-shaped railing on the winch mechanism with her right hand. Her left hand extended into the free air, reaching for Bell on his return trip.

Feltham chided herself for the hastily executed rescue of Mason, but at least sighed in relief that he was indeed alive; the aftermath of the first Ether detonation didn't give her much reason to believe anything would be left *to* rescue. All the more reason this bollixed up op shouldn't have ever come to pass; 9D reacted too slowly to subtle hints and bureaucratic sclerosis didn't predict the Confederation's close mark to success. Expending all their initial energies into the Yastanni avenue was the biggest gift they could have given the Confederation.

Self-flagellation made Feltham sick to her stomach and didn't solve any of their problems. *Spending too much time in your own skull can kill.*

Feltham locked arms with the comatose Mason, walking both he and Bell to a waiting cabin seat, lowered to accommodate Mason. Bell detached Mason from his harness and assisted Feltham with lying their stricken boss down.

"Did you spot Kindred?" she shouted into her voxlink.

Bell shook his head, readjusting his flight helmet to receive her transmission over the channel. "Like a volcano down there mixed with pea soup."

"We're making another pass now," Feltham said, turning back to Mason. She stroked his forehead, clearing the encrusted blood with sanitized wipes. Placing her palm on his chest, she felt his shallow and uneven respiration, coupled with a low heart rate. Moving her hands to his fingers, Mason's extremities grew colder by the second. Even in this broken state he gurgled and moaned, clinging to life. *If just for now....* She cracked open the nearest medkit under the seats and administered a stabilizing serum via hypo to ease his body's reaction; it would do until they reached an infirmary.

Bell dried the sweat beads dripping from his forehead and inhaled deeply to calm his nerves. Gripping the slackened zip line allowed him to focus. Drained of energy, his resolve was the sole reason his body and mind hadn't yet cracked. He wanted to believe he'd be as strong and resourceful as Mason, but his youth and inexperience caused him to doubt inside.

"Agent Feltham, we're tailing a *Toad*. It descended from our blindspot and is attempting to land a half-klick distant," Cohen's voice crackled in her ears. "There's two biosigns on the ground. One of 'em's ours."

Feltham rose with a start and manned the winch again. Bell didn't have to wait for her command; he prepped for another jump before she could reset the zip line. She clapped his shoulder and leaned close. "Make it quick, Tommy...he's in shock."

Bell nodded once and braced himself on the edges of the hatch, his eyes darting from the red light above him to the disjointed terrain far below. The first jump was fueled by pure adrenaline, enabling him to easily overcome his vertigo; this next one, duty, plain and simple. If he had to pick over every last rock by himself to retrieve Sha, than so be it.

Λ

Kindred pulled her RT-01/9V. If the idling *Toad* decided to come about and dispatch her where she lay, she could offer up little resistance, but checking out with a spent magazine wasn't too shabby. At that a man leapt out the aft compartment and approached, his trek labored by the severe gale. She held her sidearm at arm's length, tracing the path of the Russian, lining him up with her laser sight, and cocked it. He heard the click and pulled his own *Grach* sidearm before pausing several paces short behind the immobilized Tereshkov.

The two exchanged weary glances, silently assenting that neither possessed a significant advantage, nor chose to push the issue. He crouched by Tereshkov and assisted him to his feet, all the while neutralizing Kindred with his *Grach*. Deliberately the pair shuffled a few paces, pausing when the rotors of *Jiminy Cricket* lowered several meters behind Kindred, creating a wash that scoured the ground.

Looking upwards, he witnessed the jumpjet's coilgun slew directly at him.

"Sha!" Bell shouted over her voxlink.

Kindred caught the descending agent out of the corner of her eye, dangling off the zip line.

The Russian saluted her with his sidearm. *"Poka my ne vstretimsya snova!"*

Indeed. Kindred crept up and backed away, allowing the *Toad* to begin its ascent. Bell hung like a jewel at the end of a chain, ever so slowly reaching her with his hands.

She felt Bell clip her to his harness and watched him signal their own ascent. Kindred locked her eyes on the lifting Vu-1024, its occupants honoring the truce until well off over the ashen horizon. *Next time.*

The howling winds battered her on the final length up, making her forget the terrible bruises sure to develop in the next few hours. Entering the ventral hatch of *Jiminy Cricket*, she had one, sole concern.

"Stone Man, is he—?"

Feltham loosened Kindred from Bell's harness and punched the controls, beginning the hatch's closure. Dull overhead cabin lights and vented air replaced the refracted arctic illumination and brisk gale.

"By the skin of his teeth, if he's got any left," Feltham said.

"What about that boat, can we stop it?"

Feltham massaged the bridge of her nose. "We barely kept from being blown sky high along with that lorry of yours. I don't see how it could've survived."

Kindred checked Mason for herself. Seeing his prone body and the care Feltham began on him mere moments ago, she glowered back at her. "I don't believe that for a goddamned minute. Ma'am."

"We saw an island blown to nothing...I have a pretty good idea—"

"It was a dud!" Kindred shot back. "Yield was too small otherwise. They got away. The last three neutrino-capture cages—warheads—were on their way there. We failed. It's over."

Feltham pursed her lips. Toggling her voxlink, she said, "Captain, swing us by past the cloud, if you can. We to need track that boat."

"*Ionization is suspect to our systems, Agent Feltham. But we'll put our fancy skills to the test.*"

Feltham nodded. Her eyes met Kindred's and the pair swallowed air in the palpable unease.

Bell held his arms out, his hands not easily unstrapping the harness enveloping his torso. "Um, if you two are, uh, done debating, could you help me out here?"

Λ

Jiminy Cricket skimmed the seething water, its lidar prodding the Ross Sea coast for any remains or markers of the exit of *Boris Yeltsin*.

"Nothing on the floor," Cohen said, his eyes studying the data flood on his instrument panel. "Residual wave disturbance, identical to what we tracked to Mirnyy from the *Triton*."

Feltham shook her head, gritting her teeth. "Patch us through Task Force Zeta to DC on this channel." She input a sequence on his holographic interface. "We've got to help prepare our defense."

CHAPTER THIRTY

"Stone man."

Mason blinked twice, acknowledging the soft voice to his right side. Despite the ventilator breathing for him, he sighed, groaning inside the oxygen mask he wore. Moving his arm he reached out for Kindred, who started to reciprocate, but then pulled back.

"Good lord, you certainly made a mess of yourself," an agitated de Lis said, approaching from the agent's other side. The doctor's greying hair looked even thinner than the last time Mason saw him.

Mason furrowed his eyebrows. *You've got room to talk....*

De Lis took stock of the broken agent, his heart in his throat. Mason's face and head were nearly double in size and mottled in purple from the savage attack. Scrapes and welts lined his skin, which not too long ago oozed massive amounts of blood. If he looked like shit on the outside, de Lis couldn't begin to fathom how his internal organs had fared.

"I'd heard 9D just returned from Antarctica," de Lis continued. "And that you were here. I came as—"

Mason waved his left hand, interrupting de Lis' niceties. Looking to Kindred, he motioned with his right hand to write a note. Kindred rifled through her purse and produced a data ledger, which she booted up and held for him. Mason took a proffered stylus and quickly scrawled "yastanni."

De Lis pursed his lips, knowing full well Mason would be all business, even strapped to his bed. Rubbing the bridge of his nose, he answered, "Passed three days ago. Too many severed arteries and punctured organs. His daughter's family flew him back to Kermani Iran the next day for the burial."

Mason closed his eyes.

De Lis leaned close to the agent. "Look, you may be thinking this was a mistake—and maybe you're right—but we flushed out somebody who needed Yastanni dead. I, I was wrong about Nouri. When you suggested I bring him to the states. And right now I'm beating myself up inside because I exposed him to harm. But we've bigger problems on our plates now, with what Agent Kindred has told me. I suggest resting and following your physician's recuperative regimen."

Mason's chin dropped a millimeter, the best he could do to nod. His eyes found Kindred again, and he motioned to her once more. She held out the data ledger, but he waved her off.

"Oh, that. Let's see..." she took out a data cylinder and handed it across the bed to de Lis.

De Lis raised his eyebrows. "Mason—"

Mason lifted up his oxygen mask. With great difficulty, and quite a hoarse voice, he croaked, "Contact...him. The only...man I trust to finish—"

Dry coughs interrupted Mason's instructions, punctuated by staccato beeps on the vitals monitor. A holograph of Mason's internal organs flashed red, alerting the nurses at the station nearby to the emergency.

"Out of the way!" the attending nurse shouted two meters away. Her direct course towards Mason parted the visitors.

Another squad of nurses crossed the room and fell about Mason's bed, assaying his vitals as the cacophony quickened. Now the squad tossed commands to each other, checking the agent's condition and remedying the multitudes of alerts on his monitor.

His swollen form convulsed and contorted, the sausage-sized fingers flailing over the bedsheet. A nurse injected a serum into his IV drip bag, which eased his seizing with a seconds. Watching with bated breath, the nurses studied his vitals monitor until Mason's body relaxed once more, silencing the alarm.

"He's back," the head nurse pronounced to her team, effectively dismissing them.

The nurse double-checked his dressings and IVs, then stepped over to de Lis and Kindred. "We've stabilized him, but he may be rejecting the stem-cell treatment. I wouldn't go making any plans for a holiday trip with him, though. It's going to be a rough forty-eight hours."

De Lis nodded. Kindred rubbed her brow and eyes, too stunned to answer. The pair walked out of the room and into the ICU corridor.

After a few moments to digest the frenzy, Kindred looked at de Lis, eager to change the subject. "So...who is on the cylinder—?" she started to ask.

De Lis shook his head. "Maybe no one, but I have to find out. He entrusted me with this, and I won't let him down. And, make sure 'Crash' over there recovers. This isn't over yet."

The physicist took one more glance at the prone Mason in the distance before departing, leaving the vigil to Kindred.

Putting her hands in her pockets, Kindred sidled over to Mason's bed. She kneeled next to him and put her lips to his ear. A tender hand rose up and touched his cheek. "I swear I'll get that sonuvabitch, Greg. One way or another, I'll do it for you."

Λ

"We've been at Def-Con One since oh nine-twenty," Louris said, his puffy red eyes on the verge of slamming shut. "POTUS and the Joint Chiefs are convening a closed session with both Houses of Congress to plot a course of action." He paused suddenly in the corridor outside his office. "Can anyone get me a decent cup of java around here?"

Nishiyama scampered off towards the commissary.

Louris shook his head. "Dammit, could there be any worse time to have Mason holed up at Walter Reed?"

Feltham's mouth stayed wired shut, her own exhaustion overcoming any suitable answer.

"Better barely alive than pushing daisies like Yastanni," Bell blurted, laying out the truth in the most matter-of-fact manner. He knew now wasn't the time to sugarcoat anything.

"A mouth like that will get you my job someday," Louris said. "But not today. And this doesn't change the fact that we screwed the pooch. Royally. 9D's on probation, and I'm not convinced we'll be anywhere but on the sidelines for whatever happens."

Kindred whipped around ahead of the group. "Chief, that's bullshit! We gave our blood and guts to this op!"

"And the Confederation is still armed with this fuckin' new toy!" Louris' eyes lit up. "Yastanni is dead. Mason may not be far behind. And these sons-of-bitches have some WMD that scares the bejeezus out of everyone on this continent! Now, what's fair! Hmm? The DIA has been handed the task of furthering the investigation into Project Ether."

Feltham crossed her arms. "If I didn't know better I'd say we'd been frozen out."

"Lis," Louris breathed heavily, "nobody likes to be on the side of the loser."

Λ

"Nadya, you know what to do," Unat'kolarev commanded, turning towards the woman at his side. Waving his hand, ZAMYESTITYEL's holograph—one of many maintaining his many-tendriled communications web—fluttered over the old man's desk interface and vanished.

He tightened his tie knot and smoothed the seams of the black uniform jacket he wore; many decades in the past, this battered and threadbare symbol of street protest was worn in darkness as a forbidden brotherhood. Now he publicly donned it with supreme satisfaction and pride, for he would be adorning those very same web holographs.

"Yes, sir." Nadya nodded obediently and fled the *dacha*'s dim office, an armed *militsya* guard at the threshold escorting her out.

His fingers plucking his lower lip with anxious energy, Shvinskilli said, "Should we toast our imminent victory?"

Unat'kolarev half-turned in his red leather chair to his major domo, who hovered nearby. "Even Stalin waited until Berlin had been seized."

Shvinskilli swallowed, understanding that nothing save complete victory would be celebrated; too many years under their belts were at stake to squander now.

"Too bad about MOLOTOK," Unat'kolarev said after a quiet moment of thought. "But I shall spare no expense in his rehabilitation."

Shvinskilli crossed to his admirably relaxed superior. "Skimming some euros off the *PLASHCH* fund won't be a problem. Zhao's men can do the work in a matter of days, I've been assured."

"Good, good." Unat'kolarev lit his rolled cigarette and puffed a cloud of ashy smoke into the still air. "I really should quit this."

"After this many years, sir? Why bother now?" Shvinskilli clasped his hands behind his back. "Besides, a new day dawns. No one will doubt anything you do."

"You see, Dymtra, this is why I have kept you around," Unat'kolarev said, giving rare praise. He rose from the chair. "Despite our...differences."

They chuckled and departed the dark room for the bright corridor, where the lineup of blue and green uniformed men awaited the two, with Mattarov, Admiral Gyorgi Nestorov of the Black Sea Fleet and Air Force colonel general Semyon Yusupov of the Leningrad Military District heading the group. Saluting the trio en masse, they received nods in return before following the pair into a circular conference room.

Unat'kolarev crossed over to a tall executive chair at the head of a rectangular table, placing his hands on the chair's back. He looked to the men in succession. "Gentlemen, thank you for your prompt arrival. Viktor, Colonel General Kryrov of the Leningrad Military District has sworn his western armies to your supreme command. Sixty-five percent of the Ground Forces are now under our control, all having allegiance to the True Peoples of Russia. Now we will put that oath to the test."

"Yes, sir. All personnel and mechanized units are in position and on alert status, ready for your orders."

Unat'kolarev nodded his approval.

"What of the others? How should we deal with them?" Admiral Nestorov said, rubbing his hands.

"They will understand and accept our dominion, or suffer the same fate as the Yankees and their puppets—swift and brutal justice." Unat'kolarev brushed his hair to the side. "Now, at this moment, K-670 is delivering the final component." His eyes met the gaze of the assembly. He continued, "All we have sacrificed so much for will soon be at hand. Observe."

At his voice command, a holograph blazed forth from the table's center, where a circular indentation bore the Geosync Array image of St. Petersburg, focusing on the Palace Embankment of the Neva River.

"Even fabled traditions must crumble, that the revolution can be consecrated."

"Yes, sir!" the assembly chorused.

Λ

Amid the fading White Nights above St. Petersburg, a star fell from the zenith, its shriek lost in the bustle of late afternoon traffic on the *Nevsky Prospekt* and its branching avenues. The brightening glow of the curious falling star soon piqued the interest of street vendors and passersby, if only because of its rather slow velocity and novelty.

The mere moments of benignancy shifted to terror and fear; as the falling star seemed to aim directly for Decembrists' Square and St. Isaac's Cathedral, panicked pedestrians fled the streets. Automobiles stalled and aerial vehicles crashed, creating logjams none could flee.

Fortunate pedestrians at the Admiralty and Decembrists' Square witnessed the star streak over their heads, while those who strolled the Moyka River were enraptured, their minds soon to burst with the cracking of hundreds of decibels of quantum energy. Mariinsky Palace, home of the ruling *Duma*, exploded in a vast shell before collapsing upon itself, releasing a vortex of fiery clouds and magma. Debris catapulted hundreds of meters, if not kilometers, from a voluminous crater and rained down upon the four-century-year-old city buildings and monuments. The Bronze Horseman crumbled in the shockwave, its horse's limbs now shrapnel flung into the Neva River.

The spectacular port city Peter the Great himself built by hand erupted into flash fires along the Palace Embankment, hungrily consuming the brick and mortar in its path.

Λ

Hushed silence filled the conference room's atmosphere. A miniature holographic inferno soon overpowered the image of the Hero City, its realtime view from orbit now obscured.

Unat'kolarev pounded his fist upon the chair's back. "Now get to work!"

The brass bolted, taking no time to digest the sudden destruction of the government capitol, their voxlinks already sounding with cross-channel chatter. Mere seconds elapsed before the room was cleared of the de facto military council.

Shvinskilli's wrist voxlink chimed. "Sir, our *Shinkansen* awaits!" His visceral temptations for action finally realized, they were incarnated by his animated shout. "Everything is in order!"

Unat'kolarev rubbed his palms together. "I shall miss this place... it has been my sanctum for far too many days." His eyes glinted in the light of the virtual inferno at arm's length. "What a glorious hour to be alive!"

Λ

"Get in here! Now!"

9D and Louris ran down the corridor of the Glass Castle, arriving in the opulent office of Assistant Director Erin Bourgoin, where the AD waved them over. Director Harrelman scurried through the office's other entryway, flanked by his personal assistants, all of whom parted the burgeoning crowd of Company agents from other departments.

In view of the assembled group hovered a mural holograph of downtown St. Petersburg, its siege relayed by the civilian Weblinked Satellite Grid. Several other holographs orbited nearby, the primary one broadcasting the official channel of the White House, directly linked to the Glass Castle. The sixty-eighth President of the United States of North America, Frank A. Aarons, and his cabinet, along with the Majority and Minority Leaders of Congress and the Joint Chiefs, sat in astonishment, their own eyes locked to the reporting.

Carnage, smoke and fire. Shifting hues and tones flowed over the Company's collective's eyes, colors of smashed structures, detritus blown across brick, street and ground, and bodies wrapped in white plastic, with hints of red exposed beneath. A great commotion persisted over the fallen...and the cameras caught all; horror, terror, fear, sadness, hostility and anger. Pale faces, dashed with a grey pall, wandered about the scene, oblivious to their global reach, to the billions sharing their confused and wasted stares. But, most apparent to 9D and Louris was shock, sheer, godawful shock.

"The Russian Confederation is under attack—we think it's a coup...." Aarons said, his tone balanced and flat for the words he'd just uttered.

Feltham read the floating text descriptions of the scene, which alternated between surviving eyewitnesses and talking-head analyses. "St. Petersburg...this...*cabal*, has gone straight for the head. Was the *Duma* in session?"

"Yeah," Louris said. "Someone has great timing."

"Or just damned lucky," Kindred added.

Aarons held up a holobook that he recited from. "Latest intelligence report from the DIA is that Confederate Ground Forces from the Leningrad Military District have ringed St. Petersburg within the last three hours, either to participate in this suspected coup or lead a counter-offensive. Information is too conflicting to draw any definite conclusions in the meantime."

Beside the White House feed, images of various skirmishes between civilians and armed *militsya* aired, fueling the hysteria in Russia, and the growing unease in DC. A holograph of English-speaking web anchors cited, "Largest domestic terror or civil attack since the 'Season of Blood' over twenty years ago...."

"Mr President, what are our options?" Harrelman asked over the channel, tuning out the chaotic visuals.

"Director, Def-Con One authorizes me to direct an armed strike if any action is taken against our forces. So far, no evidence of this has developed. We've offered our assistance, but I doubt there will be anyone around to respond. Unfortunately, we aren't sure what the act of succession is inside the Confederation."

"Perfect...any two-bit colonel can now rile up his troops to mount a claim," Kindred said, "And we wouldn't even know who to support in that pit."

Feltham stroked her cheek. A third party...somebody *else*. "We were right, all along. There are *two* hands at play. Oh, sweet lord."

Kindred drew closer to Feltham. "Lis?"

"Put it together, Sha. The Confederation isn't our enemy. These guys are."

"These g—"

Louris craned his head back. "Cut the chatter."

A withering look grew over Feltham. She shook her head and turned to the mural holograph, where the running commentary in Russian drowned out any live audio, forcing them to listen to a shoddy, five-second-delayed and looped English translation. A female talking head in an eastern European news studio, under a banner graphic that read "New Message Confirmed" in Cyrillic caught Feltham's eye.

"Who—Chief, Chief!" Feltham clapped Louris' arm, diverting his attention.

Louris listened to the mangled English audio and waved his hand under the holograph, increasing the volume. The newscaster looked askance to a prompter. *"...Would be first details of who is responsible for attack—"*

Throughout the office room an upwelling roar emanated, cutting off the Weblinked Satellite Grid holograph feed and superseding it with a blue transmission interruption signal. Out of this dead air a globe-sized image solidified into the visage of an old man, his eyes and mouth framed by crow's-feet and craggy furrows. Spindly ivory hair on his crown was swept leftward across his liver-spotted brow. On the periphery stood four other men, three of whom in Confederation military uniforms of the highest decoration in the three branches. The old man began speaking in terse Russian, an instant English translation blasting the airwaves, leaving no wait for his arrested and disquieted audience.

"This is the voice of the True Peoples of Russia...."

Louris' jaw tightened at the name and aged face of this enemy, an organization and man he thought both long dead in the myriad Confederation internecine wars. "Bastard is back...."

The translation continued, *"We demand the attention of the world's audience...what you see is a small taste of what will come. Our cause is freedom, freedom for the peoples of Russia! The Confederation is administered by a junta of thieves and criminals, destined to crumble under the will of the people. Premier Maksimillian Vinogravich was a thief in the night, plundering our nation in the name of democracy and openness to foreigners who steal our resources and kill in the name of friendship. They smile, while behind their spineless backs they conceal the knife to strike us while we are enraptured by their so-called kindness. But, the True Peoples of Russia will never stand to allow this! The True Peoples of Russia have waited long for freedom, and will not be denied by this junta any longer! Behold our first triumphant act in the war on imperialism! We have opened the front in St. Petersburg, where the twin bastions of decadence and corruption met to further their deception on the free peoples! This is just the beginning...soon, our loyal soldiers will sweep outwards from the Confederation in liberation, wiping away the last, gasping tendrils of this regime and its influence over the downtrodden! Tonight, as I speak, Vinogravich and the cowards of the* Duma *lie dead, their downfall now complete. These men are our trophies...our just cause requires the sacrifice of their lives. The party of the people, the True Peoples of Russia, now are the conquerors of St. Petersburg and Russia! And that is our message tonight: the imperialist powers of the West—the United States of North America and its assorted cronies—will pay for their centuries of crimes!"*

The old man raised his fists above his head, contorting his face as he leaned closer to the camera, a fervid glare emanating from his eyes. *"Already, we have won against these forces, destroying an American submarine in the Great Battle of the Îlots des Apotres! Our armed forces will decimate these decadent powers arrayed against us from within and without, air, sea, land or web! So, with the power invested upon me as party general of the True Peoples of Russia, I appoint myself— Genndy Unat'kolarev—supreme commander and head of state of the Confederation of Independent States! And as my first act, I formally declare war on the United States of North America and all of her bastard sycophantic allies!"*

Feltham, Kindred and Bell stood aghast, their gazes moving from the madman to each other.

"Triangulate that feed!" Harrelman yelled into his voxlink's direct channel, seizing the attentions of the techs in the Cryptoanalysis Department. "I want to know where that SOB is hiding!"

Across the gulf of cyberspace, President Aarons and the gathered cabinet members, Congresspersons and Joint Chiefs were animated in vociferous conversation. Aarons soon drilled his eyes straight towards Harrelman and demanded, "Who is this man? Ike!"

Harrelman, having just scrolled a holobook handed to him from Louris seconds earlier, dropped it from view and answered, "Mr President, I have the boys at Crypto working on it right now. It appears—"

Unat'kolarev pointed a jagged index finger precisely at his captive audience, and after giving them a moment to digest his diatribe and pronouncement, continued. *"Now, dear President Aarons, you and your populace will experience the pain of sheer terror that you have inflicted upon the True Peoples of Russia! As St. Petersburg is in my hands, Washington, DC will very shortly fall to the same destruction as well. As I speak, a weapon of incalculable vengeance heads for your den of thieves! Your Global Security Network was much too easy to destroy, Mr President. It will be your final mistake and epitaph! Tonight, Russia is once again for*

Russians! This is the voice of the True Peoples of Russia."

"The fool!" Bell said. "What's he trying to accomplish? We can strike back with so much force it'll be ridicul—"

Feltham shook her head. "He's banking on it…forcing our hand."

"Thousands, hundreds of thousands would die…." Bell's hands slumped against his thighs in puzzled exasperation.

Kindred's eyes zigzagged rapidly, her mind racing. "My god he means an ether warhead…!" she cried.

Louris jumped over to the still-active White House holograph and barked, "MISTER PRESIDENT! GET THE HELL OUT OF THERE!"

Λ

"Kinzhal!"

Second Captain Yuri Anikiyev repeated the received command code word from Captain Vitaly Kalinin, spreading it via voxlink to all department heads, each of whom jumped to action. Within seconds *Boris Yeltsin* descended thirty meters into the depths of the Indian Ocean, escaping any remaining eyes of the fragmented North American recon satellite grid.

Steeling himself in his command seat, Kalinin whispered a prayer and commenced the next directive, straight from his superior. Oathbound, he uttered the next code word without hesitation: "Plunge!"

Third Captain Ilya Rodionev relayed the launch order to his missile technicians, beginning the sequence. Deep within the bowels of K-670, individual YV-326 *Strela* suborbital strategic missiles slid into place inside their dorsal launch tubes.

In the control room, Anikiyev looked at the holograph before him, his attention rapt. Within thirty seconds, a score of *Strela*s successively blasted forth into the upper reaches of the Indian Ocean, shoving tonnes of seawater behind them as thousands of kilograms of power poured forth. Orange exhaust plumes cracked the surface of the ocean, setting loose the tridents of mass destruction into the early morning sky.

At last, the deed was done. K-670 continued its dive and awaited further instructions, which Anikiyev could only imagine involved further strikes. In some ways he pitied the North Americans, for they could be envied for their blissful, shameless, stupid ignorance of the world. But some memories were just too raw to forget….

Λ

Dusk clouds blanketed the Potomac banks, the evening settling in uneasily in DC. Absorbing the last few minutes, Feltham and her 9D agents paced the office of AD Bourgoin, now devoid of all agents save for them and their superiors; the Glass Castle itself was already cleared of non-essential personnel, having been sent to shelters within minutes of the declaration of war against the nation. Their respective minds occupied by the procedures set down in by Company the event of a declared war, the trio beat themselves up for the failure in Antarctic Colonial Frontier.

Bell paid heed to a few seconds' worth of webmedia coverage of the St. Petersburg attack, turning back now and then to his colleagues. "I'm guessing the President and Congress are headed for Greenbriar at this moment."

"Chances are good," Kindred said, still feeling the dull ache of her injuries along her back. The analgesics helped, but the sting wouldn't subside for days. *If it even mattered anymore....*

Feltham remained mute, her arms crossed over her chest. Now tasked with the added burden of carrying Mason's flag, she struggled to define it, to live up to it. She stared out past the mural window to the cityscape, silhouetted in subtle blues and yellows and strung with opalescent pinpricks. The streaks of red and blue Air Force jets patrolling the skies now lost its novelty after the first dozen sorties.

But the fireworks seconds later at the margins of the mural compelled her forward. Her hands set against the fullerene glass, Feltham strained to see the zenith.

"Lis?" Kindred said, piqued by her superior's sudden activity.

"We've launched coastal defense drones—could be Patriots," Feltham answered. "Look at that!"

Noticing the commotion, Louris, Harrelman and Bourgoin crossed over to the agents. The six huddled in the night's darkness, their faces periodically flickering in bright red and orange hues.

Behind them the arrayed holographs broadcasted the live images from the streets of DC, the assorted commotion and speculation airing like a live autopsy.

A tremendous thud sounded throughout the Glass Castle's walls and floors before the entire structure went silent, on the heels of the Washington skyline. Another explosion rained sparkling debris dozens of klicks away, enveloped in a shell of multitudinous color that soon melted into the evening.

"Good god almighty, we just took an EMP blast," Harrelman said.

Louris clapped Feltham and Bell on the shoulders. "Then we have no time to waste! Hit the stairs and into the sublevels. I don't wanna be here when the bigger bombs start dropping!"

Leaving in the wake of the others, Feltham took a last glimpse at the black vista before her better sense prevailed and she shut the door behind her. Listening to the fading footfalls, she tracked the way to the stairs via the luminescent stripes adorning the walls and floors, knowing somehow this battle, despite its ominous start, wasn't over by a longshot.

9D would not go off into the night quietly.

Λ

"My city! My city! Welcome your son home!"

Genndy Unat'kolarev flung his arms into the air, the *Shinkansen* General HQ train car halting to a stop, the Adagio of Shostakovich's Symphony No.7 in C ringing in the ears of his subordinates. Outside, three kilometers beyond the windows and maglev tracks of the Moskovsky Rail Terminal and the wondrous, revolutionary cacophony of Vosstaniya Square, fires painted the austral sky and the Mariinsky Palace a bloody vermilion.

Unat'kolarev joined hands with Nadya and a *devushka* who couldn't be more like her mother and trotted off the car, stepping onto the marble floor. Unat'kolarev flashed a mouth full of grinning, stained teeth and danced a spirited *troika* with the two, their steps echoing through the emptied Moskovsky's vaulted hall.

A fifty-strong contingent of infantry troops exited the adjacent *Shinkansen* train cars and cordoned off the terminal, the scuffs of leather boots on the expansive marble drowning out the last civilian stragglers. Departing lastly, Shvinskilli directed Mattarov, Nestorov, Yusupov and the ten other True Peoples elite off the General HQ car, his commands clipped and sharp. The circle of men surveyed the reddened city, their eyes burning with the smoke blowing in from the near distance.

Now, above them all, Yusupov's Su-3000 *Volkvyetyer* interceptor jets patrolled the skies, layering sonic booms onto the shattered structures and *prospekts*. Resistance to the new military command would be smashed before an inkling of the reality set in amongst St. Petersburgers.

His cabal misty-eyed and awed by their accomplishments, they doffed their military caps and genuflected before the men who orchestrated this greatest of achievements...the toppling of a corrupt government, the restoration of patriotic pride and the opening fusillade on the war with the West.

Unat'kolarev pushed past the threshold of the Moskovsky's high doors and stepped out to the center of Vosstaniya Square, basking before the triumphant Hero-City Obelisk of St. Petersburg.

Unat'kolarev cupped his hands to his mouth and bellowed from the depths of his lungs:

"I have saved you at last! Tonight, my Hero City, the True Peoples have returned!"

9D Will Return

Acknowledgements

SMV, for your love and support.
AH, the "electric socks!"
Dad and Mom, for giving
all your love.

And again,
to everyone who read the first one.

Read How It All Began...

JAUNT CLASSICS

IS DEDICATED TO THE REPUBLISHING OF CHOICE, OUT-OF-PRINT AND PUBLIC DOMAIN GENRE CLASSICS. THE 2019 SELECTIONS ARE THREE VOLUMES REPRESENTING CLASSIC OCCULT DETECTIVES, PRESENTED HERE UNCUT AND IN THE ORIGINAL TEXTS.

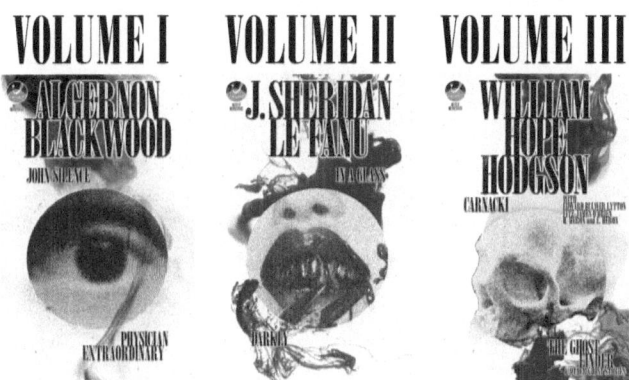

VOLUME I   VOLUME II   VOLUME III

Contemporaries of Sherlock Holmes, the occult detectives were Victorian- and Edwardian-era investigators concerned with all manner of psychic, spectral and paranormal matters, eager to separate reality—no matter how bizarre—from hoaxers and con men.

VOLUME I, renowned psychic investigator Dr. John Silence delves into five cases, ranging from the psychical invasion of a long-dead resident upon a writer of humorous tales to disturbing incidents of lycanthropy, with a twist only Dr. John Silence could conceive.
$8.99   ISBN 9780983331773

VOLUME II, esteemed German physician Dr. Martin Hesselius relates five tales, encompassing the apparition of a beastly creature only its witness can see to the unholy revenant inhabiting the form of a youthful girl, a story that pre-dates *DRACULA* by 25 years.
$8.99   ISBN 9780983331780

VOLUME III, fourteen tales of ghostly encounters with investigators Thomas Carnacki, Mr. Harry Escott and Mr. Flaxman Low, plus an anonymous story of a haunted house in the midst of London.
$8.99   ISBN 9780983331797